Wiesław Myśliwski

Needle's Eye

Translated from the Polish by Bill Johnston

archipelago books

First published in Polish as *Ucho Igielne* by Społeczny Instytut Wydawniczy Znak
First Archipelago Books Edition, 2025

ISBN: 978-1-962770-39-2

Archipelago Books
232 3rd Street #A111
Brooklyn, NY 11215
WWW.ARCHIPELAGOBOOKS.ORG

Distributed by Penguin Random House
WWW.PENGUINRANDOMHOUSE.COM

Cover art: Piotr Potworowski, *Siena*, 1955

This publication has been supported by the © POLAND Translation Program.

The authorized representative in the EU for product safety and compliance
is eucomply OÜ, Pärnu mnt 139b-14, 11317 Tallinn, Estonia,
hello@eucompliancepartner.com, +33 757690241

This work is made possible by the New York State Council on the Arts with the
support of the Office of the Governor and the New York State Legislature.

This publication was made possible with support from the Hawthornden Foundation,
the Carl Lesnor Family Foundation, the National Endowment for the Arts, and the
New York City Department of Cultural Affairs.

Printed in Canada

Needle's Eye

Chapter One

§

It was like I said. He tripped over his cane. I don't know why he looked back. No one was coming down behind him. Of course I recognized him. Though he'd changed beyond recognition – anyone would have after so many years. But I didn't let on. Maybe that was why he thought I hadn't known him. I acted as if, for me, he was just one of those people that are always going up and down the steps. I wondered whether I shouldn't perhaps warn him not to go down to the old wild green valley, because it no longer exists. But old people like to go around visiting places that don't exist, and maybe never did. I've no idea what it is they're longing for. Unfortunately though, old people's longings can be dangerous. If it'd at least been possible to walk to the valley on level ground, I might have understood him. But you can't get to a valley on level ground, that's the nature of valleys. Walking down those steps at his age, with a cane, when your legs won't do what they're told to and your eyes can't make out the world, or even the steps you're taking – it's like a young person imagining that instead of arms they have wings and they'll be able to fly down to the valley.

I was expecting somebody else; then all of a sudden he was there. I tensed up and started trembling; at that moment I'd have preferred not to be there. He felt for the first step with his cane; he placed one foot on it hesitantly, then risked his other foot. In the same laborious way he descended the next step, then the next. Doddery and stubborn, I thought to myself. Why are old folk so stubborn, can't they spare the people who're going to live on after them?

He paused at each step, looking down at his feet as if he wasn't sure whether these were the steps he'd always gone up and down, or if perhaps his memory had failed him. At his age it sometimes happens that your memory releases itself from the task of remembering, because it's been weighing you down with obligations that you're already tired of, after so many years of living. He felt each new step with his cane, making sure it was alright to continue on down. He first put his left foot on the step, then the right. The cane, which he held in his right hand, looked unsafe to me, it wobbled whenever he touched a step with it.

I was worried that on top of everything else he'd get dizzy from looking at the ground at every step. I was wondering if I should move aside, or if I ought not to let him past when he reached Needle's Eye.

He wasn't surprised to see me; he may even have expected me to overtake him before he got this far on his way from the park and through the town. He rested on the step above me and without looking me in the eye, he said:

"I checked in the park as well, but this was the last time. I don't know if you remember that sometimes she'd walk home from school through the park. I was sitting on a bench and I decided to wait. A Gypsy woman came by with a baby at her breast. Do you think she stopped like she did back then? Not at all. She didn't even ask if I wanted my fortune told, though the child whimpered as she passed me. She must have reckoned my future wasn't ahead of me but behind me, and she couldn't give me any extra years, that was impossible. I sat there for a long time, I was meaning to get up in a moment and walk through the town, because maybe today she'd go home through the town, if she needed to buy something, but an old woman sat down next to me, asking if I didn't mind. 'Unless perhaps you're waiting for someone?'

"'No, be my guest,' I said. 'I was waiting for someone, but that was a long time ago.'

"'Long ago or not, if you're in love you keep waiting.'

"'Were you in love?'

"'What a question. Is there anyone at all who's never been in love? I can see you've lived a good many years, like me. And you don't know that? I'm still in love now, though it's probably in vain. It pains me that I never told him.'

"'Why didn't you?'

"'I was sick, and the doctors didn't give me long to live, so I didn't want to burden him with my love. Especially because after he graduated high school he moved away. I don't even know where, and now he may not even be with us anymore. Would you have said anything if you hadn't been sure you'd live?'

"'I don't know, especially after so many years. Maybe I wouldn't have wanted to trouble her with a bad conscience for leaving my love behind if she happened to die.'

"'Does that mean you used to love someone?'

"'I love her still, though I'm also not sure whether she's alive. But I don't know if we'd even recognize each other if we met now. We're no longer the same people as when we were young.'

"'If a person loves, they're always the same. If people knew that when they were young, they'd live differently. As it is, they let all kinds of things go to waste. Most often love. Well, I'm off. I have to feed the cats."

"'Do you have many?'

"'Depends how many show up.'

"'I'll walk you there.'

"'No thank you. I don't have far to go. What about you, where are you heading? Maybe I could walk you? You have a cane, while I can still walk on my own two feet, thank heaven."

"'I'll be fine, I don't have as far to go as you."

He tested the next step with his cane, but he seemed not to trust it, for he moved the tip left and right across the surface before he placed his foot there. I was about to ask him why he was going down to the old wild green valley, but he spoke first:

"I feel sorry for you for having to carry on living. But maybe you'll have more luck. I wish that for you. Though in my view, wishes never did anything for anyone." He lowered himself onto the next step, again probing it with his cane. "Truth be told, every life is a repetition of someone else's life. The past is ahead of us, you must know that, we trail along behind it. Because who could catch up with their own life." He stopped on the next step. "So many feet must have come this way. Have you noticed how worn the steps are? It's taken centuries. Who knows if they're not still passing this way. Maybe I'll go along with them. You're surprised? It's always more cheerful in company." As he felt for the next step with his cane, he tottered, but it was as if someone held him up. "When I was in grammar school. . . though why should I bother telling you, you'll experience it yourself, you have to. Without that you wouldn't be able to ask yourself whether it was worth it. All the questions we ask in life boil down to that one question: was it worth it. Well, not at your age. Only years and years later. Today you wouldn't be able to answer yourself. Just remember that youth can mislead for a long time. Don't let it deceive you. It can suddenly turn out that it's been many years since you were young. Sad to say. I'm sorry for the bitter words, but they're the only ones left to me. To make up for it, I give you my life. It'll come in useful when emptiness overwhelms you. Emptiness is the worst thing that can happen to us. And the only way to cope with it is to live in someone else's life. Besides, no one begins their life from themselves. You don't understand that yet. But with time, once you spend some time there. . . I'd be curious to know your impressions. Mine have been better and worse, as is always the case with life. Once I ran away from my childhood, but perhaps you'll never want to part from yours. That sometimes happens. I can tell you, though, that it won't do you any good. Life means stumbling after yourself without any hope that you'll ever find yourself. Anyway, that's enough, because people are wanting to pass. And there are still so many steps to go."

So I moved out of his way. And at that moment the cane slipped from his hand and tumbled down the steps, and he staggered and then toppled after it. No one happened to be going up or down the steps at the time, and so no one saw it. I bounded down after him. I tried to pick him up in the irrational hope that he might still be alive. But he was heavy. He'd been a tall man when he was alive, and with the inertia of death he was all the heavier. Out of the blue I heard a voice above me:

"Leave him. The ambulance is on its way."

So I laid his bloodied head back down on the roadway, and only then did I notice there were several bystanders. Where they'd sprung from I have no idea. Maybe it's like that after any accident, people seem to pop up from the ground or descend from the sky, though when he was falling down the steps I could have sworn there wasn't a soul. There was no point questioning people then, because no one saw him trip over his cane. They might say this and that, but each of them was going to tell a different story anyway, it's always that way when people don't want to be witnesses. And as it turned out, no one did. The man who'd told me to leave him was describing a similar incident as he pointed to a nearby apartment building:

"It was in that building over there. Two buddies who weren't used to handling guns found a revolver from the war. It was so rusty the trigger couldn't even be pulled, so one of them started knocking the barrel on the tabletop. And the other one got shot in the belly. He fell down, and the first one started to try and lift him, he even managed to sit him up straight. Afterwards the doctor said that if he hadn't lifted him, the guy would've lived."

At that point his story was interrupted by the siren of the arriving ambulance. Two orderlies with a stretcher jumped out, along with a doctor who pulled the victim's eyelid back, placed a stethoscope against his chest just in case, and confirmed the decease. Right after the ambulance the police of the citizens' militia arrived, also with their siren wailing. Two uniformed officers got out, the senior one with stars on his shoulder, the junior one with bars. Then a third officer clambered out from the back seat; he was so overweight he looked comical in his uniform.

The senior officer started asking the people standing around the body who had noticed what and how it had happened, while the younger one with the bars wrote it all down, though there was nothing for him to write, because although everyone was talking over one another, no one had witnessed anything. One of them had seen only that I'd come running down the steps when the body was already lying on the roadway. And the man who'd stopped me from lifting him up had appeared right at the moment when I'd been going to do it and had said: "Leave him." He even started to say that in that building over there. The officer interrupted him:

"Did any of you know him?"

Someone wondered aloud: maybe if they'd seen him while he was still alive. . . The officer waved his hand dismissively.

"Search his pockets," he ordered.

The overweight one clumsily knelt down, took a wallet from the inside pocket of the dead man's jacket, and handed it to the junior officer, who without looking inside passed it to the other officer. The wallet had many compartments, but aside from money and the photograph of a young girl it didn't contain so much as a laundry stub.

"No ID card?" the officer said in surprise. "Take a closer look, maybe there's one in there somewhere. No?" He was more and more puzzled.

"A citizen without an ID card, it's like he doesn't exist," the overweight one said.

"There's a body so there ought to be an ID card," said the junior officer. "How's anyone supposed to investigate?"

"Maybe it fell out and he's lying on top of it. Lift the body up," the officer ordered.

The orderlies raised the body, but underneath there was nothing except a large pool of blood.

"Put him back down. The way he was lying."

"What about the girl in the photo?" The junior officer peered at the wallet where it lay open in the other officer's hand. "She's real pretty." The senior officer nodded. "Could be his daughter. People are more likely to recognize her than him. Should I show it around?" He took the photo from the senior officer and presented it to each bystander in turn.

They shrugged, they didn't know her. Someone said:

"It must be old. Those curly edges. They don't do them like that nowadays. I've got pictures like that that used to belong to my grandparents."

"What about you," he said, turning to me. "Do you know her?"

Yes, it was her, I recognized her. But I didn't let on. And so as not to arouse their suspicion, I called the officer's attention to the cane: "Maybe someone'll recognize him from the cane. Canes get connected to particular people. Everybody's cane is different. One of the teachers at the grammar school – "

The officer didn't let me finish. He eyed me distrustfully.

"We know how to identify people. Leave that to us, if you please." He gave orders to the other officers: "Just in case, search for the cane, and put the money in the evidence room. Draw a line around the body. Who knows, maybe he was a tourist and he left his ID with the tour guide so he wouldn't lose it."

They drew a line in chalk around the body, the ambulance took it away, and the junior officer and the overweight one started looking for the cane. The chalk outline of his body on the roadway, along with the bloodstain from where he'd hit his head, seemed to breathe with his breath, even to whisper something in his words; it was more stirring than when the body had been lying there.

"We'll need to drive around the town, and where there's a coach, make inquiries," the senior officer instructed, since despite a search of the steps and all around, the cane hadn't turned up. "It's Saturday, there are lots of visitors today. The coaches park under the castle, by the granary, in the new town. Wherever they're parked, go ask. Luckily there's only one hotel, ask there too. And ask at private guest rooms, get a list from the town hall, they have to be registered." He took off his cap and scratched his head as if his thoughts were itching him. "Also, it'd be good to put up posters, saying that a man aged – except we don't know his age, we didn't find his ID. Dammit, we didn't even bring a camera, we could've taken his picture."

"How could we have known he'd be dead?" the overweight officer put in. "They called in an accident, and an accident could have meant he'd broken an arm or a leg. There's no shortage of broken arms and legs on these darned steps."

"We could put up the photo," the one with bars added. "Not here, in town rather, otherwise people'll be afraid to use the steps because they'll say there's a ghost. Though a photo of a corpse – who's going to let on they knew him. It'd be better to use the picture of the daughter. Someone's more likely to admit knowing her."

"How do you know it's his daughter, not his granddaughter?" the senior officer asked sharply. The other man blinked in surprise that he hadn't thought of that himself. "From all this, it seems you're our only witness," the senior officer went on, turning to me. He added as if unsure: "And you're the only starting point for the investigation, since we don't have the deceased's ID, or photograph, or any other witnesses. Come with us, we'll get a statement."

At the station he sat me in front of his desk, asked if I'd like some tea, and picked up the phone: "Two teas," he ordered. "Do you take sugar, sir? Then I'll have some as well today. Bring sugar as well. Oh, and tell Bronka to come through and take things down."

A skinny little woman, the cleaning lady as it turned out, brought in two glasses of tea, sugar in a candy tin, and one spoon. The officer helped himself to sugar, stirred his tea, then handed me the spoon.

"I ought to bring another spoon from home. These aluminum ones break easily, there're hardly any left in the whole station," he explained.

Bronka came in too. She gave me a scornful glance, sat down at the typewriter and opened an illustrated magazine.

"I'll just check out the fall fashions while you finish your tea."

"Type. How does drinking tea prevent an interview?"

"I don't know anything about that."

He waited till I'd at least had my first sip; he took maybe his third, then pushed back from the desk, arranging himself against the backrest of his chair. He folded his hands together, visibly relaxing; he even stretched his feet out under the desk, because I felt them bump against mine.

"Go ahead."

"What am I supposed to say?"

"What you know."

"I don't know any more than what I've already told you."

"Oh yes you do, we know you do. Anyone who's being questioned says the same thing: they give their first name, last name, date of birth, and claim they don't know anything. But experience has taught us that people don't know what they know if they're not helped along. There are various ways of helping. Me though, I use ordinary conversation to, you might say, raise awareness. I start from the assumption that each person has to realize for themselves what they know. So then?"

Evidently I didn't yet understand a thing, for I decided to remind him of what he'd said to me when he brought me to the station:

"I'm sorry, but there's been a misunderstanding. I was only supposed to be a witness."

"That's true, I don't deny it, you're still a witness. But you're the only one. We don't have any other statements we could compare with yours to establish your trustworthiness. When nothing is certain, the question arises whether being a witness was your only role in this incident, or if you might be assigned another. For the moment I don't know which, but we need to try and clear that up. Both of us. So I need you to understand that I have to question you in various roles. In fact, the boundaries between the roles are fluid. Determined by circumstances. To offer a comparison, a liquid state may turn into a gaseous state or a solid state, depending on the temperature. Water, steam, ice. The same, but not the same. We can't permit ourselves to be helpless. That would incapacitate us. We'd be unnecessary. So we have to look into things, sometimes till it hurts. The truth, as you know, has the highest price; even years later it isn't reduced. So I wouldn't count on that. The truth never expires. However long the case may go on. If we only had just one more witness. But in your case that could only be the deceased. And unfortunately we can't question him. Though it'd be interesting to hear what he'd have to say. All we have is conjecture. And that's not so unwarranted. The quest for leads usually starts from conjecture, since few people are caught red-handed. Think for instance of all those betrayed husbands and wives. It's rare that any of them catches their partner in flagrante, as they say. Most betrayals start from conjecture. And it's only conjecture that leads to a search for evidence. So it's not impossible that the deceased would testify against you when you state that it was his own fault since he tripped over his cane. Where is the cane? We looked for it, as you saw. If it had been there we'd have found it. Canes don't have wings, they can't fly away." He laughed, but it was a laugh that chilled me. "Well, we'll look again. In the meantime, tell me: which hand was he holding it in, left or right, when he tripped over it? You don't remember. Too bad. You're surprised a detail like that can be meaningful? Let me tell you, a detail can tell us more than we'd expect. A little detail, yet it can undermine every statement, contradict every witness. A detail is a universe. They say the world is vast, but details determine someone will meet somebody else here and not there, that the apple fell from the tree so Newton could discover the law of gravity, that the bacteria Fleming was cultivating were killed unexpectedly by some fungus so penicillin could be invented. And so on and so forth. Did you write that down, Bronka? Then throw that sheet away."

He continued to question me, and I have to say that at times his shrewdness startled me:

"You said that no one was coming down the steps behind him, right? And yet he looked back. Maybe the sun dazzled him, because it's bright today, and he couldn't see anything so he turned away, and at that point, let's say, you offered to help him down to the next step?"

At times he interrupted the interview mid-sentence and left the room, as if giving me time to think. Or he lost himself in thought, after which he told Bronka to cross something out, though to me it had seemed important. His thoughts were clearly following a different train. Then at other moments he seemed to wish to moderate the tone of the interview and make it more like a sharing of confidences: he put in something about himself, that he had two children, a son and a daughter, with his first wife, who had died, so he'd had to bring them up himself.

"And you know how it is. Work's no picnic."

He'd remarried, and now they were expecting another child. At times he asked me questions that seemed to have nothing to do with the case:

"Your father and mother are alive? I realize you're young, but you never know. I can barely remember my mother, she died of TB. And my father passed away two years ago."

Then he'd surprise me once again:

"When did you graduate from high school? Why didn't you go to university?"

"They didn't admit me."

"You failed the entrance exam?"

"No, I passed."

"What do you mean? You passed the exam and they didn't let you in? Interesting. That should be looked into. What do you do now?"

"I work."

"Where?"

"At the canning factory. They make jams, marmalades, juices."

"I know that place. We had a case there, five train cars loaded with barrels of sour cherries stood on a siding till the merchandise went bad. Where do you live?"

"With my parents."

"Why did you come to town? Were you meeting him?"

"Who?"

"The deceased."

"I didn't know him."

"You didn't know him, yet you recognized him. That's what you said, that you recognized him. Or perhaps he only thought you didn't recognize him. Well, we can't ask him. But I'm wondering, since this was a chance encounter, why you happened to meet at Needle's Eye and not on the street, in the park, in a cafe or restaurant or wherever, the way chance meetings usually go. Think about that. I'll be right back." He left the room.

It's not going to be easy with him, I thought to myself. After all, I couldn't tell him that I was waiting for her, and that he'd shown up unexpectedly. I'd actually thought he was already dead, as a year had gone by since the time he was supposed to die, according to the Gypsy woman's prophecy. But the officer would have jumped right in with: who is she, first name, last name, where does she live. And did she turn up? How is that possible, you knew she wouldn't come yet you were waiting for her? People wait for people who might be late or might not come that day because something unforeseen cropped up, but they'll come another time.

After a short while he returned. Right from the door he barked out an impatient question: "Do you have something to tell me? Let's say for the sake of argument that you didn't know him. We'll follow a different line of thought. You saw him coming down, yes? Where was he going?"

"Toward the bottom."

"Obviously, if you're coming down you're going toward the bottom." He sat at the desk, staring into my eyes with a strange intensity. "Toward the bottom, you say? How would he have gone back up, since he could barely make it down, have you not thought about that? At his age, with a cane?"

"I don't know. Maybe he wasn't planning to go back up."

"He wasn't planning to, you say. How do you know he wasn't?"

"I'm supposing."

"I have to tell you that these suppositions of yours can also be evidence. And we can use them against you, despite the fact you're supposing something that supports your own innocence. Everything has two sides, every thought and every word. Nothing is unambiguous, contrary to what you might think. Unambiguousness is an illusion. The fact that you're just supposing gives you away, it shows there's something behind it. And what's behind something is the most important thing. True, you safeguarded yourself with that 'maybe.' But sometimes 'maybe' just pops out – though even then it isn't without a reason. Words rule us, you ought to know it. You don't need to graduate high school to learn that. Sometimes you don't want to say a particular word, yet it says itself. So how is it then, because something here doesn't add up." He fell silent, as if waiting for me to answer.

I felt unnerved: he was silent for a long time, staring at me and not saying anything. In those eyes that were fixed on me, I thought I detected a question he wanted to ask me, but he was worried he'd get mixed up in something himself. I was afraid of that question and waited nervously for him to put it to me. He didn't. He merely cleared his throat:

"Hmm..." And for a long while that was the only sound that came out of his mouth. A moment later he repeated: "Hmm..."

His "hmm" made me flinch. A "hmm" like that can conceal anything, even an accusation for which, admittedly, there was no evidence, yet still it rang with a conviction that evidence would be found, if not sooner then later. Later it might actually be easier to find. Investigative techniques would improve, methods would be perfected, new equipment would appear that would be able to read automatically, without the need to ask questions. And without Bronka, for there'd be no need to write anything down, the suspect would be projected on a screen. If he had a soul, the soul too would be there for all to see. Be patient: what moves away will also come closer. And in the meantime there was no harm in dreaming. During that time, for the suspect too years would pass, he'd experience all sorts of things, understand all sorts of things, he might even come of his own free will and confess, he wouldn't need to be arrested, there'd be no need to go anywhere or investigate anything. You'd just sit at your desk and receive the guilty parties like you receive applications for benefits or for an apartment. All you'd have to do would be to gain access to consciences, because up till now consciences rarely open up of their own accord, and if they do it's only in old age. Perhaps, instead of the citizens' militia there'd only be offices and administrators, so salaries would go up as well. The police wasn't doing so well, especially with the younger people. The young are the hardest to question: they're evasive, deceitful, they deny everything; laws and regulations mean nothing to them, they believe that youth makes everything permissible. They have no regard for the police. They would see, when we become the beacon of the world.

At this point an officer with one extra star came in and laid a note on the desk.

"Have you got him?" he asked, glancing at me.

"Almost."

"Tough one, is he? Maybe let Edek have a go at him."

"No, I'll be fine."

"As you wish."

After the superior officer left, the other one glanced at the note he'd brought, put it aside with suppressed anger, and then turned that anger on Bronka:

"Put the magazine down, Bronka! Type!"

"I've been typing the whole time," said Bronka grumpily. "There's nothing to type right now."

He stared at me just as angrily, as if expecting that at the very least my hands would be shaking.

"Let's go back to the cane."

"'Let's go back to the cane,' I've got that," repeated Bronka.

"What did it look like?"

"'What did it look like?'" That was Bronka again.

"Stop reading back what you're writing, goddammit!" He was furious. "So then, what did it look like?"

"Like a regular cane."

"Be more precise. What color was it?"

"Black, I think."

"You think, or black?"

"It could have been black."

"'Could have been' isn't an answer. Listen pal, you don't seem to realize you're being questioned about an incident that who knows, may even be murder. You might just as easily have stuck your foot out as he could have tripped over his cane. Because up till now we haven't found the cane."

"Black," I said, a little scared. He seemed to be slowly getting closer to my thoughts.

"Good, so now we have the color. And?"

"And it stayed black."

"Are you taking the mickey? And here I am trying to give you a chance."

No, I wasn't taking the mickey, I wouldn't have dared. Maybe it had been a stupid thing to say, but I'd been confused by his suddenly calling me 'pal,' and wondering what that might mean.

"What about the handle?"

"The handle?"

"What shape was it? There are different shapes. There was a guy here, young fellow like you, carried a cane, and the handle was in the shape of a snake's head."

"No, it was round and smooth."

"What else was there about it?"

"It had a rubber tip to prevent it from slipping."

"So he couldn't have slipped, it would have stopped him. And he still fell?"

"Maybe it stuck when he tried to go down a step. And he got tangled up in it."

He looked at me like he was thinking, You're a wily one, pal, but you're not going to pull the wool over my eyes.

"Fine. Let's forget about the cane until we find it."

He started drumming the fingers of his right hand on the desktop, as if wondering whether he shouldn't pass me along after all to Edek, as his superior officer had suggested when he brought in the note. I didn't know who Edek was, it was just a name, but the idea of Edek having a go at me didn't sound good. Up till now he'd been easy on me, friendly at times; I even had the impression he was sorry to be questioning me. And I felt a rush of fear. He'd said no to Edek, but maybe there was an Edek there inside him, since he'd said he could manage on his own.

"No doubt you're aware that confession is a mitigating circumstance," he said in a voice that sounded weary. He may even have yawned.

"But what am I supposed to confess to?"

"That's not for me to say. I'm not the one that needs to confess. Truth is, everyone has something to confess. Even if we pulled some random person off the street to be questioned. Maybe it'll be like that one day. For now we're limited in how we can operate."

He stopped drumming on the desktop with the fingers of his right hand and shifted to his left hand, and as if in a burst of energy his drumming grew louder and faster, till my heart was in my mouth.

"Oh, I forgot to mention that on the cane, beneath the handle there was a gold plate. It had an engraved inscription –"

"Gold, you say," he interrupted. He picked up his phone. "Send Tubs in to me. See. You have to keep digging till it hurts." He stopped drumming, appeared to smile at me even. "That will settle the matter for us."

The overweight officer appeared at the door.

"Sir?"

"Go look for the cane. It has a gold plate."

"If it's gold there's no point in searching, it won't be found." He explained: "Gold prices are high these days. Trading's banned, so there's a flourishing market. All those gold rubles and dollars we've seized, and still they go on selling them. We've put away any number of people, and what's it achieved? They even steal stuff from churches and melt it down to make rubles and dollars."

"Shut the hell up and go. That's an order."

"Yes, sir." The overweight officer clicked his heels so hard he tottered. His body was too heavy for his thin legs.

"I don't smoke, otherwise I'd be glad of a cigarette," the senior office said, appearing to flag. He took out a comb and ran it through his hair, which was thick and black, though graying at the temples. "I used to smoke. But my first wife was always saying, 'You should quit, we have small children,' the second one says, 'You should quit, I'm pregnant, do you want the baby to be born a cripple?' Anyway, we'll wait till they bring the cane. Best not to skimp on time when you're going after the truth."

Time, though, was stretching into infinity, not only for me but for him too, because he kept going out and leaving me alone with Bronka, who grabbed the opportunity to thumb through her magazine every time he left, and didn't say a word. I asked her if she had any idea how long it might go on.

"Oh, it might, it might," she said, not lifting her eyes from the magazine. "If they don't finish by nighttime they pick up again in the morning. I've only written one page. With Edek there'd have been five already. Edek doesn't muck about. He'll whack you or throttle you a bit if you're not telling the truth. And no one does. You're not being straight either, I can see that. It wasn't the way you say it was. Edek'd get it out of you. Edek can bend horseshoes. Me, he can lift me up all the way to the ceiling like I was a feather. When Edek's running the interview it's never boring. Next to Edek, they're pretty much all wimps here. Everyone spills the beans with Edek. You see life. What you learn when you're in with Edek, you can't read it in books. People say more with Edek around than they do in the confessional. If Edek was dealing with you you'd find out all sorts of things about yourself. Edek wouldn't let you just sit there the way this guy does. He's a decent person and he's not dumb, but sometimes he doesn't know himself what he's after. He asks and asks, but there's nothing to write down. Gives you tea. Edek wouldn't give you so much as a drop of water. And he was calling you sir till you made him mad. With Edek the interview would be over by now, I could have gone home. With this guy who knows. He's having them look for the cane, but what will the cane tell him. It's starting to get dark. If you confessed, he might get his promotion, because he's been waiting forever for an extra star. He'd get a raise. Two kids from his first wife to bring up, and a third on the way with the new one. You too, you'd feel better if you got it off your chest."

Except what was he supposed to confess to so as to make himself feel better? He'd never felt better, not since he let the Gypsy woman tell his fortune; she foretold a long life for him, but he didn't care about that, whereas when he heard that today she wouldn't be walking home from school through the park, that she'd go via the town, because she needed to buy something, hooks and eyes or press studs, he virtually flew up from the bench.

At that time the park was generally empty, plus it was small, like most town parks; in addition it had been thinned out by an almost apocalyptic storm that had struck the town a few years earlier, and that people still shuddered to remember. So the park wasn't as popular as it had been before. There was nowhere you could hide away, so it wasn't often used for dates these days. Young people preferred the bushes down by the river, while older folk missed the park from before and no longer went strolling there or sat on the benches. Before, the trees would have been filled with birdsong at this time of year, but now the silence was rarely broken, so he was certain he'd hear her footsteps when she came by.

He half-closed his eyes against the glare of the sunlight; he knew that in the silence nothing would escape his attention. He'd hear any footsteps from a long way away, so he didn't have to keep opening his eyes to check whether it was her or not. He knew her footsteps by heart. Her feet seemed to touch the ground only lightly, you'd think she was in sandals, though she always wore heels for she couldn't abide flat-soled shoes. When she walked, she placed her toes on the ground first, not her heels; he'd have recognized that step even in a starless darkness.

Behind his narrowed eyes he gave himself over to his imagination; he wasn't expecting her till after the last class was over. He had the advantage of that one class over her, for he'd cut Latin so as to wait for her in the park, which she usually went through on her way home. He often skipped his last class – not just Latin, which he didn't like, but also physics, math, classes in which he was one of the top students. Whenever he left the school at the same time as her, after the last bell, he would lose sight of her among the various classes all getting out at the same time. There were quite a few concurrent classes, each with a lot of students, so when the school day ended a whole crowd would always pour out. Then when he'd spot her, she would almost always be walking with someone else. There were a lot of boys, including from the older classes, who waited to try and walk a little ways with her at least, or to accompany her all the way home.

What he might have been dreaming about is probably not worth mentioning, since dreams at that age are rather commonplace and familiar to everyone, so anyone can use their own dreams as a reference. All at once he heard approaching footsteps, or rather the padding of bare feet. It wasn't her, he'd have recognized her at once. These steps were unhurried, almost furtive, and he would have continued with his daydreams if he hadn't heard a child whimper almost within arm's reach from him. He opened his eyes so abruptly he was dazzled by the sunlight, then in the brightness he saw the Gypsy woman in front of him with a baby at her breast.

She was directly in front of the bench where he sat, and she would have continued on her way, for her footsteps betrayed no intention of stopping beside him. Experience must have told her there was no point telling the fortune of someone like that, she wouldn't get one zloty from him. If he had any money he'd hold onto it for the cinema or the circus. Though what girl would have agreed to go to the cinema or the circus with him? The better looking ones were only interested in someone with a future. Whereas what future could he have? Pale, hollow-cheeked, he seemed somehow broken down, maybe even sick, except he didn't yet know it himself. She could only tell him that he'd live a long life, because that couldn't be verified other than by living a long life.

So perhaps it wasn't an accident that when she drew level with him and was about to walk on, her baby whimpered because the nipple had slipped from its mouth; she put it back in and it quietened down. But she'd had to pause for a moment and right then her eyes met his. Only briefly, for his gaze chilled her and she looked down at the head of the suckling child, and stroked its head tenderly. She was skilled at overcoming people's distrust, even disdain, toward herself, but his eyes seemed to her not to match his years. Something sorrowful shone in them. She'd never before seen so much suffering in such a young gaze; often you didn't encounter it even in older eyes. The best proof of which being the fact that he only opened his eyes when he heard the baby cry. Could he have inherited that suffering from someone else? After all, every person is an endless inheritance. Since she'd stopped in front of him, though, she couldn't just walk away without a word. The child's cry had been the first word to him. So as if continuing, she said:

"If you let me read your fortune, I'll tell you whether she'll walk home this way."

Without waiting for his consent she sat down on the edge of the bench. With a practiced movement she took her right breast out of her blouse and shifted the infant to it; the baby whimpered again at being pulled away from its suckling but didn't have the time to start crying, for the other nipple was already in its mouth.

"When something's troubling you, it's best to have your fortune told. No wise man was ever born who doesn't believe it'll make things better. Having your fortune told can bring you comfort, and it doesn't take anyone's hope away. It can change many a thing. And you, you have your life ahead of you. If you give me the money for a rattle, I'll tell your whole life."

Again without waiting for him to give permission, she freed her left arm from the shawl that, looping around her waist and the back of her neck, held the child at her breast.

"Give me your hand," she said. "Not that one, the other one."

She drew the hand onto her lap, took it in both her hands, turned it palm upwards, and began to pass her index finger over it.

"You have a long life line. Really long. From here to here." He didn't even look. "You'll live and live." She mentioned how many years; it happened to fall last year. "See, from here to here. If your hand was longer you'd live even more. But it's long as it is. You'll live a lot." She must have seen disbelief in his eyes, for she closed his hand up and whispered with something like dread: "There's another line here, the heart line. A Gypsy isn't mistaken. A Gypsy always tells the truth."

But he showed no interest in the second line either. A longer or shorter life made no difference to him. He was immersed in the one moment he'd been waiting for as he sat by the main path through the park. For that moment he would have exchanged the longest life. There are moments that, like the sun through a lens, concentrate our entire life into a single point, burning a mark into us for all time. Who knows, perhaps we live for those moments alone, not for however many years.

He was barely listening to the fortune she was telling, for in his mind he was leaving the school along with her after the last class, passing the door of the building, then going out through the gate; he walked down the sidewalk for a while, crossed to the other side of the street, then turned in the direction of the church; he was already in front of the church, in a second he'd enter the park, he was in the park already, so now he ought to hear her footsteps moving toward him. He thought he could already make them out, quiet as anything to begin with, for she must still be near the start of the side path, but those were her footsteps, he'd know them anywhere, when suddenly, like a blow to the head the Gypsy woman's words reached him: "She won't be coming this way today. She meant to, but she remembered she needed to buy something, hooks and eyes, press studs, so she'll go through the town."

She didn't finish, because he pulled his hand away, jumped up and moved off in the direction of the town.

"What about the rattle?" she shouted after him; the nipple must have slipped from the baby's mouth again, for it started crying loudly.

He turned back, dug a coin from his pocket and tossed it in her lap.

"This won't buy a rattle!" she exclaimed. "A curse on you!"

If the Gypsy woman had been telling the truth about her going through the town, then her way home led down the steps and through Needle's Eye to that old wild green valley that lay between the hill on which the town stood and the much lower one opposite where her house was.

It didn't take him any longer to reach Needle's Eye than it took me, though from the market square, where I'd had tea and an apple charlotte in a cozy cafe, it was less than a hundred yards to the steps. He'd had the whole length of the street to cover after he left the park, then the path from the hill opposite down into the valley, then a stretch across the valley, then he had to go up to the road that ran along the foot of the steep steps and climb to Needle's Eye.

True, in his case the earth itself ran beneath his feet, as they say, whereas I was trailing along one step at a time, leaning on my cane. Not to mention that he was in a hurry in case she reached home before he got to the steps. Me, on the other hand, I'd given up hope long ago, and I was only going to visit the old wild green valley. It's been so very many years, I'm no longer sure if she'd been coming back through the park or through the town the last time I walked with her. I'd asked her as I always did:

"Can I walk you home?"

"I'd like that," she said with a smile, though it wasn't the kind of smile I'd have wished for. "Is that why you skipped Latin? Really. I'll have you on my conscience."

Afterwards, when we'd already said our goodbyes, I lingered by the garden gate till her footsteps had completely faded down the well-worn path that led through the orchard to her house. Sometimes she'd already have vanished among the trees when she'd call to me:

"Bye!"

The officer came back in; I don't know if he'd heard or if he was guessing, but right from the doorway he barked at Bronka:

"How many times have I told you, no talking with interviewees."

"Why would I. He was only asking what's in my magazine, so I told him: dresses, coats, blouses, skirts."

There was a noise outside and the overweight officer appeared in the doorway.

"We didn't find it, sir." He withdrew at once, closing the door behind him, as if expecting the other man to be furious and lay the blame on him for not finding the cane.

He wasn't furious, he seemed dejected rather. He took his head in his hands, lowered his eyes to the desk and sat like that without saying anything. Perhaps he was waiting for me to speak first, to lead him on to some question that would change the course of the interview. At that moment he might even have preferred to be the one being questioned rather than the questioner, that way he wouldn't have been at such a loss. All roles are interchangeable, after all, and it's easy enough to imagine ourselves in any one of them. Especially if he took off that uniform of his. I felt sorry for him. But how could I console him, bring him out of his helplessness? Let him at least start interviewing me again from the start, ask me the same questions. I preferred that to a helpless silence. And so I said rashly:

"The cane wouldn't have told you anything. It was simply playing the part of fate. The Gypsy woman – "

He didn't let me finish. He jumped up from his chair, exclaiming:

"What fate? What Gypsy woman? You're talking gibberish! I'll lock you up for forty-eight hours, that'll knock some sense into you! Gypsy woman! Fate!" He brought his fist down on the desk and left again, slamming the door behind him.

Yet a moment later he came back. He'd gotten a grip on himself. He turned on his desk lamp, sat down, and said to Bronka:

"Give me a cigarette, Bronka. I know you smoke."

He drew the smoke deep into his lungs, letting out a string of smoke rings at each puff. The smoke rings triggered a memory: Every Christmas my mother would make a chain of colored paper rings for the tree, then father would lift me up to the top of the tree and I'd drape the chain over the branches. He may have associated the rings with a Christmas tree also, because he blew them with relish, then watched as they dispersed over my head. When he finished the cigarette he said: "It would have been good to know the deceased from childhood, because the key may lie there. And only then, with that key, open the door to what happened today on the steps."

I have to give him his due: at last he'd hit on the right track, and my heart started pounding. Luckily for me, another thought seemed to lead him in a different direction:

"Though whatever approach you take, it's always maybe, maybe, maybe. As if we maybe existed. And maybe this station. Who knows, the whole damn world could be maybe. Nothing's for certain. Goddammit all!" He grabbed hold of his empty tea glass and seemed about to crush it – Bronka let out a gasp – but fortunately all he did was hurry out of the room with the glass.

"There, he won't be back for a while now," said Bronka. "Now he's really mad. Before, he was only pretending to be so as to scare you. Who knows how long this interview's going to last. And I've got a date with my guy. He's also a police officer, but at a different station. If I don't show up he'll be furious." She opened her magazine again.

I thought about asking her for more tea. My throat was dry, my lips were cracked. But I realized it wasn't in Bronka's power to make tea for an interviewee. I raised the glass to my lips, hoping there might still be a drop left at the bottom.

"I'd make you more tea," Bronka said without taking her eyes off the magazine, "but that isn't the way here. When the interviewee's thirsty they're more likely to confess. This guy is only different from the others in that he offers people tea. Because of that he doesn't get promoted. What sign are you? I'm a Capricorn. Last week it checked out, maybe this week it will too. You have to believe for it to check out. Once I went to see a fortune teller and it came true. She said I'd get married in the fall. And that's happening. I have to think about a dress and a veil. I want one like I saw in a movie once. Two children were carrying the train behind the bride. I just need to take out a loan. There's a benefit fund here. But what should I say it's for? They won't give me money for a church wedding, they'd fire me more likely. What kind of wedding is it at the registry office. Personal differences and boom, they give you a divorce. Then I'll be on my own with the kid. Because I think I'm pregnant. We'll have to go somewhere different. That's what people do, they go away. Far away, to someplace in the country. Then they have their kid baptized in one of the villages. Shall I read you yours? Don't worry, he won't be back for a while, I told you. Your horoscope says you're going to have problems. You should've told him where the cane is. What do you want a cane for? You're not going to use it to walk with. You're too young. People'd make fun of you. Anyway, what do I care. All I can think about is the wedding. I'm wondering what it'll be like afterwards, because you never know. Some of them beat their wives. Maybe mine won't. He wants a son, I want a daughter.

I don't know how we'll square it. I'll just keep having babies till we get a son. One guy here at the station, he's got four daughters. He's a senior officer, but still, it must cost the earth when they grow up, buying clothes for all of them, seeing them married. A senior officer's salary is enough for one or two daughters tops. He comes to me sometimes, I need your advice, Bronka. I'd give him my advice if he weren't in the police. Send them all away to be nuns. I'm worried because my guy's a head shorter than me, and that's when I'm not in heels. I can see it bothers him, but I can't shorten my legs. I promised him I'd only put on high heels for the wedding, then never again. I said I'd buy him a hat and we'd be the same height. Are you nuts, he goes, a hat with a uniform? Then join the secret police, they wear civilian clothes. At school I played basketball, they say that was why I grew so tall. Do you have someone? A girl, I mean?"

"I did."

"What happened, she dump you?"

"I don't know."

"What do you mean you don't know? If you had her and now you don't, then you don't. You're not bad looking. You could have someone. Maybe you'll find a girl. There's no shortage."

I thought about the day we said goodbye before she left for the sanatorium. She'd already opened the gate, but then she paused.

"Maybe, when I come back. . ." She trailed off, as if afraid to finish her thought. Then she quickly closed the gate and disappeared into the orchard. From that moment on I never heard from her again, she didn't even send a postcard with snowy mountains or a meadow strewn with crocuses. It could have been blank, with no greeting, no indication it was from her, it still would have been some sort of confirmation of those last words of hers: "Maybe, when I come back. . ."

As Bronka predicted, it was a long time before he returned. Shutting the door behind him, he said:

"Take that sheet out of the typewriter, Bronka. And for the moment don't write anything."

He crossed from the door to the window, walking as if he were half asleep – you'd never have known he was an officer if he hadn't been in uniform. He stood at the window and watched the dusk that was turning into darkness. He stayed like that, not saying a word. In the end, without looking around, without even turning his head, he said as though to himself:

"If it were up to me I'd keep you here. Who knows, it might yield something. Though truth be told, people should be questioned throughout their lives, at different times of the day and night. When they're young, when they're old. Then their statements could be compared. Keep picking at their memory till they're no longer sure of themselves: was it them or wasn't it, are they remembering themselves or do they just think they are. Because what they hide is more important than what they say. You, I feel you're hiding something, but I'm not finding a path to you. And I've been wondering whether interviewer and interviewee oughtn't to get to know each other better. Sometimes even change places. First you'd be questioned, then me, so we'd grow more familiar with one another, because without some give and take there's no getting at the truth. We need to show each other more understanding – recognize that in other circumstances you could have been me, I could have been you. It's against regulations. Can life be contained in regulations, though? In each of us there's a tiny bit of the other, even the interviewee in the interviewer. Anyway, maybe one day. We're not parting for good, after all. We have your contact information. For the time being you're free to go."

No doubt I'd have been pleased, if it hadn't been for that "for the time being," because for the time being never ends. Everything is for the time being. We're young for the time being, we're free for the time being, we exist for the time being. True, they didn't bring me in again, but for almost my whole life I was waiting for that summons, since I was free to go for the time being. Looking through my mail I'd feel a kind of temporary relief that it hadn't come. But I could never rid myself of that expectation, to the point that I began to suspect I was the one conducting an inquiry into myself. And I'd often feel a sense of dread in what would seem the most innocent situations. Yet are there in fact innocent situations in our lives, since not even dreams are innocent?

He suddenly spun around from the window.

"You'll be given a note from the police for your place of work to say you were a witness to an accident and we had to take your statement. Put some paper in the typewriter and get typing, Bronka."

"I don't need a note," I said. "I'm on night shift today. I'll be there on time."

Chapter 2

§

There were three shifts: the first was from six in the morning till two in the afternoon, the second from two till ten, and the third from ten in the evening till six in the morning. They switched you around from week to week. Night shift was my least favorite. Often I was so sleepy I could barely keep on my feet. Whenever the crew leader left to see somebody or check if anyone had brought in vodka, I'd need to doze for at least that quarter of an hour. There were five of us in the crew including the leader; two of them were seasonal workers. Someone would always manage to wake me when the leader was on his way back. But I didn't like the morning shift either. Dragging yourself out of bed at dawn required an almost superhuman effort; even after I'd gotten up, sleep would drag me back down into the sheets. The alarm clock did no good: it rang and rang, yet slumber was like a wall between me and the clock. Luckily, along with the alarm clock mother was keeping watch over me. Father went to work at eight, so he could stay in bed longer. Mother used to say she had an inner alarm clock that was set at the same time summer and winter, she didn't need dawn or daybreak or darkness to wake her.

When I was in high school I did seasonal work every vacation, then when I didn't get into university, my father arranged a permanent job for me in the drying plant. He worked in the same factory, but in the offices. Sometimes I was temporarily reassigned to another department, when the drying plant equipment broke down, or they were rinsing out the sieves, or if there was no fruit to dry. In season we dried apricots, sour cherries, plums, pears, and most of all apples. The apples were sliced then washed in a solution of sulfur so they wouldn't discolor. The best varieties were dried and preserved. The others went directly to the press to be made into juice. Onions and potatoes were also dried, after being sliced like the apples. There was a special crew of peelers who prepared the fruit or vegetables for drying. In the winter there were two shifts, morning and afternoon; all the seasonal workers were let go then, and some of the permanent employees, including me, were moved to other jobs, even cleaning and sweeping.

The hardest task was breaking up the pomace left after the apples were pressed. The pomace was also dried, then made into pectin. The dried product was packed in paper sacks and sent off somewhere. It came out of the press as rocklike rectangular blocks that first had to be broken up with hammers, then loosened with a pitchfork. Today there are probably machines for the job, but back then we only had hammers and pitchforks.

My arms would ache so much from all the breaking and loosening that the pain would wake me up in the night whenever I turned over in bed. Sometimes I was unable to carry a pail of water, or screw in a lightbulb on the ceiling because I couldn't reach up so high; I couldn't button my shirt, and I was always cutting myself shaving. My mother would rub my shoulders with agave extract, or a capsicum liniment the pharmacist had recommended, but while she did it she'd lament over me so much it made the pain even worse.

"How's it come to this, son? You should just up and quit. It breaks my heart to think that my son is a laborer."

"But don't forget that as a laborer it'll be easier for him to get into university," my father would put in. "This is a workers' state, as a worker he'll be at an advantage. And his muscles will grow from the pitchfork. People have to know what times they're living in. He must have answered the wrong way when they asked him. Because they ask questions according to the times, and you have to answer the same way. Everything comes with a price. You have to learn how to live. Look around, there's no shortage of smart people. To this day he hasn't told us what they asked him. Apparently he wasn't capable of being humble, so he didn't get in. The pitchfork'll teach him humility too."

I don't know if it was the wisdom of experience that spoke through my father, but when I'd been up before the admissions committee, right from the get-go the chairman asked me:

"You're applying to major in anthropology. Tell us what a people is."

"All of us," I answered without hesitation.

The committee members exchanged a smirk, and the chairman said:

"Thank you, that will be all."

And that was the end of the exam.

One day I was walking to work for the second shift when I heard a kind of whimpering sound being made by a child. I stopped in my tracks. On the left-hand side of the street there was an empty lot with a pile of bricks, rocks, boards and beams, at the far end of which was a cottage. I walked across the lot; it was only then that I saw a pit filled with slaked lime, and in it a drowning child. Only his head was visible. A moment later and it would disappear beneath the lime. I rushed forward, lay down at the edge of the pit, put my hands into the lime up to my elbows, grabbed the child under his arms and tried to pull him out, but it was too much for my arms. By an effort of will, not of my muscles, I kept the child's head above the surface of the lime. My heart was pounding, my mind raced, because there was no time to lose: slaked lime burns, and it drags you down like quicksand. Not to mention that I could be pulled in myself, because I wasn't going to let go of the child. One half my body, more or less up to my waist, was lying at the edge of the pit; the other half was leaning over the lime, my outstretched hands hooked under the child's arms. Maybe I was imagining it, but his teary face, his little blue eyes narrowed in fear, seemed to be coming closer and closer. My head must have been drawing nearer to his little head, as if I were embracing it.

All at once I heard from a distance, as if emerging from my innards: "Dear God!" Footsteps thudded, there were shouts and curses. The mother and father and the grandfather were running from the cottage at the end of the lot. A strong pair of hands seized hold of my ankles. And a powerful male voice, the father as it turned out, exclaimed:

"Don't let go! I'll pull you out!"

He snatched the child from my arms and ran over to a well. He pulled up a bucket of water and emptied it over the child, who started crying even louder than when he'd been drowning in lime. The mother ran back to the cottage and returned with an armful of old clothes. She wasn't crying so much as wailing: "My Lord! Oh my Lord!" The grandfather, meanwhile, shuffled back and forth by the lime pit, repeating his lament again and again:

"I said, cover it over. Cover it over, I said. Cover it over."

That wasn't enough for him, because he went down to the edge of the pit, where the boy had fallen in, and started beating the ground with his cane till dust flew up.

"You monster! You devil! Take that!"

"Have you gone mad, father-in-law?" The boy's father snatched the cane away; the old man stumbled and almost fell into the pit himself. "You're knocking soil into the lime!"

They were slaking the lime for their new house. The house was going to have stone walls and a cellar, a steep roof, a high-ceilinged attic, big windows, and a glassed-in veranda. It was going to stand on the street, in front of the lime pit, with only a small flower garden separating it from the roadway. No lilacs or jasmine, so as not to block the view. Life's always more cheerful when you can see who's walking or driving by; windows should have some life in them.

They'd been eating lunch in the kitchen, which was on the other side of the cottage, so they hadn't heard anything. Besides, the boy had been eating with them, but he was a bad eater, always wriggling about, and at some point he'd slipped out. They thought he must have gone to his bedroom at the other end of the house, because at mealtimes he often hid under the quilt or crawled beneath the bed. He needed to be dragged out by the ear, or you had to stand over him with a belt. He was an only child; if you didn't beat him he'd get spoiled. And who knew if there'd be another one. Maybe after the house was built. Children are expensive. If there were two or three of them, and all such bad eaters, think how much patience you'd need before they grew up. And when they grew up it'd be the same, you had no idea whether they'd bring you joys or worries.

My father was right. As a laborer I got into university easily. I didn't apply to anthropology like before. I chose history instead; or rather, history chose me, though the times didn't favor history. For of all the branches of knowledge, history is the most at risk from those who want it to conform to their own wishes But it also has the advantage of being the most demanding test of a person's character.

One time, after I had gotten my doctorate, I decided to go see my father. My mother had died two years before, so while I was home I took the opportunity to visit her grave. The cemetery wasn't far. All of a sudden I see a strapping young fellow stomping towards me. He was taking long, vigorous strides. With him was a frail-looking little woman who took two steps for every one of his. I didn't recognize them – how could I have, so many years had passed. She'd been much younger then, taller and broader; her chest made her bigger, she carried herself erect and she looked like she could give birth to many more children. Now she was hunched and skinny. It turned out it was the house that had worn her out. They stopped in front of me and she said to the young man:

"This gentleman saved your life. Say thank you."

He looked at me without a shadow of gratitude, irked that he, a giant of a man, should have to thank anyone, especially a stranger, for the fact he was alive. What had I done? Pulled him out of the lime? Ever since he could remember, he'd overflowed with a sense of his own strength, so he could have pulled himself out without any problem. At dances he'd grab two or three guys by the scruff of the neck and toss them through the window. And here some type in a hat and glasses, walking with a cane, was supposed to have saved him? True, I was only carrying the cane for the visit to my father, I didn't need it to walk with at the time.

"Go on, say thank you," his mother urged him.

Without a word he offered me his large hand; I gave him mine, and he shook it so hard I saw stars.

"If this gentleman hadn't been on his way to work right then, you wouldn't be here today." The woman was moved; her face shone with gratitude on her own behalf, that of her son, and of her late husband and her father, for it was their graves they'd been visiting.

I looked him up and down – this huge figure of a child saved long ago – and I said:

"Today I wouldn't be able to pull you out."

"Today I wouldn't fall into the lime – the house is already standing," he answered, and his expression, which up till then had seemed indifferent, showed something like a gleam of fellow-feeling for me. "Maybe I'll pull you out one day."

"Well, I'm not planning to build a house, so I won't be slaking any lime."

"It doesn't have to be out of lime." He gave a good-natured smile.

Then he took the cane out of my hand and read the inscription on the gold plate. As he handed it back to me he said: "I wouldn't believe that. Your own legs remember you better."

The moment I crossed the threshold, my father expressed his surprise that I was already walking with a cane: "Are you having problems with your hip, or your knee?"

After he'd made me some tea, he poured us each a little glass of his plum *nalewka*, mentioning that it was the last half-bottle, which he was keeping for me and no one else, but which ought to last for the rest of his life, since I wouldn't be visiting often. He picked up the cane and tried to read what was written on the gold plate. Since my last visit he'd gotten even thicker glasses, but he still couldn't make it out. It was only when he helped out the glasses with a magnifying glass that he was able to read the inscription: "To Our Dear Professor, We Will Always Remember You. Your Students. Oh, so you're a professor already. You didn't tell me."

"Well, I'm not yet."

"When you do become one, this'll be just right for the job. A professor ought to have a cane. Otherwise how would you know he's a professor. He'd just be someone walking along. That's a really nice message they wrote. Though let's hope they do remember you, because all sorts of things can happen when it comes to memory. Me, I'm no longer invited to the factory when there's a special occasion, not since the new director came. The previous one used to invite me. What can you do, people's memories are short. If you could just remember about yourself. Though what can you do after your body dies? Your memory would have to live on without it. But wouldn't it suffer more than it'd live?"

After my father died I had no more reason to go there, except to visit their graves from time to time. So I also only rarely visited the old wild green valley. Especially since with the passage of time it was harder and harder for me to walk down the steps. I sometimes had the impression there were more of them since my last visit, and it was even harder to walk back up, not to mention that the hope we'd one day meet was fading. I was drawn there only by the memory of walking her home to the gate and waiting till she'd gone down the path through the orchard and reached the house, and she'd shout from amid the trees:

"Bye!"

But it's not good to visit places from before, they're not the same places. Places come to an end, like everything else. So I'd start off by visiting a cafe on the corner of the market square that I knew from my previous visits. I'd order tea and a slice of hot apple charlotte with whipped cream, and to buck myself up I'd drift into thoughts of my youth, when I'd bound down to the valley, then run back up to the town taking several steps at a time. I'd get vexed when someone was in front of me and got in my way going up or down, and it wasn't possible to pass them because they'd tack from one side to the other as they watched their footing, and I'd have to traipse along behind them. In addition some of them would stop when they reached Needle's Eye, as if pausing halfway through life, because that's usually when our first fears of the future come to us, and we begin to look to the past. And Needle's Eye was about halfway up the steps. Plus, it was only wide enough for two slim people or one stout one, so I'd pause too, though I had nothing to look back on, and the future didn't fill me with anxiety.

A young couple came into the cafe, a man and a woman with a small child, and sat down at the table next to mine. They started talking loudly, as young people do, and I couldn't help overhearing that they'd just come back from a walk. At first I couldn't figure out if it had been to the old wild green valley. They were singing the praises of the walking paths, the benches, the bike path, the children's playground. They bantered about which of them was more suntanned, he'd taken off his shirt, she'd removed her blouse, and the little boy had gone to play with the other children. Then they'd eaten a nice and reasonably priced lunch, because a bistro had opened in the old fruit processing plant built into the hillside.

Could they be talking about the old wild green valley? My suspicions were confirmed when they started complaining that the only problem were those steps, especially going up. Young people, and they were complaining about the steps – I couldn't believe it. At one point I was so annoyed that the teacup I was raising to my lips shook in my hand: one of them, I think it was the woman, sighed and said that if it wasn't for Needle's Eye they could install an escalator like they have in department stores and train stations. Then the man, or maybe it was the other way around, said he hoped the regulations would change and no one would have to pussyfoot around with listed monuments. He would put escalators all around the hill that the town was built on, because they'd be useful here, and there, and there – he named a handful of places – because what's most important is convenience. Especially if you bear in mind that a lot of people are sick or infirm, and there's more and more of them. And thanks to advances in medicine people are going to live longer and longer, even when they're sick and infirm. He himself already had varicose veins, despite his young years.

I couldn't forgive them for Needle's Eye, which was one of the most precious sites in the town. Everyone called it Needle's Eye, but in fact it was an old Dominican gate, preserved in almost pristine form, that had been part of the town's medieval defensive wall. It really did have the shape of the eye of a needle, narrower at the bottom, widening toward the top, with a semicircular vaulted ceiling. On either side of it there were two-story apartment buildings that were much younger, probably by several centuries. Since the buildings were crooked, it looked as if they'd leaned on Needle's Eye and made it so narrow only two slim people or one stout one could pass through at a time. It did have a good side, though: in such a narrow space, even complete strangers meeting there felt obliged to exchange a hello or a Christ be praised. They'd often swap pleasantries or even begin a longer conversation, for who knows if such narrow places aren't conducive to words. If one person so much as murmured that you need the strength of a horse for those steps, then because one word leads to another, after that horse they'd open up to one another about their illnesses, their families, the world, loneliness. Words have a power to unearth our secrets, even if our will doesn't wish it. So acquaintances and friendships were struck up, especially if two people met frequently on the steps. Two men who'd had a permanent falling out were reconciled at Needle's Eye, people said. One of them was coming down, the other was going up, and since both of them were on the portly side they got stuck, because neither would let the other pass and they both tried to squeeze past one another, so they got squashed together like best friends greeting each other after a long separation, and they had to make up.

In the window of the local photographer there were two wedding photos of a couple who'd met at Needle's Eye. One of them showed the man carrying the woman up the steps through Needle's Eye, as if he were carrying her across the threshold, with her veil trailing behind; in the other picture he was also carrying her, but down the steps. Had the photographer instinctively captured a metaphor for their lives, or did he simply figure he'd make more money from two photographs than one? The banal and the sublime are Siamese twins. Thanks to those pictures the couple became famous in the town. I'd sometimes see them walking along holding one another by the fingertips; everyone would look their way, and even older people would greet them first. I don't know what happened to them later – it may have been what happens to the majority of couples in love – because I moved away from the town after I graduated high school. When I came back many years later, the pictures had gone from the photographer's window.

On an impulse I had the curious idea of going into the shop and asking him about those photographs. But he didn't remember the pictures.

"Listen mister, I've taken any number of wedding photos since I started this job. I can't be expected to remember one or two of them in particular. You say it was at Needle's Eye? I've taken pictures there too. Nothing unusual about that. Newlyweds dream up all sorts of locations. I could tell you stories. All I do is perform a service. They want it here, be my guest. Over there, likewise. Every photograph is a matter of price, not metaphor. A metaphor, you say? What's that? These days I'd be too old for certain photos that I maybe would have taken previously, for the right fee. It's a hilly town, everywhere's uphill. Even if they want the pictures down below, afterwards you have to go back up. Couple came in here one time, wanted their picture on top of the town hall. They'd climb up there on a ladder. Where was I supposed to get a ladder like that? The fire brigade would've had to be called out, like for a fire. A wedding isn't a fire. We'll make the arrangements, they said. Luckily the mayor wouldn't have it. What about those two you were asking about, at Needle's Eye: were they a family? They didn't even know each other? I've probably got the negative somewhere, I keep all the negatives. But it'd take forever to go through them. You should come by when I close the business. I might have time to search for them then. I could take a look through my own life while I was about it. Though I'm not sure it'd be worth the effort."

As I stood on the first step and looked down, all of a sudden I started wondering how those two met here. Was she coming up and he was going down, or vice versa? What difference does it make, someone might ask. From a detail so small, trivial even, from the fact that she was going down and he was coming up, or the opposite, could anything be concluded other than that was how they met? All the same, it'd be good to uncover the beginnings of your fate even in a tiny seed that hasn't yet started to sprout. Alas, by its very nature the beginning is unseizable, you might say imperceptible, so who knows if the end doesn't constitute the beginning.

The fortune told by the Gypsy woman, when she pulled my hand into her lap and started tracing out my life, seemed barely worth listening to. Yet when I reached the year she'd predicted for my death, I was dismayed to realize that it was now. And with that sense of dismay I tried to see my life as a whole, though it's quite possible that it was only then I began to put it all together, often missing the truth. For example, when I heard that she wouldn't return home that day through the park but would go via the town, and I raced panting to Needle's Eye, was I still hoping to meet her, or had I given up hope? Was it not earlier that we'd parted, after all? And our parting: did that take place the way I remember, or another way that I'm trying to cover up?

I never told her I loved her, nor she me, as if some fear was holding us back. Whenever the words were right there on my lips – I love you – they refused to sound in my mouth. Did she guess? I'm certain she did. It wasn't hard to: I kept skipping the last class so as to wait for her after school, I'd walk her back to the old wild green valley, invite her to the movies when a new film came out, though she often turned me down. True, I suspected (though it was low of me to think so) that for some reason she was shielding herself against my love. Yet at the same time I doubted my suspicions. She once declared as we were walking back from the cinema: "They say that when you love someone you love the whole world. But I couldn't fall in love with the world."

Perhaps I was incapable of understanding those words, which she'd uttered out of the blue after some film or other. All the same, after she'd said them it was even more impossible to declare my love for her. Yet I continued to hope that a moment would come when she herself would say:

"Would you like to fall in love with me?" I'd be stunned into silence, and she'd continue: "You have no idea how much I need love."

I know that after all these years I'm putting words in her mouth that I myself wasn't capable of pronouncing, not so much from lack of courage, as from the world, if it's supposed to go on existing. You might ask whether the world deserves to exist. I can't say. What I do know is that we don't have to love the world, it's enough that it's so hard for us to part from it.

She only came to our school in the final years. In those days high school was two years. Before that she'd apparently gone to school somewhere in the mountains. Why the mountains? People said various things, as always happens when no one knows. She didn't talk much about herself, and I was too timid to ask. Especially since she usually dodged the question, as if any answer would take away a little part of her life. She was the best student in class, especially in Polish. Add to that her good looks and her large sorrowful eyes, even when she smiled, it was no wonder she was popular. Yet another reason was the mystery of why she'd been at school in the mountains when she'd been born in this town and had gone to elementary school here. Her parents were here – everyone knew them – and her family home, supposedly built by her grandparents, stood on the hill, surrounded by its orchard.

Some in school called her the Jewish Girl, though she wasn't Jewish. People had known her grandfather, who'd been an army physician. Certain folk remembered him as being almost a miracle worker. It was said he could tell a patient's illness just from their appearance and behavior and speech. Legends circulated about his methods of treatment and how effective they were – he'd often snatch people from the jaws of death. In addition, he wouldn't take money from the poor, and would make it up by charging the rich. He even gave poor patients the money to buy the medications he prescribed. He died right at the beginning of the war: he'd been posted to the front along with the regiment that was stationed in town.

Her two uncles on her mother's side were also in the military – a captain and a major. They were shot in a mass killing of prisoners of war in the East, a fact that after the war could only be whispered about. She told me about it one time, asking me not to pass it on, since it could cause problems for me. When my father mentioned it to a friend in confidence he was subsequently called in for questioning. He was working in the municipal administration, in the accounts department I think it was called back then, and he was saved by the fact that he'd won various awards, even a medal for being a model employee, which had been presented by the provincial governor himself. My mother was a librarian in the town library. Thanks to her efforts to organize various kinds of competitions, incentives, and other forms of encouragement, literacy improved considerably in the town.

The name "Jewish Girl" came from a homework assignment that the Polish teacher gave us one day. It was something like: "Which incident from the war stuck in your memory the most?" For her it was the liquidation of the Jewish ghetto, which was on the rim of the hill behind the market square; that hill was separated from the one where her house stood only by the old wild green valley through which I often used to walk her back all the way to her garden gate, and toward which I was now descending step by step, first testing each step with my cane.

When I started high school, for the first year I lived in one of those tumbledown houses that had belonged to some Jewish families and had remained unoccupied immediately after the war, then the poor of the town had moved in. From there you had a bird's-eye view of her house in the orchard on the opposite hill, which was much lower. Later on, as the years went by and it was harder and harder for me to go down to the old wild green valley, and even more to climb back up, I'd sometimes stand at the edge of the hill where the ghetto had once been, and in my mind's eye I'd watch her walk from the gate where we parted and pass through the orchard; the trees would hide her and show her by turns till she disappeared through the door of the house. One time it even seemed to me that amid the apple trees, which happened to be in blossom, she stretched out her arm and waved to me. Another time I heard her call from among the trees:

"Bye!"

I stood waiting for her to reach the house, in the hope that she'd wave to me from there, but she never got as far as the door.

The column was just leaving the ghetto, accompanied on both sides by dogs and by men with machine guns at the ready. She and her mother, hearing that the Jews were being led to the train station about two miles away, ran up there and stood, out of breath and crying, at the top of the steps. When the column had progressed some distance, though its end still couldn't be seen, a little girl broke away and ran toward them. She didn't make it to them, though, for one of the dogs went for her and would have sunk its teeth into her had it not been pulled away by one of the machine gunners. He lifted the scraped-up girl and thrust her back into the column. It was Sara, her friend from elementary school – they'd sat next to one another till Sara had to move to the ghetto.

The Polish teacher said her essay was the best in the class. She had her stand up in front of the other children and read it aloud. As you listened to the essay, it was hard to believe it had happened in this world, in this town – which had seen all sorts of things in its centuries-long existence – and on top of it all in front of Needle's Eye. Her childlike sensitivity had enabled her to remember it all so intensely that the rest of us were plunged in a silence that lasted until the end of the lesson. When something imprints itself on your memory as a child, it stays. When you're still discovering your existence in the world you wonder at everything, and wonder is the root of memory. Alas, that root dries up as the years go by, and eventually nothing makes us wonder anymore.

When she finished reading, the Polish teacher's eyes filled with tears; she excused herself and left the room. A moment later she came back and announced that we'd end there for today. During the war she'd been arrested and sent to a concentration camp, where she was apparently subjected to medical experiments. People claimed that incisions had been made in her legs, as a result of which they were covered in scars, and all year round she wore ankle-length skirts.

People came down the steps, others went up; some of them said hello though I didn't know anyone. Everyone looked young to me, whether they were going up or down. I thought to myself, has the world gotten so young? Then what am I doing in it? Somebody took me by the arm and asked: "Are you wanting to go down or up? I'm going down, I could give you a hand."

"Thank you, I'm not sure yet. For the moment I'm just standing here."

He gave a laugh, let go of my arm, and continued downward in rapid strides. A moment later someone else, this time coming up, asked me the same question: "Are you going up or down? I'm going up, you could take my arm."

"Thank you, I don't know yet. I haven't made up my mind."

I really was making my mind up: what in fact had I come for, since I no longer had any hope. Yet I thought, I'll go down, because I'd just remembered that it was in the old wild green valley that no longer existed, after I'd walked her back all the way to her gate and we were exchanging our goodbyes, that out of the blue she'd said in a kind of muffled whisper:

"I'm going away to a sanatorium. But perhaps when I come back. . ."

I placed my foot on the next step, after probing it first with my cane. Before the following step I suddenly felt afraid I wouldn't manage it as well as the previous one. I looked downward. The steps went down and down as if they had no end. On top of which, they were much steeper than before. I couldn't believe I'd ever been capable of running up and down, taking two or three steps at a time.

All at once, from that invisible bottom way down there, I see someone running up toward me, taking long strides, precisely two or three steps at a time. He's close, only a few steps separate us. I recognize him, how could I not, I search for words because I'd like to greet him. Someone on their way down comes between us, someone else who's coming up. All the same we draw closer, he's already at Needle's Eye, and I'm only three or four steps from him. He lets somebody pass who's going up, but it seems he doesn't intend to make way for me. He stands in the middle of Needle's Eye and stares warily at me, as if asking, who are you? I realize he doesn't recognize me, and I'm not surprised, how could he from such a distance of years, since he'd just come running from the park where he'd been waiting in vain for her till the Gypsy woman told him she wouldn't be returning home through the park today, she'd go via the town because she needed to buy something, and I was going down to the old wild green valley that no longer existed. He may even have tried to remember me, but how could he make out his youth in an old face like mine? It doesn't seem possible. And yet...

I was no further than two steps away from him when I detected something hateful in his eyes. I didn't hold his hatred against him, he may not have known yet that old age was waiting for him too, somewhere. At his age it might even seem that the elderly are unnecessary in the world; people ought to free themselves of them, that way the world would always be young. Or perhaps the hatred was his defense, so he wouldn't see his own future in me, and that was why he refused to recognize me. He was unaware that his future and also his childhood and his youth, were contained in my old age, that I'd already lived them, often worrying myself over him, troubled throughout my whole life by that future of his, just as I was about my own past.

I'd been as full of hope as he was, waiting for her at Needle's Eye, to see if she'd appear. Was I to take that hope away from him now, tell him she'd never come, that she'd left him nothing but emptiness?

I often experience that emptiness. Even my dreams have abandoned me. I wake in the morning, not believing that I'm waking, and it takes me several minutes or more to get used to myself, to the fact that it isn't someone else who's woken up in my place. What's the point of living in such emptiness, without even dreams? Just for life itself? After all, dreams are life just as much as our waking hours, it's merely that they're concealed. Once I used to dream of her every night. She was just as young, with those large sad eyes, with a row of white-white teeth whenever some word made her open her mouth; that was how my memory had preserved her. For me the years were passing, while she didn't change a bit. I could have made my life out of dreams alone, and it probably would have been more interesting than my waking life, for what is life when everything seems to be no more than a dream? When I was sitting back then in the park, on the bench, was I not dreaming that I was waiting for her on her way home from school? Then the Gypsy woman tells me she won't be coming that way today, she'll go via town because she needs to buy something, hooks and eyes or press studs, so I jump up, run off, reach Needle's Eye, and she's already waiting for me there.

"I'm here," she says. "I didn't buy anything. I was in a hurry, as much of a hurry as you were. I'll buy it another time. And you, in future don't believe the Gypsy woman."

He stepped aside, not completely out of the way, but I was slim, I would have been able to move past him. Yet after so many years it was only right to say: "We haven't seen each other in a long time, sir. Let's greet one another. Or perhaps we should say goodbye. What do you prefer? You don't recognize me. I understand. I understand and I forgive you."

They were paltry words, but nothing else came to mind, and so instead of saying anything I felt sorry for him, for I could see how anxiously he was gazing toward the top of the steps, not looking at me. I was on the point of passing him, making sure of the next step with my cane, when suddenly a bell began to sound so loudly that everything around shook, and all the hills and orchards rang with the echo of the chimes. I felt the steps trembling underfoot, and the cane quivered in my hand. I stopped. Someone climbing up toward me, panting as if he were dragging the steps up attached to his heels, also stopped when he reached me and said between gasps: "You have to stop when the bell rings, because death is pulling the rope." He panted further: "The glazier."

"What about the glazier?"

"He died. They're burying him." Then, when he'd recovered a bit: "Are you going to the funeral maybe? You could say goodbye to him from me. Take these gerberas. I have a greenhouse, down that way. My son runs it now. Say they're from Leon, the gerbera grower. It's too bad you don't have an umbrella, it's likely to storm. One time there was a storm. Real big one. Trees were blown down, roofs torn off. My greenhouse got smashed to pieces. Hail like chicken's eggs, I'm telling you. And it blew so hard you couldn't stay on your feet. All the panes were shattered. He put new ones in for me. There were so many of them – he used a cubic yard of putty alone. And now they're burying him. I don't mind giving you the gerberas – they're about to wilt anyway. It'd be good to go. But my legs aren't what they used to be, they won't carry me. I'd have liked to go for all those panes. I used to be ramrod straight when I walked, people said I looked like an officer, though I only ever made corporal. If he'd died sooner I might I have been able to go. They die too late. Too late. It's a ways to the cemetery, over cobblestones. You wobble this way and that, plus there's all those potholes, it's easy to trip. They could at least put some gravel down. But they don't have the funds. Though when you go to the town hall the place is crawling with staff. They've got enough to pay themselves. How are they going to carry the casket over that? He's not that big, the deceased, but it'd be hard even with an empty casket. All right, I've got my breath back. Let me past, if you will."

After the chance meeting with the gerbera grower, one night I had a dream about the glazier's funeral. There was no storm, contrary to what the gerbera grower had predicted, but it was raining, pouring in fact. Everyone except me had an umbrella. I was walking in the middle of the procession, carrying a huge bouquet of gerberas, when behind I heard someone whisper in reference to me: "It's so nice that a young person came."

Somebody next to me urged me to move forward, closer to the casket. Since I didn't show willing, they began to propel me through the whole procession, and some of the gerberas fell to the ground. Now someone whispered instructions, their hot breath burning my ear:

"Closer, closer, or you won't make it in time. Surely you'd like to say a few words. It'd be only right for you young people to bid farewell to the deceased too. He put so many windows in the schools."

I felt a tap on my shoulder.

"Are you from abroad by any chance? Apparently somebody flew in. It'd be great for someone from abroad to speak as well, that would make the funeral look good. We can say you're from abroad. No one's checking ID here."

Then another attendee virtually forced his way between me and a woman in black who may or may not have been the wife of the deceased, and who had taken my arm and held her umbrella up to shelter me from the rain. He said:

"I'm terribly sorry, are you close family or distant? Not that it matters. We're all family in the face of death. And you can't have a family without young people."

I was surrounded by older and older faces, drawing ever nearer, insisting on my youth. There was no way to fight it, youth was what they wanted, as if no one could admit that youth ages as quickly as fashion. True, some people hold onto youth with all their might, submit themselves to torments, forgetting that they're aging from the inside. Whatever they do, they can't hold back the passage of time. But evidently faith in fashion can sometimes be stronger than faith in the passage of time. Who knows, maybe the first can even defeat the second.

I knew someone who was the same age as me. When he reckoned his youth was over, he committed suicide.

"The only thing awaiting me now is waiting," he said to me in farewell.

What can you do: it's not old age's fault that it isn't fashionable, nor youth's fault that it is. Maybe somewhere in all this lies an idea for the present world. Whether things will ever switch, I don't know. In the

Middle Ages – the period I specialize in – old age wasn't just a repository of memory, but also an oracle in matters of the highest importance. Whereas today the old are said to be hampering the world's forward march. Except if you think about it, it's only in old age that you realize the world's march forward is nothing but an illusion of youth. The globe merely turns beneath our feet, while we mark time, pretending to march. Because what would "forward" mean, if not toward death.

I even wanted to inquire what it's like to be old. But when I started looking around for someone to ask, all the faces suddenly disappeared beneath their umbrellas. The procession had already passed through the cemetery gates and had stopped next to a freshly dug grave. The casket was lifted down from the bearers' shoulders and placed by the hole. Wreaths and flowers were put on it and the funeral speeches began. I was certain I'd be asked to go first, since I'd been appointed spokesman for youth. I planned to lay down the gerberas from Leon at that time.

I'd already worked out what to say. In my childhood I'd visited a glassworks with my parents, and we had our picture taken. I had that photograph till not long ago, me between them in my little beret. The photo went missing eventually but it was preserved in my memory. Behind us, in the background there's a glassworker, I would say it was the deceased. He was holding a large pane of glass in both hands; it had just come out of the press, and he wanted to offer it to us as a gift, so we could watch the world through the glass, and it'd be less painful to us. Unfortunately, a crowd formed in front of the casket, as though everyone wanted to speak, and I was pushed so far back I couldn't see myself any longer. I looked around anxiously, where was

I? I may actually have cried out, Where am I? Where am I? But I was nowhere to be seen. I remember, though, that people kept interrupting each other, elbowing one another back from the grave; they even stepped on the casket. Some, inflamed by their own words, rose up onto their toes, craned their necks, waved their arms, and were moved to tears, as if their toes and necks and hands and tears were bearing their words to heaven.

Soaked to the skin in the dream, I decided to buy an umbrella. I went into town and, walking down the street, I saw an open umbrella in a shop window. It was identical to the one carried by the woman in black at the funeral who'd taken my arm and sheltered me from the rain. It was big enough for two people. Over the window there was a large signboard with pictures of umbrellas of various colors, above which was written: "Umbrellas and Parasols for Every Season, Men's Women's Children's Classic and Modern."

I pushed the door open. A bell rang.

"I'd like the one from the display," I said. Then all at once I fell silent, for I couldn't see umbrellas anywhere. It was like an office. At the far end a bald man sat at a computer; all I could make out was his hairless head. Without lifting his eyes from the computer screen he said:

"You must be looking for a funeral speech, sir. For what age?"

"No, I'm after an umbrella," I answered uncertainly.

"Umbrellas are next door. You got the wrong entrance." Then, still from behind the computer: "But since you made the mistake, I suggest you take advantage of it. Mistakes often lead us in the right direction when we're lost, or we forget where we were going. Now that I look at you. . ." Though he still wasn't taking his eyes off the computer.

"A Gypsy woman, when I was young – " I broke in, thinking that the Gypsy woman would disturb his composure.

But he didn't let me finish.

"Let's not bother one another with the Gypsy woman. Her slogan is: A long life. Mine: Ye know neither the day nor the hour. Help yourself to a brochure. They're on the table under the mirror. Take a look while you're here."

I went up to the table, picked up a brochure and noticed that on the wall nearby there was a large baize bulletin board on which were pinned thank-you notes – some hand-written, others printed, some short, some longer.

"Are these thank-yous from the dead?" I asked.

He fired back wryly:

"If you decide one day that you'd like to thank me, your note will be added to the board."

"I'm sorry."

"Don't worry. I've had to put up with all sorts of sarcasm, I still do. The important thing is that business is flourishing. People need speeches. And since such a need exists, someone has to write them. Not everyone's capable of making one up out of their own head. Often emotions are of no help, and the tongue trips over itself. Besides, most human minds are overgrown with the weeds of newspapers, radio, television, the internet. A speech shouldn't be an outrage to death. Plus, there are fewer and fewer words in people. Have you not noticed how they're disappearing? So words too need someone to help them out. You see how many dictionaries and reference books I have here." He gestured toward the shelves behind him at the far end of the room. "A mine of words, you might say. It's not so easy, this business. But other things aren't easy either. The factory was sold and they started letting people go because the workforce was too big. I worked in planning, but they said that now there wouldn't be any more planning, only production. And I found myself unemployed. The benefits weren't enough; I had a wife and children, and often there wasn't food to put on the table. Let me tell you, I was close to suicide. But I suddenly realized that no one would come to a suicide's funeral, and they'd bury me right by the wall. And on top of that, everyone was saying that people should take matters into their own hands. So I did. During my engagement I'd bought this book, *The Art of Letter Writing*. Perhaps you know it? I used it when I wrote to the woman who later became my wife. Till she wrote back one day to say that if those letters reflected my feelings for her, she'd marry me. But I thought to myself, letters are an uncertain business. Outmoded, you might say. These days, instead of writing letters to someone you go to bed with them. I need to find something more permanent so as not to worry about finding work anymore. And what's more permanent than death? That was how I came up with funeral speeches. There are more and more people, not less and less, so there won't be fewer funerals. I rented this place, put up a signboard. Before I opened the shop I wrote and wrote and wrote. I didn't have a computer back then, it was all by hand or on the typewriter. A friend lent me the money for a typewriter, because I couldn't afford it. I had to have a supply of speeches in case somebody wanted something ready-made. In any company you need a stock of goods for the beginning. If people started coming and I didn't have anything to show them, what kind of business would that be? Whereas now I could say, there's this one, or this one, or a different one. In a ready-made speech like that, often you only need to change one detail or another, add or remove something. One death isn't that different from another, and funerals even less so. Today, those shelves over there are filled with pre-written speeches." He pointed to a row of binders behind him. "If you'd like to take a look, I can pull out a binder or two." He got up from the computer and reached toward the shelves, but I stopped him:

"Please don't bother. First I need to think about your advice."

"Then come back whenever you're ready. I may have umbrellas too by then. I heard a rumor that my neighbor's going bust; if it's true, I might buy his stock along with his shop. It likes to rain during funerals. People would be glad to buy an umbrella along with their funeral speech. You know, I even thought of writing a book, Funeral Speeches. I've built up quite a collection. But who would patronize the shop then? I'd sell my entire experience in a book, and then what? All that toil, sweat, mental strain, all those sleepless nights spent fitting everything into categories. Because you ought to know that every deceased person can be placed in a categories. People don't differ very much from the point of view of death. And for a ready-made speech like that I only charge a third of the price of a custom job. Occasionally I give a discount as an incentive. Though people are getting more and more ambitious. When you go to the cemetery on All Saints' you see that people are building bigger and bigger tombs. It's no different with speeches. So more and more people are ordering custom ones. And longer and longer. Some of them want poems in there. As if there weren't enough formalities already. So I had to take on a poet too. He used to publish his poems in the factory newsletter when the factory was still going. He had a full-time job as arts and education coordinator. Once he even won a prize in a competition about some national holiday. But how was he going to earn a living now? From poems? Come off it. He'd have made more money begging on the street. I'm not denying he has talent; I give him carte blanche, all I do is tell him the requirements. My father told me that in the old days people like that went around the church fairs. Sometimes they'd sing their poems. About wars, plagues, other catastrophes. My family remembered one poem about a man who kills his wife, the wife has previously poisoned her husband, then they each appear in the other's dreams. The whole fair would listen. And the coins would roll in, often they'd fill their cap. I give my guy twenty-five percent of the price for a custom speech. I ask the client, do you want a poem? And let me tell you, most of them do. You just need to explain to the client that a speech with a poem will be fancier. The Lord God is more likely to listen to a poem. Priests come to me too, they do. A priest is only human. How many speeches like that can he give from memory? When he has two or even three funerals, one after the other sometimes. So what if it's his job? In every job there are limits to how much you can do. They come from the provincial government, the administrations of counties, towns, villages. One time a limo pulled up. I won't say where from, client confidentiality. These days, I'm telling you, a director or a CEO, a minister even, they're not going to spend time over a speech when one of their employees dies. They've got more important things to worry about, and here they have to speak at a funeral. So they send someone to me, and that person buys one of the ready-made ones or puts in an order, depending on how important the deceased was. I've got speeches for believers and non-believers, and for people who are half and half. At first I only wrote them for believers. But one time this fellow comes to me and says he needs a speech for a secular funeral. What does that mean, I ask. Secular, he says, what's not to understand? What world are you living in? He got mad. Listen pal, I said, here everyone's a believer, even the people who used to be party members, they're believers too. No one's ever asked me for a secular job. Take a look at what I have, maybe you'll find something. I give him one binder and another. He looks through one of them and tosses it aside, leafs through the next one, tosses that aside too. That's how it is when there's no competition, he says; he curses, and slams the door on his way out. I tell you, that thought of competition gave me the willies. I told my wife, I said, we need to write a few speeches for secular funerals. What does that mean? You know, without God. I'll give you without God, she says. I'll go live with my mother and you can write what you like. Cook your own meals, do the housework, wash your own clothes. I sweated bullets over it, let me tell you, hammered my fists against my head till it rang, I had nothing. I didn't eat, didn't sleep, I wrote and tore it up, wrote and tore it up. Then one day she says to me, you must be hungry; your eyes are closing from lack of sleep. And she takes that empty head of mine and cradles it against her chest. What can you do, she says, the world's heading toward godlessness. You won't hold it back with speeches. I'm telling you, sir, women understand the world better. She didn't go live with her mother. Then another time she says, in a shop you can't just sell regular bread, you need to have whole meal loaves too. You could use a bigger shop, two rooms, a bathroom with a toilet. Because if someone's caught short, where are they going to go? These days everyone's remodeling, redesigning, expanding or reducing. If the umbrella man goes bankrupt, we could knock down the wall. Why would he go bankrupt, I say, it's not going to stop raining or snowing. Then we should look for other premises. One room could be a waiting room, the other one your office. We could take out a loan. Obviously you're not going to go bankrupt, so we'd be able to pay it off. We should do it. We could buy three armchairs, a rug for the floor. A coat rack. Take your coat off, you'll say to the client, the rack is right there. Some pictures for the walls. A magazine rack. What magazines, I say. You know, when you're waiting at the dentist's or the barber's, you look through a magazine and you lose track of time. Though only the ones with lots of photos of actors and actresses. Changing them every six months would be enough. They can even be from last year. It'd look more serious with magazines. A fan for when it's hot, one in the waiting room and one in here next to you. You'd have a breeze, you wouldn't get so tired. I do get tired, it's true. It's not like it was in the planning department: there, we always had time for coffee, tea, the paper, news, gossip. Whereas here, I'm telling you, before one client leaves there's already another one waiting. And you have to listen and listen about the life of the deceased, even though only a fragment of it is any use for the speech. If I put everything people tell me into the speech, no one would make it to the end of the funeral. Even the people invited to the wake would opt to eat at home. But if you want business to go well, you have to be patient. And it is going well, I won't deny it. Some even envy me. Is it my fault people die? I don't kill them, I just write speeches for their funerals. Though let me tell you, I sometimes wonder what direction the world is going in. Yes, people have always died, but these days funerals have become an industry. I ought to be pleased I've got a product like this, but my conscience troubles me more and more often. Think about it: every life is different supposedly, yet I have to fit each one into a category. I even gave them labels – A1, B3, C5, and so on – so I wouldn't waste time looking. I've got models for different ages, from infants all the way up to the very oldest, when someone's really lived. Truth be told, though, who really has lived. Everyone's as thirsty for life as a mushroom for rain, as the expression goes. I've got models for husbands, wives, mothers, fathers, grandfathers, grandmothers, sons, daughters, grandchildren, distant relatives. Neighbors, acquaintances, close friends. I've even thought about writing some for partners, as they say today. I give each client the relevant binder and let them choose. I don't impose, at most I offer advice. I'll admit that at times I think about preparing something suitable for myself also, so no one talks a bunch of nonsense about me afterwards. Some people choose the shoes they want to be in, or their suit or shirt, occasionally their casket, while they're still alive. Though I wonder whether I should write a custom speech or take one of the ready-made ones. What do you think? Be honest – what would you recommend if it were for yourself?"

"What would I recommend for myself? Silence."

Chapter 3

§

I can't say for sure if it was after or before. It doesn't really matter. I could have gotten the times muddled up. Time has a tendency to switch around. It's as cunning as a fox, and it can be malicious. It can flow in one direction and simultaneously in the opposite one. We only think it's always flowing along with us, and that our life sets its boundaries. Nothing could be further from the truth. It pulls us where it will. Backwards, to when we didn't yet exist, and forwards to where we'll no longer be there. It plays with us, fully aware that there's nothing we can do about it. It's not hard to play with human beings.

He was pleased to see me, and he halted in his tracks.

"I brought my umbrella just in case," he said. "It's big enough for both of us. Because it looks like there's going to be a storm. Can you feel how muggy it is, sir? It's hard to breathe. You should buy yourself an umbrella too. In these parts it can storm without any warning. The sun's blazing, then all at once the storm's upon you. On this side the land is hilly, over there it's flat as far as the eye can see; places like this evidently favor storms. It's stifling today. No one even feels like talking."

I did in fact have the impression that he was short of breath. He kept pausing as he spoke, and each word sounded a little hoarse. His forehead was speckled with perspiration. Taking out a handkerchief, he mopped his face and wiped his nose.

"When I was your age," he began after a moment, but he seemed to forget what he'd been about to tell me. He stared at the hills and orchards that lay before us, with houses among them, a church to the left, another church farther away, and a cemetery; and I was convinced he wouldn't say what he'd meant to. "When I was your age," he went on, "it made no difference to me whether I was going down or up. I'd leap up and down these steps."

I thought to myself, he could have come up with something better than that ritualistic "when I was your age." Do old people always have to begin with "when I was your age"? It sounds like a reproach or even an invitation to a contest of strength, a "let's measure up against each other." And I felt like retorting that when I'm his age it won't make any difference to me either whether it's up or down. But I held my tongue.

"I can guess what you meant to say yet didn't." He'd read my thoughts. "I don't hold it against you. I even understand you, I used to think the same way myself, because youth is believing that you'll always be young. But I have to warn you, it's a belief that passes. All the same, when you look at today's world, it's no surprise that it believes in youth, since it's drawing closer and closer to its end. And over there" – he pointed toward a two-story building in the distance – "or near there anyway, was the hostel. Not a dorm, like they say today. What was wrong with hostel? For me it'll always be hostel. What can you do, though, the world changes from words, not just words from the world. Though it's amazing how it can happen in the course of a single lifetime." He glanced up at the sky. "What's going on with that storm? You really should buy yourself an umbrella."

It was as if he'd foreseen that I would need it. One time I'd walked her back to her gate and we couldn't bring ourselves to part. There was a flash somewhere, another, and a roll of thunder, even though the sky was crystal clear – yet who would have looked at the sky. All at once it began pouring down. Quick, run into the house, I said, it's just up through the orchard. But she wouldn't, because she knew that before I reached my hostel I'd be soaked to the skin, and she couldn't bear the idea that she would already be home. Come on, let's take shelter under that chestnut. She pulled me under the tree. Its leaves are broad, we can wait out the storm here. There were all sorts of trees in the valley back then: chestnuts, ashes, elms, even a linden I think.

But I didn't buy an umbrella as he'd urged me. I borrowed one from my father. True, my wage packet had been bigger on the first of the month because I'd put in a lot of overtime – it was strawberry season and they'd transferred me from the drying plant to the strawberries, where production was going full steam ahead, so some days I worked a double shift. But I was saving money for university, and I didn't want to spend it on an umbrella. The weather wasn't the best, so it was smart to carry an umbrella. Standing with the umbrella at Needle's Eye, I was watching to see if she'd arrive from the direction of the valley, or whether she'd come down from the town. I would have greeted her with:

"Now we can stay dry."

But she didn't come that time either. Even today I'm often troubled by the darkest thoughts, that maybe that's how you die. You just don't show up, don't reply to a letter, don't pick up the phone. I knew a man, he was sick, it's true, but he used to joke that he'd outlive all the healthy people because his illness made him stronger. He never lost his sense of humor. His death too I missed. He quite simply didn't open the door when I went to see him one time. I rang and rang the bell, till his neighbor came out and scolded me:

"What are you ringing like that for? He's dead."

Another man lived abroad, we corresponded regularly. He was a professor of history like me. We studied the same period. We used to let each other know about new publications, new sources that had appeared, we'd sometimes meet at conferences. One day I sent him a registered letter, but after a while it came back with a note from the post office saying, addressee unknown. Though as an academic he was very well known.

The same could be said of more distant acquaintances or people I'd met in passing or known only because I'd read their book, seen their paintings, heard their music – from everything we encounter, even subconsciously, we take something away for ourselves. Thanks to which it might be said that in each of us there's a little bit of all humankind. It doesn't matter if they're people who are alive today or if they lived in another time, long ago. It's thanks to them that we too live now, and in another time, and long ago. And we're all the richer for suffering less, as it were, from the passage of time.

Once, in the winter, during Carnival we organized a party in the hostel. It was a modest affair, with a phonograph. The phonograph had a big tube; it was one of the later models that worked by electricity instead of being wound up. In the hostel, if I remember correctly there were eight rooms with six or eight beds each, and a larger one that contained over a dozen beds. Before the war the larger one had apparently been the rec room. After the war though, there were so many new students, especially from the surrounding villages and small towns, that the rec room was converted into another room for sleeping. Some classes had their lessons in the afternoon; each one had up to forty students. Everyone was going to school back then. Apart from us there were several accelerated classes of day students for older children making up for the lost war years. Some of them had begun school right back before the war and only now were finishing. Some had been with the partisans, others in prison. In a word, the hostel was bursting at the seams.

We stacked the beds from the big room elsewhere and brought in chairs from the canteen, which was down in the basement. We put them around the walls, so the girls at least would have somewhere to sit. We cleaned the room, of course, washed the floor, shaved off some candlewax and trod it into the floorboards till they shone. We hung up garlands made of colored tissue paper, and covered the lamps with it too. It was a lot of work, but everyone chipped in. The sense of excitement spurred us on.

There needed to be as many girls as there were boys at the party. So we invited a lot of girls. They all showed up, except for her. I thought maybe she was running late. The party began, a tango played on the phonograph, everyone paired off. I sat on a chair against the wall and waited, hoping she'd appear during the tango. Because even if I'd wanted to dance, I wouldn't have had a partner. What could have happened to prevent her from coming?

In the end I went outside and started walking in the direction she ought to come from. There was no other route to the hostel. The snow creaked underfoot; I stopped and listened to see if her footsteps weren't by any chance approaching. Especially because footsteps are heard much sooner in winter than in summer: the silence carries them from far away. There's no comparison between winter footsteps and summer ones. The winter was severe, the frost stung my ears and cheeks, the stars glared in the sky like they do when it's really cold. And the moon shone like a lamp. If I hadn't been afraid of getting frostbite, I would have taken off my shoes and walked in stockinged feet so as not to miss the faintest footstep when it reached me in the silence. Because there wasn't a single sound. The music from the hostel had stopped following behind me; I could virtually hear the stars rubbing against one another in the sky. For if you look up at the mass of stars, it's hard to imagine that they don't rub up against each other.

I didn't realize that I'd gotten chilled to the bone. I went back to the hostel. Not all the pairs were dancing now. A dozen or more girls were sitting on the chairs around the walls, while my schoolmates had disappeared somewhere. I guessed they'd gone down to the canteen in the basement, because there were a few bottles of wine down there. It wasn't right for me to sit when so many girls had been abandoned like that. So I asked her best friend to dance.

"Why are you so cold?" she said when I took hold of her. It was only then that I began to shiver. "They should play something fast." She called over to the other girls: "Put on some boogie-woogie!"

I warmed up a little and I asked her if she maybe knew why her friend hadn't come. She would know. The result was that she refused to dance the tango that followed. I asked another girl and it was the same story. She was miffed that I was asking about another girl.

"So how was the party?" he asked me when we met again some time later. "Some time later" could have been two or three years or more. "You know, at the hostel. Was it a success? There, you see. We met too late. I could have warned you she wouldn't come. But there's nothing I can do about it: you yourself have to live through what I already have behind me. I'll just say that with girls, friendship is one thing, but when you're dancing with one girl you don't ask about another one. Excuse me, but I'm in a hurry. My son's waiting for me at the cafe. He gave me a ride. Myself, I no longer drive. I don't have the confidence I used to. And we have to visit the art exhibition at the castle. Paintings of the town since last century. Seemingly it's a large exhibit. While I'm there I may meet up with Mrs. Zofia, the director of the castle. A person of great merit. She's spared no effort in returning the place to its former glory. I may also see Mr. Jerzy, who runs the Museum of Literature at the castle; he's such a kind man, always so helpful. I should also definitely look in on Mrs. Alicja. Do you know her boarding house? Artists and scholars often stay there. Worst-case we'll drive back by night. As you see, there are still a few people I'm attached to here. While for you, it's probably only her. It was like that for me too once. Today, though, I only walked this way out of habit. It's hard to free yourself entirely from your youth. Youth holds on to people with an iron grip. I have a son, a grandson, yet youth keeps growing back in me, so to speak. My grandson's a marvel, as you can imagine, like all grandchildren. Yours will be too. You shouldn't say it won't happen. Young people often say this or that won't happen, it's typical of them. But life will draw you in and won't stop to ask for your opinion. So what if the world is uncertain? It's always been uncertain, yet people go on being born. As if they were thumbing their noses at wars, revolutions, mutual slaughter. We'll have more than one war yet, more than one revolution, people won't stop killing one another, but they'll still go on being born. I should say goodbye, my son will be getting impatient. I promised him I'd only be a moment. Oh, you know what, the house has been sold. Lord, how many years has it been since she waved to me from amid the branches as she walked up the path through the orchard, or called 'Bye' to me when she reached the door. Some young people have bought the place, apparently they have some kind of arts project that involves the house. I hope people like that will become the future of this town. But you should wait, you should wait, if despite everything you haven't given up hope."

I didn't know whether to believe him or not. A son, a grandson? It somehow didn't sound plausible. Especially because when I tried to take his arm, saying, I'll walk you back, he pulled away and replied:

"No, no thank you. I can manage. I'm not in such bad shape. You can see I'm walking without a cane. I'll manage."

"Maybe to the top of the steps at least?"

"No. Because you'll say, a little bit farther. Then another little bit. Then, just one more block. Just to that apartment building, to that tree, that bench, and we'll never part."

Despite his unwillingness I walked after him. After a few steps he looked around, and as much as he could he hurried on, as if running away from me.

"Stop following me. Stop it. Don't be cruel. My son would never forgive me if he saw me with you. How could I introduce you? That you're who? He may well step out of the cafe if he's wondering what's become of his father. Go back and wait. She may be longing for someone to wait for her. And who could still be waiting for her if not you? I don't have long left. My time isn't counted in years anymore; it might be months, weeks, days."

It was only after he died that I finally grasped the fact that, though I'd waited for her so many times and she hadn't come, now she surely never would. He was gone, so why would she come? For whom?

When I reapplied to university I needed certification from my high school. On my way to fetch it I went by Needle's Eye. For the first time since he'd fallen down the steps. No, I had no hope of meeting her. I don't even know what I would have said to her. I just wanted to see how my memory would behave regarding what had happened on the steps. You should check yourself in relation to former events, even ones from long ago, from before you were born. And who knows, maybe also with regard to your own ideas. Especially because he had been the one to urge me to major in history. It seemed right, then, to come here and whisper:

"Thank you. The future will tell if I was right to follow your advice."

He often tried to convince me that history was not the past. However distant it might be, it's always happening now, in our own lifetime. History alone can help us find ourselves on the map of time. History is the discipline of all disciplines. Thanks to it I've come to understand many a thing in my own life, and in numerous cases it helps me bear the pain of its weight. I've felt that weight more and more, precisely since the first time I didn't get in to university, when I wanted to study anthropology.

Besides, how long could I go on living at my parents' place. At some point you have to find your own life. The sooner the better. Every wasted day shortens your life. Was I not wasting days like that at the drying plant? I'd head out for the first, or second, or third shift, always with the feeling that this was not what I'd been born for. Yes, I was earning money, but earning money isn't what people are born for either. When I think about it from a distance of years, I don't know if I was living my life, or whether perhaps I was constantly running away from it.

It was the summer vacation. My mother had rented out a room at our place to a friend of her cousin's from before the war. The friend had decided after all that time to come back here for a vacation; before the war, the two of them had taken part in the public works program, repairing the levees after a great flood. My mother was unwilling at first, but her cousin came with a letter from the friend and read it to her. The friend was asking the cousin to find him a room to rent somewhere because he and his wife would like to come and stay. It was probably the last chance they'd have to meet up, after so many years. No he didn't want to stay at the cousin's place, because if he remembered correctly there was only one bedroom and the kitchen, and you entered the bedroom via the kitchen, whereas he'd prefer a room with a separate entrance, for his wife's sake. He asked how the levees were holding up after the big flood, because there were still often floods. He'd hear about them from the papers and the radio. The truth is, he said, I don't have time for a vacation, I've got so much going on at work, but my wife keeps saying, let's go there, let's go. She wants to see the levees, walk on them. I've often told her I left a good piece of my youth on those levees, sweated so much for them, it always touched her. Who was I then? Nobody. Without hope that anything in my life would change. Whereas see how things are today. I used to think, if war breaks out – because people were already talking about war at that time – then I'd go to war and maybe I'd die. And it would be better that way. I didn't go to war, though I volunteered. When I see you I'll tell you why the army didn't take me. So I joined the partisans instead. I was wounded three times, one time it was serious, but I recovered.

Well, my mother was touched too, and she rented them the biggest bedroom, with a separate entrance off the hallway to the right.

In the same letter the friend asked my mother's cousin how Krysia was, though he said not to mention her when his wife was around. Remember, you introduced me to her. Good-looking girl. She was from a nearby village. They didn't have anyone to work the farm, her father had died and it was only her and her mother, her older brother was a noncom in the professional army and he was stationed abroad somewhere. We were going to get married. Is she still alive? She wasn't.

The flood had been immense. Apocalyptic, some people said. It broke through the previous levees, swept away houses; people and animals drowned. The oldest folks couldn't remember anything like it. When it receded and the river finally returned to its banks, a whole trainload of unemployed workers arrived to repair the broken levees and build them up higher. Barracks were constructed for them and they worked through till late fall, when the first frosts were just starting. The town grew busier and livelier, there were dances more often, almost every Sunday. They drank, they fought with the locals. My mother's cousin had met him at one of those dances. The cousin had no money but he wanted a drink. The other guy bought him one, because he'd just gotten his wages. Then a second, a third, till they swore friendship and kissed each other on the cheek. Oh, and he also mentioned in the letter that as far as the rent for the room was concerned, money wasn't a problem.

So then, one Sunday just after midday they arrived with two suitcases. He was in a trench coat, she wore a matching outfit. The weather wasn't good, the sky had clouded over and it was windy; there were rain showers. My father had just gotten up, because on Sundays he caught up on his sleep from the whole week. I was scheduled for nightshift that evening. I won't lie, I liked the look of the wife. At first glance she appeared ten years younger than him, perhaps even more. Plus, she had a nice full, shapely figure, blond hair, and a pleasant smile.

On the second or third day my mother wanted to register them as guests with the authorities and asked for their ID cards. They said it wasn't necessary.

"But if the police come, I'll get a fine."

"They won't come," the man declared rather forcefully.

"What do you mean?" my mother asked in surprise.

"We'll swing by one day and register ourselves," the wife said gently, to mitigate her husband's tone of voice. And she invited my mother to their room for coffee.

They'd brought a big can of real coffee, and from that day almost every morning they invited my mother, and me when I wasn't on first shift, for coffee in their room. My father had work every morning. Plus, he didn't like coffee. He said he remembered coffee from before the war, and he hadn't liked it then either. He drank tea in the morning. For my mother, though, there was nothing she missed so much as real coffee. Otherwise there really wasn't that much to miss from before the war. Her husband was an educated man, but for several years he'd been unable to find work. He'd traveled about playing the guitar. Here it is, she said, and she brought it in and showed them. There were three of them, fiddle, clarinet, and my husband playing guitar and singing. He had a nice voice. Still does. Occasionally he gets asked to sing at some official celebration or other. That was how I met him. Through the window I heard music and singing. I went out to give them a few pennies, and my husband, he wasn't my husband then, said they'd prefer a hot drink, or maybe some soup, instead of money. It was only after we were married that he confessed they hadn't been hungry, he'd just taken a fancy to me. I invited them in. My mother grumbled, who was I bringing into the house, they could be thieves and the music and singing was just a cover. I made them tea, cut some slices of bread and spread them thickly with butter.

They ate, then they asked if we'd like them to play and sing for us. So they did, and my mother cheered up to the point that when they got up to leave she stopped them and invited them to stay for lunch. They started talking about themselves, where they were from, what they'd studied. The fiddler had been to conservatory, the clarinetist had attended commercial school, while my husband had had to break off his studies because his father had died. My mother felt sorry for them and gave them a sandwich and an apple for the road. My husband to be, when he kissed my mother's hand as they were leaving, said, We'll come visit you again, ma'am, if you don't mind. Perhaps I'll have found work by then. But he hadn't. We moved on, because he couldn't just go on playing and singing under people's windows. We were young, and that carried us along. Except that youth alone doesn't feed you. Youth won't put a roof over your head. It won't put clothes in the closet, or shoes, it won't provide a bed. Luckily they built the canning factory here and we came back.

Right after breakfast my mother would get ready for the coffee. She'd curl her hair, put on lipstick and mascara. She'd pick out a fresh blouse and a skirt to go with it, clean her shoes till they shone. She'd study herself in the mirror, pinch here, brush there, tug at something or smooth it down, till there was a knock at the door and a warm voice:

"Come have coffee with us."

She drank the coffee almost devoutly, as if transporting herself back to pre-war times, to her youth. She relished it rather than drank it, in small mouthfuls, barely opening her lips. She lent them her best china for the coffee after she saw them drinking it out of glasses.

"You can't drink coffee from a glass! Before the war we always used cups," she said, not surprised so much as almost upset. "Coffee loses its taste in a glass."

They explained that they only ever drank coffee at work, and at work everyone used glasses. Cups would have to be brought from home, whereas glasses were provided. If one got broken it was replaced. Besides, in a job like that you sometimes bang on the desk or slam down the telephone, or jump up from your chair, and a cup could easily get cracked, while glasses are stronger. So they'd gotten used to glasses. And everyone knows that when you get used to something. . .

"What kind of job is it?" My mother was inquisitive and would often ask questions.

"One that's just as essential as any other. Except the hours are irregular. You work as much as is needed. Sometimes till late at night."

"I'm sorry to hear it." My mother liked to sympathize.

Oh, and she also lent them a pot to make the coffee in, because she couldn't bear to see them pouring boiling water over the ground coffee in their glasses. The pot was from before the war, and since the war it hadn't been used. You put the grounds in, added boiling water, and the coffee was made under pressure. Also, it kept the coffee hot. The pot lived on the bottom shelf of the laundry cabinet, behind the sheets and pillowcases. When my mother was taking something out of the cabinet she'd lift out the pot as well, just to gaze at it. Occasionally she'd let slip a word of regret, saying we ought to throw the pot out or give it to someone who collects old things, because there probably wouldn't be coffee anymore. One day, as she sat savoring the coffee, my mother said timidly:

"I wonder where you can buy coffee like this nowadays? Around here there's only the ersatz kind."

"There are shops," the wife replied, glancing at her husband, who frowned. As if holding her back from going where she shouldn't, he added sharply:

"There'll be places like that here one day. Right now there are more important things than coffee. The country has to be rebuilt after all the destruction, people must be guaranteed jobs. They need to be given faith that things will be better than before, because everything's been in shambles since the war. Also, there are quite a few people who get in the way. Coffee will come later. I worked on the levees before the war and I didn't drink coffee then, even though it was in the shops."

"You're right." The zeal with which he spoke had convinced my mother. "In our town several buildings burned down. And there were any number of smashed roofs and broken windows. Some people still have their windows boarded up today. When it rains they have to put down pots and bowls because there're holes in the roof. And quite a few people died."

But my mother recovered from her momentary wartime sadness when she drank a little more coffee. The coffee brought a new expression of delight:

"I couldn't even say if the coffee from before the war was as good as this."

At that, the wife announced out of the blue: "We'll send you a can of the coffee. We'll send a coat for your son and some coffee for you."

"Thank you. But I'm not sure I can afford it. How much would a can of coffee and a coat cost?" My mother's voice was tinged with misgiving.

"Nothing," said the man.

The wife added with a smile: "It'll be a gift."

"Then you should say thank you too." My mother turned to me.

"Thank you," I said reservedly, though few things could have pleased me more than that coat.

The day after they arrived, right away they'd decided to go for a walk on the levees. They went by the kitchen to say they were going out and would be back in a couple of hours. The man asked my mother if the same road led there as before the war. He was wearing a coat. The weather wasn't looking good. Windy, the sky overcast. My mother was surprised they felt like going out on a day like that. It might rain. See, it was sprinkling already.

"We have umbrellas," the man said.

"But do you really have to go to the levees? There are no trees to shelter under. It's all bare. There are so many other places to take a walk." She mentioned some possibilities: "You could go here, there."

He seemed irked. "I've already been to all those places. I don't need to go again."

My mother realized she must have touched a nerve. To make up for it she said: "That's a lovely coat you have. My son could really use a coat like that. I've looked in all the stores but I've never seen that kind. It's good for rain and dry weather both. He's planning to go to university, he ought to have a coat."

"Where's he applying?" The man was suddenly interested and alert.

"He doesn't know yet." She turned to me. "Unless you've made your mind up, then tell the gentleman."

"He doesn't need to right now. We'll talk about it later," he said, as if he didn't want me to have already made my decision. "And we'll send you a coat."

His wife turned to me: "You should maybe try it on to see if it's the right size. You're about the same height as my husband." And to him: "Take it off."

He took the coat off and I tried it. It was a perfect fit – length, width, shoulders, waist, sleeves not too long and not too short.

"Then you should join us for lunch today." My mother's eyes were shining from gratitude. "You needn't go to the restaurant. We're having noodles made with fresh eggs. I always make them myself, nice and thin. I was going to keep the chicken for Sunday but I'll roast it today, with potatoes. And there'll be black currant kompot." She was so thankful that she threw in a cake: "This afternoon I'll bake a *topielec*."

"Topielec? 'Floatcake'? What kind is that?" The wife's eyes opened in surprise. "I've never heard of it. Why's it called that?"

"If you like it I'll give you the recipe, though I never share it with anyone. All I'll say for now is that you have to put the dough in a pot of cold water and wait for it to rise to the surface. Sometimes it takes more time, sometimes less. You think it's never going to rise, but it does. It can just be a bit stubborn. I don't know what determines it."

"Let's leave the topielec for now," the man said, as if sensing that they'd be waiting and waiting for the dough to rise to the surface. And from his wife's curiosity he knew she'd start asking what next, after it rises. "I'm going out, you can do as you wish."

"No no, let's go. You can tell me later, ma'am. I'll write it down."

After they left my mother didn't know what to do with herself, she was so pleased by the coat and the coffee. She kept taking things out by mistake and putting them back where they didn't belong.

"What nice people they are. Offering us a gift like that. And here I am charging them so much for the room. I'll drop the price. Maybe I should put Christ in the Garden of Olives on their wall? I could move it from our room. Why aren't you saying anything? These days everyone's always taking whatever they want, while these people are generous as anything. Though you didn't seem all that pleased about the coat. I had to remind you to say thank you. Then you just mumbled it. It made me uncomfortable. They might think you weren't brought up properly. And when someone isn't brought up properly, whose fault is it? The mother's. Not the father's. Your father works eight hours a day in the office, when he comes home he needs to take a nap, then read the paper. As if he couldn't read it at work. If he'd at least teach you to play the guitar. It's just hanging there going to waste. You should teach him. You never know when it might come in handy for him."

Here my father put in: "What for? He's not going to go around the streets, playing under people's windows. A guitar's no substitute for a trade."

"How do you know there won't come another time when he'll have to go around playing to put bread on the table."

"When he graduates from university he'll earn enough for bread and for butter too. Do you know what university studies were like before the war?"

"Your father might be right," my mother conceded. "But I can remember people wandering around playing music, and they'd been to school. You never know when the world might change. You have to protect yourself from what came before and also from what's ahead. But protect yourself how? We had some savings set aside, then the war happened and they were gone. Perhaps it's only what's in your head that remains. But when your head is empty, there's nothing that can remain there. Study, son, study. We'll manage somehow, if only you graduate from university."

It was in my mother's nature to fall easily into joyous excitement when a bit of good fortune came her way. At moments like that she was prepared to make a special dinner, even bake a topielec. Sometimes, though, after an onset of sudden delight she'd start to doubt whether she truly had a reason to celebrate. And she would give up the idea of a special dinner and the topielec. She'd make potato soup followed by kasha and bacon.

One time father came home from work and declared the moment he walked through the door: "Stalingrad. There's hope."

She didn't let him go on: "What about Stalingrad? What's happened, why are you puffing like that?"

"Just let me catch my breath. Put your hand over my heart. Can you feel it pounding? The moment I heard, it started thumping like that. Plus, I was walking quickly." After a moment he told us what he'd heard. "But don't say a word to anyone. Not a soul, understand? They could get arrested, deported, shot. Someone told me in confidence. I won't even say who."

"Then tomorrow I'll bake a topielec and make a special dinner. Come home early. I hope to God it's true."

"What's God got to do with it, the foreign radio said so," he huffed.

But mother was already beset by doubts.

"Do you think the foreign radio is telling the truth? Foreign or not, maybe they're just trying to cheer people up. Remember, you once came home and told us they'd said – I don't know if it was the foreign radio – that the war would be over by Christmas. And how many Christmases ago was that?"

It was the same when they promised to send the coat for me, and the coffee for her. She couldn't conceal her pleasure after they left the house. Then all at once, as she was already making the noodles for the soup, she said supposedly to me, but really to her own misgivings: "Do you think they'll send those things? Maybe they're just making promises. Some people like to promise this and that, then they count on it being forgotten. But I'll make the dinner since I invited them. And I'll bake the topielec. Maybe they'll be more likely to send things if they enjoy the meal."

Naturally they did enjoy it, both of them. The wife went into raptures, what a delicious cake, she'd love another slice if she may. She oughtn't to, she had to watch her figure as she'd recently put on weight, but she wouldn't say no to seconds. She must have eaten three helpings. The man also said he liked it, though he restricted himself to a single slice.

While the wife was singing the praises of the topielec, my mother added that it would have been even better with raisins and orange peel. But where were you supposed to find raisins and oranges?

"We'll send some," said the wife, lifting another forkful to her mouth. And to her husband: "Remember, raisins and oranges." Then to my mother again: "Anything else? Please don't hesitate to ask. It's no trouble for us to send raisins and oranges. Perhaps some almonds too? And lemons maybe?"

"I could use them, but I wouldn't dream of it."

"You just need to give us your full mailing address," the man added.

"I'll write it down." My mother went into the kitchen, wrote the address on a slip of paper and brought it back. Handing the paper to the man, she said:

"Perhaps you can give me your address too. I could at least send you a card at Christmas. And Easter. I'd like to be able to repay you somehow or other for so much kindness. And on holidays it's as if God adds to the wishes you send."

The wife looked at her husband uneasily, but he didn't move a muscle. His face was cold and stern. Or perhaps that was only my impression, especially as I was seeing him from the side. Because for someone to come on vacation, especially after so many years, when it was a different age now, just so as to visit the levees he worked on as a young man – something must be smoldering in a person like that, and their face is a map of what's inside. I evidently hadn't yet learned how to read that face, because not a day went by without them going

for a walk on the levees. Come rain, or wind, or the worst heat, when
it was best to stay indoors, because outside the sun drew you up into
itself. The man would cover his head with a handkerchief with knots
tied in the corners, because the front part of his head was entirely bald;
his wife would put on a headscarf, though she had a thick head of hair,
and each afternoon they'd go off to the levees. What was there, aside
from the fact that it was a flat place to walk?

"We don't have a permanent address," he said with a slight frown,
as if warning his wife, who was about to say something more. "I was
recently transferred from another town."

"To a higher position," the wife put in.

"We're waiting for an apartment. And you know how hard it is these
days with apartments. People have to share. For now we're living in a
hotel. It's no matter, in the future there'll be apartments for everyone.
They're already being built. The bricklayers are beating records. Perhaps
you've heard?"

At this point my father came back from work and joined us.

"Your wife has baked us a delicious cake," the woman said to him
right away.

"The two of you work at the same factory," the man said, not so
much asking as confirming.

"But my husband has an office job," my mother hastened to add, as
my father had a mouthful of cake and was just taking a sip of tea. "My
son, though, is a regular laborer. He insisted on going to work when
he didn't get into university. It's not much of a job. He breaks up the

pomace. Even though he graduated from high school. My husband and I have encouraged him to try again. He's already wasted a couple of years in that job. But he's still young."

"Yes indeed," the man said. "The world is wide open for young people today. They just have to be given new faith that it can be a better, fairer place."

"There's faith already," my mother said, starting to bristle. "What need is there of another one?"

"What faith?"

"In God."

"In God you say, ma'am. It's just that that God of yours built the world we're now raising from the rubble. And he didn't move a finger when it came crashing down. Before his eyes there were massacres, villages and towns burned, people tortured and set upon by dogs. They even pulled gold teeth from the victims' mouths. And he didn't help. They carried his name on their belt buckles to show he was with them. Nothing can be built anymore on that faith of yours. A new faith is needed, one that'll inspire people with hope, allow them to regain the strength they've lost." Previously he'd been stern and taciturn, but now he flared up.

"The old faith is two thousand years old and everyone shares it. Who's going to share this new faith of yours?" My mother, though a little taken aback, was not giving up.

"Young people, young people will share it, ma'am. The old can't be counted on. They're burned out, overcome by the fumes; let them rest. When the young people come to believe that the future depends on them, nothing will hold them back."

"Let me tell you something," my father put in, finally joining the conversation. "Everyone's always said: it'll be the young people. But young people grow old, new young people come along, then after them other young people. And things are as they were before. Sometimes worse. Because the newest young people have to grab as much for themselves as the previous young people, sometimes even more." The man tried to get a word in, but my father wasn't easily derailed when he was certain of his own position. "Wait a moment. In our plant, if you count up, there are just as many loafers among the young folks as among the older ones."

"That depends on who's counting."

"The inspectors do the counting, Wait just a moment, though."

But the man wasn't letting himself be put off so quickly either: "What age do they count as still being young?"

"That I don't know. But this young guy came to work in our office. In the office you have to stay put for your eight hours. Him though, every few minutes it was, I have to pop over to the production line to check, because something isn't right in the paperwork. Turned out he'd found himself some girl in the sorting hall and he was running off to see her. They caught them in the warehouse on the sacks of dried fruit. Let's face it, all these youngsters care about is hanky-panky." Here he nodded toward the man's wife: "Begging your pardon, ma'am."

"How could you?" my mother huffed. "And in front of a lady. You should be ashamed."

"I said I was sorry. Though there's no need to be ashamed of the truth, am I right ma'am?"

She didn't answer, just sipped her tea. The husband on the other hand cut short my father's reflections on young people, saying: "Let's come back to your son." He turned to me. "So what are you planning to study?"

"History," I said hesitantly, though I'd already made my mind up.

"Hmm, history. We do have history. But wouldn't psychology be better? We need psychologists. You could study, and at the same time have a job. The work wouldn't be hard, and it'd only be a few hours a week – casual work, really. You'd have free board and lodging in the dorm, and free tickets for the cinema, the theater, other things. We'd pay for your train tickets too, if you wanted to go visit your parents. Twice a year. And a few zlotys for personal expenses. It would ease the burden on your parents."

"That really would be good," my mother said enthusiastically. "With my husband's salary we'll not be able to help him much."

"Exactly. In time you'd be the one helping them out."

"He wouldn't have to do that. He only needs to study." My mother was joining in his efforts to persuade me.

"In time, like I said." And to my father: "I'm sure you sometimes wonder how the two of you will manage after you retire."

"I still have a good few years left." My father didn't hide his irritation at this outsider sticking his nose in uninvited. I knew him. More than anything else he'd have liked to say: What business is it of yours? Are you family, or a neighbor at least? But he merely scooped a piece of topielec from his plate and declared: "When the time comes we'll give it some thought."

"I'm not trying to convince you one way or another, I'm just offering advice. It's always good to think things through in advance, so as not to be taken by surprise when the inevitable happens. Illness, for instance. Though I wish you both all the health in the world."

"Thank you," they both said almost simultaneously. "Same to you."

"Thank you." He nodded. "Unfortunately, everyone has to count on being sick. Even the healthiest person. I had this stabbing pain in my lower right side. I ignored it. They barely saved me. And that was only my appendix."

"Oh, that was what that film star died of – Rudolph Valentino. His appendix. Fine-looking man. And what a dancer." My mother was pleased she could give a famous example.

"That may be. My wife's brother wasn't yet thirty when she lost him to TB. If he'd been able to afford a doctor or a sanatorium, he'd still be alive. But their father was unemployed, and their mother had no trade, she only made a little money from laundering clothes and cleaning. How were they supposed to pay for TB treatment? Especially because he came down with it all of a sudden. You feel healthy, you've just got a bit of a cough. Maybe it's a cold. Maybe you've been smoking too much, and cheap cigarettes at that. You feel dizzy sometimes – well, perhaps that's your stomach, you ate something to upset it. Then all of a sudden you have blood in your mouth. That's how it was with my brother-in-law."

"I don't smoke," my father stated. "As for eating, I don't use the canteen. I eat what my wife prepares. And she doesn't make anything that upsets your stomach."

"I'm not talking about you. I'm just giving examples. Or let's take accidents. Someone loses a couple of fingers or a hand, or they fall from a ladder and break their back. They're confined to a wheelchair for the rest of their life."

"How can you fall from a ladder in an office?" my father retorted. "The most you'd do is bump into a chair. Or how could you lose your hand, like you say. You might trap your finger in a desk drawer if you're not careful, no worse than that."

"But you don't live only in your office. You walk through the streets. Besides, a back can give out in an office too, just from sitting, from lack of movement."

"He already slouches," my mother commented. "He always used to be straight as a ramrod."

"Plus, I see you wear thick glasses. It's in offices that eyesight worsens the quickest. Look around at your co-workers. I'm sure the majority of them wear glasses. It's the same in every office. And what then? They pension you off. It's not even half your salary. Plus, you can just as easily have a stroke or a heart attack in an office."

"You're right," my mother put in again. "You need to think of everything ahead of time. And we're no longer young."

"They thought and thought about how to prevent war from breaking out, and it happened anyway." Annoyance sounded in my father's voice.

"If you'd thought about it, you wouldn't have let him be a manual laborer," my mother said almost aggressively, indicating me. "The director wanted to put him in accounts, have him keep track of quotas, but no. 'Your son has a high school certificate,' he says, 'accounts is almost like office work. Or maybe he could be a controller? He'd check when everyone leaves the plant, make sure no one's taking anything with them.' 'What could they be taking sir, a jar of jam, some kompot? No, he ought to get a taste of real work.' 'What do you mean real work? Is your work not real?' 'Mine isn't real.' You were up for a raise, and because of that you didn't get it. Just because he needs a bit of paper that says he's a worker."

They started to argue; my father could give as good as he got with my mother when she pinned him to the wall. He was likely formulating a response when the man interrupted: "Excuse me, both of you, but I'd like to say a bit more to your son. You wouldn't need a certificate. We'd give you a place without an exam. There are always two or three spots in every major, all that's needed is a recommendation. History's the same, as far as I remember. Besides, even if it isn't, we'd arrange it somehow or other. I can take care of that. We have our professors, associate professors, assistant professors. History's needed too, if you should opt for history. Every age depends on history, ours in particular. History's responsible for the state of our minds, our convictions, our engagement. Because you can't build anything without changing history. It'd risk the breakdown of society, the collapse of morality, of faith in the future we've started to construct. Besides, the war laid bare all history's falsehoods up till now. That's why we had to take history into our own hands, set it on the right path that would lead to a more just world. Generations have dreamed of that world. They spilled their blood for it, rotted in prisons. And up till now, it was in vain."

Previously he'd been cold and severe, weighing every word before he uttered it; now he seemed quite unlike himself. He'd grown passionate, as if it wasn't history so much as his own speech that had stirred him so. I'd never have imagined he had so many words in him. He spoke to us as if he were addressing an auditorium full of people. My mother listened wide-eyed, my father with his head lowered. The man's words exuded such power that it occurred to me to wonder if he wasn't a professor of history himself, since he could pick history apart like that; I even had a suspicion that it was a dangerous discipline. And I started to have doubts. Maybe I'd be better off trying for anthropology again. All at once he mellowed and said, perhaps with a hint of bitterness:

"It's all changing too slowly. We need to get a move on, or history will pass us by and leave us behind the rest of the world."

His throat must have been dry, because his wife asked my mother: "Would you mind making some more tea for my husband?"

"Of course." My mother took his teacup. She'd been so moved that the cup rattled against the saucer as she walked into the kitchen. Luckily her hands had stopped shaking when she brought it back and placed it in front of him. He thanked her. She was about to put another slice of topielec on his plate, but he said no thank you, it was delicious, but he couldn't manage any more. The tea, on the other hand, he drank at once, virtually emptying his cup in a single draft. It was as if he needed to put out a fire.

"Another cup?"

"Yes please."

This time he drank at a regular rate. In a calm, rather subdued voice he turned to me and said: "You'll just need to go through a probationary period. It's not long – six months – though it won't be easy either. Some people don't make it, parts of it can be tough. But in your case I'm sure you'll succeed. When we send you the coat I'll write about the initial formalities."

"And the coffee," his wife added.

"And the coffee," he repeated, nodding toward my mother.

"Thank you." My mother smiled.

"And raisins, oranges, and almonds, don't forget," said his wife.

"Raisins, oranges, almonds, of course. If I'm wrapped up in work and forget, remember it for me. We'll send it all, we will, don't you worry about that." He looked at my mother again.

"And lemons," said his wife.

"And lemons." His face stiffened when he had to repeat her words again; he'd have preferred to hammer his fist on the tabletop and yell: "And lemons! Otherwise. . . !" But instead he took another sip of tea and said to me in a voice that was still a little muffled: "If you decide to go ahead with it, just send a short message saying, Yes. No more. If not, don't write back, so there's no trace of your having refused. It'll be better that way."

On the day of their departure they decided not to take a walk, even though their train wasn't till late afternoon. Yet there hadn't been a single day when they'd not taken themselves off to the levees. My mother, who ought to have gotten used to their daily walks, never concealed her surprise whenever they went out. Her expressions of astonishment must have been annoying, but they didn't let it show, and the wife even felt obliged to justify each walk: "My husband's drawn to the place. At first I couldn't understand it either, you know, ma'am. But now, believe me, I'll miss it. You have no idea how lovely it is there."

"I've been there, but it didn't seem that way to me."

"Oh, you feel as if the world were endless. You could walk and walk. You have earth under your feet, not asphalt or concrete. My husband finds it calming. Sometimes he takes his shoes off and tells me to as well. And we walk barefoot. Once he asked me: What does it make you feel?"

When they'd finished packing their bags, she asked if they could take one final farewell walk, saying they had plenty of time till the train.

"Who do you want to say farewell to?" he replied frostily.

"To the levees you're so fond of."

"Places we're fond of are a liability. People are where they are, not where they were before. Let's go to the station and buy our tickets."

They'd spent their entire vacation on the levees, day after day he'd taken his wife with him till she shared his attachment, and here he seemed to be abruptly cutting himself off from them. It was hard to understand, especially because when my mother's cousin came to see him, usually with vodka, they spent each visit reminiscing about repairing the levees. The cousin was a blacksmith, but back then he'd given up shoeing horses, as he made better money repairing tools – wheelbarrows, spades, pickaxes, blunted saws; later he'd had to go back to what he called his daily slog, which is to say, putting on horseshoes. In any case they painted an emotional picture of those times, as if they owed their youth to them.

"I tell you, sometimes it's hard to believe we were so young back then," the cousin would say as he poured another round.

To which the other man replied as he raised his glass: "Then here's to our youth. It won't come back, but there's no harm in drinking to it."

"I tell you, if people hadn't ever been young, they wouldn't be able to handle being old. You remember things and it cheers you up."

"How old are you anyway? Right, same age as me. We still have some life ahead of us. And the times are favorable. Work is looking for people these days, not the other way around. There're all kinds of jobs that need doing. You only have to be willing to pitch in. Don't sit around, or you'll go to seed. Anyone who isn't with us is like the finger of – well, I won't say it since I'm not a believer. You used to be different, you had the fire in you. I remember you saying to me once, I wish all the horses would die. Hammering and hammering, what kind of life is that. There won't be any horses, I guarantee it. What would you like to do instead?"

"I've no idea. Maybe nothing. Ah, life was good once. A dance every Sunday, and when there was a dance there was vodka."

"And other things too. I won't talk about it in front of my wife, because it's best not to remember too much."

"Your health, then, ma'am."

"You don't need to pussyfoot around me." She pouted. "I know what I know already. Say whatever you like, the two of you. I'd rather go talk to the lady of the house than listen to you." And she left the room.

"She's gone, but here's to her again." He poured another drink for himself and for my mother's cousin, and they downed it. "Let me tell you, my wife is wonderful. You couldn't find another woman like her anywhere. At least I had good luck in that department."

"Congratulations. Choosing a wife is the toughest thing. It's even harder than choosing a government. The government's always chosen already, before you even cast your vote."

"You didn't hear that, young man," the man said to me, because sometimes they asked me to join them when I wasn't at work, and it didn't cost them more than a glass or two. Actually I never liked vodka, I preferred wine, even the awful stuff that was around back then. Occasionally they'd invite my father too.

"We're old friends, and when you're drinking vodka you can be a bit freer. What about you?" he asked, turning to the cousin. "Are you married?"

"I was."

"What happened?"

"She died."

"I'm sorry."

"Just imagine, my wife was chosen for me by a flood. There was a flood during the war..."

"What do you mean? We did a good job repairing the levees, built them higher."

"Still, they broke and the water burst through, it came all the way up here. Flood like that, you'd need a levee that reached all the way up to the sky. Even then you couldn't be sure it wouldn't burst. The train station was like an island. When the trains came in from one direction or the other, they couldn't signal for them to pull in till they'd checked the tracks weren't under water. The railway workers were running this way and that, testing the ground with spikes, tapping the rails, and people were ferried to and from the station in boats. The inbound trains were usually full, and the outbound ones even more packed, because everyone was carrying flour, kasha, beans, lard, anything they'd managed to buy. They'd deliver the stuff to the surrounding towns. The boats went back and forth whenever a train came in. You made more money on the boats than you would shoeing horses from dawn till dusk. There was one train that I made three or four trips to and from the station for. There weren't many boats. They were moored by the roadside chapel. You remember the chapel that had the Eye of God inside? It was kind of at the edge of the flood, the water reached all the way there. It's still there, why wouldn't it be? People even said that God had held back the flood, stopped it from going any further. Nonsense, you say? Maybe it is, maybe it isn't. It's not for us to decide. You remember, I had a boat from before the war. It had belonged to a fisherman who died, I'd bought it for a few zlotys. It had dried out, so I mended it and calked it. It was in that boat that I met my future wife. I was taking some people to the station with all their luggage one day, and she had only a small suitcase. Little brown thing, and it was light as a feather. She said she didn't need help, but I carried it into the station for her. The train was held up at the signals for a good three hours. You should go, she kept telling me. No, I'll wait till you board, miss. We went on talking, till finally the train rolled into the station. She found a place, I handed her the suitcase through the window. There was such a crowd, I had to push her through the door when she was getting on. Then when the train set off, she shouted to me that she'd come again. And when she did, she stayed. You know what she had in that suitcase of hers? Soap, a towel, a toothbrush, toothpaste, some lady's things. It was only after the war that she told me there'd been secret papers hidden in a false bottom in the suitcase. If they'd caught her, I wouldn't have had a wife. I tell you, I didn't believe she'd come back. Days, weeks, months passed, the flood receded. I'd sometimes go down to the station when a train from those parts was due, but nothing, she hadn't come. I wondered if I shouldn't maybe look for someone else, but I doubt I'd have found anyone even by now, because I couldn't get my mind off her. Till one day I'm eating my lunch and all of a sudden, there she is. 'I promised I'd come and here I am.' She didn't live long, didn't have time to have a baby; if she had, I might still have felt like shoeing horses."

You could see the station from our kitchen window. When they left to buy their tickets, my mother pulled the net curtain aside and looked after them for a long time, as if making sure they were far away.

"Why're you spying on them?" I snorted.

"I'm not spying on them, I'm just looking to see if they go to the station."

"They said they were going to buy their tickets."

"There's no harm in checking something that someone's said. Keep an eye on them, I'm going to make sure they haven't left anything behind. People sometimes forget things. Let me know if you see them coming back." She left and returned almost immediately, trembling. "Lord in heaven, who did we invite into our home?"

"What is it?"

"I'm not even going to tell you. Don't go there, God forbid. That's what happens when you take in someone you don't know. That darned cousin of mine. Before the war this, before the war that — what do I care about before the war. People have changed since before the war. And to think I made them a topielec. It was all a show. And here she was so sweet. Coffee, raisins, oranges, almonds, they're going to send it all. What else was there? Oh yes, lemons. I don't want them to. And I don't want that coat for you. You can manage without it. I'm afraid to think what's going to happen."

"Nothing's going to happen. Take it easy. They came and now they've gone."

"What do you mean, nothing?" she almost shouted. "I heard what your father was saying. And that cousin of mine. Besides, what kind of cousin is he anyway? His grandmother and mine were sisters, that's all. You too — it seemed you weren't saying anything, but he dragged all he could out of you. They need young people, isn't that what he said? Young people are supposed to build something for them, believe in something. Without God. The devil must have made me bake that topielec. I'm never going to make it again. I need to find a different cake. Once they've gone I'll look through my recipes. Maybe gingerbread. You like gingerbread, don't you? I wonder if they'll send those things or not?"

They did. And quickly. The mailman brought a notification to say there was a package for my mother to pick up from the post office.

"Big one," he said. "Weighs a bit too."

"Could you go fetch it for me, son?"

"It can't be your son. It's addressed to you. You'll need your ID."

My mother brought it home on a cart. We knew the carter – he delivered our coal in the winter – and he took my mother down to the post office and drove her back with the package. As she carried it in, she seemed scarcely able to conceal her delight. She didn't set about opening it right away. First she examined it on every side.

"Look at all these stamps and postmarks. And it's taped up every which way. If someone had wanted to steal something at the post office there's no way they could have gotten into it. They'd have had to cut it open. Though they have their ways. One time an old friend of mine from childhood who'd emigrated to America, she sent me a few dollars in a book. Well, the book arrived, I mean who'd steal a book. But there was no sign of the dollars. I went through page by page, nothing. And that was that, though I did read the book. I had my father read it too. I didn't like it, there was one corpse after another all the way through. And no one could figure how they'd gotten those dollars out. See, here it says express mail, and here's the value. But I don't see their address. Maybe it's inside, or they didn't get that apartment. Perhaps you should open it."

They'd sent everything as promised. My mother had me try the coat on right away.

"It's just like his." Her eyes glowed. "Coffee, goodness, what a big can. I think it's bigger than the one they had with them."

"It's the same size."

"No, it's much bigger. You're not remembering. Two pounds of raisins." She weighed them right away. "I can give a few ounces to the neighbors, remind them what raisins are like. We'll still have enough for a long time, even if I bake more often. Your father's nameday is coming up, I'll make him a proper topielec. And what's this? Pineapple – well I never. Three whole cans of it. They never promised that."

I don't remember how many oranges there were. But my mother took each one in her hand, and repeated:

"It's like a sun, it really is. Look at this one. It's beautiful. I'm not sure they were this good-looking before the war. True, we used to buy the cheaper kind. We'll peel one when your father comes home from work. Heavens, when did I last eat an orange?"

"Are you not going to weigh the lemons?"

"I'm not going to check, I'd be embarrassed to."

"See, you have almonds here. And there's something else." I took out a large tin. "Chocolates." There was a card stuck to it that read: "In return for the topielec."

She picked up the tin eagerly, but she couldn't get it open; she broke a nail trying to prize off the lid. Her astonishment took on a note of disbelief.

"Maybe they put them in by mistake? They meant to send them to someone else, and they mixed up the parcels?"

"But you see the card on top. 'For the topielec.' And there's a letter here, read it. They say there are chocolates too."

She didn't read the letter right away. First she tipped all the chocolates out onto the tabletop – each one was individually wrapped – and set about counting them.

"There's so much of everything. Who would have expected it? I've never been sent so many things in all my life." All at once this excess seemed to trouble her. The letter deepened her unease, though other than the greetings it didn't contain anything in particular. The wife had written. She thanked my mother, saying they'd felt at home with us, and she listed what was in the packet. She apologized for not giving their address, because they didn't yet know where they'd be living. For the moment here was the address of a relative of theirs who'd be sure to pass on the letter when I wrote to him as I'd agreed to. She dwelled most of all, with great enthusiasm, on the topielec. She said she'd made one too and everyone had found it irresistible. She shared it with some friends and they were speechless. Her husband took some to work, and now his co-workers' wives were calling her to ask for the recipe. The husband had added a postscript at the end of the letter: "Waiting to hear from you."

"You see, he's waiting." The "waiting to hear from you" had scared my mother. "What did you say to him? Tell me now. I didn't hear everything, I had to go out to the kitchen to make the tea and cut the cake. And a couple of times they invited you to join them over vodka. He was drinking too, but men like that can handle their drink. Tell me."

"I didn't say anything. He asked me questions and I gave him honest answers."

"You have to know who to be honest with and when. Plenty of people have ended up behind bars for honesty. I never heard of anyone going to prison for lying. When you've lived a bit longer you'll see."

From the time the parcel arrived she grew more and more worried; she couldn't sleep, she was dejected and distracted. Then one day she said to me:

"Go away, son. If they ask about you we'll say we don't know where you went. Your father has a cousin who's a forester, we could write to him. You could stay there for a year before you go to university. You might get in this time. If not, you could be an apprentice there. Forestry isn't a bad line of work." She went on at me most when she was making a topielec, while she added raisins or orange peel, as if the fear was rising in her again.

Despite my mother's constant fears, no letter came for me. And I only left the following year, when I got into university. I don't know if my mother instilled her own fear deep inside me, or whether it was only my own fear from that interview when the police officer had said:

"We're not parting for good, after all."

I was in my last year of university when my mother wrote to tell me that the man's wife had visited on her own. At first my mother hadn't recognized her: she'd aged, lost weight, she was dressed untidily and her hair was unkempt, whereas when she'd stayed with us she'd been stylish and smart. When my mother asked where her husband was, the woman's eyes filled with tears.

"Please don't ask. I can't bring myself to talk about it."

My mother was chilled by her words; it occurred to her that something like that could have happened to my father too. He could have died, disappeared, they could have arrested him – though for what? She was not at all worried he'd leave her, because she knew my father well enough to be sure he couldn't manage without her. In any case she tried to learn a little more.

Naturally she welcomed the wife cordially, glad that at least in this way she could repay her for the parcel. She put her in the same room with the separate entrance where they'd stayed all those years before. She told her she'd prepare the same bedding they'd slept in back then. The woman smiled, but it was a bitter sort of smile, my mother wrote. I even said I'd cook for her, she said, why go to restaurants, what was one more person for dinner. She served her meals in the guest room, because the woman would probably never have come through to join them; she never even asked for tea. But when her guest was going out – every morning she left to take a walk – my mother made sure she had some tea before she left, then she brought her a second cup in the afternoon. My mother guessed she must be going to the levees, but she never asked about that either.

It was May, the weather was sunny. My mother's cousin came by one day and my mother suggested that maybe he could sound out the wife a bit about what had happened to the husband. He'd been his friend, she was more likely to open up to him. So the cousin joined her on a walk.

"Did you ask?"

"Yes."

"And?"

"Nothing."

"What do you mean, nothing? Not a word?"

"She started crying."

"Then you should've – "

"Should've what?" The cousin was annoyed. "If you're so smart, explain how tears can be translated into words."

I had a friend. You could say we'd known each other forever. Our friendship had something of love about it, though unlike him I wasn't gay. He hid it from me for a long time; I don't think he realized that I knew. In fact that wasn't the only thing he hid; he concealed his whole life. When he spoke about anything, it was always: someone, somewhere, sometime. Never who, never where, never when. When I asked him, sometimes brusquely, to tell me who he was talking about, where it had been, I could tell he found it hurtful.

I wasn't asking out of curiosity. I feel that when something isn't named, it doesn't exist. Naming is knowing. We need words if we want to know. What possibilities do we have other than words to look inside ourselves, understand others, imagine the world to ourselves? Take hope, for instance: what is it if not words? Or conscience: is it not a torment inflicted by words? And what about our thoughts – would they even be possible without words? Our feelings, if they were devoid of words? Our dreams, if they were wordless?

He often irritated me with his fear of words. He'd break off mid-sentence and fall silent. Sometimes he'd barely begun when he would stop, excusing himself with a "Well, anyway..."

At the beginning, when we hadn't known one another long, I tried to understand it. I thought that with time things would change, he'd learn to trust me. But it was like that throughout our entire friendship, up till his death.

He was a few years older than me. Unfortunately, his bad health began early in life. Plus, he didn't like getting treatment. Going to the doctor or even having the most straightforward tests done, was torture for him. The thought would eat at him for weeks in advance. That he didn't keep secret. Evidently he couldn't handle it on his own and needed others to sympathize with him. His helplessness in the simplest matters meant that, though he made no demands, he needed to be looked after like a little child.

Friendship with him was hard. But perhaps every friendship is hard? His affection for me showed in the fact that he spoke less and less, as if it was enough for him that we thought of one another, remembered the other, and sometimes also missed each other; that from time to time we'd meet up, spend time, eat and drink together. As if we didn't need to validate our friendship with words. The decline of words between us may also have come from the fact that my life and his life began to overlap, so to speak. People receive signals beyond words from others, and send such signals themselves. It's not hard to imagine what happens between two people when they fall silent together; why then, on top of everything else, should we strive to speak, when whatever one or the other might say wouldn't be the right thing anyway. It'll never be the right thing. A friendship isn't measured in words.

Someone might suggest that this was rather a sign of a growing distrust between us; what's it got to do with friendship? Even if that were so, friendship grows stronger through distrust. For at the root of friendship there lurks a constant fear that something will happen, just a single misplaced word will be spoken, there'll be a disappointment and the relationship will suddenly founder. And the deeper the friendship, the more painful such a disappointment can be, to the point that you'll stop believing in friendship at all. Fear, then, is a kind of guardian angel to friendship.

One time he invited me out to a restaurant. The place wasn't far from his apartment. We ordered food, mineral water, and a shot of vodka each. He even asked solicitously if vodka didn't disagree with me. Maybe I'd prefer wine. It disagreed with him him, true, but he felt obliged to drink on such an occasion.

After a few vodkas, he said out of the blue:

"I'd like to meet your parents someday."

"Nothing could be simpler. We'll go visit them," I said. "They'll be pleased. We just have to decide when, so we can let them know."

But time went by and he didn't bring it up again. I thought he must have said it just to be nice. Besides, I'd started writing my doctoral dissertation and it wasn't convenient for me to leave town. Plus, autumn was coming, which wasn't the best time to be going away. In this way, two years or so went by. I was sure he'd forgotten. Then one day he said: "We were supposed to go visit your parents. Remember?"

"Then maybe next Sunday," I replied without a second thought, because I felt embarrassed. "Otherwise we'll forget again."

"I hadn't forgotten," he sniffed.

It was Thursday. I had no way of letting my mother and father know. A letter would have taken at least three days; it would have arrived on Saturday at the earliest, but on Saturday the post office was closed. So we made a surprise visit. My mother panicked. She was just getting lunch ready, and it was an ordinary lunch, potato soup followed by noodles with bacon and cheese. But she didn't let it show that she'd been taken unawares. She was a master at bluffing. She could feign sorrow, regret, joy, even shed tears when the occasion called for it. That's why she was hard to read, even for me. Perhaps that was wise though? How often do you make a show of interest in something that somebody's saying, or complaining about, or laughing at, though you don't actually care about it and you're thinking about something else. It helps in life, makes other people better disposed toward us, even makes some of them like us. And who doesn't want to be liked.

To enhance the potato soup and the noodles, my father brought out a bottle of his plum nalewka. He only did so on grand occasions, when he wanted to offer special hospitality. He served it one evening for the couple who later sent the coat.

"It's excellent." The husband actually smacked his lips after taking a sip. "Excellent. I've tried all kinds of drinks – Polish, foreign – but I've never had anything as good as this. Truly excellent."

The wife sang its praises too, saying it had cheered her up right away, because for some reason she'd been feeling down since that morning. Flattered by their compliments, when they were leaving my father gave them a small bottle to take home with them.

"Perhaps they'll send that coat," he said later to my mother to justify himself, for she doubted whether they'd send anything.

"Promises promises. You always were over-trusting."

So he was triumphant when the package came – thanks to his nalewka, as he said.

"You see what my nalewka can do. Requests and prayers don't work. You could pray and pray for them to send it. I went back and forth about whether to give it to them or not, because I knew you wouldn't approve."

It had never happened before that he'd given anyone even the smallest bottle, even the kind they put stomach drops in. Oh, he would serve it, a little glass for a taste. But if anyone failed to admire it, he'd never give them it again. Not out of stinginess, he wasn't stingy, but it was an expensive drink to prepare and he only made it infrequently, once every few years. I don't know where he got the recipe – he said it was very old, from before the war. He didn't feel the need to specify which war, everyone ought to know – as if there hadn't been any others.

The nalewka was made from dried plums. Plums for drying were only picked after the first frosts. That was when they were at their best. Just like the best jam is made from plums that have been lightly frozen. For the nalewka they need to be unpitted. And not dried too much or too little. The imported kind you get these days won't do for nalewka. Once in a while my father would manage to buy plums like that somewhere or other; at other times he'd bring some home from work, where they'd been drying the late ones: the last batch so to speak. He'd get them on account as part of the allowance each worker was entitled to once a year.

He'd put ten pounds or so of fruit into a big jar and fill it to the brim with pure vodka. It took about a gallon and a quarter. The vodka needed to be a bit stronger than the regular kind – it had to be a hundred or a hundred ten proof. You could sometimes get it in the stores, it was called "extra strength." If he couldn't find that, he'd use distilled spirit. He would borrow an alcoholmeter from the factory lab. The alcohol had to be heated almost to boiling; then came the crucial moment. Pure spirit boils at about a hundred seventy degrees. When it's mixed with water, I don't know what the boiling point is. In any case you had to watch out, since the escaping steam could catch fire.

One time it did; my father got burns on his hands, and when the fire was put out, all that was left was water. Anyway, he would pour the almost boiling liquid over the plums in the jar. Then he sealed the jar, and it stood for up to three weeks. Because of the stones you couldn't leave it longer than that. Afterwards the nalewka was decanted into bottles and left to stand for some time. From the ten pounds of plums and the gallon and a quarter of alcohol you got three quarts of nalewka at most, sometimes less. The plums left in the jar, swollen from the alcohol, were sprinkled with powdered sugar, and eventually yielded a quart or so of stronger liqueur.

After the nalewka had stood awhile in the bottles, it was filtered through gauze and lignin and rebottled. You needed to leave some room in each bottle, because it would be topped off with a glass of dry white wine, or, even better, brandy, except that the brandy had to be top shelf, as they say, meaning French. You could buy that kind for dollars. My father would buy dollars on the black market without telling my mother, to buy the brandy. My mother didn't know French, and even if she saw the label she'd think it came from a regular liquor store, since sometimes those stores sold Bulgarian or Albanian brandies. Then the nalewka had to stand for some time again, till it acquired a ruby-red color. When you lifted a bottle to the light, the rays would refract in it like in precious crystal. Very few of those who tasted it guessed it was made from dried plums.

"I've brought a friend," I said as I greeted my parents. "He wanted to meet you."

"Welcome, welcome." My father got up from his chair and offered his hand, though I could tell he wasn't too pleased about the unexpected appearance of a stranger. Years later, after my mother had died, he admitted to me that that Sunday when I'd shown up with my friend, he was supposed to meet with someone who was also visiting from out of town, and who was bringing him dollars so he could buy brandy for his nalewka.

My mother on the other hand, as always in such cases, found it in her to be hospitable; she was bursting with joy, as if she hadn't been taken by surprise one bit.

"If he's a friend of yours, let me give him a kiss." She brought his head down and kissed him on the forehead. In return he took her hands and was about to kiss both of them, but she pulled one away, saying she wasn't done manicuring it; if we'd come an hour later, both hands would be ready. Luckily she'd finished one, but she hadn't had time for the other because there's always something to do around the house.

He gave an open-hearted laugh of a kind I never heard from him either before or after. Something familial, so to speak, came out in the way he behaved toward my mother. Perhaps she reminded him of his own mother, about whom he never talked. He never talked about his father either. He must have had close and distant relatives, everyone does. Sometimes he'd start to say something but break off, so I could only guess that his parents were no longer alive. But I wasn't certain. He wasn't even middle-aged then; could he have lost both of them? Or perhaps for reasons of his own he preferred not to have any family?

To show how pleased she was by the visit, my mother chided me for not letting them know in advance. They didn't have a telephone, they were on the waiting list and they'd been told they'd have one in three years, but if I'd called the post office and had them deliver a message, she could have cooked something special.

"We only decided two days ago. Don't trouble yourself, mama. We'll eat whatever you give us. Or we'll just drink tea. We're not staying long. Our train back is at eight this evening."

"What do you mean?" she said indignantly. "You only just got here and you're already leaving?"

"We have to, mama."

"Not on your life. What kind of mother would I be? There are beds to sleep in. Tomorrow I'll go shopping and there'll be plenty to eat. I'll make the kind of meal I ought to have made today, if I'd known. And in the afternoon I'll bake a topielec. I haven't made one in ages. This is the time to do it." Then to my father: "Come on, say something."

"Like what? You already said what needs to be said."

"You could chime in too. Say you'll give them a glass of your nalewka. You still have some, don't you?"

"There's one bottle left. I was going to make more in the fall."

We ended up staying four days. My mother, of course, made the topielec that same day, so my friend could have some for supper. That evening she explained to him – in detail – how it was made. If he hadn't said it was delicious, she might not have felt encouraged to tell him.

I thought he was only listening out of politeness. But one time, recollecting our stay at my parents', he said:

"That topielec really was marvelous. But if I had to choose between the topielec and the story about how to make it, I'd choose the story. Only mothers can talk like that about baking a cake."

Father was proud to serve his nalewka at dinner. When he brought the bottle up from the cellar he stressed the fact that it was the last. Though his words may also have been an apology: he'd have been glad to offer his guest a bottle to take home with him, but alas, this was the only one.

"Come visit again, by then I'll have made more."

We almost finished the bottle in the course of our meals. It had only been three quarters full to begin with. He poured us small servings, to make it last longer. We polished off the little that was left as a stirrup cup the day we were leaving, standing up, just before we set out for the train station.

"To memory," he said. "May we not forget."

"No one has the right to forget a nalewka like that," my friend responded. It wasn't just flattery on his part: he could tell different flavors of alcoholic drinks even in the dark. With pure vodka, for instance, he knew at once if it was made from potatoes or rye, or another base, as well as what its alcohol content was. The same with flavored vodkas. Nalewkas too – he'd take a sip and at once he'd say: chokeberry, sloe, quince, black currant. Though it took him a day or two, he was the only person who ever worked out that my father's nalewka was made from dried plums. The only thing he didn't identify was the brandy, but my father told him that part.

"Right – I could tell there was something beyond the plums."

My father's heart melted when he heard my friend say that no one had a right to forget his nalewka. My mother alone was supposed to walk us to the train, but my father said he'd go too, because how could he not accompany such a guest to the station. So they both waited till the train pulled out. They were still waving when the last car had left the station. I opened the window to wave back, and over the clatter of the wheels I heard my mother shout: "Come see us again!"

We were sitting opposite one another, at the window. There were two men and a woman in the compartment with us. Even though it was only just dusk, all three of them were asleep. It was a long-distance train, and they must have been on it for a while. They woke up when we came in. Their legs were stretched out, and we couldn't help bumping into them as we made our way over to the window. They looked at us through bleary eyes; the woman opened her mouth wide in a yawn, revealing gaps in her teeth. One of the men asked what station it was, the other looked at his watch.

"Is that the time? I thought it was night already. We've a long way to go still."

When the train picked up speed and began to rock, they fell asleep again. To avoid waking them we barely talked, sometimes just a word or two in a whisper, leaning toward one another. It was more me saying something to him than him to me. He stared out the window the whole time at the meadows, woods, villages, and towns growing dim in the twilight. Even when they were hidden completely by the dark of evening, he didn't move his eyes away. When he occasionally spoke it was as if he was talking to the window, and his words were so quiet they didn't reflect off the pane for me to hear.

The conductor came through and turned on the light, asking: "Anyone get on at the last station?"

We showed him our tickets and he clipped them. He didn't wake the other passengers, which further showed they'd been on the train for a long while and he'd already checked their tickets. He turned off the light and left. If they hadn't been sleeping I'd have asked them where they were traveling from and where they were going – almost obligatory questions when you find yourself on a journey with someone.

"It's dark already," I said. "Surely you can't see anything."

He didn't answer. He didn't even look in my direction. I had the impression he was clinging to the window. I leaned in close to his face and saw tears. I wasn't mistaken – he was crying. Almost completely silently, as if stifling his sobs, so as not to wake the other passengers. He couldn't stop himself, for all at once his whole body shook. Yet he kept staring out of the window, attaching himself ever more firmly to the darkness outside, it seemed.

I didn't know what to do. I felt more and more helpless, just as he was more and more overcome by his tears. I had the impression they were running down the glass, though it could have just been rain.

"Why are you crying?" I tugged at his sleeve. "What happened? Don't cry."

"Let him be." The man sitting next to him had woken up. "Let him cry. He must need to get it out."

"But he's my friend."

"What can anyone know, even about their friend."

The other man stirred too.

"What's up with him?"

"Nothing. He's crying," the first one said.

"Yeah, sometimes it builds up in you. Then it bursts out when you least expect it. Times like that, it's good to have a bottle with you."

The woman also woke up.

"What is it, has he lost someone too?" she said in a general sort of way, more to show that she was awake as well.

She sat up, reached for her bag on the shelf, took something out and started to eat.

"It's two years now since I lost my daughter. Only God knows how much I've cried. He's just crying quietly; me, I tore my hair out. I knelt in front of Our Lady yelling: God doesn't exist. God doesn't exist! Then I went on a pilgrimage. We walked and walked. My feet were covered in blisters. They burst and wet my socks. She wasn't yet twenty. All the guys chased after her. One of them had a farm, machinery, people working for him. But she didn't want a country boy. What kind of life is it in the country. You slave away dawn till dusk, for a pittance. They still owe us for milk from back in the spring. She went to a dance in the next village and never came back. They pulled her out of the river, a long way from us. Her body had almost rotted away." She crumpled up the paper her food had been wrapped in, dropped it into her bag, and took out an apple. It crunched in her mouth. "It was in the reeds by the bank. Men were fishing there, and one of them, his line got caught up."

"Enough," muttered the man who'd woken up first. "Everyone's lost someone, ma'am. There isn't anyone who hasn't."

"Should I put the light on?" The second man got up from his seat.

"What for?" the woman objected. "It's nice in the dark. We might get back to sleep." A moment later she was snoring quietly. The two men followed suit.

I don't know if the rumble of the moving train had calmed him, or if it only muffled his crying, but when I leaned toward him again I couldn't hear any sound other than his breathing. I felt relieved, and I drifted off myself. It wasn't sleep, I was just dozing, for I heard the woman snort and then murmur as if to herself:

"Is he crying?"

To which the man sitting next to her, who'd been roused from his sleep, said: "I can't hear anything."

"Maybe he's crying inside?" The woman was completely awake.

"No, I think he's sleeping," the man said.

"Then let him sleep, let him sleep. There's no better medicine than sleep."

Chapter 4

§

As usually happens, at first I was given the lowest position, that of junior assistant curator. My main duty was leading school groups – and only from the elementary grades. The assistant curator took the middle school visits, the high school students were led by the senior assistant curator, while the head curator himself showed special guests around.

It wasn't an easy job, contrary to what you might think. There were tours every day. Often one would arrive before the previous tour had left. Of course, it had all been scheduled ahead of time. But I'd never dealt with schoolchildren before. They wandered all over the place, shouting, running, and it was all you could do to keep them in order. Even their teachers were unable to control them. Often one of the children would go missing, and we'd have to search for them in every one of the innumerable rooms, many of which were not actually open to the public – though that didn't stop the children from straying in there too. Worst of all was when the head count didn't add up before they left, because then the entire mansion had to be combed. Not to mention that they dropped candy wrappers, paper sandwich bags, pear and apple cores. One of them knocked over a Greek amphora, another shot a catapult at a portrait of some ancestor, poking his eye out; a third peed on the floor in the bathroom. The responsibility for all of this fell on me.

Fortunately the head curator was understanding, and reassured me by saying that learning isn't just gains, but also losses. Besides, after I'd been through experiences like that with schoolchildren I'd have a better grasp of history itself, because history begins with children, little ones still at their mother's breast. They're the ones who pay for it with their innocence, much more than the adults, for whom history is only a game. I'm not sure what he was getting at, but there were times when I'd had enough. To raise my spirits he promoted me to the rank of regular assistant curator and I moved on to the middle school tours. I still felt unsatisfied, though – leading school groups wasn't how I'd imagined my working life to be.

One time, though, when I was waiting for her at Needle's Eye, he came by too. Whether he was coming up from the old wild green valley, or on his way down there, I can't say – all my meetings with him have gotten mixed up.

"You're waiting for her," he said, not so much asking as stating. "You're waiting. Of course – at your age you still wait. At mine, there's nothing to wait for. Say hello to the head curator."

"From who?"

"He'll know." And he continued on to the next step, upwards or downwards, I don't recall, though I ought to, since every step of his meant something. All at once he paused. "I was forgetting. I think you ought to do a PhD. Surely you don't mean to stop at a master's. The fact that you have to lead school groups is neither here nor there, it'll come in handy in time. I have a research topic for you that hasn't been touched by the scholars. You wrote your master's thesis on the Middle Ages, right? I thought so. From your expression, I'm guessing you'd have preferred contemporary history? I wouldn't advise it. The present day isn't history, it's a battle over history, because everyone's seeking to rise to the top. With the Middle Ages you're dealing with those who are long dead – which is a condition for true history – with their long-dead fears, tribulations, ambitions, their long-dead despair, and traces of hope. You wouldn't have to feel sorry for anyone, to praise or criticize anyone falsely. A disinterested period, a beautiful period, for beauty is always disinterested. Think it over. While you're young, time still flows slowly. But soon it'll start to get faster and faster. The next time we meet, you'll give me your answer."

To tell the truth, I wasn't intending to go back to school. I had to earn a living; the salary of an assistant curator wasn't much, but it freed my parents from having to help me out. It bothered me throughout the time of my studies that they were taking food from their own mouths to share with me. Amid the monotony of that job, something nevertheless happened which, though it didn't seem particularly noteworthy at the time, often came to mind later on.

The regional authorities had decided to organize a celebration for a local eighty-year-old man. The reason was not that he'd turned eighty, which he denied, but because he'd written a book about his life, which also included the life of his mother, and to a lesser extent that of his father, who had died when the man was still an infant. All of this was set against a broad social backdrop.

A program was devised, and I was given the job of looking after the honoree and his family during the event, an assignment which I took as a distinction. There was a generous budget, and a large number of guests were invited, both from the town and outside.

The honoree – spry and sharp as a tack – came from a nearby village. His entire education had been four winters of elementary school. Winters, he stressed, because from spring to fall he minded the cows at the manor. Yet his life had been so rich you could say he'd had no need to graduate from any school.

I knew him. Everyone there did. He sometimes came to the mansion, joined a school party, and accompanied the children on their tour. When I wasn't sure who was who in some portrait or photograph, he would explain whose bedroom this had once been, talk of the dances that had taken place in the ballroom, describe who used to visit and from where, and mention the hunting trips the various trophies came from – in Asia, or Africa, or the local woods. Most often, though, he'd be seen on a bench under the chestnut tree, waiting for somebody to sit down next to him. I'd join him myself occasionally when I was tired after a school group and needed a little break in the fresh air. He'd immediately shower you with stories from his life, as if the pressure of the experiences that had built up within him demanded words. It was hard to break away: he drew you in with those tales of his. A short man – or at least of less than average height – he had an extraordinary sense of humor, as if language were compensating for his lack of stature.

Every sentence of his brimmed with irony, sarcasm, irrepressible wit. He came to the mansion, he'd say, because he was bored at home, and his wife was tired of listening to him.

His knowledge of life and of the world was impressive. He'd fought in the previous war, had earned no promotion and laughed at every rank; he was constantly being put in the blockhouse or sent to the rear, thanks to which he was never once wounded. He said he'd never had such a laugh as when he was in the army. He'd been here and there in search of a living – as the expression goes, he'd eaten bread from more than one oven. Often he'd gone wandering because he was quite simply bored – boredom alone had driven him from the house, because tell me, you get up and you go to bed, get up and go to bed, don't you get sick of it? Take a job? There were no jobs. We only had two acres, my mother and sister worked the land on their own.

As I bring him to mind all these years later, it makes me sad to think that soon we'll need a dictionary to read Polish. In his case you didn't just hear his words, you saw them. You had the impression that out of language he was building a world that was unique, not something copied from somebody else: it was like a multicolored painting that you gazed at as he spoke, in which you actually saw yourself at his side as he traveled about that world of his; for words can draw you into someone else's life, however distant it is from your own. Especially because traveling with him seemed to release you from all your sorrows and troubles and weariness.

He made fun of everything and everyone, including himself. One time he asked me what I thought: Was it better to be born tall or short.

Me, he said, I was too poor to be born tall. But maybe that's a good thing. Because see how people grow these days. If they keep on at that rate, we'll need to build houses without ceilings. Then how would we live without a ceiling over our heads? Where would we hang the garlic, the onions, or even the baby's cradle, if there's no beam? Also, a tall fellow needs twice as much food, and the earth won't give that much. Plus, staring at the underside of the roof all your life? If it were thatched it wouldn't be so bad, but with tarpaper or roof tiles or tin, you'd have to make holes in it to let the sky in a bit.

"My nose is crooked, it's shaped like a potato – as you see. But when they give me one thing or another to sniff, it's cabbage I smell. You've no idea how good my mother's cabbage was. Your eyes won't tell you that, your mouth won't tell you, words won't, but your nose will smell it. I could eat cabbage every day."

When it came out that he'd written a book, everybody was amazed; they found it hard to believe that someone like him – a man who you'd think could barely sign his own name – had done that. Four winters of schooling and he'd written a book. And what was education like back in those days? All four classes often learned all together in a single schoolroom. Somebody even said that there's no justice in the world, what was the point of getting an education at all, graduating from one school or another? Someone went into town to look in the bookstore, but they came back empty-handed. The book had been there, they'd stood in line, but by the time it was their turn the store had run out. Check back in a week or two, they said, they'd ordered more.

The same day that person failed to buy the book at the bookstore, a copy arrived at the mansion in a package addressed to the head curator. There was a dedication, not to the curator though, but to the mansion, as if hinting subtly that curators come and go, while mansions endure. The inscription was written in a regular, in fact vigorous hand, which surprised people even more. Some suspected that another person had written the dedication for him – maybe even the whole book, because it was hard to imagine him writing it after only four winters of schooling. With that little education he'd barely have been able to write, and no one had ever seen his handwriting.

After the book was published, its author stopped coming to the mansion, as if he was afraid for having written it. The doubts and suspicions were only dispelled when the local powers-that-be decided to organize a celebration for him. A three-person delegation, including myself, was sent to inform him, but he wasn't in. Where was he? His wife spread her hands. She didn't know where he'd gone, he hadn't said. When would he be back? He hadn't told her that either, so who knew, it might be this evening, it might be any time. Once before he'd left like that – and she began to tell the story chaotically, mixing things up so much you'd have been forgiven for thinking that to this day he still hadn't reappeared. We said our goodbyes and told her we'd come back in a couple of days. Perhaps by then he'd have returned.

"God willing, God willing," she said hopefully.

A few days later the delegation visited again; it was even bigger this time as the head of some department had taken charge. But he still wasn't back. Luckily I wasn't part of the delegation that time, the head curator himself had gone in my stead. They didn't know what to do: give up, or say they'd try again in a day or two. Then all at once a clattering sound came from the attic.

"What was that?" someone asked.

"Just our cat, the rascal," said the wife. "It must have knocked something over while it was hunting mice."

"Cat?" They were surprised, but they might not have believed it if a cat hadn't sidled into the room through the half-open door and meowed. Someone else in the delegation asked: "How many cats do you have?"

"Just the one," the wife said without thinking.

"And it's in the attic and downstairs at the same time? It must lead a double life," somebody joked.

"It must have dashed down the ladder in no time."

"We didn't see a ladder in the hallway."

"It's not up."

"Then put it up and we'll go take a look."

She went out into the hallway, made a clucking sound, and the ladder dropped from the attic, seemingly of its own accord. The whole delegation went up there; the rungs creaked, but they held. It turned out that the honoree had been hiding up there all that time. He had a straw mattress, a quilt and pillow, his wife brought him his meals, and when he needed to come down to relieve himself, his wife stood guard in front of the cottage to make sure no one was coming. They found him on his makeshift bed, his head under the quilt. Since he was small, and the quilt was thick, they might never have known anyone was under it. All the more because the cottage was roofed with thatch, and there was only a little bit of light coming from the hatchway to the attic. But one member of the delegation lit a cigarette lighter, pulled back the quilt, and the department head, as leader of the delegation, addressed the honoree, who was lying there in his shirt and long johns, as follows: "Dear honoree, don't hide any longer. You've written a book, and we checked up and found that you're eighty years old –"

"I'm not eighty yet," the honoree said.

"If the authorities say you are, then you are."

"I'm not. My age belongs to me, not the authorities."

"Then show us your ID."

"I don't sleep with my ID."

"Where is it?"

"Downstairs."

"So let's go down."

They went down. He searched for his ID everywhere but couldn't find it.

"Someone must have stolen it, or I misplaced it somewhere."

He was at a loss, seeming genuinely concerned.

"Look behind Our Lady," his wife suggested.

"What's Our Lady got to do with my ID? Don't mix up worlds," he retorted.

"This is a serious matter," the head of the delegation said sternly. "You ought to know you can be fined, or even go to prison. A citizen without ID, it's as if he was trying to hide his existence from the authorities. And that's a crime."

"Then what should I do?" The honoree was alarmed.

"All you can do is go report it."

He didn't go, either the next day or the one after that. His wife couldn't say where he was. She shrugged helplessly and promised that when he returned she'd make sure he went. That time they didn't find him in the attic. And he might never have appeared, but yet another delegation went there and said that if he showed up they'd buy him a suit, a white shirt, a necktie, shoes and socks, and it would all be his to keep, he wouldn't have to give it back. Who wouldn't agree to their own celebration once they were offered such an incentive. He stopped denying he was eighty years old. He even agreed to let an artist paint his portrait. He was meek now, he consented to everything.

The event was held in the ballroom, the largest and loveliest of all the rooms in the mansion. Tables were arranged in a single row along the entire length of the room, in the middle, while at each end there was a much shorter line of tables at right angles to the others. At one of these shorter tables sat the honoree, with his wife next to him, then two male cousins of his, a female cousin, and myself, charged with caring for the guest of honor. At the other short line of tables, opposite us at the end of the long row, were the local powers-that-be, though there were said to be some out-of-town bigwigs too, the most important of whom was some kind of secretary, who had no need to show he was the most important person there, since he was the one to raise the first toast to the writer.

There was a mass of guests; they barely fit along the two sides of the long table. There were representatives of various committees, councils, associations, organizations, but also writers, poets, critics, journalists, and two or three professors of literature. The event promised to be very grand indeed, not to say festive, though it was a regular weekday, Wednesday or Thursday. In any case the mood was lofty; everyone was dressed in suit and tie, and wore an appropriately solemn expression. The atmosphere was enhanced by the ballroom itself. On the walls were sconces that seemed to be flowering in springlike fashion; between them hung portraits of ancestors of the mansion's former owners. You might have been forgiven for thinking these were the ancestors of the honoree, who in this way were participating in his eightieth birthday celebration. Crystal chandeliers of an exquisite opulence hung from the ceiling directly over the tables, which groaned under a multitude of dishes of every kind. Your head spun at the number of serving plates, salad bowls, and trays, once they began circulating among the guests. They seemed to float through the air, while dozens of hands reached out and pulled them back onto the tabletop.

In front of each guest was a bottle of beer and a half-liter of vodka. Though it was afternoon, all the lights were on. Sunlight streamed in through the windows, and the glare from the chandeliers and the sconces made the whole room dance before your eyes; instead of seeing more clearly, your vision was blurred. At a sign from the table where the powers-that-be were sitting, the waiters began to open the vodka bottles and fill everyone's glasses. In those days they still sealed bottles with wax, and everyone marveled at the skill with which they were opened. One blow of the hand on the bottom of the bottle and the cork broke the resistance of the wax. The waiters' attire was also admired. Pale gray tuxedos, white shirts, red bow ties, black pants, and patent leather shoes. Where they'd sprung from, no one could say; it was rumored they'd been brought in specially. Their hair was brilliantined down, with a part in the middle. When all glasses had been filled, at the table facing the honoree, the secretary who was the most important of the dignitaries seated there stood up and began a toast. It seemed this would take the form of a brief greeting; at least his opening words suggested so: "Respected honoree, respected guests, I greet you in my own name and that of our leaders."

He picked up his glass; everyone followed suit and stood. The glass in his hand seemed to inspire him, for his voice suddenly grew louder, the words began to flow rapidly, and from one sentence to the next they took on the tone of a speech at a rally.

The guest of honor stood with everyone else, glass in hand, though he was so short it wasn't easy to tell if he was standing or sitting. It looked more like his wife was standing for him – she was quite tall – and of course the rest of his family, who were even taller than the wife. His hairless head inclined to the left as if it was weighing him down. At every other moment he closed his eyes and opened them again, fighting back his amusement at the fact that this was his birthday party. He looked like a drawing of a grandfather made by a first grader. Only the glass trembling in his hand showed that he was real.

Meanwhile, the secretary went on with the toast: "This mansion, respected honoree, would never have allowed you to enter its rooms, had it not been for the rule of the people. The masters would still be at play in this chamber, while the downtrodden commoners would be slaving from dawn till dusk providing for their luxuries, their carousing and their entertainments. Who then would remember that you were turning eighty? A fine age, by the way, a venerable age. But in order for your years to be celebrated as they should be, first it was necessary to lift the people from their knees, and toss their oppressors on the trash heap of history. It's also thanks to the rule of the people that your talent awoke. The rule of the people liberated your faith in yourself from the tyranny of class, so you too believed you could write; it gave you the courage to take up the pen; it freed your heart with its sensitivity to suffering, and the work-worn hand with which you write. Just as all of us here are grateful to you for what you've written, so you too should be grateful for the rule of the people. Without it – " At this moment the glass he held – which up till now had remained steady despite all those words that had roused him over and again – his glass shook, scattering drops on his hand. "Anyway, it's time to drink, comrades!" he exclaimed. "To the health of our honoree! Long may he live and write!"

His glass was already at his lips when the person standing next to him abruptly cried: "To the health of the rule of the people, in the person of the comrade secretary standing here among us!"

The secretary, irked that someone had presumed to finish his toast for him, retorted sharply: "The rule of the people doesn't need its health to be drunk. We have an obligation to be healthy." He tipped the contents of his glass down his throat.

Everyone drained their glasses, set them down, and applauded. The applause went on for a long time, falling into a rhythm, till the secretary raised his hand as a sign that that was enough. He sat down. Everyone else sat too, and began to eat.

It was hard to eat much, however, since simply eyeing all the dishes and choosing what to have was time-consuming in itself, then serving yourself also took a moment. Meanwhile the ever-vigilant waiters topped up everyone's glasses without a second's pause. And already somebody was jumping to his feet as he swallowed one last mouthful of food, preventing anyone else from going before him, and reminding everybody that the sequence of toasts reflected each person's position in the hierarchy. He raised his glass, but apparently hadn't quite finished the mouthful, because he coughed once and twice, excused himself for having a sore throat, and as if forgetting what he'd meant to say, began by mentioning the secretary who was above him in the hierarchy. As the latter had stated, and rightly so – as he had phrased it so profoundly, enlightening us with such wise words. . . The sentences refused to join together, so eventually the secretary took pity on him and interrupted: "You should drink. It'll be good for your throat. And let's eat."

"Then here's to the honoree's health!" the man rasped out with an effort. After which he collapsed back into his seat, drank, and lowered his head, perhaps wondering if he'd dropped in the hierarchy, to the point that the secretary nudged him in the ribs:

"Why aren't you serving yourself? Don't think, eat. Everyone's eating. You won't get food like this at home, or in the canteen. Today it's tomato soup and egg fritters."

The clatter of knives and forks filled the room; everyone was attacking their meal in a rush so as to try and get something down before somebody else rose to their feet. Despite the fact that the waiters kept refilling their glasses, though, no one was moved to make a toast. Nobody was even talking to anyone else. All that could be heard was the chewing of food, as if some terrible hunger had emerged in people's stomachs, forcing them to eat for several days in advance.

Only the honoree was not eating. He wasn't eating, wasn't drinking, and looked to be dozing off. His wife noticed and shook him by the arm.

"Don't sleep."

"I'm not sleeping."

"Yes you are. Your eyes are closed."

"They are, but I can see what I need to."

"Then have something to eat. Shall I serve you?"

"I want cabbage."

"What cabbage?"

"My mama's."

"Are you crazy?" she said. "You say you're not sleeping, and here you're dreaming of cabbage." She piled his plate with a variety of dishes. He didn't touch any of it.

It was hard to tell if anyone had eaten their fill, especially since you grow hungrier with every shot of alcohol you drink, and the waiters kept refilling people's glasses, knowing from experience it would stoke their hunger.

All of a sudden a tall guy in glasses stood up. He was no doubt thinking it had been a long time since the last toast. Seemingly timid, or perhaps to make himself appear more dignified, he didn't raise his glass, pushing it aside and gazing around at those present as if waiting for them to put down their knives and forks and turn their attention to him. Then he took a bundle of papers from his jacket pocket, put on a different pair of spectacles and, at first stumbling over his words, started to read.

"All my life I've been concerned with literature." Hearing someone clink glasses with somebody else, he repeated distinctly: "All my life I've been concerned with literature." He wasn't old, barely middle-aged, so what could "all his life" mean? You have to live all your life before you can speak of it. True, a person can't be sure that their life, however old they are, isn't coming to an end. I've lived through mine, I know this. Alas, mine has been too long. At least by that one year more than the Gypsy woman foretold. So in that last year I had to live it anew, from the beginning up to the point where, standing at Needle's Eye, I was deciding whether to go down one final time to that old wild green valley that no longer existed, or if perhaps I shouldn't. And I may well have chosen not to take the next step down if I hadn't noticed a glint of derision toward my old age in his eyes. That was when the cane wobbled in my hand. "On the basis," the speaker went on, stopped at some sound that interrupted him, then began again: "On the basis of many years of research I arrived at the sad conclusion that literature has reached its end and is only repeating itself. I never imagined I would after all live to see the emergence of a crystalline talent. Here I bow low to our honoree." He bowed, his head almost touching the table. "A talent that is not entangled in any movement, trend, program, theory, and that alters the face of literature, refreshing it with his simple heart. He shows us a world that we do not know. Because everyone sees the one we're familiar with. As for us – his admirers gathered here – he inspires us with an optimism that is essential in life. For we are all weary of pessimism, upon which up till now literature has fed, in ever more violent renderings. And so, turning to our honoree with the greatest respect – "

Someone shouted: "Long may he live!"

"Just a moment, I haven't finished." Out of nerves he must have mixed up his pages, because he began shuffling them back and forth. The silence he had insisted on suddenly came to an end, however. There arose the sound of knives and forks, there were bursts of laughter, conversations. "A little more patience. A little more patience," he said, almost begging.

"Perhaps you've already said all that's needed, learned comrade?" the secretary said, attempting to rescue him.

"No, no." His hands were shaking as he continued to shuffle his papers. "No, no."

"Have a drink and you'll find the page you need," the secretary urged him.

"No, no."

At this someone jumped up and in a hoarse bass voice cried: "Keep on looking, and in the meantime we'll sing *Sto lat* for the honoree. Everyone rise."

There was a commotion as people stood, pushing back their chairs; some of them were already the worse for wear and it was a struggle to rise up and assume a vertical position. Some needed assistance from their neighbors, others found it so hard to stay on their feet that they sat straight back down again. When *Sto lat* finally came from every throat, the song was uneven, raucous, as if stripped of its tune. The worst of it was that the moment they finished they started up again. "May he live a hundred years. May his happy star shine on, And forever with him go. Whoever does not drink with us, Let the lightning strike them low!"

The honoree also stood, along with his whole family. When the song started again from the beginning, though, he gave up and sat back down, and his family followed. True, he was smiling; he smiled throughout, as if his smile formed a barrier between him and everyone else.

Fortunately the singing began to die down. Two or three individuals were still on their feet, but the others went back to eating. The waiters stepped forward to fill the empty glasses. It appeared we'd finally be able to eat and drink as much as we wanted without any more interruptions; plus, the dishes themselves were hard to ignore, they stirred not just our appetite but our imagination. In both eating and drinking the imagination plays an important role. With your imagination you can anticipate telling your friends later about what you ate and drank, and even experience it again with them. In fact it all tastes much better in the telling than when you were actually eating and drinking.

The celebration was becoming less formal – livening up, you might say. Everyone was talking together, clinking glasses, changing places, sitting down by one another. Some had taken off their jackets and loosened their neckties; they were exchanging embraces and drinking to friendship. Only the honoree and his family behaved with dignity, for even the secretary had slackened his tie and unfastened the top button of his shirt.

The talk grew louder, shifting from one side of the table to the other, drawing closer, moving further away, splitting into multiple conversations. Here, there, nearer, farther away, along the entire length of the table people were speaking over one another, yelling, slurring their words, and downing the glasses that the waiters methodically replenished. Here people were exchanging kisses, over there they were at each other's throats, as if they'd have fought it out had it not been for the table between them. In the end two incensed, red-faced men grabbed one another by the lapels. Luckily they were restrained by others. The dispute had been over the relative merits of their poetry. They were only finally pulled apart when someone suggested they each read one poem. They didn't agree right away. They sat there, still muttering; eventually, seemingly calm, they had a drink and began to eat.

All at once one of them jumped to his feet, pulled a sheet of paper from his pocket and announced he was going to read a poem he'd written for the honoree. The poem was about youth, in fact, but the honoree had been young once. There were a few "bravos," though they were rather feeble; all the same, the author bowed gratefully on all sides. His thanks were interrupted by the other poet, with whom he'd almost come to blows, calling out:

"I'll read you a better poem!" And he began to read, or rather stammer, stumbling over his words again and again, raising his voice then running out of breath, as if the poem itself was lame, crippled, unable to keep pace with its author's confident belief he was reading something extraordinary. It was hard to even figure out whether he was reading a poem or a speech.

In the end one of the other guests couldn't take it anymore and shouted: "Put the poems away! We didn't come here for poetry! Here's to the honoree's wife!"

The whole room stirred at this toast. Someone even proposed a toast to all wives. It didn't end with their health. The toast turned into a speech on the role of writers' wives, with the conclusion that if it weren't for the wives, the husbands wouldn't write, for the wives are their inspiration. Someone said in a loud drunken whisper that he'd had three wives and it didn't help a bit with his writing. To this, his neighbor replied: "Maybe you picked the wrong wives? Try a fourth and a fifth. Keep going till it works."

"Till it works? Death's more likely to come before inspiration."

"Still, we should stand up, it wouldn't be right not to drink to the health of wives."

All glasses were raised, and the waiters hurried forward to refill them, for when you're toasting wives, one drink isn't enough.

From that moment on, everyone started jumping up and raising toasts. They toasted anything that came into their heads. Their words were jumbled, sometimes chopped up into individual syllables, and had to be forced out of their mouths; they had the hardest time staying on their feet, while the glasses in their hands looked like flags waving in the wind, spilling their contents – though a waiter would spring forward at once to top it up. At times two or three attendees would leap out of their chairs at the same moment, one at one end of the table, one at the other, one in the middle, or even two people sitting next to one another, as if their vision had grown so hazy they didn't notice each other. The contest was won by whoever was loudest, whoever stood most firm and held his glass with the greatest confidence. Right at that moment somebody with a voice that rang like a bell, though a cracked one, was drowning other voices and roaring out not so much a toast as an admonition:

"May our wives be happy with us! And vice versa!"

Alcohol sometimes takes away speech, but the opposite also happens: a taciturn type becomes an orator. The fellow with the voice like a cracked bell turned out to be one of those. He spoke and spoke, though everyone stopped listening. Even the representatives of the rule of the people were deep in conversation about some plenum that had just taken place or was about to happen, I couldn't make out; while the other man went on talking. Someone slid from their chair onto the floor, others hurried forward to help him, but their own strength had clearly been sapped, for the moment they lifted him up he sank back down to the ground, and the waiters had to come to his rescue and put him back in his seat. The other man was still speaking. Heads fell to the tabletop as if mown down, and still he went on. One man rose from his chair so quickly he staggered. He looked about to fall over, but after rocking this way and that, he stood firm. Perhaps he'd meant to interrupt the other guy, but his words deserted him, and all he did was strike himself a swinging blow in the chest with his fist, after which he flopped back down and started crying, as if his soul was in great pain. At such moments, aching souls too can feel a need to vent their grief. Especially when nothing can be said to counter words, yet silence is too much to bear.

Cake was brought in.

"Dessert already?" the secretary said in surprise. "Time flies."

The waiters placed the cakes on the tables at more or less equal intervals, putting the largest one in front of the honoree. This cake rested on a tall serving platter; it was covered with candles, to the point that the guest of honor disappeared behind them. One of the waiters lit the candles. I didn't manage to count them, but there was probably one for every two years of his life, because there wouldn't have been room for eighty.

The honoree's wife grumbled: "How are you supposed to eat it with all those candles? It must be for show, not for eating. I've never seen anything like it."

"You have to wait till the candles burn out," one of the men at the family table said.

I don't know what it meant, but the honoree wagged his finger at the cake.

"Now then, you little devil. Don't cheat us now, don't cheat us." Then he took a few candles out of the cake, blew them out, and said to his wife: "Here, there's a slice free, help yourself."

"Shall I cut you a piece too?"

"No."

"What about them?" She indicated the family.

"They can take out their own candles and put them out."

People spent a long time eating the cake. In fact, it wasn't exactly eating; the process did not go well. Some of them dug in with a spoon, others couldn't seem to get the spoon to work and tried to use a knife and fork.

At a certain moment the secretary rose to his feet, tugged his necktie up, fastened his jacket, and announced resoundingly to the whole room: "Everyone rise! The crowning moment is here!"

Anyone who still had the strength stood up; those who didn't, at least tried. People helped one another, for getting up wasn't easy. Those who'd been dozing, head resting on the tabletop, had to be woken up, and bringing them back to consciousness took some time. Some of those on their feet were still asleep, their heads lolling as if they didn't belong to them. The secretary waited patiently; he himself was swaying slightly.

"Very good. We're up," he declared at last. "Now, I ask you all to pay attention." He turned to someone standing in readiness behind him, holding in both hands a stiff red binder opened for reading. "The envelope's for after," he said. Despite his efforts to lend his voice a lofty tone, the reading did not go entirely smoothly. Some sentences came out loud and clear; others descended into a barely audible murmur.

It was a congratulatory letter from the powers-that-be to the honoree. The secretary was visibly relieved when he got to the end. Applause rang out. Whoever still had the wherewithal, clapped for two. Others though could scarcely tap one palm against the other, their hands seemingly refusing to obey them, along with their heads and legs. Some didn't applaud at all but merely stared, not fully understanding what was going on.

The secretary closed the binder, took an envelope from the other man and set off toward the honoree. He moved as if forcing himself to take each step, though to his credit he didn't stumble even once. When he reached the honoree, he handed him the binder containing the letter, gave him the envelope, and embraced him, towering over him, for the honoree's head only came up to his chest. He even laid his hand on the honoree's bald head and stroked it. Then he returned to his place and raised a toast: "To the health of our honoree once more! Long may he live!"

The honoree's wife immediately grabbed the envelope from her husband and peered into it under the table. She must have been counting the contents, under cover of the animation in the room after that solemn moment, and the further toasts it had engendered; her gaze remained lowered for some time.

"They could have given more," she said in a disappointed whisper. "We could have put in some stairs to the attic, we wouldn't have to climb up and down that ladder. We're too old for that."

"It's good they gave that much. They could have given nothing at all," the honoree replied.

She didn't return the envelope, but slipped it under her blouse. The junior assistant curator now went up to the secretary, leaned in and whispered something in his ear; the secretary nodded. Somebody stood up to propose another toast, but the secretary waved him back down: "Sit now. It's not the time."

A moment later the head curator himself entered the room solemnly, flanked by two young women dressed in folk costume, with wreaths of wildflowers in their hair. They were the two youngest female employees at the museum; one worked in the administration, the other in bookkeeping. They were perhaps also the best-looking. The curator bore before him in both hands a silver tray on which there was a laurel wreath. They walked up to the honoree, and the curator said something like the following:

"In Ancient Rome there was a tradition by which the victor in battle was awarded a laurel wreath. The wreath we are offering our guest of honor is also made of laurel leaves, from our orangery. The wreath was placed on the victor's head by the most senior senator, accompanied by two virgins."

The room burst into laughter, making the crystal chandeliers ring beneath the ceiling. The dignitaries laughed too, though not so loudly, for the secretary at once exclaimed: "Quiet!"

All the same, more or less amusing comments came from here and there: "Have they checked? Don't take anything on trust! Not these days! Make sure! Make sure! Long live Rome!"

The girls were embarrassed; they flushed and looked down. The head curator, though, maintained the gravity appropriate to the moment; he waited for the jokes and laughter and heckling to die down, and didn't even stir when someone called out: "Even virgins are officially appointed these days! How can that be good?"

When things had settled down somewhat, the curator resumed: "Today the victor is our beloved honoree – it's on his head that the laurels will be placed. I'm not a senator, but this privilege has fallen to me, so if I can be so bold. . ."

The honoree stood up, came out from behind the table and placed his bald head beneath the wreath.

"Ah – it's a bit big," the curator said. "Let's leave it like that for the moment, we'll adjust it later."

"There's no need. My head's going to swell from all of this," the honoree replied. He shook the curator's hand and kissed each girl on both cheeks. "What a treat," he said.

When he sat down again, his wife grumbled at once: "You didn't need to kiss them. Old codger like you, and that wreath is giving you ideas. You look like a scarecrow."

Unfortunately the wreath kept slipping down over the honoree's ears – first to the left, then to the right. He tried to straighten it, but to no avail. In the end his wife, who'd forgiven him already, took the wreath and twisted the leaves from the outside to the inside, making it smaller. It didn't work though, for the leaves were strung on a piece of steel wire and slid back outwards.

"If you had hair like you used to once, I could've fixed it with a hairpin. You ought to take off that greenery, people are laughing. How embarrassing."

The honoree didn't appear embarrassed, though he did in fact look funny. He smiled out at the room, which was still applauding him; he was aware his appearance was comical. In fact, from the very beginning of the dinner there'd been something clownish in his behavior. I had the impression he'd decided to amuse himself with the crowd. The drunker they were, the more obviously he acted the fool. Who knows, quite possibly it was part of his wisdom: it was only in the role of clown that he could bear to be at his own celebration. And perhaps not just the celebration, but his life. Maybe even the entire world he'd found himself living in. Besides, do we not all play certain roles, and it's those roles that live in our stead?

"Where's the portrait?" the secretary said abruptly to one of his neighbors. "We ordered a portrait of our guest of honor."

"They're just bringing it in, comrade secretary."

A moment later both wings of the double doors opened. A man came in with an easel and set it up right next to the secretary, but the secretary told him to move it further away, so everyone would be able to see. Then two men brought in the portrait, which for the moment was hidden under a white cloth. They placed it on the easel. Only then did the painter himself make a formal entry. His hair was tied back in a pony tail; on his head he wore a broad beret, and in place of a jacket he had a long black robe. He bowed, and the secretary addressed him: "We now ask the artist to unveil his work for us."

The artist untied some ribbons at the back of the frame and the cover dropped away, revealing the guest of honor to the eyes of those present. People crowded forward curiously around the portrait. The secretary on the other hand, as if struck dumb, looked for a moment at the painting and then, struggling to suppress his vexation, said curtly to the artist: "Who's this supposed to be?"

"The honoree," the artist replied in a triumphant voice.

"On his knees?" The secretary was seething. "Surely you were given instructions?"

"I was indeed. To show the honoree at his work. So I painted him at work."

"What's he doing there?"

"Writing."

"He's not writing, he's praying. I'm not falling for that. You write at a desk, not kneeling down. What kind of painter are you?" He was furious. He jabbed a finger at the artist. The other comrades sat hunched over, heads lowered. It looked like the secretary was about to push back his chair and leave, but he merely grabbed a glass angrily and drained it. He poured himself another and downed that too. His tablemates breathed a sigh of relief and also drank.

"Pour him one as well," the secretary said to a waiter, his voice still charged, indicating the artist. "He should sit down and eat something. Somebody must have been having him on. We'll need to look into it. Take care of that." He turned to the man sitting next to him, and the man replied at once: "We already have an idea where to look, comrade secretary."

"Good. Do that."

In my view the portrait captured the honoree as he really did look when he was writing. In old clothes that he wore about the house, barefoot, he was kneeling on an old blanket, elbows resting on a stool. In his hand he had a penholder, and if you looked closely you could see that a roundhand nib was fitted in the holder – there were nibs like that back then. At the edge of the stool there was a pot of ink, while between the writer's elbows lay a sheet of white paper half covered with handwriting. In his quest for accuracy the artist had included a wedding portrait of the writer and his wife hanging on the wall, though I'd been in their house several times and I'd never seen any picture like that. In front of the writer, just above his head was a window with a small open pane. Outside the window the heads of sunflowers sent rays of light onto the honoree's head and the hand that held the pen. The artist must have placed his easel in the right position to stimulate his imagination, for the honoree's face bent over the sheet of paper was more than half hidden – his nose, ear, and one temple were visible, but not his eyes. On the other hand, his bare feet, worn and wrinkled, big as spades, were in the foreground. In this way, I thought, the artist meant to show how much of the world the writer had had to travel in order to write that one book.

"Couldn't you have put a desk in there?" The secretary, merely glum now, turned to the artist, who was still standing by the portrait. "We were switching out the desks at the committee offices. One of those would have done. Now you're going to have to redo it. He can't be on his knees. We spilled our blood to raise them up from their knees, and boom, there he is kneeling again."

In the meantime, the portrait had been taken off the easel, and a place was being sought for it on the walls.

"Let's put it in place of that one," somebody suggested.

The honoree's portrait was big, but the painting they wanted to remove was also pretty large. It showed someone in a thick curly wig, in a frock coat bearing a medal in the shape of a star. The man wore white stockings; two greyhounds lay at his feet. It wasn't easy to take the picture down, though. It was hanging too high. A stepladder was needed. Yet it wasn't right to bring in a stepladder during such a dinner. Besides, everyone was drunk. Even the secretary was yawning, as if he too had had more than enough. Drunks, though, sometimes have bold ideas. Two of them lifted up a third. The third guy almost managed to reach the greyhounds at the bottom of the picture, but then he slipped down. They told him to climb onto the shoulders of the other two men. As he clambered up, holding onto the wall with his hand, all three of them suddenly crashed to the floor.

"What an embarrassment," the honoree's wife said. She started scolding her husband. "I told you, put a suit on. Did I not say that? I did. I ironed a shirt for you. I said, put on a tie, shoes. I polished your shoes for you."

"In a suit and tie and shoes," the honoree said, still beaming unchangingly at the company, "who'd believe I was writing and not praying?"

"You should have been sitting at the table. I scrubbed the table with lye for you."

"He wanted me to be writing. I don't write at the table."

"Just for once you could've been at the table."

"At the table I'd have been thinking about cabbage, not writing."

"What if they make us give the money back? Dear Lord, what then?"

"They won't. I didn't sign for it."

"He can't be kneeling," the secretary repeated, yawning again, as if the air had gone out of him. In fact, everyone had grown sleepy. Glasses stood empty yet no one was asking for them to be refilled; besides, the waiters had disappeared too. Maybe someone had instructed them to stop topping off the drinks, stop serving – had decided it was time to bring the dinner to a close. A glance around the room suggested that most of the attendees were already dozing, that they needed to be roused, helped up from their seats, shown the way out, perhaps even accompanied outside so they wouldn't tumble down the stairs and break an arm or a leg, for the ballroom was on the second floor. Then all of a sudden, as if from an unexpected puff of wind, the last spark flared in a seemingly dying fire. I don't know where the voice came from, because no one had risen to their feet, but a cry rang out: "Speech!"

"Let the guest of honor speak! Speech!" others chimed in.

"He doesn't need to!" The secretary too had stirred. "We should have one for the road rather. We need to be wrapping things up." He came to a sudden realization. "Where the hell are the waiters!"

The waiters hurried in en masse and quickly started filling glasses. The secretary took his drink and stood up.

"Your health, respected honoree. But our comrade artist needs to paint you again so you won't be kneeling."

The honoree rose too. He took the laurel wreath off his own head and placed it on his wife's.

"She's the one who deserves it for spending her whole life with me," he said. "Not me." Then he took his glass. "Well, you certainly all drank to me today. Now I offer a final toast to you all. You wished me many things; I send you my wishes in return. May each of your lives stretch like rubber so you never reach your eightieth birthday. What I had to live through in order to write that one book can be seen from the fact that I'm kneeling. I'm not praying, I'm writing."

Many years later, long after the honoree had passed away, I was invited to join a committee of experts tasked with determining the authenticity of certain objects the museum was considering buying from a private collector. I arrived a day early so as to visit the mansion and see what had changed there since my time as assistant curator. I was shown around by another assistant curator, as young as I had been back then.

In one of the rooms I couldn't believe my eyes when I saw the portrait of the honoree, not repainted the way the authorities of the time had wished, but kneeling in front of his stool, pen in hand, over the half-written page, his spade-like feet in the foreground. The assistant curator hurried to explain that no one knew why this painting had been hung in the palace. It was no antique. But up till now, though curators changed, no one had actually taken it down.

"Do you know at least who this is?" I asked him.

"Yes I do."

"Then you've probably read his book."

"No. I've not been working here long. And the job keeps me so busy I don't have time to read. But I've heard this and that about him."

"Such as what?"

"That he didn't write the book himself."

"Then who did?"

"There are various candidates. But most often people mention the curator at that time, who also came from a peasant background. Apparently the dedication in the copy of the book that's here at the museum looks like the curator's handwriting."

"But in the portrait it isn't the curator who's kneeling at a stool, who's holding a pen and nib in his hand – besides, he didn't use pen and ink but a fountain pen, as I recall. And those bare feet don't belong to the curator."

"The truth of portraits and the truth of life are different, professor. Like all these portraits of beautiful ladies and worthy gentlemen here in the museum."

"Yes, but surely the manuscript of the book is still in existence?"

"They did search for it for a long time after he died, thinking it must have been donated somewhere. But in the end his widow let on that he'd ordered it to be put in his coffin with him."

Chapter 5

§

I'll do my best to remember, but I don't know if it'll be the truth. Unless it's a truth by acceptation. What does that mean? Well, often one thing or another is accepted to be the truth, though no one knows if it really was like that. Or if it even existed at all. But somebody wanted it to be that way, someone imagined it that way and not otherwise, or they may have purposely preferred things to be one way instead of another. Though it occasionally happens that something accepted as the truth, and corroborated by witnesses and evidence, turns out years later to have been a mistake that condemned somebody to death. In history such truths by acceptation are legion, and the closer they are to us in time, the more of them exist.

I don't deny such a thing. But this is the only way I can remember it. To ask my own memory to work against me would mean I was betraying it. And betraying your own memory is unforgivable, for nothing can atone for it.

He said I'd appeared to him in a dream. I couldn't have cared less. So he gripped my arm and repeated: "I had a dream about you."

"What kind of dream?" I asked, though I don't like dreams.

I never sleep well when I have dreams. Sleep ought to be like death. There's nothing, then when you wake up it's an ordinary day, as if life were just beginning. Dreams weigh you down, discourage you, they often make you think goodness knows what. Sometimes they even force you to try and track yourself down. I especially don't like it when other people dream of me. Because what lies behind the fact that I appeared in their dreams? It couldn't have happened for no reason, that's clear. But try finding the reason. Mull the thing over, rack your brains over the fact that they're trying to lay some burden on you – to cast something off their own back and onto yours, so as to lighten their burden, but increase yours. Especially since we're not responsible for our own dreams. Maybe we should be. Maybe one day someone will extend our sphere of responsibility to include our dreams. In fact, we're already heading in that direction. They see us walking down the street, they hear us when we whisper, and even the walls of our own dwellings may not be able to protect us. Yet we're one with our dreams, just as we are with our thoughts, our words, our feelings, and so on. They've already made inroads in some of these things. So it won't be long before they'll do the same with our dreams.

What had he dreamed about me? I'm not sure if it was the way I remember it. He ought to know, since it was his dream. I didn't consent to being dreamed about. He didn't ask. He usurped my rights. Just because we sometimes met at Needle's Eye? Anybody could have met anybody else, in any place, not necessarily there. He was going down to the old wild green valley, and I was waiting. Or maybe he was waiting and I was going down. Though what could he have been waiting for at his age?

"I died," he said.

"What do you mean, you died? You're right here, you're going somewhere."

"But I dreamed that I died. That's why I decided to visit the old wild green valley, which apparently no longer exists. Because who knows if it won't be for the last time."

Oh well, I thought to myself, once you reach a certain age dying is nothing unusual. Though from the outside he didn't look as if he'd reached the age that the Gypsy woman had foretold in his youth. Life hadn't yet faded within him. His complexion was till rosy, his forehead relatively smooth, his eyes clear and bright, his hair peppered with gray in a way that only made him look more distinguished. No, he wasn't yet walking with a cane, he held himself erect; true, he moved a little more slowly than he once did, but perhaps he'd merely decided it was better to walk more slowly since these days he had nowhere to hurry to. In addition, he wore some fancy cologne. It might have been Fahrenheit. It's quite strong-smelling, not all that subtle – and not for every pocket. Yet when at a certain point he leaned in toward me, lowering his voice to a murmur, though I don't recall what he was saying, a different smell mingled with the Fahrenheit.

Every age has its smell, beginning from babyhood. Sicknesses, moods, anger and joy, success and failure – all have their smell. In company I could smell when a woman had her period; her perfume couldn't hide it. People always revealed themselves to me more through smell than through words. Words can rarely be believed. Smells are truthful. Most of us are only capable of that kind of truthfulness. What can I say – nature made me that way. Someone once said to me: "You're like a dog. You should get that treated."

"Get what treated?"

"Your nose. It's bad enough that we see too much and hear too much. Smelling it all into the bargain? It'll drive you mad."

"The thing is, my sense of smell is the only thing that never lets me down."

"It will, it will, they'll find a way somehow or other. You'll smell things normally. Or everyone will smell the same. And you'll completely lose your sense of smell. Give a dog a sausage and it loses the trail."

"What do you say to that?"

"To what?"

"That I died."

"You said you dreamed it."

"True. But what is a dream? Right – you don't know yet, how could you? At your age, what can anyone dream. There's no material for it, so to speak. But there'll come a time when you too are afraid of your dreams. You'll start to shield yourself against them. How can you do that? Only by not sleeping. Let me disclose something to you. You died with me. You didn't know? See, you don't know anything yet. You were standing over my grave, the gravediggers were about to shovel in the earth but you told them it wasn't yet time, not all life had died with me. The wind was blowing, shaking the trees, while you threw handfuls of earth on the coffin from time to time, and you were saying nothing.

I couldn't stand it anymore, because each time the earth fell, it almost smashed the coffin to pieces. I begged you, please stop. Why are you taking your revenge on me like this? For what?"

At that moment the cathedral clock sounded. It chimed once for each quarter hour, then after four quarters it rang the hour. We got carried away listening to the resonant chimes, counting to see what time it was. As if he couldn't wait, he took his watch from his trouser pocket. He carried one of those old-fashioned watches on a chain, an Omega – my father had one like it – and he said dubiously: "Can that really be the time? Maybe the cathedral clock's wrong? It's hard to trust even clocks these days."

I glanced at my wristwatch. "No, that's not the time. It's fast."

"We're evidently living in different times," he said, slipping his Omega into his pocket. "Let's hope one day, though, that our two times come together. If we assume everything moves in circles, even time. You see what an advantage dreams have over reality. Even from the coffin you see and hear what's going on above you. Such things aren't possible in our waking life. Dreams are an infinity of dimensions. They may even be dimensionless."

Then she appeared. And she went with him. I couldn't believe it, because I was the one waiting for her. Yet I had the impression she didn't notice me. She gave me a fleeting glance, then she smiled at him. He was already getting on in years, while she was as young as before, with the same smile brightening her face, revealing the same row of gleaming white teeth.

It's just that I don't remember whether it was still his dream, or mine already. What can you do – no one can cope with their own memory, much less force it to remember what they want. Besides, memory serves to forget as much as to remember. And just as well. If we had to remember everything we experience, memory would destroy us. Add to that the fact that memory is constantly working on what happened yesterday, the day before, and before that, all the way to childhood, then if we weren't able to forget, our whole life would be moving inside us like some unimaginable river that has no banks and flows in every direction at once.

Our neighbor from across the street was dying. He often used to come over, and he seemed fond of me. He'd bounce me on his knee like I was galloping on a horse. Or he'd give me a piggy-back ride, jolting me up and down as if we were running as he carried me from the kitchen to the living room, the living room to the kitchen. He used to call me grandson and I'd call him uncle, though we weren't related. When he came into the room, right from the door he'd ask: "How's my little grandson?" Not, Good morning, or Good afternoon, or Christ be praised, but: "How's my little grandson?"

Sometimes he'd come early in the morning, right after my father had left for work: "I see my little grandson's still in bed. Shame on you! Well then, we should have some fun." He'd sit on the edge of the bed and make the sounds of different domestic animals. He'd meow, bark, bleat, neigh, crow; or he'd form his hands into a trumpet and play reveille for me. "You're laughing, grandson, that's good. It's good to laugh a bit in the morning, because you never know if you'll be crying by evening."

"Don't go frightening my child," my mother would scold him. "He can't even read or write yet, and here you're talking to him about crying."

"Children cry from an early age, don't forget."

"That's a different sort of crying. Put his mouth to the breast and the tears would be gone. Or give him a rattle or his pacifier, and he'd stop. Unless his diaper was wet, and I hadn't had time to change him because something was boiling on the stove or needed draining. It's always like that when there's no maid or nanny. Housework is endless, you never know what to turn to next. I always dreamed of having a maid, and if we had a baby, then a nanny too. My husband said we would, before we were married. Promises, promises. Then afterwards we couldn't afford it."

"I never promised my wife anything. I asked her if she'd agree to not having any money. We'll be together, I'm not afraid of being poor, she said."

"You can put up with being poor at the beginning, but what about afterwards?"

"Afterwards I went to the war. Straight from the wedding, pretty much. You don't have a nanny or a maid but you've got the little one, while we don't have any children. He's getting bigger and smarter all the time. He's grown such a lot since he was born. And he's gotten past all that crying. Now a different sort of crying is coming."

"You're back to that? I told you not to scare him."

"I'm not scaring him, I'm just saying. Without crying you wouldn't know what life is all about. Crying doesn't have to be seen or heard. It's like blood, you don't feel it flowing inside you. You're asleep and it's flowing in you. You can even be laughing, it's still flowing. One guy had his legs blown off in the war, and he laughed like somebody was tickling him. Even the doctors couldn't figure out why he was laughing like that. Maybe he was glad because for him the war was over now. But two legs for a war, I don't see it. It's another matter that in wartime everything gets turned upside down, so crying can be different than in civilian life too. When they came at us with tanks, some men threw themselves under the caterpillar tracks. I mean, I'd get it if they'd been students or something. Going straight from books to tanks, that I'd understand. But there was a blacksmith who went mad too, and he'd spent his whole life forging iron. A railroad engineer went mad, though in civilian life he drove a train, what's a tank compared to one of those trains. Men were always going mad. Whether they became themselves again after the war, that I couldn't say. As for me, I changed out of my uniform and went back home but I still couldn't believe it was me. I looked the same in the mirror. The missus knew me right away. But to me, even my name didn't sound like mine. There it had been private, private first class, corporal, be-cause I made corporal, and here she starts calling me Franuś. Who's Franuś, I asked? Have you been seeing someone? Fess up. 'For God's sake talk some sense! Take the cross down from over the door and I'll swear to you.'"

"Come off it, uncle," my mother said. "You think auntie would have let someone come here? And I'd not have seen it, with our windows right opposite yours? She lived like a nun. Whereas you, who knows if all you did was go into battle. There's plenty of stories about what men get up to in wartime. No one comes back innocent from war. You're the one should've been beating your chest in front of the cross the moment you got back. Mama was always sending me over with dinner, take this to auntie in case she forgot to cook, and there was nothing but cats there. You had two of them, right? Well, there were two cats. She was sitting there, her hand stroking the cats and her lips praying for you. One time I go over and she's whitewashing the walls. What are you doing that for? I ask. You just whitewashed the walls last spring. They're clean. Well, she says, maybe my man'll come back. Another day the whole place was covered in feathers. What on earth's been going on? I've been filling a new pillowcase, because my man might come back. The old one was losing its down. Every day she dusted and she washed the floor, because maybe my man would be coming back. She planted little flowers in the window boxes, it should look nice when my man comes back. When it snowed in the winter, she shoveled it straight away so the path'd be clear when you came back. The gate was creaking, and she went and cleaned at the inn after some wedding so she could buy a new one that wouldn't creak when you came home. You saw the wall hanging she embroidered for you? It's on the wall, where else would it be. Husband in the home, God in the home. There was an artist going door to door, she ordered a wedding portrait. I don't know, maybe she had a photograph. The two of you look like saints on it. Another time, I knock and try the handle, the door's locked. I look through the window, the curtains are drawn, but I tap on the pane. I think I see some movement, then a moment later the door opens. Oh, it's you, child. I haven't been out all day, it's still locked from the night. Have you been crying, auntie? I say. Because I can see tears in her eyes. Why? Well, sometimes your thoughts just cry of their own accord. What kind of thoughts cry like that, tell me? What can I tell you, you're still a child, enjoy it while you're young. If you tell me, I'll tell you something too. What kind of thoughts could you have, you're not waiting for anyone. So you're crying from the waiting? I wish he'd get wounded there, not too badly, just enough so he'd come home. Come in and help me braid my hair, I'll put it up in a crown for when he comes. After he left I let my hair grow, I haven't cut it since, and he could be back any day. I'm telling you, there were only cats there, and you keep asking everybody if she was seeing someone."

"Asking everybody? Who have I been asking? What are you talking about?"

"I've heard, yes I have. People have told me. And all these years since the war. You really should leave it alone. They're saying there's another war coming. While you're still stuck in the old one."

"Because when you're a soldier at the front, you stay that way all your life. You can't forget it. Army memory's different than civilian memory. You think I don't want to forget? But one time I wake up in the night and I shake her by the shoulder, where've you put my rifle? Go back to sleep, I'll find it in the morning. In the morning she gives me a hoe. Here, here's your rifle, go and till the vegetable garden. Dear Lord, what did that war do to you. Were you wounded? In the head? But I didn't have so much as a scratch. If I had, I might have forgotten a lot. As it is, I remember every little thing, I see it all. Clear as I see you here before me, grandson. One time a sergeant got blown to pieces as he was standing right next to me. His blood was all over me. I had to brush bits of his body off of myself. Another guy that was wounded, I put him over my shoulders to take him to the Red Cross tent, and he begs me, take me home. I'm not going to tell him it's a long way from the war to his place. I'm taking you home, I say. You said you're from the village. I can see it already. I think that's the bell ringing in the church tower. Can you hear? Hold on. Your family lived in a cottage with a thatched roof. I see it. There's a stork's nest on the barn. Two storks on it. One of them just flew up, it's coming towards us. That must be your mother standing in front of the cottage, waving at us. She's glad you're back. Did your brother-in-law go to the war as well? Because your sister just came out, but alone. No, there's a little girl with her. You said they have a little girl. Oh – now your father's coming towards us. Stay where you are, I called. I'll bring him to you. I didn't have far to go, truth is – no further than from our place to yours across the road – when he died on my shoulders. He suddenly became so heavy I staggered, and I'm no weakling. I still carry his death today – here, on these shoulders. It's been so many years, and still it's heavy as ever. Another time we were gearing up for a bayonet charge. Most of the time we'd just be sitting around in the trenches, all damp and moldy, thinking about what our wives were up to. Thoughts like that are poison when you're damp and moldy. She makes me all kinds of different teas with herbs, but I can't see that it's getting any better. She had me go see some healer that was supposedly real smart. He feels me over, mumbles something, tells me to look in his eyes, and says he knows what's wrong with me. But I asked him: have you been to war? Not me, pal, he says. War's for mugs. Then you don't know what's wrong with me, buddy. How could a guy like that know. He hadn't carried death home on his shoulders, he hadn't brushed off pieces of someone else's body, hadn't rotted away in a trench. I'm not saying he wasn't smart, maybe even very smart. It's just, what use is being smart when you haven't paid for it in blood? There was this one professor. Oh yes, there were professors too, engineers, judges, lawyers, directors, aristos. There was even one guy that wrote books. His pack was full of those books, he didn't carry any canned food so we had to share ours with him. He gave out the books and told us to read them, said they'd lift our spirits. It happened not to be raining, the sun had come out from behind the clouds, the other side wasn't shelling us, so we opened up the books. All of a sudden someone fired a flare, I don't remember if it was a green one or a red one, to signal an attack or a retreat, but instead of going upwards it shot along the trench and landed right on the book he happened to be reading. It tore up his hands and burned his eyes. Seems someone had accidently bumped against the guy with the flare gun just as he pulled the trigger. I brought the book he gave me home, he swapped it for half a can of food. You can read it when you grow up, grandson. Will you? Then that half can of food won't have gone to waste. What professor?"

"You said there was a professor," my mother prompted him.

"Professor, you say? See, I'm starting to forget, thank heaven. Maybe it's those teas she's been making me. Hang on, I think he wore glasses, because how else could he have been a professor?"

"He went to war when he wore glasses? My husband was rejected by the army because of his glasses, they said he wasn't fit."

"Toward the end they accepted anyone, the half blind, the half deaf. There weren't any more men who could see and hear, they'd all been killed off, so they took whoever they could find. War needs more and more people. Maybe one day wars will manage without people. But luckily I'll be gone by then. They made him tie his glasses on with string so they wouldn't fall off, and we attacked with bayonets. The first time, he didn't kill anyone. Follow behind me, professor, I said to him, because I knew he hadn't learned how to use a bayonet yet. But once he did learn, he could stab two men with one thrust. He marked each one on his rifle butt. He was only one short of twenty when a sniper spotted him. Glasses are a lot easier to see than eyes. And he got him in the glasses. Some people said it was just a stray bullet, no one saw or heard where it came from, but it hit him. Maybe he shot himself after he counted up on his rifle how many people he'd bayoneted. There are soldiers like that who start having a bad conscience. Though in wartime there aren't any consciences, there are only orders. Maybe that's what wars are for: to free you a bit from your conscience, because in civilian life it gives you enough trouble. But that wasn't mentioned when they awarded him a medal, they just said he'd given his life in a sacred cause. It had been snowing, there was a frost, and here the order came: fix bayonets. The lieutenant jumped out of the trench; I had to help him up, because he slipped. I followed after him. He ran a few steps, then he made the mistake of looking back to see if we were behind him. He stumbled, fell backwards, and landed on my bayonet. You attack with your bayonet fixed to your rifle, so the bayonet goes first, the rifle after it. I pulled the bayonet out and ran on. You can't stop an attack even for a lieutenant. I don't know what rank you would stop for – general maybe. But generals mostly sit tight in the rear. In the trenches I never had any dreams, then when I came back home I couldn't get through a single night without dreaming. One time I dreamed about that lieutenant. I pulled the bayonet out of him and he got up and said, ah, that feels better. You stabbed me deep, but living without blood is easier. He looked at the snow around him. I think it's all gone out of me now. Then, just two nights ago the artillery started up, we were under such heavy fire that I wanted to wake up but I couldn't, the dead bodies were pressing down on me and I couldn't, wake me up I shouted. . ."

"Enough with that war of yours," my mother broke in. "I'll be late with dinner because of you. War, war, war. Then afterwards the little one'll be waking up in the middle of the night, if he keeps hearing about those wars you fought."

I didn't know whether to side with uncle or with my mother, so just in case I laughed.

My mother turned on me. "What are you laughing at?"

"Let him laugh, don't stop him. When else can he have a laugh? Any day now another war could come along, then he'll stop laughing."

"Your wounds haven't even healed from the last war and already you want another one."

"I didn't say I wanted it. But if it broke out, I'd go again."

"You're too old for war now. War needs young people. Young people would –"

"What about young people?" he said, annoyed. "Who's going to teach them how to be a soldier? Who's going to show them how to make a bayonet charge? That you have to aim for the belly, because that's the softest place."

"Stop, dammit!" My mother was furious.

"There's no substitute for seasoned men."

He got up and left. He was fortunate enough not to live to see the next war. One day – it was May, the sun was hot and there wasn't the tiniest cloud in the sky – my mother changed out of her kitchen clothes, put on a black skirt and blouse, tied her hair up, put on makeup, dressed me in my Sunday best too, looked out of the open window and said: "Your father ought to be here by now. He was supposed to take time off work. Something must have come up. Oh well, we'll go on our own. If he doesn't die, father can go say goodbye to him after work. Come on." She took me by the hand.

"Who's going to die, mama?" I asked, though I didn't know what it meant to die. To me it seemed that dying was going somewhere far away. A bricklayer we knew, who'd built our veranda, came to say goodbye because he was leaving for America.

"For long?" my mother asked.

He thought for a while. "Who knows if it won't be for good. There's no work here. No one's building houses, all I do is make some steps or do a bit of plastering."

"They say there's going to be another war. Maybe you should wait. After the war you'll have plenty of work."

"What if it doesn't happen? You have to make a living. Wife and four kids. Later on I'll bring the parents over if they're still alive. My brother-in-law wrote and said they're forever building over there, taller and taller buildings, some of them go all the way up to the sky and you can see the sea on both sides. I'd find work on one of the smaller buildings, because the highest I've ever been was up on the church that time the bell tower came down in a storm. They're building the whole country afresh. They didn't have any war there, but still they're building."

"In that case, you've no reason to come back. You'll probably be there till you die. I hope the earth over there is light?"

"You'd have to ask the dead."

"Uncle," she muttered, as if annoyed I'd asked who was going to die. "Stop looking around for your father. If he was going to be here, he'd be here. And death may be in their house already."

She knocked on the door and tried the handle. It was locked. She tried it a second time, still no luck. She looked in through the window, tapped on the pane, nothing. It was only after a short while that the curtain was pulled aside, auntie shifted a flowerpot and pressed her face against the glass. She stared at us for a moment, then closed the curtain again. The key squeaked in the lock.

"There wasn't anyone following you?" she said in a fearful voice. "Come in." She peeped outside, then locked the door again.

"Why are you locking it?" my mother asked.

"He told me to. 'Lock up and don't let them in.' 'Don't let who in, Franuś?' 'Them.' That's all I heard from him. 'Them, Franuś?' He said something again. I bent over him, put my ear close to his mustache. I may have misheard because of the mustache, but he said it was the men he'd bayoneted. Lord in heaven," said the widow, though she wasn't a widow just yet, for uncle seemed to be sucking at his mustache with his lower lip.

His head appeared much bigger than when he would visit us and put me on his knee, which was a horse. Perhaps because he was lying on two huge pillows, while his head on those pillows was surrounded by a dense mass of gray hair. It was the same with his mustache, which must have gone untrimmed for a long while: it had grown out to the side, beyond his hollow, pale cheeks. If I hadn't known it was the same person that called me grandson, I wouldn't have recognized him. And I would never have believed he'd been a soldier. His long, scrawny white arms lay on the counterpane, which was pulled up to his chest. I imagined him holding a rifle with a fixed bayonet in his big hands, but lacking the strength to stick it in someone's belly.

"Go up and touch uncle's hand." My mother ushered me toward the bed. "He might not be able to see us anymore, but if you touch his hand he'll feel it."

Uncle's eyes were closed the whole time, but I didn't believe him, he had to see us through his eyelids. He'd told us that in the trenches, when they dozed off from exhaustion, they saw what was going on in front of the trench. A soldier has to be able to see even through closed eyes. Not like a civilian, whose eyes flip back in his head when he sleeps.

I went up and touched uncle's hand, and at that moment he raised it with an effort, as if along with the hand he had to lift a body that was already dead, and he placed it on my head. I felt such a weight that I buckled and looked fearfully at my mother, hoping she'd free me from the hand, or else uncle would take me with him. But my mother's eyes only ordered me to stay where I was, don't move till he takes his hand away himself. He never did though, I can feel it still, heavy as ever.

The widow stepped forward, took the hand from my head and said: "He's gone." She laid his hand back down. She tidied some loose feathers from the counterpane between uncle's chest and his feet. Then she put his hands together, and took a rosary down from where it hung on a nail on the wall.

"See how worn it is." She passed it to my mother. "That rosary alone knows how much I prayed for him to come home."

"Wooden ones get worn like that," my mother said. "I had one like it from my grandmother. It hung as a memento, because you couldn't pray with it anymore."

Auntie took the rosary from my mother and wound it around uncle's hands. Then she perched on the bed and broke out in quiet, murmuring tears. After a moment she got up, took a jug, filled it with water and watered the flowers on the window sill. She moved a pot on the stove-top from one place to another, looked into the drawer of the sewing machine, took out needle and thread and thimble, picked up a broom from the corner as if she was going to sweep the floor, then started crying again. My mother went up to her and put her arms around her.

"Don't cry. There's nothing you can do. At least he won't see the new war."

They stood for a moment like that, as if fastened to one another. I wanted to go and hug them too. But who would have seen us then?

"Come on, don't cry," my mother said. She sat her down on a chair, gave her a glass of water, straightened her headscarf, wiped her tears away with the hem of her apron, and told her to blow her nose on the apron. "I'll come back and give you a hand. I'll just take the boy home. My husband should be back from work soon. He was supposed to take part of the day off. Don't lock the door. If those people haven't come yet they're not going to now."

We left. On the way we paused briefly and my mother as if instinctively looked left and right. "Really, there isn't anyone. Why would they come?"

"Mama." I pulled my hand out of hers. "How did death get into uncle's house if the door was locked?"

"Death doesn't have to go in. Give me your hand." She held me more firmly.

"It wasn't at uncle's, was it?"

"What do you mean, it wasn't? How else would he have died?"

"I didn't see it."

"The person who's dying sees it. Other people don't need to."

"Maybe uncle died without death, mama."

The war that uncle hadn't lived to see, broke out a couple of years later. Who knows if he wouldn't have been a soldier again. I could read and write by then, and I read on his gravestone that he'd been forty-eight years old. For a child that was a lot. But as I grew older it was less and less, as if instead of aging he was becoming younger. Today people would say he died at a young age.

Uncle's widow died a few years after him. Perhaps uncle had told her to die before the war broke out. Her death was unexpected. My mother often said she was still good looking, she could have remarried.

She often came by, but she never said that her time had come too, or complained she wasn't feeling well. Not once. Even the last time she visited, no one could have imagined it was the last time. Though when she was leaving, as she stood up from her chair she said: "I dreamed about my man last night. He asked if grandson was big now. He's surely a young man, he said. Time must pass faster there than here."

"Stay awhile," my mother urged. "You can eat with us. The potatoes are almost done."

"Thank you, dearie, but I'll be going. I've got some dumplings left over from yesterday, I'll heat them up. I'm off my food for some reason."

That was the only time she complained. But even my father couldn't eat sometimes because he'd lost his appetite. It happened to my mother too. She explained it by saying it was from all that smelling and tasting before the food was ready. Not to mention me: I never felt like eating. I'd sit over my plate and poke at my food with my fork, and my mother would stand over me and beg me to eat, eat up son, eat up or you'll stop growing. She'd mention for example someone they'd used to call Midget, who hadn't grown up because he didn't eat. If my father happened to be at home he'd take my side, or maybe he'd simply had enough of hearing it: "It wasn't because he didn't eat. They were all runts in that family. They should have been in the circus. He's not going to go to the circus. Let him be. He'll eat when he's hungry."

"But I'll have to heat it up again."

"Then you'll heat it up."

At that point my mother would get upset, I don't know if it was at father or at me, and she'd burst out angrily: "I'm not cooking for either of you anymore! That's it! I work my fingers to the bone. I do everything I can to please you. Then on top of everything I have to beg you both to eat. Or I'll take a belt and skin you alive!" That was to me. "Eat up this instant."

When uncle's widow already had her hand on the door handle, she paused.

"You were good people. May God reward you."

Aside from expressing her gratitude, no one would have heard her words as a farewell. My mother went to see her almost every day after uncle's death; she took things over for her, helped her out. My father too: he never put off a job if he felt she needed a man's hand, even if it made him late for work. Often he clocked off early, went by and chopped wood for her, oiled the hinges on the doors at her place, went up on the roof when she said she had a leak, changed a fuse or a light bulb, because we had electricity even before the war, thanks to their having built the canning factory. True, the word "were" should have made my father or my mother think. Sometimes a single word can say everything. Words suffer when they're in vain. But at that time everyone was talking about the war that was supposedly going to break out any day, and in fact already had, it just hadn't reached us yet. The radio was already saying where they were, they're in this place or that, they're on their way. Who would have paid any attention to that one word "were," when there was such a torrent of words, each more fearful than the last. It was no surprise, then, that the widow didn't visit, she didn't even appear in her window. It was only a couple of days later that, standing in the kitchen stirring a pot of kasha, my mother suddenly exclaimed: "Dear Lord! Never mind the war, we should go check in on her."

"Who?" My father didn't cotton on at first, he was so wrapped up in the war and what would happen when it reached us.

"Mind things here. Keep stirring so it doesn't burn." She ran over. She knocked, called, banged on the door, because it was locked, but there was no movement inside. The curtains were drawn. She stood on tiptoe but she couldn't see anything.

Early the next morning my father went to the authorities to let them know the widow wasn't opening her door despite their efforts. Some officials came to see, along with a police officer, and summoned a locksmith. When he opened the door, they found the widow sitting as simple as can be, in an armchair by the bed. The bed was made, it was covered with a throw, and on the throw was the wedding portrait that she'd taken down from the wall – the picture she'd had painted by the traveling artist when uncle was away at the war so long. The armchair was still in good shape; uncle had bought it for a song from the factory when they'd switched out the furniture in the director's office after a new director came.

"This is for the war," uncle had said, "for having waited for me all that time. Now you can sit in an armchair like a lady, not on a hard chair."

He decided to have the chair reupholstered, so, as he put it, she wasn't sitting on some director's backside, but her own. He took so long about it, though, that the chair never was re-covered, though the old covering had been taken off.

What most surprised the people who entered the house was the fact that the widow, who was so small and frail, had dragged the armchair all the way from the storage room to the bedroom, because my father testified that it had been in storage.

"See?" He showed them where the cover had been removed as proof that uncle had planned to replace it with a different fabric. The new fabric, though, was nowhere to be found.

There were long discussions about what to do. They started by forming a commission, because only a commission was entitled to open an inquiry. And since the commission also felt unqualified to establish whether the widow was dead, a doctor was summoned. The doctor took the widow's hand, looked into her eyes and confirmed her decease.

"There's no doubt," he said. "She's dead."

It's no easy matter to die by commission, though, since the question of the death certificate came up. Who would write it? One of the officials volunteered. Except it turned out he didn't have anything to write with, or any paper. The doctor only had a prescription pad. The police officer did have a pencil and blank receipts for fines, but it wasn't right to record a death on prescriptions or receipts. Also, those are small, while a certificate required a large sheet of paper and needed to be in two copies. The younger of the two officials was sent back to the office to bring some paper.

The widow had died just in time, for a couple of weeks later the war came to us. People were surprised it appeared so soon. Since it was on the move, it could have just kept going, especially since it hadn't given any sign it was so close. First, a plane appeared in the sky; planes fly fast, as everyone knows, so the infantry could be walking and walking before they arrived. The plane didn't even drop a single bomb. It circled once and twice, descended lower, and the other children and I actually waved at it, till one of the neighbors came out with a stick and shooed us all back to our homes, so that when the plane flew off immediately it looked like it had been frightened off by the stick.

There was a silence. My father said: "It'll take a while longer. They won't be here right away. They may still be fighting with our boys somewhere or other." We sat down to lunch. We ate the soup, mother started serving the main course, when all at once the window panes started rattling, then a moment later the plates on the table too.

"Lord in heaven, what's going on? Go take a look outside."

My father was annoyed, because his food was already in front of him. He went up to the window. There, like a mountain of iron, a tank was moving past, slow as anything – one step at a time, so to speak.

"How about that? They're here already."

There was a soldier in the turret, visible from the waist up; he was smiling left and right as if he was saying hello to everyone. He smiled toward our window too. My mother stuck her tongue out at him, and my father cursed.

'Not in front of the child," she said. "Sometimes you have to cuss, but you should do it when you're alone, or in your thoughts."

"You think he hasn't heard worse things? You know how everyone curses on the street – old people, young folks, children too."

"Don't listen, son. Cover your ears."

"I will, mama."

"And don't play with those sorts of children."

"Who's he supposed to play with? There aren't any other kind."

A second tank drove past, then another and another. The main course was getting cold, but father stayed at the window counting.

"How can I not swear," he said. "There are seven of them already."

"Sit down and eat. They'll have gone by the time you finish."

"I'm not hungry anymore."

After the tanks came the artillery. Each gun was drawn by four horses, the bigger ones by six.

"They've got horses and horses. Their hooves are big as loaves of bread, their manes are like lions. They're shining too – they must have rubbed oil on them. There's no sun today, it can't be from the sun." My father seemed filled with admiration, but then he caught himself. "The sun was smart to hide. There aren't any horses like that here. Our horses are old nags. They couldn't pull a cannon. Though we don't have cannon like that either."

After the artillery came the soldiers. They were walking loosely, not in time and not in ranks; they moved in a mass. They kept coming and coming. They were talking and laughing with each other; there was a clatter of hobnailed boots. Some of them wore their helmets tipped back on their head, some had them strapped to their belts. Their packs were covered with a kind of horsehair leather, on top of which was a rolled-up blanket. They looked cheerful, as if they were returning from the war, not just setting out.

"I wonder how many of them won't come back?" Concern sounded in my father's voice.

"Don't you have anyone else to fret about? Sit down and eat. Your lunch is completely cold."

"Do they even know where they're going?"

"They know full well, don't you worry. If they didn't know, they wouldn't be walking there."

"Could that be the general?" my father said, almost in a murmur.

At the word "general," my mother hurried over to the window. She was too late though: the car had driven past, sounding its horn mercilessly, making the soldiers jump aside to let it pass. After the general came two trucks covered with tarpaulins. Father tried to guess what was in them: maybe ammunition; maybe provisions; perhaps one was bringing the general's bed. Two field kitchens brought up the rear, each drawn by a pair of horses like those pulling the artillery. The cooks wore helmets, but they had white coats over their uniforms. They sat on stools; one of them happened to take off the lid of a big cauldron as they drove past, and stirred it with a huge ladle. My father caught a whiff of pea soup.

"Can you smell that? I think they're making pea soup."

"I smell my own cooking. I don't need to smell someone else's."

"You might make pea soup once in a while."

"I like that. The doctor told you what you can eat. Pea soup isn't on the list."

"Just once, what harm could it do. Add in a can of army grub as well: delicious."

"How do you know? You weren't in the army."

"The guys that were told me. It tastes best from a mess can."

"Then go ask them for a mess can. And leave me be."

"They'd want something in return. It smells good." He sniffed loudly. "They'd probably take eggs. A dozen or so. You've got eggs."

"I don't keep chickens, where would I have eggs?"

"You went to market last week."

"I bought eggs for the cake. Do you know how much they're charging for eggs these days? But with all these terrible things going on I'll bake you both a topielec. It might be the last one."

My mother didn't manage to distract my father's attention from the pea soup with the topielec, though. Long after the column had disappeared, he was still saying: "It smells really good. I wonder how many cans they'd need to put in a cauldron like that?"

My mother must have had a sense of how the war might go, but for some reason she preferred to keep her thoughts from my father. If he'd had heart problems I'd have reckoned she was concerned for his heart. But he only had problems with his liver. There was a doctor at the factory and every so often the office workers went for a checkup; the labor force less often, unless one of them was complaining of something. My father never complained, even about his liver; he said my mother was putting ideas in his head. He was strong: he could lift a hundredweight sack of cement and put it on his shoulder. He held himself straight. He walked a bit slowly, but he never got so much as a headache, whereas my mother often did. If it hadn't been for his eyes he would have gone into the army, he was the right age for the draft when he went up before the commission shortly after he married my mother. The commission decided he wasn't fit for service, though, because of his eyesight. He'd left his glasses at home and didn't admit to wearing them. But he was unable to read one of the rows of letters. My mother said that when he was traveling around playing the guitar under people's windows with his band, he hadn't needed glasses. His vision started to get worse after they married. Later, and for the rest of his life, he put drops in his eyes twice a day, morning and evening, and ever more frequently he got new, thicker lenses. Where reading was concerned, for a long time he managed without the glasses, though he had to hold the book or newspaper closer and closer to his face. He ate without his glasses too, although in his old age he knew what he was eating more by taste than by sight.

I think my mother liked my father in glasses, and not just as a young man. When they were already gray and bent over, shuffling their feet, one time she said: "Those glasses suit him, don't you think? He looks like a real office worker."

I agreed, though for some years my father had in fact been retired. I'd often wondered, even long before then, whether my mother wasn't protecting him in this way from her imagination, which would often hint to her that there was some kind of fear hidden in my father; though it could have been her fear for him. Because my mother worried about everything except herself. Any little matter was enough – for instance, the business with the rat. My father once spotted a rat in the yard and hurried in, alarmed: "There's a rat! Can you imagine it? A rat!"

She was so upset by the news that she dropped a plate, as if who knows what had happened, though she was afraid for instance of spiders and whenever my father made fun of her, she'd beg him: "Catch it! Get rid of it! It makes me ill to think of. Don't kill it though, it's bad luck."

It was only when she'd picked up the pieces of the broken plate that she said, seemingly in surprise, but also as if to reassure him: "Where could a rat have come from? We've never had rats here before."

Yet there were rats. I'd often seen them scurrying across the yard.

When I mentioned it to her, she'd say: "Just don't tell your father."

During the war, if so much as a gendarme came down the street she'd hustle my father up into the attic to hide. Actually, it wasn't much of a hiding place: an old folding screen put up in the darkest corner. One day a motorcycle and sidecar pulled up in front of uncle's house, which had been empty since the death of his widow. In the sidecar there was a civilian in a leather coat and a hat, while two armed and helmeted soldiers were on the bike. They started hammering at the windows and doors and shouting: "Come out!" My mother hurried my father into the attic, then went out to the men. She walked up to the one in civilian clothes: "Nobody lives there, sir. They died."

"What do you mean, they died?" the civilian asked angrily. He spoke Polish.

"They passed away."

"How can they have passed away? They're on our list." He pulled a sheet of paper folded in four out of his pocket, opened it, and read out uncle's first and last name, though it was so hard for him the words crunched in his mouth. "Is that the right name?"

"Yes," my mother confirmed.

He glanced at the number on the door. "This is the address. It has to be him."

"Did he do something bad?" my mother asked timidly.

He cursed at her. "You ought to be shot, all of you."

The fact that uncle was dead meant nothing to them. They broke down the door and searched the house from cellar to attic. In the cellar they even shoveled the coal from one corner to another. In the attic there was a chest; they tipped out all the contents. In the living room and kitchen they threw everything on the floor and stomped over it with their boots. They pulled the mattress off the bed, shook the straw out of it, ripped open the pillows and quilt with their bayonets. It didn't look like a search so much as revenge. For what? The fact that uncle had gotten away from them by dying? Was he really such a threat?

"To think we had no idea," my mother said.

"Maybe it was because he fought against them in the last war?" said my father.

It was just that uncle had died so many years before. Could he have taken some secret to the grave that had only now, with the next war underway, been uncovered? What could it have been that it needed a new war? No one would have suspected uncle of hiding a secret. Secrets usually gnaw away at you, whereas the only thing that gnawed at uncle was the war, and that was why he kept talking about it, as if he wanted to get it off his chest. True, it didn't do him much good; he sank deeper and deeper into that war, dwelling in it as if in a separate world, until the very end. Maybe uncle's secret lay concealed in those stories, and we just didn't understand?

They took the whole house apart, arrested the former police officer who'd been a member of the commission after the widow died, as well as the doctor who'd confirmed the death, and the official who drew up the death certificate on behalf of the rest of the commission.

"Sometimes it's good to have bad eyesight," my mother said when they went away. "If they'd let you into the army it could have been the same thing for you. Besides, I like men in glasses better than men in uniform."

"It's such a pity." My father couldn't forgive himself for not having been a soldier. "Maybe I'd have been promoted? It could be useful these days."

"Useful for what?" My mother was starting to get mad.

"What do you mean, for what? It's obvious," he answered loftily, though he was usually cowed by her words.

"If I'd wanted to marry a military man, there was one with two stars who liked me."

Those two stars must have really gotten to my father, because after that he didn't speak to her for days.

My eyesight isn't the best either, though I only started wearing glasses in middle age. During my time at university, in army training classes I was always one of the top students when it came to target practice and distance shooting. I didn't long to join the army, though.

All the same, I felt bad for my father, because even in old age he used to complain about not having been a soldier. When I was small I always took his side. I'd get angry at the army for not taking him, and I sometimes imagined him as a general. After I went to bed and my imagination could run riot, I'd picture him on a fine white horse, a golden saber at his side, a gold cord hanging from his shoulder, gold medals gleaming on his chest – for the sun shone only on him – gold epaulettes, golden spurs on shiny riding boots; and behind him countless battalions. They marched and marched, with no end in sight, as if all the armies of the world were marching; the field kitchens hadn't even come into view yet, though they were making pea soup for my father back there. In the end, tired by the parade, I'd fall asleep before I could see its end.

I regret never having told him. I had plenty of opportunities to, whenever I came to see them. It wasn't that I forgot. But I had the feeling I'd be burying my childhood if he laughed, because in his boldest dreams he never imagined being a general. Who knows, he might even have been afraid of a promotion like that. His glasses were getting thicker and thicker, and the eyes behind them seemed more and more distant. Old age is never seen so clearly as in a father and mother growing old. Theirs is an old age that hurts us, that we suffer from along with them, that we're condemned to gaze into and find ourselves in. Perhaps it's thanks to their old age that we come to terms with our own and bear it with greater understanding.

At times I had the impression that his eyes were setting behind those glasses, so to speak, the way the sun sets over the horizon, and it was a smaller and smaller part of them that I could see. I had the notion that at some point he'd stop seeing completely, because there aren't any glasses that you can see through from the other side. I sensed that in what remained of his sight, words were lurking that he finally wanted to say to me. Alas, he never said them. Or maybe they weren't words? Though I don't remember ever seeing tears in my father's eyes. Of course it wasn't right for a general to cry, for what would the men think if they saw tears in his eyes? Would they be willing to carry on fighting?

Even at my mother's funeral, as we stood over her grave, at a certain point he simply took off his glasses and wiped them, but his eyes were dry, so maybe the glasses had just fogged over? Then he put them back on, looked around at those present, nodded to someone he perhaps hadn't expected to see there. Then when we came back from the funeral, he said: "Did you see how many people there were? I didn't think he'd come too."

"Who?"

"The new director from the factory. I'd retired by the time he arrived, but he still came. Maybe he'll be able to do something."

"About what?"

"The factory's on the verge of bankruptcy. I'm surprised he agreed to the appointment. There were several before him, and none of them succeeded. The factory was concentrating on black currants. People had planted acres and acres of them. Seedlings were handed out freely. There were inducements, contracts. The money was good. You could do well off black currants. People even planted them in their vegetable gardens. They cut down orchards – apple trees and plum trees and pears – and planted black currants. You'd go out into the fields and not recognize the place, there were black currants everywhere. When the black currants ripened they were picked and brought to the plant. Then all at once they stopped taking black currants. There was no longer a market for them. They only wanted red currants. But not many people had planted red currants. Production was stopped, they started laying people off. Before, people would bring produce from far away, and the factory delivered to all sorts of distant places. You found a job there easily yourself. I went to the director, he asked: 'What skills does he have?' 'None. He's planning on applying to university and he wants to save up some money.' 'Fine, let him come.' They even laid off permanent staff, long-term workers. New directors kept appearing. Managers were switched around, foremen became ordinary workers on the production line in the washing room, or they were assigned to cleaning. Bonuses and supplements were cut wherever they could be. People cried, cursed, complained that the land had died. So they started cutting down the black currants. We used to have twenty bushes ourselves right here in the back yard, you remember. Your mother wouldn't let me keep them, though I said, let's wait a year or two at least, maybe something'll change. I might plant some new ones now."

He stopped talking. We walked on in silence for a while, then suddenly he said more to himself than to me: "How's it going to be now without her? I hope it won't be for long."

I worried about him, about how he'd manage. Especially because when my mother was alive he'd ask her about the simplest things; thanks to her he never felt helpless. I remember visiting one time. I said my hellos to him and to my mother. She was peeling potatoes, while he seemed unsure whether to take me through into the living room or stay there in the kitchen. In the end my mother said: "Bring him a stool. I want to listen too."

He brought a stool, and he took me by the hand like he did when I was a child, then he decided I was too far away from my mother, so he moved me closer.

"Sit here. Is this all right?" he said, turning to her. Then back to me: "How long will you be staying? Tell us everything. I'm sure you've a lot to say. We want to hear what's been going on with you. Though even when someone tells everything, there's always something that goes unsaid."

"But maybe tell me first what's been happening with the two of you?"

"Us? Well, we. . ." He turned to my mother. "Tell him what's been happening with us."

"What could be happening? Old age," my mother said. "Oh, your father had to get stronger glasses. Not just the lenses but new frames as well, because they were too thick for the old ones. The doctor's prescribed him some new drops. The new glasses suit him, don't you think?"

After he died, time seemed to start flowing more quickly. One day I was startled to realize I'd reached the same age as him. It's a very strange feeling to realize you're the same age as your father or mother. You almost refuse to believe it. You always want to be younger than them. It feels like breaching a natural law of life by which you're always younger than your parents, and always will be till you die. As when you were young, you still think they're your shield, behind which you can seek protection, though they're no longer there.

Another decade or two must have gone by when I passed the time at which according to the Gypsy woman's prophesy I was supposed to have died the previous year. She might have given me a bit more time if I'd allowed her to tell my fortune from the cards. As she showed me the longest line on my hand she said: "Here's where your life ends. It's a long, long way off still. If you'd let me read the cards it'd be longer still. The cards know more than the lines on your hand."

She even took out some cards. Luckily, at that moment her nipple slipped out of the baby's mouth and it started to cry. By the time she'd shifted it to the other breast I was gone. I ran through the old wild green valley to Needle's Eye. He was standing on the verge of the steep steps, tapping the step below him with his cane to check how far he needed to descend. How can anyone be that old, I thought to myself. It annoyed me. At his age there's hardly anything left of the world. So where was he going, and what for? If I'd known I was going to meet him there I'd have preferred to wait for her down there, on the bench in the park. The Gypsy woman would have gone away in the end, when she saw I wasn't going to let my fortune be told from the cards. Especially because, when he only had one last step before reaching me, he stopped and said: "I truly feel sorry for you when I think that one day that youth of yours is going to turn into my old age."

When I'm unable for instance to tie my shoelaces without sitting, because my back prevents me from reaching down to the floor, I remember his words. The same with my pants. I sit down to get the legs on, then I stand to pull them up to my waist. To think that when I was young I would pull my socks and pants on standing up, one foot or leg at a time, then I'd lift my foot up to my hands so I could tie my laces. One time on the beach, as I was putting my clothes on like that, I heard my friend's wife say in amazement: "He's a stork! Look: he can get dressed on one leg!"

My friend, who was dressing sitting on a blanket, jumped up. "Wait a sec, you can hold onto me. Whoever saw such a thing! Even his shoes. Without wobbling!"

I wonder though if at a certain age you don't lose the right to compare yourself to your own youth. From a distance of several decades, are you allowed to say you're the same person you used to be? Your hair, for instance – that's where the comparison comes off worst, from a rich full mop to complete baldness. When I was in high school there was a regulation length for hair. Not like today, when anyone can wear their hair any way they want: completely shaved off; in a buzz cut; down to their neck or shoulders or down their back; tied up behind in a bun like a girl; or even dyed red or green or other colors. Young people weren't always that free. Every so often our home room teacher would pass among the rows of desks and sweep the hair from our forehead over our face. If it reached as far as the tip of your nose, he told you to have it cut. Otherwise you ran the risk of a lower grade for conduct. If someone was stubborn, they were sent to the principal. I don't know if that was a general rule or the home room teacher's idea. Luckily for us the principal didn't hand out punishments but explained in a kindly way that the requirements were for reasons of hygiene, and he recommended not just having your hair cut regularly, but washing it frequently, since there was a danger of head lice: the effects of the war still lingered, and would continue for some time yet. You don't come out of a war when it ends. And he told me to be understanding toward the homeroom teacher, who'd spent the whole war in hiding. The principal was a lovely man, gentle and calm; he had no children of his own, and he was lenient with the students at the school. Before I graduated he was removed from his position, supposedly precisely because he was incapable of maintaining discipline, though people said various things. I was sent to him perhaps three times, so he knew me.

"Your hair again? Are you being rebellious? Studying should come first, rebellion can wait."

I think it happened to me most frequently out of our class, because she liked my hair longer. One time I gave in to the homeroom teacher and got a haircut, and she said: "I prefer you with long hair."

So I hit on an idea. I took a pair of scissors and cut short only the hair on my forehead, so it didn't reach past the end of my nose, as the rule required; whereas I let the hair at the back grow down over my neck. The homeroom teacher wasn't fooled, though. He took hold of all my hair, including from the back of my neck, and it turned out it came all the way down to my chin. He growled: "Buzz cut. And don't come back till it's done."

In fact, I had an experience with my hair at university too. There was a barber shop a few yards from the campus. I always had my hair cut by the same barber there – I'd decided in the end that it was good to have short hair – and over time I grew fond of him. His name was Stanisław. One day I made the mistake of going for a haircut on his nameday. He was excessively polite with me that day.

"Good morning, good morning dear sir." He leaped forward the moment I appeared in the door, a big smile on his face, though his eyes seemed a little dim. "Is our hair getting long? No problem – we'll take care of it right away. It's a great honor that you've been so kind as to choose me again. I apologize for having made you wait till I came back from vacation."

He'd never called me "dear sir" before, though when he was ill one time, instead of going to someone else I waited till he was better and went to him. It was true that my hair was down below my neck, because in those days it still grew thick, but that certainly wasn't the reason he was calling me dear sir.

"Take a seat, dear sir." He moved the chair closer to the mirror. I sat down and he smiled at me in the mirror. I smiled back. Strangely, he kept gazing at me and smiling, instead of getting on with the haircut. His hazy eyes seemed to be clinging to the mirror, as though he couldn't bear to part with his own reflection. When he finally looked away, he seemed to sway slightly, as if from an excess of energy after his vacation. Or maybe the mirror made the movement look different, since I could only see his reflection. A moment later he appeared carrying a white cloth, which he began to wrap around me. All at once he yanked it off.

"Let's find a bigger one, nice and fresh."

At this point he was concealed behind my own reflection; I heard only the bang of a drawer and a sort of complaint: "Darn it, why's the floor so slippery today? They've put too much polish on it."

It may seem strange that I still hadn't put two and two together, hadn't thought that it was the nameday for Stanisław. But I'd been going

to him for several years, and fondness can sometimes prevent you from
noticing things. Whenever he happened to have another customer, and
more were waiting, I didn't go to one of the other barbers if they were
free. We became almost friends from the fact that I only ever went to
him to get my hair cut. Even the words he always opened with bound
me to him: "The usual?"

"The usual."

"Longer sideburns are in these days."

"Then leave the sideburns longer, please."

And he'd already be setting the comb and scissors in motion, beginning a dance around my head. I'd actually feel regret when he announced: "All done. Thank you. It looks like something from a fashion
magazine."

Especially because while he was cutting my hair, he'd always have
some interesting story to tell. I think that drew other customers to
him also. And I don't think he told everyone the same stories, because
there were generally two or three other clients waiting for a haircut
after me who heard what he was saying to me. He had an extraordinary
imagination, and most of the stories he told he probably made up. At
most he might have heard or read something, from which he then
fashioned a tale that would last the whole haircut, sometimes including
a shave. And if even the haircut and shave weren't long enough and
the customer asked what happened next, he'd say: "I'll tell you next
time you come."

He had an exceptional gift: his stories were colorful, rich, vivid.
Once I suggested he should write down the tales he told.

"It'd be a waste of time, sir. Who would read them? Everyone's in a hurry. Whereas they have to listen while I'm cutting their hair. Often they don't intend to get a shave, but they ask for one anyway. Who'd read a barber? I tell stories because it's as much a part of my job as the comb and scissors and razor. Or the mirror, the chair you're sitting on. Plus, I don't have time to memorize it all. Whatever stories I told yesterday, today I don't remember them. I've lived many more years than you, yet I could fit my life on half a page, a footnote to a life if you like. But when I take someone's head in my hands, I always have some story to tell. There's something in people's heads, don't you think? Maybe I tell what those heads remember, what they think about and dream about. There was only one time when I sensed it was better not to get anything out of a head. During the war I used to cut the hair of a Gestapo officer. He wore a black uniform with a skull and crossbones on the cap, and a red armband with that broken cross of theirs. I have to tell you, those people were the worst of all. I was scared, believe me. If he wasn't satisfied he could have shot me. Make no mistake: they'd shoot people for nothing. I finish his haircut. 'Danke schön, Herr Offizier,' I say. He doesn't say a word, just looks at himself in the mirror, turns his head this way and that, while I'm standing behind him, beside myself with fear. Then all at once – I knew a bit of German – as if he's talking to the mirror, he says: 'I never imagined there were barbers like that in Poland.' He jumps to his feet. 'Heil Hitler!' And he left.

"I moved to a different shop all the way across town, because who knew, he might come back. You meet a guy like that once and you never know if it's for the last time or not. Him, I didn't tell any stories to, it was just the haircut. If I'd known German better: you can make different languages get along together; not so much with people. I've had all sorts of customers, including some strange ones. Before the war, during the war, afterwards. There's no shortage of them even now. One time this man comes in. Older type, stylish I must say. It was winter, he was wearing a fur-lined coat with a beaver collar. Before he sat down he handed me his card. I took a look: a count. If he's a count, he needs to be treated with kid gloves. He tells me he isn't able to sit still for the whole haircut. He'd been to various barbers; they even sat him on cushions. Till in the end someone recommended me. 'Mr. Stanisław, is that right?' 'Stanisław's the name, yes, Count.' 'It seems you tell such interesting stories that one can make it all the way through a haircut and shave, even a hair wash. I'd like the full service, then, and wave my hair too, please.'

"In those days everyone wore their hair smooth, straightened out with brilliantine, like it was stuck to your skull. That was the fashion. You've maybe seen it in old films and on postcards from back then. This fellow seemed to be going against the grain.

"'Yes, Count, haircut, shave, wash, wave.' But what tale could I tell him, I wondered. Anyway, let's get started with the haircut. It's not easy to find the right story for a count. I search high and low, rack my brains, but you know sir, a barber's brain is like anyone else's, filled with all sorts of trash, while here I needed to come up with something worthwhile, it's not every day you have dealings with a count.

"'Why aren't you telling me a story,' he says. 'I'm listening.'

"'Right away, Count, I know just the thing.'

"'Do go on.'

"'There was a couple, a husband and wife.'

"I knew a story like that, taken straight from life. But maybe it was too ordinary for a count. He'd say, It's not refined enough. Tell me something better. You should know, dear sir, that truth shouldn't be presented just as it is. It always needs seasoning. A little salt, a little pepper, so to speak. The truth has to taste good. The truth is like gold, you need to work it all kinds of ways before it becomes jewelry. And it depends who makes the jewelry. A master craftsman or a bungler. The same with a diamond before it becomes a diamond. Likewise, a marriage can go various ways. They live together till they die. Or they split up soon after the wedding. What's interesting about that? Nothing. So the married couple wasn't going to work for me, though like I said, it was taken directly from life. Maybe the fact that he was a count was paralyzing me. I barely made it to the part where he grew up poor, she grew up poor, because that's how it really was. To begin with he was smiling whenever I checked in the mirror. Then all of a sudden he's making a face, frowning, narrowing his eyes, pursing his lips – he had a little mustache – and I start wondering: could he be having some kind of fit, is he ill? Finally he says: 'Your haircut is hurting me. It's too much. Your scissors are dull.'

"My scissors had just been sharpened. A barber with dull scissors – can you imagine? It was as if he'd slapped me. He didn't know how to listen, that's what it was. Or maybe there were problems in his own marriage? Perhaps he'd married outside his class, with his own maid! He stood up abruptly. 'No, it's too much. You've disappointed me.

I need to find another barber.' And right then I had the idea that the wife wore fake jewelry. She died tragically, and in his grief the husband found himself in even greater poverty. One day, instead of keeping at least the fake necklace as a memento of her – after all, memory's more precious than any necklace, even if it had been a real one, memory is priceless – I have a cameo that belonged to my late wife, it only cost pennies, I bought it for her nameday back when we were engaged; it hangs on the wall over my bed and before I fall asleep I always look at it. For me it's the most precious keepsake, you don't look a keepsake in the mouth like you do with a horse. I don't know if you know, but after the January Uprising Polish women used to wear these little cast iron crosses, and today they're worth more than if they'd been made of gold. Anyway, the man takes the necklace to a jeweler. The jeweler tells him how much he can give for it, and the man turns pale. Can you guess why?"

"Mr. Stanisław, I know this story."

"How? I've never told it to anyone before."

"There was a French writer by the name of Maupassant. He wrote a short story – "

"I don't know French. I've never read it."

I felt I'd touched a nerve. He stopped talking, and didn't even look at me in the mirror. I decided to surrender to his story after all, in order to cheer him up, and I asked: "So what about the husband?"

His eyes flashed in the mirror, he half-smiled. "You weren't interested in hearing the end, dear sir, but it's only now that it gets interesting. What did the husband do? He took out his pistol and threatened to shoot her."

"But she was dead."

"No no, she wasn't that foolish. She admitted that one of her lovers had given it to her. Shoot me if you like, but then I won't bring anything more back home. Whereas we could sell it. Think how much better our life would be. We could get a big new apartment. Have rugs on the floor. Buy fancy furniture, hang paintings on every wall. You wouldn't need to go to work, what for? It'd be enough for me to work. He laid his gun down and put his arms around her head. What a brain you've got, he said. You should know, dear sir, that if truth doesn't convince the heart, it doesn't convince the reason. Actually, reason and truth never go well together. I'm sure you've noticed that the truth is disappearing. So more and more people like to hear my stories. You're one of them, dear sir; in addition you know how to listen. And listening is an art."

It was true, I always enjoyed listening to him, whether or not I believed his tales. Even if the story was a trashy one, I found it soothing. It's not only in childhood that we like fairy tales. Fairy tales are an antidote for everyday life, which is often hard to bear. We make our world out of fairy tales. Many of the truths we're offered to believe in are fairy tales. In addition there was his warm, kindly voice, that seemed to be almost caressing my head, and put me in such a torpor that before I knew it I was feeling sleepy and my eyes were closing despite myself.

It was like that on his nameday. All at once he moved my head backwards, bringing me out of my doze. I was horrified to see that my hair had been cut only on the left; the right side was untouched. He followed my gaze in the mirror.

"You nodded off, dear sir. I wonder what you were dreaming about?" His eyes seemed to waver indistinctly deep inside his head. At that moment he lost his balance and, steadying himself by holding on to my head, he mumbled: "I once dreamed. . ."

"Mr. Stanisław, you've only cut the left side of my hair. What about the right?"

"Don't fret, dear sir. We'll get to the right side. There's just a little bit to finish here, over the ear." He went on cutting the left side, and not just over the ear. "I had a dream, I don't know if it was then, that I was in the cinema, they were showing some action film, and I was on the screen chasing a villain – "

"Mr. Stanisław, please do the right side now."

"You haven't noticed, dear sir, that I'm done with the right side. Look in the mirror if you please." He smiled crookedly at my reflection. Then he picked up the razor so as to shave the back of my neck, which meant the end of the haircut. I felt the razor touch me. Then all of a sudden he staggered, grabbed at my head, and he would have fallen, except one of the other barbers, who happened to be unoccupied, rushed over and snatched the razor from Mr. Stanisław's hand. He called to a colleague in the back room. They took Mr. Stanisław by the arms and led him away. Then one of them came back and apologized to me.

"I'll finish your haircut, sir. It's on the house today."

Unfortunately it wasn't possible to completely match the right side to the left, and I felt like a casualty with my uneven haircut. I never patronized the place again; I found another barber, although it wasn't the same anymore. Once however, when I was passing by I looked in to ask after Mr. Stanisław. I might even see him, I thought, though I wasn't needing a haircut just then. He wasn't there. But both the other barbers greeted me like the prodigal son.

"Ah, you're back, sir! We're glad to see you. Welcome!"

They didn't have any customers right then, so I asked: "Where's Mr. Stanisław?"

"He doesn't work here anymore."

"Why not? What happened?"

They exchanged glances and one said to the other: "I think we can tell the gentleman. Generally speaking, he's in a secure place."

"What does that mean?"

"A mental hospital. You didn't notice that time when he was cutting your hair?"

"He was afraid to move from the left side to the right when you asked him to."

"And he hadn't had that much to drink, just a small one for his nameday."

"We told him to stay home, lie down and rest. But since he had an appointment with you, he wouldn't let himself be talked out of it."

"A couple of times now he's run away from where he is and come back here to see if you might be by for a haircut."

"It was about a month ago, we were just shutting up shop for the day. He appeared, saying he had to wait for you, because your hair must have grown long since the last time. 'The shop's closed, Staś.' 'Then I'll sleep here, in the back, because he might have an appointment with me tomorrow. I get mixed up with the days.'

"We've got a couch bed in the back, he went and lay down there. We come back in the morning and he's sitting in front of the mirror, cutting his own hair. It was the left side he cut back then, sir?"

"Yes, the left."

"So this time he was doing the right. 'What are you up to, Staś? Leave it be. One of us can cut your hair for you.' 'No, no. If he comes he'll see that I've cut the right side of his hair for him too.'"

Chapter 6

§

People say, the last one. But the last one hasn't happened yet. The world is only now moving toward the last one. The last one will mean no more and no less than the world's end, if the word "last" is to recover its proper meaning. So when we hear only about wars that are happening here or there or somewhere else, we can sleep easily. It's like with an artillery shell: if you can hear it in the air, it won't strike you. I once heard a moaning whistle like that, I ducked down instinctively, but it flew overhead and exploded beyond me; all it did was deafen me a moment, no more.

For now they're not happening here, but what the future will bring, no one can tell, since they have to happen. The world has shrunk almost to our own back yard, and it's shrinking still. So it's all the harder to imagine a world without wars. Who knows, wars may be the only available remedy for our passions, our hatreds, the sole compensation for all our defeats, failures, unfulfillments. They don't cure fully, but until we find a more effective way, for some of us at least they may stir our consciences.

Luckily, on average an individual will live through two or three wars at most, and even that's too much for one person's memory, so often they muddle up which war was which. Not to mention how much of that memory leaks out along the way. Which way? Well, they say life is a journey. What direction the journey leads in: that I wouldn't recommend imagining, since all directions lead to death. Do they go further than that? I couldn't say.

Also, strange things happen sometimes with memory. So far I've only experienced one war, but I remember several. For memory is a function of collective responsibility, and collective responsibility obliges us to remember far more than we've experienced. Collective responsibility even sets a norm for our memory that is appropriate for the time we live in. I'm not sure how much my own memory fits within that norm. I've lived through different times, so I've been subject to different norms. And the norms knead people's memory like dough, so that whether we like it or not we adapt our memory to the norms laid down by one or another time.

The front was approaching, the first shells had already started to reach us. They'd exploded here and there, though they hadn't done too much damage for now: one hit a cart standing outside somebody's house, another went off in someone else's garden. Still, my mother decided we should move out, since our house wouldn't be safe when the front drew closer and started really pummeling the town. So we moved into the basement of an apartment building where a neighbor lived, a few doors down. It was a two-story construction, recently built, with a metal roof rather than tile like our house; its walls were thick and solid, and there was plenty of room in the basement. I didn't want to go, I said I'd run away; my parents all but dragged me there.

"We can survive here," my mother explained. "In our house who knows what could happen."

I hated the neighbor. I couldn't forgive him for the fact that he killed horses. He slaughtered pigs, calves, cows, and made meat products out of them, all through the war, buying and selling whatever came his way. People said he had the military police in his pocket; they were often seen going to his place, you'd think they were about to arrest him, but they'd come out laden with food. One time my mother sent me over for a piece of meat on the bone, to make soup with. He wasn't in; only his wife was there.

"I don't know if he's got any beef today," she said. "Go behind the sties, he's there. Ask him."

I went. There were two horses; the neighbor and another man were blindfolding them. The other man finished putting the blindfold on his horse, then he took a big blacksmith's hammer from by the wall. He placed the hammer against the horse's forehead, and despite the blindfold the horse trembled. It was a lovely sorrel. Its coat gleamed, its hooves were like big loaves of bread, its long mane lay on its neck. It's hard to forget a horse like that.

"There's no beef today," the neighbor said after he'd put the blindfold on the other horse. It was a fine-looking creature too, black, with a white blaze on its forehead.

"Come tomorrow, I'll be slaughtering for beef. Tell your mama to make vegetable soup today." He laughed.

At that moment the other man hoisted the hammer and brought it down with all his strength on the first horse's head. The horse dropped to its front feet, and I burst out sobbing and ran off. Pigs weren't ever blindfolded, or cows; why horses? And those ones had simply been yielding to death, as if demoralized, instead of kicking and rearing. I ran crying to my mother. She was unable to console me. She tried to explain everything to me, but I couldn't stop the tears. I didn't believe her when she started saying that all the horses they killed had a bad heart. Healthy ones wouldn't have been slaughtered. A horse with a bad heart? I couldn't associate horses with any kind of illness. There's even an expression in Polish: healthy as a horse.

"Oh well, I'll make vegetable soup," she said. "And you, don't cry. This is a time for crying over people, not horses. I wouldn't eat horsemeat, though it's a lot cheaper than beef."

One time several families took shelter in the basement with us. Some of them had grandfathers and grandmothers with them, though for them it shouldn't have made any difference whether they died from bullets or in their beds; there were also babies still at their mother's breast. When the shell bursts grew more frequent, everyone quickly began praying: they said their litanies, sang hymns, while the babies mostly wailed. There was one candle – a big one that had been blessed at Candlemas – and people knelt around it. Someone lit it and led the litany from the prayer book, or directed the singing, because folks were getting the tune or the words wrong, or weren't keeping time with each other. Despite the candlelight it was dark in the corners, darker even than before the candle was lit.

Amongst us was the Polish teacher from our school. I was in his class. He was young, and he liked to joke around. He gave us forbidden books in secret – mostly historical novels. I remember *The Teutonic Knights*. There was also a young woman gym teacher. While the others were praying and singing, the two teachers kept out of sight in the darkest corner of the basement.

"Those two are at it again. God'll punish us all because of them. We won't live to see the end of the war."

What did we eat? By night the women would go back to their homes and bring whatever they had in their larders; sometimes they'd cook. The bombardment wasn't as heavy during the night; it was only once in a while that a shell would go off. In the nighttime you could go outside, get some fresh air, stretch your legs, relieve yourself. The guns usually started up at dawn, or sometimes just before the sun came up. Evidently the soldiers needed to rest too. The dairyman would bring us cans of milk from villages farther away that the shelling hadn't yet reached. He said he wasn't afraid because he believed in destiny; according to him, his death wasn't going to happen in wartime, because if he'd been destined to die it could have happened many times in the last war or the one before it. Besides, destiny paid pretty well, since he charged three times the regular price for the milk. Sometimes even more, depending on whether the day was quieter or more dangerous.

One evening the landlord of the apartment building took his wife by the hand as she was kneeling and praying with the others by the light of the candle.

"Come on, let's go sleep at home."

"Are you looking to die?" someone said among those praying.

"It'll be a nice way to go."

Dawn came, yet here there was silence; the sun rose, still nothing. People were afraid what it could mean: was this not the proverbial calm before the storm? We stayed where we were till midday. Then the landlord burst into the basement.

"Why aren't you coming out? The war's over!"

I was first out the door. I ran onto the road. It was deserted – there wasn't a living soul. All of a sudden I saw three soldiers. They were walking in single file, hugging the buildings. They were strung out a couple of yards from one another, bent over, glancing from side to side; their rifles were angled ready to fire. A cat meowed somewhere and they dropped to the ground; the cat emerged from one of the yards and stopped in the middle of the road. The soldiers burst out laughing. The one in the lead spotted me and shouted: "*Shto, mal'chik? Gyermantsa nyet?* Hey, kid – are the Germans gone?"

When all three of them came up to me, I asked if they'd like some milk. They nodded, their helmets bobbing. I didn't ask if they were hungry, if they'd like to pick some apples. There was an apple tree just behind the apartment building bearing fruit like never before. No; I just asked if they'd like milk. Why I thought of milk, to this day I can't explain. I led them down to the basement.

"Bring milk!" I called, as if I were one of them.

The landlord's wife took some mugs and was about to serve the milk, but her husband stopped her.

"Mugs? They're soldiers. Bring the big pots." She brought the pots and filled them with milk. Each of those pots was half a gallon. They laid their guns down, took off their helmets, and stuck their heads in the pots. They guzzled the milk down, as if drinking it wasn't just quenching their thirst, it was a long-awaited relief from the toil of war. And who knows, maybe the milk took them away from the death that was lurking everywhere. They didn't put the pots down till they'd drunk every last drop.

"*Spasibo*," the senior one in rank said.

Then they took out little bags of tobacco; each of them tore off a piece of newspaper and rolled himself a cigarette. As they walked away, one of them called back: "*Ostavaytyes's Bogom*. God be with you."

Soon after, the first tanks appeared. We all came out of the basement and waved at them till the last one passed; they waved back. After the tanks had gone we went back to our homes. Our house was still standing, thank goodness, though all the window panes had shattered. There was broken glass everywhere: on the windowsills, all over the floor, the table, the beds, even the chairs. It crunched underfoot wherever you walked. Other houses were in worse shape, roofs torn off, walls brought down; some were nothing but ruins, some had burned to the ground.

The moment we crossed the threshold, my mother crossed herself and my father said: "Well, we're alive." And right away he told my mother to sew a white and red flag.

"Maybe I'll make lunch first? We haven't had a cooked meal in such a long time. I can peel some potatoes in a jiffy."

"No, the flag needs to come first."

"Have you gone crazy?" she said, annoyed. "What am I supposed to make it with? There might be a bit of lard, we ought to eat something with the potatoes."

"No, the flag." He swept the glass off a chair, sat down, lost in thought for a moment, then said as if to himself: "Otherwise I won't believe it."

"Believe what?" my mother said uneasily.

"That we survived."

"You're sitting on a chair in your own home – isn't that enough?"

All the same, she started to search. I thought she was after the lard, but she said: "What can I make it out of, eh? For the white I could maybe use a piece of bedsheet. But the red, I have no idea."

"Why did they drink so much milk?" my father asked. "Funny kind of soldiers they were."

"Soldiers'll drink anything. You didn't serve, you don't know. That man who came here to try and convert us to his religion, he said something about it, didn't he? At the start of the war, remember? Some soldiers found themselves at a creek. They lay down on the bank, the bullets were whizzing overhead, while they all dipped their heads in the water and drank. The line of them stretched for half a mile. Some of them never got up again."

"Those were our boys."

"It makes no difference, soldiers are all the same. Here, sweep up some of this glass, that'll help you come to your senses. Ah, I know what I can use for the red. A pillowcase." She snatched up a pillow from the bed. "Come outside with me, we can empty the feathers into a sack. There should be one in the entrance hall."

When mother finished the flag, my father stopped doubting that we'd made it through. He attached the flag to a piece of beanpole. My mother had a vegetable garden in the back yard, with some beans among other things. Those kinds of beans were called *jaś*, I don't know why. In any case, they grew up attached to tall poles. Father went into the woodshed, took a roll of wire and the ladder, and told mother to go out onto the road. He leaned the ladder against the roof on the other side of the house and climbed up. At the highest point of the roof, he fixed the pole to the chimney with the wire.

I watched from the yard as my father clambered onto the roof, then I ran to join my mother on the road. She was watching his every move, growing ever more anxious. In the end she shouted up to him: "For the love of God, do you want to make a widow out of me? Come down! If I'd known you were planning to hang it up there I'd never have sewn it! Come down! What's gotten into you?"

The neighbors hurried out, drawn by my mother's voice; they craned their necks, curious whether he'd fall or not. One of them called to my father from below: "You should mend the tiles first! Your roof got damaged too! You'll fall through if you're not careful!"

That spurred my mother on to further lamentations: "Lord in heaven! What a waste of a pillowcase! A waste of a sheet! Come down!"

Like most of the other houses, ours was roofed with tiles. And tiles are terrible to walk on. You take a step, a tile slips out from under your foot, and there's a hole. The least gust of stronger wind, not to mention a storm, and tiles come crashing down. Plus, a whole lot of them had been broken by hail. Now, in addition the roof was pitted with holes from bullets and shrapnel. But my father was young, he managed to avoid the holes. When he emerged over the ridge of the roof with his flag, I jumped for joy, for which my mother slapped me on the head.

"You're going to grow up to be just like him, I see."

Someone must have been annoyed at my father's triumph; maybe they were hoping he'd fall. A malicious voice rang out: "Goddam office worker. They go mad from all that paperwork. Not from tiles and flags."

"What's it to you?" my mother snapped back at the speaker. "Leave my husband alone." With the same fury she turned back to my father: "Come down! Will you listen to me?"

But he didn't seem to hear mother's cries. He was holding onto the chimney with one hand and wrapping the wire around it with the other, fixing the flag in place. All eyes were on him, heads tipped back, as if he were running that flag up a flagpole to honor them for having survived. Somebody said anxiously: "How's he going to get down, though? Climbing down is harder than climbing up. One time – "

But someone else interrupted: "Don't talk, watch."

I had never been so proud of my father as on that day. Once he'd put the pole in place, he leaned against the chimney and stood there, the flag flapping above his head. There was a light breeze which down below could barely be felt; up there though, as you'd expect, it blew in stronger gusts, and each one wrapped the flag around my father's head. He didn't remove it, he just waited for the next gust to unravel it. With the flag above his head, holding onto the chimney with one hand, he looked like a statue of the victorious father, while our house with its chimney appeared to me like a plinth supporting my father atop it. Of all the monuments I've seen in my life, the only one that can compare is the Statue of Liberty. Even my mother no longer dared to shout at him, Come down this instant. She merely made a request: "Please climb down now, you've stood there long enough."

One time when I was perhaps in my third year of university, I spent the long vacation at home. As usual, I asked my father to get me a summer job at the factory, because I couldn't imagine being idle all that time. My mother objected: "Honestly! It isn't right for you to do manual labor now." She turned to my father: "I won't let you do it!"

"But he wants to."

"Well, maybe office work."

"Office work? During the season? No way. Seasonal labor's all in the production section. There are masses of strawberries, the black currants will be along any day now."

My mother made a topielec; she still had a few raisins left. It was a Sunday. As we shared tea and cake, I reminisced about the time father had stood on the roof attaching the flag to the chimney. And I said that even now, all these years later, I still sometimes felt afraid for him the way I had back then. I don't know if my father meant to say something or not, but my mother spoke first: "What are you talking about? When would your father ever have gone up on the roof? After we had the storm and all those tiles got smashed, I had to hire a roofer."

"It wasn't then that you hired the roofer," my father said in his usual calm, emotionless voice. "And the storm was a different day too. You were sound asleep at the time. Lightning struck the ash tree by the co-op and split it in two, and all you did was roll over. That time lots of trees were hit, roofs came off, there was one lightning strike after another. Luckily we didn't lose a single tile on our house. When you woke up in the morning you couldn't get over the fact that there'd been a storm in the night. And then the flag – "

"What flag?"

"You made it out of a bedsheet and a pillowcase."

"I don't remember."

"Maybe you're forgetting I was still young back then?"

He still wasn't old. His glasses were thicker than before, that was all. He didn't strike me as old till much later. When I myself was no longer young, in fact. I never asked him about it, though perhaps I should have, for who would have given me a more honest answer than my father as to whether he was already imagining the end of his own life. Though even if his imagination had been inclined to do so, why would he have weighed himself down with what was to come? After all, there's so little of youth. And aside from youth, all the rest involves forcing yourself to live, at most growing accustomed to it. If it weren't for our youth, what would we feed on during what's left? If you put all the rest on one side of a scales, on the other our few years of youth, youth would certainly weigh more. At most the sides would balance. That may be the whole meaning of existence, in my view at least. And that was why I never had the courage to ask him, because it wouldn't have been right for me to disagree with my father.

The truth is, I only noticed he was old after my mother died. He didn't despair, didn't cry, didn't complain; from one day to the next he simply went gray. He accepted her death with a restrained calm. He didn't want to be consoled. He spoke few words, only what was necessary. But though only a few days beforehand he'd had no more than a bit of gray at the temples and a few streaks here and there, by the time of the funeral he'd gone completely gray. I'd just been promoted to associate professor. He didn't want to move in with me.

"You have your own life and your own problems," he said. "What do you need mine for as well."

I stayed with him for a few days. We didn't reminisce much during that time, as if memories brought pain rather than comfort. I had the impression, though, that, helpless in the simplest matters, he was asking my mother about one thing or another in his thoughts. How much salt to put in the soup, how long to let the tea steep, how thickly the bread should be sliced, whether a shirt collar needed to be ironed on one side only, what setting the iron should be on. Washing the dishes was hard too; he dropped a plate and broke it while he was drying up. I tried to do one thing or another for him, but he wouldn't let me, as if it meant he'd have to stop asking my mother those questions. When he went shopping he bought everything as if mother had written it all down for him on a list. One day he bought celery. I asked him: "What's the celery for? What are you going to make with it?"

"I don't know; we used to buy it, so I bought some."

When I tried to insist that he couldn't live on his own, he answered: "I'm not on my own."

That really set me thinking. Maybe being alone and feeling lonely were two completely different things? I mean, it sometimes happens that you have a wife, children, grandchildren, friends, and yet you feel lonely. Maybe we impose loneliness on ourselves as a sort of refusal to accept the world we find ourselves living in? Perhaps its roots lie in our vulnerability in the face of that world? And also in the face of our fate, over which we have no control?

I don't remember if it was earlier, or in that final year. And a year like that doesn't consist of days, weeks, months, as you might suppose A year like that never ends of its own accord. It fills itself up almost completely with our life and makes us live it over again from the beginning. It has no understanding for the fact that we're tired, that we've lived enough already. So I thought to myself, let him get on with it. He's young, he'll manage; he has his whole life in front of him.

He happened to be standing at Needle's Eye, waiting for her as always. He didn't recognize me, or perhaps he chose not to; it makes no difference. Though suspecting me of having something to do with his death is baseless, unjust in fact. Of course, I'm not saying I don't have a bad conscience. I still feel that even today. But don't people have a guilty conscience simply because the world is the way it is, not otherwise? Even if they think they play no part in it. It's not true that others are the only guilty ones. Claiming the virtue of innocence for yourself shows a lack of understanding of our connections to the world.

So what was bound to happen, happened. What can I say: no one lives only their own life. You might even say that we repeat what others have experienced, from our birth to our death. Perhaps it's this repetition that allows us to survive. Because it's hard to imagine how the world could begin from us. Behind us nothing, and in front of us, what? There'd be no one to rebel against for the fact that we're alive.

We'd be walking into the future blind, filled with fear and anxiety, not knowing where we're going. This way, at least we're following in someone's tracks, whatever direction they lead. Tracks are more important than any direction.

He was the one who marked out tracks for me. And I followed them step for step, you might say. I could have been walking in darkness, his footprints alone would have led me. Though I wonder if he made those marks that I was following, or whether it was me making a trail by which he tracked my youth like a hound tracking game. When I got into university, I decided to free myself of him at least a little. That's why I didn't apply for a dorm room. It was another matter that I was no longer capable of living in a room with a lot of other people; I'd lived like that before and I knew how taxing it was. At the same time, I couldn't afford my own room in town, and I didn't wish to burden my parents, though they probably would have helped me out. I had a little money saved from when I worked at the factory, but I needed to buy a few things for the winter – coat, shoes, socks, plus a few books – and I needed to leave enough for food. I put up an ad on campus saying I was looking for accommodation in return for tutoring, but I got no responses.

I spent most of my days in the library, while at night I went to the train station to sleep. At the station there was a canteen, and a bathroom with wash basins, so if need be I could wash up and get something to eat. Sleeping was harder. Almost every night a police patrol came around; they woke anyone who was sleeping on the benches and checked their ID, asking what they were doing there, since the last train had already left. I usually explained that I'd missed that train and I was waiting for the next one, which wasn't till morning. I had to memorize all the train times. Some of the departures I still remember today. The last train left at ten thirty pm, the first one in the morning at six seventeen am. Everyone knows how the trains were back then. It wasn't unusual to wait all night for a connection. Especially when an incoming train was delayed and the ten-thirty didn't wait for it, then the next one wasn't till morning. Trains were late all the time, because on their way they'd have to let through an express or a freight train carrying some important load. There was only ever a single track; it's the railway workers who deserve credit for somehow making it all function.

Luckily, when the police entered the station word traveled through the waiting room that they were coming and we should wake up. It was a kind of communication chain that stretched across the room and had been perfected by those who slept there regularly. One or another of them was always awake, keeping guard by the main door; each night it was someone different. Except that the police knew the waiting room regulars and didn't bother asking for their ID. Any new person, on the other hand, was immediately suspect, even if they weren't sleeping, they might simply be sitting on a bench, or reading a newspaper. Something like that happened to me one night.

"A student?" one said in surprise when he opened my ID card. He was with another officer. He shone his flashlight in my face, then trained it on my ID. He went back and forth a few times between the card and me, as if checking whether the two faces matched. He evidently wasn't sure, because he turned to the other guy: "Take a look. It's hard to say."

Now both of them turned the beams of their flashlights from my face to the face on the ID and back again, trying to see a resemblance between me and myself. They were dazzling me, and I could see them less and less. In the end the second one, who seemed a bit friendlier, said: "We could take him in, but it's already full down there."

"There'd be room. Though then we'd have to write it up."

"Can you be bothered? Gimme that ID. Let's have a closer look." He started again, shining the light on the photo and on my face. "He's still a kid in the picture. It doesn't really look like him."

"Maybe this ID's stolen, eh?"

"That was the only picture I had, I swear, officer."

"It needs looking into."

"It'll have to go to the lab. Maybe he hasn't slept, and that's why it's hard to say if it's him or not."

At that moment the PA announced that the train for such-and-such a place was leaving from platform such-and-such.

"That's my train, sir," I mumbled desperately. "Let me go."

They reluctantly handed back my ID. One of them wagged his finger at me. "You haven't seen the last of us, pal."

I jumped onto the train when it was already in motion. I rode to the next station and came back on foot. After that I stopped sleeping at the station. I spent a couple of nights in a lecture hall, under a bench seat, so the janitor wouldn't see me when he did his final check at the end of the day to make sure the place was empty. One time I slept head to tail in the bed of another student I'd just met who lived in a dorm; another time with someone else; two or three nights I slept in the stairwell of different apartment buildings. Back then the buildings weren't locked. Sleeping there wasn't any more uncomfortable than at the station. At least the police never showed up. Plus, in the waiting room, sometimes there was no free bench to lie on and you had to crouch against the wall. Or someone would plop down next to you, usually a drunk, and start spouting nonsense. Then there was no way of getting to sleep.

One time one of the regulars sat by me like that. He had his own bench. Even if people were squashed up on the other benches, his was always empty, waiting for him. They were afraid of him – he was a strapping guy. Word was, one time he'd stabbed someone there, but there hadn't been any witnesses to say it was him. If anyone accidentally sat on his bench, when he turned up he'd tip them off like a piece of luggage.

"You're not asleep, buddy?" He pushed my legs onto the floor. "Then let me tell you about my life. You're young, how can you know what life is. From newspapers and books? You carry your life inside you. If you don't tell it, it doesn't exist." There was no chance of sleeping at that point.

Every day, with less and less hope I'd check the notice board at the university to see if anyone had responded to my ad. Time passed, and there was nothing. Then one day, I see a little card pinned to a tree in front of the main entrance to the university, with a note in clumsy handwriting: "Need a place to sleep? Will give half my bed in return for lessons." There was an address.

He was a student at auto technician school. Thick as two short planks. Aside from the practical classes, in which he got by more or less,

I had to tutor him regularly in all his subjects, because he was always getting Fs, once in a while a D minus. When he saw how much time I devoted to helping him, he shared not just his bed but also his meals with me. He was from the country, and every two weeks, sometimes more often, he got a food parcel from home: eggs, butter, lard with crackling, sometimes sausage or bacon, sometimes jam or honey, and always a loaf of dark bread marked with the sign of the cross. Every package also contained a letter from his mother that always ended in a sort of entreaty: "Study, son, study. People here are saying they're going to take the land away from us. I'm afraid to even think what'll become of you if that happens. I'm praying that God will watch over you because He's obviously abandoned us. Have pity on us, Lord. Mama."

He'd mumble his way through the letter – he wasn't able to read silently. Every so often he'd break into a sweat, get angry at his mother for her chicken-scratch handwriting. Along with the poorly formed letters, she didn't put in any gaps, as if the whole message were one long word from beginning to end.

"There isn't anyplace to take a break. Give me a hand with it," he'd often ask. He'd sometimes go so far as to say: "It'd be better if she didn't know how to write at all, that way I wouldn't have to read it." One time he let on that when he'd started his program, his mother had taken a literacy class so she'd be able to write letters to him.

I felt sorry for him, and even more for that mother of his. I spared no time or effort in tutoring him. Often we wouldn't go to sleep till the early hours of the morning. I could at least sleep late, whereas he had to be up for school. The bed we slept on had an iron frame and springs, and it wasn't wide enough for us to be able to lie comfortably without our bodies touching. Also, the springs in the middle were worn, so we kept sliding towards each other. When he turned onto his other side, I had to turn too. Each time we did, the rusty springs would creak horribly beneath us; it would wake me up, and I couldn't get back to sleep till he got up. Him though, his breathing didn't even change when he turned over. If he was having a dream, I'm pretty sure the same dream continued on his other side. He was such a sound sleeper that the alarm clock would ring and ring and he wouldn't even budge. If I hadn't woken him to say it was time to go to school, he'd have just slept on.

There was no space for a wider bed. It was hard to even call the place a room. At one time it must been the maid's quarters, or the bathroom of some rich people who'd occupied the whole floor. Maybe the entire building had been theirs, but after the war they never came back and many families lived there now, mostly poor people. It was from one of those families that he rented his tiny space. Aside from the bed there was also a narrow table with two rickety chairs that wobbled every which way when you sat on them. On your way to the bed you brushed against the wall, or you had to move sideways, it was so cramped. There wasn't a separate entrance either; the only door led through the kitchen, and it barely opened half way. Fortunately we were both skinny; the landlady was a tiny thing, and her two sons also managed somehow to squeeze through when one of them needed to come by our room. In fact, you rarely saw fat people anywhere those days.

There was one window, which happened to be behind the bed. Not only was it on the north side of the room, it was so narrow that even on sunny days very little light came in, so we worked by the light of a lamp that hung over the table. During the day it had a forty-watt bulb; at night, when the family went to bed and we were still working, the mechanic would climb up onto the table and put in a hundred-watt bulb then, before we went to sleep, he'd change it back to the forty-watt one. Since he paid separately for electricity, he'd agreed with the land-lady that he'd use a forty-watt bulb, and she'd worked out somehow or other how much he should pay her each month.

There was only one meter for the whole floor. It hung on the wall in the stairwell. There were six apartments on that floor, three on each side of the landing. I don't know how all those families worked out the electricity bill, whether it was by the square footage of the apartment or according to the number of residents. In any case, whenever the man came to read the meter and collect what was owed, everyone seemed to disappear from all six apartments. There were three door-bells on each side, with the names of the occupants on each one, and he'd ring each bell in turn, but no one answered. He knocked and knocked without any response, as if no one was home. He rattled the door handles, even banged on the door with his fist; he knew the people who lived on that floor and knew they were pulling the wool over his eyes, probably sitting there holding their breath till he went away. He'd even lay an ear against the door to see if he couldn't hear anything. In the end he'd give up and tuck the bill behind the meter, with a note saying payment was urgent, otherwise there'd be a fine. He was stubborn, but it was no wonder, he received a commission from the bills that were settled during his rounds. At times he'd get so mad he'd call the residents every name under the sun, saying that all sorts of riff-raff had been allowed to live in a nice building like that, they ought to be in kennels, plus on top of everything they'd been given electricity to light the place.

"You ought to be sitting in the dark, you so-and-sos! Or using candles!" He could still be heard in the courtyard.

That, though, was nothing compared to the arguments that broke out after he left and everyone was sure he'd moved on to the next street. Whoever got to the bill first, called everyone else out of their apartments. Once I witnessed such a scene. I was on my way back from class, and here the landing was in uproar. Someone was whining: "How am I supposed to pay? How? And for what? I come home late and go straight to bed!"

"Lemme see that." The speaker snatched the bill from the man's hand. "Who's been using so much? Who is it, goddammit! Not me! All my bulbs are twenty-five watts!"

Someone else grabbed the bill from him in turn. "Screw that! I'm not paying a penny! Over my dead body! Last month it was only half that much."

"How much is it?" someone asked. They'd all come out of their apartments by now.

"Maybe the meter's broken? We should have it replaced."

"Course it's not broken. People make tea with immersion heaters, do you know how much electricity those things use up?"

"As for you, you've got an electric heater for your feet, because they're always cold. I've heard you complaining to your neighbor."

"My feet? My feet? How dare you! I'm so hot I have the window open all the time! It's that lady, she's always washing and ironing clothes for her clients." He pointed at our landlady, who was so scared she didn't say a word. "She's the one who runs up the bill."

"Well, those people in number three are up all hours playing some kind of games." The speaker lived on the same side of the hallway as our landlady, and he was trying to stick up for her.

In the end somebody got so furious they virtually screamed: "The heck with all of you! We should just share it equally like we agreed!"

"What do you mean, agreed? An agreement has to be on paper. Do you have anything on paper? No, you don't."

Amid all this masculine ferocity a squeaky female voice was heard: "Some higher authority has to step in, because it'll never be fair. Why should I pay equally? I hardly have the light on at all. I spend all evening praying. Prayers reach God best when they're made in the dark. I only need enough light to wash and get ready for bed."

"What's fair is paying equally, ma'am, you must realize that. There's no need of any higher authority. We spilled our blood for that sort of fairness."

The spilled blood was too much for one of them: "You spilled blood ratting people out! You think we don't know?"

The other man didn't say another word.

"If it's to be equal, we should check the list of residents to see how many people are in each apartment. There's a whole horde of people living with that man" – the woman speaking pointed at someone – "supposedly his family. All they do is drink and play cards. You think

I don't hear? Oh, I hear. Who has that kind of family these days. Me, I'm a widow, I live alone with my daughter."

"Your daughter has visitors too, every night. The moment one of them leaves, another one comes knocking. I hear too."

She might have snapped back, because she had a mouth on her, that woman, but one of the other men said with a guffaw: "That daughter of yours, just looking at her would give a guy the droops. Those men are better off in the dark."

The woman was touched to the quick. She screeched at the top of her voice: "Monsters! Degenerates! Perverts! You've no respect, not even for a married woman! Did my late husband not sit boozing with you all? That's what killed him. Lord in heaven! Lord in heaven!"

I don't know how they all made up after those arguments. In any case, the whole time I lived there the electricity was never turned off, except the days when the whole street lost power, or the neighborhood. So they must have paid the bills on time; whether they paid equally, I can't say. Maybe they let some people pay less, maybe they bargained it out.

Across the hallway lived a mystery tenant about whom various things were said, though it was never possible to get to the truth. Some people claimed they knew a lot about him, others more still. Their truths could have caused an even bigger scene than the ones over the electricity bill. But he never let himself be dragged into those quarrels. He'd come out onto the landing, ask how much he owed, take his wallet at once, count out the money, hand it over, and disappear back into his apartment. Though one time he became annoyed when the row was about to get physical. He stepped forward and said that this month he'd pay the whole bill, because otherwise someone would end up calling the police. He always dressed smartly: coat, necktie, or sometimes a bow tie. He lived with a lady who also wore elegant clothes; she was pretty, and much younger than him. Every day they'd go out to eat in a restaurant; he would offer her his arm, she'd hold him close and cuddle up to him. They occupied the largest apartment on our floor – three rooms, plus a kitchen and bathroom – though it was just the two of them. No one could understand why more tenants hadn't been assigned to their place. Apparently there were paintings on the walls, in gilt frames, and a Persian rug on the floor in the living room. Their furniture was different from everyone else's too; it was all curves and shapes and carvings, and the chairs were upholstered. People said that she worked for him; some reckoned she was a singer in some bar, others that she was a whore, but not an ordinary one, like the women that waited on the streets in the evening, or like the widow's daughter. One tumble with her cost more than the daughter could have earned in a month, even if she'd had clients twenty-four hours a day. Others still put the two things together and said she sang and whored as well. Every day they'd leave just after dark and come back when everyone was already asleep. The auto mechanic and I often worked till it started to get light, and we never saw her coming home. The mystery was solved when one day she left him, then less than a month later, he disappeared too.

He used to call in often on our landlady; he'd bring his laundry and ironing. He was polite, cheerful, friendly; he'd always ask if he could help her out in any way, then pay her a little extra, and in thanking her he'd kiss her bony, wrinkled, work-worn hand. She toiled hard to provide for her two doltish sons. The younger one usually slept till noon, then he'd get dressed and go out, announcing to his mother that he had business to attend to; I'd often meet him strolling about the city. Whenever he saw me he'd either turn away or cross to the other side of the street. The older son had some sort of job, but he was forever short of money and was always borrowing from his mother, saying he'd pay her back after the first of the month. The fact that their mother spent her life slaving over a washtub meant nothing to them. Exhausted, soaked in perspiration, her clothing disheveled, she would rock her tiny figure back and forth over the huge tub as if she had no more strength left and was persevering on stubbornness alone. Aside from that she also had to make dinner in case one of them came by; they either did or they didn't. Once she hadn't had time to cook. The younger one happened to put in an appearance and he bawled her out for not having dinner ready. She had to give him a few pennies so he could eat in a cafeteria.

The kitchen was quite big, as was often the case in those pre-war apartment buildings. Parallel washing lines ran the length of it; she had to climb up on a stool to hang her laundry out to dry. One time she fell and was unable to get up on her own. Luckily I happened to have gone to fetch something from the kitchen, and I helped her up. When I lifted her from the floor, she was light as a feather. She couldn't have weighed more than ninety pounds. I wanted to carry her to her bed but she wouldn't have it; she said she had to finish hanging up the washing. She rubbed the places she'd banged when she fell and climbed back up onto the stool. I lifted her and set her down.

"Hand me one thing at a time and I'll put it on the line." She burst into tears.

Whenever one of us went into the kitchen – we'd wash there in the mornings and evenings, or boil water for tea, warm up something to eat, or borrow a plate, a knife or fork – we'd have to steer through all that drying laundry, bent double beneath it. If we had to straighten up for some reason our heads would brush against a bedsheet, a quilt cover or tablecloth, a shirt or a pair of long johns, a slip or some underwear. I sometimes had the feeling I was on a sailing ship, though I never had the desire to go sailing. One time I had a dream that I was at sea, and my boat was driven by the wind in those sheets, covers, tablecloths, shirts and long johns and underwear.

As well as taking in laundry, the landlady also worked as a cleaner. Twice a week she left for the whole day. She never mentioned who she cleaned for, but since it took her all day it was probably some big apartment, perhaps a detached house. They must have been important people, the more so because she always came back with some gift. The younger son would always be waiting for her that day. He'd go roam around the city till midday, then come back and stay home. When his mother returned, he'd ask seemingly out of idle curiosity: "What's that you've got?"

She'd hand him the bag or package almost without thinking: "Take a look, I don't even know."

He'd unwrap it, and express his satisfaction when it was for instance some cologne or a box of chocolates. He'd take the cologne for himself; the chocolates he'd open and stuff himself till they were coming out of his ears. He never offered one to his mother. When she brought back something he regarded as useless, on the other hand, he'd get mad, bark at her and leave, slamming the door behind him. One time she brought a bronze horse with wings.

"The hell you take that for? It's got wings! Whoever saw a horse with wings! No one'll give two cents for a thing like that. The guy you clean for must be nuts! Find someone else!"

"Well, he gave it to me so I took it," she explained meekly.

Another time he jumped down her throat the same way when she brought home a book. "The idiot went and put his name in it too. Otherwise someone might've bought it."

"I didn't dare say no to a book. I wasn't going to tell him you don't read."

In fact, he must have sold the book for a good price because the next day, when he came back in the evening after wandering the city all day, from the doorway he called out: "Take books, mother! But have them sign their name in them!" He kissed his mother's forehead as she leaned over the washtub. "If they try to give you something else, say you'd prefer a book."

His mother was up to her elbows in suds, and she splashed him with them accidentally as he leaned in, unsure whether she'd heard him above the noise of the washboard, and yelled in her ear: "A book!"

In this way the sons fleeced her of everything: her gifts, her money. Yet she never complained.

When she didn't have a penny left, she'd come ask us if we couldn't give her at least half of next month's rent in advance. She didn't know I was only giving lessons in return for staying there. We didn't tell her. I don't know what arrangement he'd come to with her for letting me sleep on his bed. Maybe he was paying her more; after all, I was washing, boiling water for tea, heating up food sometimes, and also borrowing a mug, a knife or fork or plate, here and there. One time she mentioned timidly that he wasn't paying much for the room, that other people charged more. So maybe he topped up what he'd been paying before, because when his final exams were getting close – he had less than six months to go – he told me that he needed to find a third person who'd share the bed in return for help with his practical classes. He was doing okay, but he wanted to review every subject. He found somebody who'd graduated from another school like his, and who in addition had already worked in the trade in a few different factories, so he had experience.

One day, then, the guy for the practical classes appeared. He was a beanpole: skinny, but so tall he had to bow his head when he came through the door. He was stooped and surly.

"Name's Zbychu," he grunted when I met him the first time. "Where am I supposed to sleep? I don't see a second bed."

"The three of us'll share this bed."

"You didn't say there'd be three of us."

"Yes I did. You said, let it be three then, since you didn't have any-where else to sleep."

"Well, I thought you had a big bed. There was this movie where a guy was with two chicks, he was in the middle with one of them on each side, and none of them fell out. He was a big round guy, and the chicks weren't exactly on the petite side either." He guffawed with a kind of rattling laugh, like dried beans in a sieve. "Pity they didn't show what came next." And he laughed again, as if absorbed in imagining what followed. All at once he broke off and rubbed his eyes, because all that laughing had made them water. "How often do you want these lessons, because I need to look for work." He went up to the bed and jiggled it. He checked the mattress. "It's fucked. The straw needs changing. I can get hold of some for you, special stuff for mattresses."

"What do you mean, special?" my automotive student asked.

"You're from the country, you should know. Threshed with a flail, not in a threshing machine. But that's not part of the lessons. Where's the crapper?"

"There are two outhouses in the courtyard."

"Fine. Though I'm used to an indoor toilet. All right, get on the bed and we'll give it a try. You two put your heads at that end, I'll lie the other way. I don't need a pillow, I sleep flat."

We lay down the way he told us, and he squeezed in between us. At first his feet were by our heads, but when he stretched out and straightened his legs, his feet reached beyond the head of the bed, through the iron bars and out the other side. "Godawful," he said. "But you can't live without sleeping."

Young people can put up with all kinds of things. But sleeping three to a bed – even they might curse. I never imagined it would become a landmark among the memories I shared with that student of mine. Yet shared memories are valuable, because they're the hardest to come by. I had a painful lesson to that effect when my old school celebrated its four-hundredth anniversary: when my classmates and I reminisced about our days in student digs, none of the events would match up.

When we mentioned that the feet he'd placed by our heads smelled, he didn't deny it.

"I'd lie in the same direction as you, but my shoulders are too wide, there wouldn't be enough room. Anyway, I'll sleep in my socks."

The socks actually smelled worse, because who knew if they'd ever been washed, and there were holes in the heels and toes. You wrinkled your nose up even in your sleep.

"Don't bother with the socks," we suggested.

"What's the problem?" he said, taking offense. "If I was married, my wife would wash my socks and darn them. Except that then I wouldn't be sleeping three to a bed."

But that wasn't even the worst of it. The worst thing was that whenever he changed position, turning on his other side or onto his back, he had to take his feet out of the bars and stick them back through. In his sleep it was hard for him to find the gaps in the bars, so he'd feel with his feet, sliding them over our heads and waking us up. Half-conscious and furious, I'd take my pillow and my blanket and move to the table. But the table was too short to sleep on; on your back it wasn't possible, your legs hung down and went numb. The only thing you could do was sleep on one side or the other, curled into a ball as if you were back in your mother's womb. At moments like that it helped to be young.

Somehow we made it through till the end-of-school exams. And though only one of us was taking them, it could be said that all three of us were.

As the exams drew close, naturally I started looking for a new place. I put another ad up on the notice board at the university, saying I was looking for a room in return for tutoring. I listed the subjects I could teach, and this time I gave my address. Weeks went by, the exams neared, and there was no response. I was getting more and more anxious. One day I asked Zbychu: "Where are you going to live after the exams?"

"Maybe he won't pass?" he said, something like hope entering his voice. "Another year would be good." The hope evaporated, though, when he thought for just a second. "No, even a moron can pass if they grease the right palms."

"So what'll you do?"

"Probably go back inside. I'd have a roof over my head, my own bed, grub, someone to do my laundry. Even a few zlotys if they choose you for the shops. A guy with a trade does fine in the slammer."

"You said 'back'?"

"Well, yeah. If you've been there already, you go back."

"What were you in for?"

"Nothing. Other people were stealing, I got put away. Whenever a car came off the production line, almost every one had something missing. The radiator, or one of the silencers. I could tell you things. They stole ashtrays, bulbs, door handles, floor mats. Anything that could be swiped. There's plenty of stuff in a car. I had a bit of luck when I was in the joint. The governor's car broke down; different people tried to fix it, but it was me that got the job done. So they let me out early for good behavior. Though now that I think of it, I'm not sure it was good luck. Maybe I should have done something to get a longer sentence. They wouldn't hire me back at the auto plant. I tried a building site, but they were stealing there too. And I got put away again. If you've done time, whenever something goes missing you're the first one they look at. You're marked for life. What about you – where will you go after he does his exams?"

"I posted an ad at the university. But I've had no takers."

"You should put it up at bus stops and tram stops. People wait and wait there, they read things out of boredom. If you don't have a book or a newspaper you'll even read the timetable. Books and papers cost money, the timetable's free. There was this one guy inside with me, he'd memorized the timetables of all the buses and trams and trains. He'd pace up and down the cell from early morning, repeating over and over: eight twenty-three, twelve fifty-eight, four eleven, on and on like that, he could keep it up for days, then he'd start all over again. I asked him, I said, why do you keep going over all those times? When I repeat the timetables to myself, the time goes faster, he said. He was in for life. He'd killed his wife and her lover. If you found another blockhead like ours we could both live there. Even if it was two to a bed, that's still better than three. If he wasn't at trade school I could teach him some life skills, practical stuff I mean, how to hammer in a nail, screw in a lightbulb, how to use a mallet, pincers, a screwdriver, how to measure stuff. There's no shortage of guys with two left hands, even when they're not left-handed."

I followed his advice. I put my ad up at several stops. But I didn't think anything would come of it. My student was coming to the end of his exams and he let us know he'd be moving out soon; whereas I still had three exams to take before the vacation. Zbychu was always restless, he'd go out and come back testy, as if someone had crossed him. When he heard that our blockhead had passed yet another exam, he exploded with all the anger he'd accumulated: "How the fuck is anything supposed to be fair! No wonder innocent people get put away."

Many years passed. I was already a professor. One day I received a letter at my university address. My hands trembled slightly as I opened it; I thought it might be some kind of summons. There was no return address. The whole letter was written by hand, which was a great rarity. All the same, as I sat down to read it, it occurred to me that it might be a witness to the incident on the steps from years before, when I was young, saying that now, toward the end of their life, as often happens, they want to confess that they saw us back then at Needle's Eye, and that the truth was different from the way I'd presented it when I was questioned. They understand that I'd had to act in my own defense, anyone in my situation would have done the same. And they don't want to drop me in it, they'd never do that. I'd sooner have believed in something like that than what was actually in the letter.

 Dear Professor,

 After so many years, I'm sure you've forgotten me. It's hardly surprising: why wouldn't you? In the decades since, you must have given lessons to so many people. I was wondering how I might best remind you, and I reckoned the one thing you might recall is that we slept three to a bed. I'm sorry to bring it up, but what else might have stuck in your memory besides that bed? It was awful, when all's said and done. And awful things – even if we experienced them when we were young – sometimes they come back to mind. Perhaps I shouldn't go on about such disagreeable matters, but I admit that even today

I still sometimes wake at night with aches and pains just as I used to back then every morning. I sometimes also imagine a whiff from the feet of our fellow sufferer, the one who tutored in the practical subjects. Zbychu, was it? Or maybe Zyga, from Zygfryd? No, I don't think it was Zygfryd. Yet I owe him a great deal too. He gave me a lot of practical tips that weren't in the textbook, and which saved me more than once during my exams. Do you know what happened to him? Were you in touch after we went our separate ways? I'm asking because I could repay him today, even find him a job worthy of his talents – I saw him in action when he reviewed all the material for my exams, at a time when he had no job, no place to stay, no means. I don't know if you know, but he'd just come out of prison when I took him on as a tutor. I'm also asking because whenever you part ways with somebody, especially if you've slept in the same bed, you're always curious what happened to them later. Or at least to know if they're still alive.

I wasn't a good student, but thanks to you and him I passed my exams. You might be surprised to hear that afterwards I graduated from the polytechnic. My major was shipbuilding – it was a fashionable choice at the time. I didn't think I'd get into the program, people advised against it. Even my mother (who's no longer with us, alas) urged me to pick something easier, because in the village there'd never been anyone who built ships. But I thought to myself, I'll give it a shot, sometimes you have to reach higher than yourself, otherwise you fall even lower. And it worked. After that, though, my ambitions were hampered. Promotions passed me by, prizes too, so I seized an

*opportunity that came along and signed up with the merchant marine,
first on one of our ships, then on a foreign one. We delivered cargo
from Europe to Asia, Asia to America, America to Africa. I spent
most of my time in the Pacific. It was an international crew; they
were from various backgrounds, many had university degrees, but
I was the only marine engineer, so I earned good money and didn't
spend much. Despite my mother's concerns my parents' land wasn't
taken away from them, so I convinced them to start a chicken farm.
A good period for agriculture was beginning back then, and chickens
are easy to raise. I started sending them money. I was also thinking
that when I was finished with the sea I'd need somewhere to go back
to, and parents aren't eternal, so when they got old, what then? Let
it not be an industrial farm to begin with; when I came back I'd
develop it. You can't work at sea too long, old age comes quicker there
than on land. Perhaps too I was starting to miss home. Missing can
take various forms, I'm sure you'll agree. Even that of imagining
your native country as a chicken farm. Sometimes, as I stared out at
the boundless ocean I'd see thousands, millions of chickens crowding
together on its surface, and hear them clucking amid the murmur of
the waves. I was already figuring out how much income I could expect
from a farm like that, and what I'd build on my family's land with
the money: a health clinic, a hospital, a new school, an arts center, a
firehouse. Another year or two and I'd be done with the sea. But the
stock was wiped out by chicken cholera, and my dreams lay in the
rubble. My mother passed away soon after, of despair. When I came
back home my father was dying too. I sat gazing at that devastated*

chicken farm like Marius before the ruins of Carthage, wondering if I should weep as he did, or if I should tell myself I wouldn't submit to fate. You're probably surprised to see a reference to Seneca, after I barely scraped through my graduation exams. While I was at sea, though, I acquired learning in all kinds of disciplines. I might say that what I learned on the seas and oceans, I'd never have learned on land. I know four languages. And during my few years in the merchant marine I read more books than I'd have read in a lifetime here. It wasn't a big crew, but there were all sorts of people, of every race and every occupation, each one from a different country. Many of them were experienced sailors who'd worked on different ships, under various flags; others were fresh out of university and just learning their trade.

When the sea was calm and there wasn't so much as a haze on the horizon, the ship would follow its course and if only out of boredom you'd be glad to learn, to read, to listen. For instance, there was one guy who'd majored in classics. I don't know how he ended up with us; I think his uncle was the captain of a ship that used to be in port sometimes at the same time as ours. He performed the most menial tasks – scrubbing the deck, cleaning the cabins and the toilets – but he told me one day that it was only here at sea he felt free. Or there was an assistant cook who'd graduated in law, and said he'd gone to sea to escape the lawlessness. I could go through the whole crew like that. Though there was one fellow who jumped in the sea and never came up again.

I'm boring you, I'm sorry. But it was because of my time on the ship that I didn't give in after the failure of the chicken farm I'd placed so much hope in. I'd brought back a decent amount of money, so I decided to buy a few more acres of land. It was going for a song and was lying fallow, because our village was dying. The young people had all moved away, while the old couldn't manage the land anymore; in fact, they were on the verge of becoming part of it. I started with strawberries – a risky crop – but I laid down plastic tunnels as I'd seen in other countries, and I grew good-sized early fruit. I bought more land and added tobacco and hops. I became more and more convinced that working the land had a future. The world is always hungry, and it'll grow even hungrier, as there are ever more people. Today I own five thousand acres. I rent out part of it. I bought a tumbledown manor house, restored it, and added two wings in the same style. The vegetation had been cut down; I planted new trees and bushes. In my view, all these manor houses and mansions that are springing back these days, often from ruins, never looked like that before, because almost all properties of that kind were deep in debt and usually run-down. To think that these days the descendants of serfs are re-instituting feudalism. Could history be going backwards? Or perhaps it moves in a spiral? I wonder: would you be prepared to share your professional insight with me? In your opinion, is there not something like a longing for servitude? You'll say that's ridiculous. If so, is it not then an unconsciously inherited, generations-old desire for revenge that is only now manifesting itself? A wish for compensation on the part of the lowly for all the wrongs and humiliations they suffered over the centuries, which is being realized in the only bloodless way possible – their enriching themselves so as to be the equals of their former oppressors? These perhaps ignorant thoughts went through my mind after I read your latest book. I came across it by chance. Thank you. All the more so because it became the reason for this letter I'm writing to you. By the same token, I'm grateful for being able to share my conjectures with you. And above all to share the story of my life, for I don't have anyone to confide in. My only son went out into the world, and my wife left me. She was an actress; actually, she came from the neighboring village. She claimed I'd stymied her career. She'd wanted me to build a theater for her. I asked her, who around here is going to come to a theater? There wasn't anyone in these parts I could hire, I'd have had to bring them in from elsewhere. Though maybe she was right. Perhaps one day there'll be theaters in the villages. Even now, people are starting to move away from the cities. Cities are becoming unlivable. And you can imagine what the future will look like. More and more people, everyone living their separate lives. In my view there's a limit, and when you cross it, things begin to fall apart.

I'm writing and writing, yet at the same time I'm wondering if you'll believe me. Zbychu, or whatever his name was, didn't even believe I'd passed my exams when I showed him the certificate. How much did you pay for that, he asked me. So you too may have your doubts whether this letter really was written by the blockhead who gave you so much trouble, and for whom you spared no effort or time. I'm sorry to make that comparison. Our voices only mature when they drop after the transitional period of childhood. People's lives undergo a change in the same way, when we understand something, begin to feel something, discover that our fate isn't in our own hands alone. True, despite our efforts and plans, our struggles even, we don't know

the meaning of our lives, though we're constantly posing the question.
Yet the answer is only provided by death.

　　I don't expect you to write back. I wouldn't dare. I admit, though,
that it would bring me true joy to welcome you in my home. Just
in case, though with little hope, I'm sending you my address, phone
number, email. If you should ever decide to visit, it goes without
saying I'd send a car for you. With deepest respects, in remembrance
and gratitude.

His signature followed.

I was moved by the letter. I recalled those times. I'd seen Zbychu
one more time, then afterwards I don't know what happened to him:
whether he went back to prison as he said he would. I remembered not
just the bed – the bed, after all, was unforgettable – but also the last
conversation we had before I moved out. Just as Zbychu never told me
where he was constantly going off to, I didn't let on to him that I was
looking to give private lessons even without accommodation, since I'd
had no response to my original ad. I needed the money. My parents sent
me a food parcel every now and then, and they always included a few
zlotys too. But I knew things were hard for them, though they never
said anything. I'd divided my summer earnings into equal installments
for each month, but what of it, since I often had to borrow from the
following month, and for that month from the one after it, so that in
the end I had nothing left to borrow from. Seeing me fretting one time,
Zbychu read me like an open book and guessed what was bothering me.

"No money, huh? I don't have any either, or I'd lend you some. The
landlady's stupid son wanted me to sell that horse with the wings, he

was going to split the dough with me, but no one was buying. There's only one thing for it: find a chick that's loaded. You could promise that as soon as you graduate you'll marry her. Later on you can wriggle out of it. They're wild for students. Students have a future. Not like me, no future and no past. Even better would be an older babe, not too old, no more than twice your age. Just make sure she has money, or jewelry. Woman like that, you wouldn't even need to promise marriage. It'd be better than giving private lessons. After the war, I'm telling you, all these chicks are looking for a guy. They lost their husbands and fiancés at the front or in the camps. They don't have anyone to be faithful to. Even if they did, what's faithfulness when you've got the urge? That urge, one day the world's gonna go mad from it. Reason won't hold anyone back. What good is reason? They keep telling you, use your reason. But if you don't know where you're going to sleep, how can reason help? The urge, that can come in useful. In the joint I read all kinds of books. On the outside I wouldn't have bothered. In there though, you have to. Because either you read, or you count the days you have left inside. There was one guy, he counted and counted, then in the end he slit his wrists. The only one I actually liked was *Ali Baba and the Forty Thieves*. They say books are good for your reasoning. But I don't think I understood any more after they let me out than before. What I understand is already enough for this life."

Of course, I could have picked up the phone and thanked him for having written. But I started wondering if it wouldn't be better to write back – one letter for another. A letter forces you to say more about yourself in return, to repay the first with some confidence of your own, not as long as his, perhaps, but not too short either, since he'd told me his whole life story. If I called him up I'd have to decide whether to accept his invitation. But to make that decision I'd need to check my calendar, find some free days amid the various obligations – meetings, lectures, committees, and articles which were constantly overdue as it was – not to mention all the conferences here and abroad. In a word, the web that entangles you. The next vacation wasn't even an option: I'd set it aside as time off. A fellow historian who worked on the same period as me had invited me to stay at his Renaissance villa outside Florence. Aside from everything else, I wasn't too good at replying to letters, especially by hand. I had a backlog of several of them from the last months. So with this one too, though I'd resolved to write back soon, I put it off till the following weekend. And so it went. In the end I felt so embarrassed, and perhaps guilty, I made up my mind that on the following Sunday I'd call after all, thank him for the invitation, and say I'd visit. When? As soon as I could find a few clear days in my calendar, I'd call again. Yes, of course, I'd be glad if he could send a car. Then one day I'm reading the newspaper and among the death notices, like a bolt from the blue I see a memorial written by his son, entitled "My Father." It turned out he'd died in a car accident. He'd been driving at night; it wasn't clear whether he'd dozed off or taken ill. The memorial mentioned my name, saying how much he'd been in my debt, and that he'd been looking forward to having me visit.

Chapter 7

§

He didn't so much as glance at me. At the very least he ought to have asked: "This is your son? Is he an only child? What grade is he in?"

When children are present you need to start with them, when you visit someone's home, because it shows from the get-go that your intentions are good. When uncle used to visit, the moment he crossed the threshold the first thing he'd ask was: "How's my little grandson?"

Uncle was virtually family; this guy, who knew who he was. He was dapper, I'll give him that: hat, pinstriped suit, necktie, gloves, cherry red shoes with white tips and buckles, an equally stylish leather case in his hand. Without taking off his hat he said a polite good morning and looked about.

"Your husband isn't in?" he asked.

"He's at the office," my mother replied. "What's this about?"

"I'm in luck, then," he said. "It's always easier with a woman."

"I beg your pardon?" my mother said, bristling.

"You misunderstand me. I just meant that it's easier doing business with a woman."

"What business?" My mother fumed even more at the mention of business.

He took his hat off, apologizing for not having done so before, hooked it over the back of a chair, and began to explain.

"Because unlike their husbands, my good lady, women are the main-stay of the family, its foundation you might say. Since ancient times they've been the priestesses of the hearth. It'd be hard to imagine a world without women. Without men, on the other hand, the world would do fine. Nature would find a way for women to have children without men. But since things are as they are, we have to accept it. The essence of the matter lies elsewhere, as it happens: women have come into possession of a gift unavailable to men. Men merely bring home their pay, while women know what to spend it on. The man often drinks away part of the money before he hands it over to his wife, yet the woman's able to keep house even with what's left. She knows what to give up, what to put off buying till next month, what's essential. Does your husband have a taste for alcohol? I'm sorry to ask such a personal question, but I also have anti-alcohol preparations."

"He has a glass from time to time. I wouldn't have married a drunkard."

"It usually comes out once you're already married, dear lady. Often only after you've been together a long while."

"I'd never have anything to do with a drunk. What an idea."

"So I understand you have the whole salary at your disposal?"

"It's not that much, but I don't complain."

"Then you're in the fortunate position of being able to allow yourself more than other ladies. My congratulations. It's rare to meet such a well-matched couple. I wish you many more years like that."

"Thank you." My mother had been listening to him only reluctantly, about to show him the door, so it seemed. Now though, she softened, and offered him a seat.

"In a moment, perhaps," he said. "In a store, behind the counter the clerk's always on his feet when he serves a client. You can't convince people to buy things when you're sitting down. It's not just a requirement in this line of work. It's a mark of respect, which gives rise to a shared bond. And since we've come to trust one another a little and reached an understanding, I'd like first to offer you something essential for health and beauty. At the same time, I'm not insisting. That's not my role. My duty is to help women out. My case contains every kind of medicament you might desire. Shall we take a look?"

I don't know whether my mother was won over by the flow of words. As for me, I didn't understand a thing. No doubt I was too young, and in addition I was angry that he'd pushed his way in and taken my mother away from me – that was how it felt to me. Are sales pitches aimed at reason, though? If they were, no one would buy anything. In fact, they're the clearest indication of how low reason has fallen.

"By all means." Anticipation glinted in my mother's eyes.

"Where might I put it?"

"Here on the table. Just a second, I'll make space."

She moved the vase of small flowers, took off the tablecloth, and gave the top a wipe since against the light she thought it looked dusty. He put the case down, opened it, and we beheld a mass of vials, tins, sachets, jars, all arranged in neat rows and held in place by a piece of pasteboard with separate shapes cut out for each vial and tin and sachet and jar. It was only then that he seemed to notice me.

"I'm afraid I don't even have a candy for your little boy. Next time I come I'll bring some chocolate."

"What's it all for?" my mother said almost anxiously.

"It depends on what you're after."

He began to list which preparation was for what ailment, pointing at things, from time to time taking something out and letting my mother have a closer look. "This is for heartburn, if you've eaten something you shouldn't have. This is for bloating, for instance after cabbage or beans, if they disagree with you. This is for the kidneys, it helps you pee sooner. These are the famous 'rooster pills' that are for headaches and more." He brought his lips close to my mother's ear and whispered something. "This is to calm you down, let's say after a tiff with your husband or a quarrel with the neighbors. Or when you don't know what to do with yourself, when something's troubling you. This is for bad breath. It's popular, especially with young unmarried ladies and gentlemen. What can I say, in this country not everyone has perfect teeth. This is for swollen feet; it's most often purchased by shop assistants and anyone whose work involves standing. This is for hemorrhoids. Your husband works in an office? There you are. It's a complaint of office workers. This is for bunions; this is for eczema, it clears up after three applications. This is for scabies. Rub it in gently and don't wash it off. Within three or four days you're better. This is for heels, it softens them, makes them smooth as a baby's skin. This one you rub on your hands when they're dry from housework. You have lovely hands, but I'm sure you have to wash and do the laundry like any woman, you should always rub some on afterwards. Here I have eye drops for when your eyes gum up. One drop per eye is enough; if it doesn't work the first time, repeat for a few days. This is for colds. For coughs. For a sore throat. For earache. And all this range is for beauty. Day cream, night cream, cream for your neck. This one is for wrinkles under the eyes. I don't see any wrinkles under your eyes, ma'am, but I'd advise you to start early. This is to go under face powder. This one under lipstick. I also have powders and lipsticks. The best color for you would be this one. Please, give it a try."

My mother went into the living room, where there was a big mirror; she put the lipstick on and came back smiling.

"I knew from first glance that would be your color. I also have mascara, eyebrow pencils. Rouge. What kind of powder would you prefer? Show me the kind you use."

My mother brought it in.

"That's a nice compact, silver I see. It must have been expensive."

"It was a present from my husband, from before the war. He had some good luck one day, he won at cards." My mother's eyes lit up with pride.

"But that's not the right powder at all, dear lady. Here, I have the perfect shade for your complexion. Take a look and compare."

My mother compared the two powders, and in a sort of moan she said: "People need so many things."

To which, certain already that she'd buy more than just the powder if he pushed, he responded with something like exaltation: "Women, dear lady, women do, I cannot stress it enough. A woman is a flower, a man at most the stem."

My mother smiled. "You're very eloquent. I'll take the powder. Mine's running low. And maybe something else too. You say that lipstick suits me? Perhaps I'll take that as well. What else do you have?" She leaned over the case, as if it alone had finally opened her eyes.

Seeing that she'd taken the bait, he said: "I have something special. Only for customers I feel comfortable with. Something for you and your husband together. It helps in certain situations to avoid mutual disappointment, so to speak." He took it out of the case and showed it.

My mother, not knowing what it was, spelled out from the label: "Yo-him-bine. What's that?"

He glanced at me, then, leaning in to my mother's ear, whispered something for a long time. I felt as if he went on for too long, though it may only have been a second. I was angry because I thought he must be saying bad things about my father; maybe the two of them were plotting something, taking advantage of the fact he wasn't there, that he was in his office struggling with all his bits of paper, that he'd come home for dinner but there'd be no meal because my mother wouldn't have time to make it. I wanted to grab my mother's hand and pull her from him, when all at once she laughed and pushed him away herself.

"Well I never. A smart, well-spoken man like you, saying such dirty things. I'd never have expected it."

Unfazed, he put it back in the case and explained with professional calm: "People suffer from various maladies, ma'am. That's a form of sickness too."

How old could I have been then? In any case, yohimbine meant nothing to me. I doubt I'd even have been able to repeat the word. I'm not saying it didn't stick in my memory. I was just mad at my mother for letting someone whisper in her ear – and a stranger at that. I only got suspicious later, when my father came home from work and my mother showed him what she'd bought.

"Where?" he asked indifferently, because he must have been hungry. Luckily she'd had time to make the dinner.

"There was this man going around. He had a suitcase full of all sorts of things. I could have spent all of your wages if I hadn't been careful."

"Then what would we have lived on?"

"I didn't buy much. This, this, and this." She showed him each of the items she'd purchased, holding them up almost at the level of his eyes, explaining that this one she'd run out of, she only had enough left for two more uses; this one was better for her skin; this other one, she'd noticed she was already starting to have wrinkles. "Don't worry, I'll economize. What a talker – I'm telling you, I never met anyone like him. He tried to get me to buy all sorts of things. Some of it would have been good to have around the house. He even tried to sell me. . ." Here she leaned in and whispered something in my father's ear.

My father turned red. My mother flushed. They both glanced at me, as if wondering whether I'd guessed what she'd whispered to him. My father lost his appetite, though he'd come home hungry. He only ate his soup, he said he'd have the main course later, for supper.

I know it's not right to suspect your parents of anything. Even after they'd both passed away, though, I sometimes wondered if my mother hadn't perhaps cheated on my father at some point. The fact that she liked good-looking, smartly dressed, well-spoken men – that meant nothing. Besides, she never hid it from my father. But did she tell him about every man of that sort? I was already in elementary school, in fourth or fifth grade. When I came home from school one day my mother wasn't at home, which had never happened before. She returned soon after, out of breath from walking quickly, her hair messy. She always tied her hair behind with a ribbon, pinning it up in a bun, then my father bought her a silver clasp to replace the ribbons. This time, though, it was only at home that she took the clasp out of her handbag and pinned her hair up with it.

"Forgive me, honey, I lost track of time talking to someone, you don't know her." She mentioned a name. "She's visiting her sister, she's leaving tomorrow, and we hadn't seen each other in years. You must be hungry, I'll make something right away. Just as well I prepared dinner this morning. I'll heat it up in a jiffy." She stroked me on the head, kissed me and gave me a hug. "My little darling. You're not mad at Mama, are you? How was school?"

She was just as affectionate toward my father when he came home from work. He was even a little surprised: "What are you so happy about?"

It didn't make him suspicious, though, for when my mother was happy it always put him in a better mood too. If he'd had difficulties at work he found them easier to bear, telling himself that things would work out, there was nothing to get upset about, he'd been through worse. My mother would be the one to worry: "So what'll happen?"

"Nothing'll happen. Serve the dinner."

"Would you like a second cutlet?"

"Sure, stick it on, I'm starving."

When she was happy it actually improved my father's appetite. The problems he'd had at work would melt away as if by magic. Was it really so easy for him to adapt to whatever life brought him, virtually every day? Once in conversation, I don't remember who he was talking to, though it must have been someone special because he'd served them a glass of his plum nalewka, out of the blue he declared: "Whatever anyone says, people are made of plasticine, otherwise they wouldn't be able to put up with it all."

When I would think about those words of his years later – because I often recalled them – I'd find myself wondering who he was, aside from the fact that he was my father; and I was always inclined to agree with him. Adaptability is a condition of existence. If you don't have it, you usually end up paying a price beyond your means. I have to say that for me my father is a more mysterious figure than my mother, harder to figure out. Because I don't believe he suspected nothing in my mother's sudden outbursts of affection, even if they put him in a good mood. Yet what right do we have to judge our fathers and our mothers? Their secrets die with them and will never be revealed to us. Perhaps that's for the better.

One day I came home early from school. I'd skipped gym, which I didn't like, and which was the last lesson of the day. Through the kitchen door I heard a conversation in the living room. I recognized my mother's voice, but the other one, a man's, was unfamiliar. At the very beginning I thought my father might have returned from work sooner than usual. No, it wasn't him. My father's voice was strong, whereas this one sounded hushed. So I didn't go in. I waited till my mother would realize I was home. Instead of that, though, she laughed once and twice, and the other voice laughed with her. I even pushed a tin cup off the table onto the floor so she'd hear I was back. But if she heard it – and it was hard not to from the next room, despite the closed door – she might have thought that the cat had knocked something over chasing after a mouse. We had a cat, though it wasn't big on catching mice, it preferred being fed from a saucer. One time a mouse came through the open door; the cat was sunning itself on the windowsill, and it didn't move a muscle. My father pushed it off onto the floor.

"Go get it! Come on, after it, lazybones! You see it? It's right there!"

He snatched up the cat and tossed her in the direction of the terrified mouse, but she simply meowed and walked out of the house. We had to hunt the mouse ourselves. My mother closed the door so it couldn't get out, my father grabbed the broom and managed to trap the mouse against the wall with it. My mother went looking for the poker, because it had gone missing somewhere; I ran into the living room and snatched up a plaster figure of Our Lady with the baby Jesus. My mother whisked it out of my hand.

"Are you crazy?" She went to take the meat tenderizer out of the table drawer, but the drawer got stuck.

"Kill it, or it'll run away again!" my father said. "I can barely keep it where it is."

So my mother took a log from the kitchen stove. We leaned over, ready for the kill; my father lifted the broom with a swift movement, but the mouse was gone.

From the living room I heard the scrape of chairs being pushed back, then footsteps coming toward the door. As I stared at the handle, waiting to see when it would move, I heard the man's voice: "The wife's taking the kid to her cousin's at the seaside. I'll be alone."

My mother replied: "But I won't. I have to be a model wife and mother. My son'll be back from school soon, my husband'll come home from work."

To which he said: "The summer vacation's coming. Your son could go away to camp. And I could give your husband some well-paid overtime."

At that moment the door handle creaked and my mother stopped in her tracks in the doorway.

"Aren't you in school?"

"I got a headache and the teacher let me out of gym."

She was clearly relieved at the news of my headache, and grew tender at once.

"Does it hurt badly? I'll make you a compress with a cabbage leaf. I just need to go get a cabbage. Excuse me, sir."

The man was the manager in charge of the office where my father worked. I knew him. He said, as if not at all surprised by my appearance: "Hi. How's it going? You should come by some time when you're visiting your father at work. You can have some orange juice. See you." And he left.

There are some strange coincidences that can be hard to explain. You'd be forgiven for thinking that people enjoy setting them up deliberately for themselves, though they don't know to what end. That morning, when he left for work my father had forgotten some important papers he'd brought home to work on, and he had to come back and get them during working hours. He was so wrapped up in looking for them that he wasn't surprised to find me at home, nor that my mother was dressed more nicely than usual, in a new blouse, a nice skirt, high-heeled shoes, without the apron she always put on first thing in the morning, because first there was breakfast, then she would set about making dinner. He couldn't remember where he'd put those papers. In the end he turned to her: "You don't know where I put them, by any chance?"

My mother went into the living room, though he'd looked in there already.

"Here. You can't have been searching very carefully. They were right there, in plain sight."

Perhaps out of gratitude, to repay her he said something about having met his boss on the way.

"I even said he should come by, that we could go back to work together."

"What for?" my mother objected instantly. "The last thing I need is your boss here. I have to get dinner ready."

I clamped my mouth shut so as not to say: He was here.

After my father left, she remembered about my headache. She

fetched a cabbage, cut off a couple of leaves, took a fresh tea towel from the linen chest, then crushed each leaf with the handle of a knife. As she was putting the compress on my head, I said: "It's stopped hurting, mama."

At that point it was like the devil got into her.

"Leave me alone, all of you! I don't know what to do with you!" She ran into the bedroom, threw herself on the bed, and didn't get up again till it got dark.

There was no dinner that day. When my father came home from work he took the news calmly.

"Making dinner day in, day out like that, it's easy enough to be tired of it. And not just dinner. Breakfast, supper. You can get tired of yourself too."

I don't remember what we ate that day. Perhaps he bought bread and milk at the store. Or maybe we went to a restaurant. Though I don't think we'd have gone without my mother.

He hated writing letters; he said that the writing he did at the office was more than enough for him. My mother, on the other hand, could have written a letter every day. She wrote for him and for herself. At Christmas or Easter she'd buy a pile of cards. Sometimes she'd write so much her dough would burn.

"Who are you writing all those cards to?" my father would ask, seeing her sitting at the table with the pile in front of her. "Wouldn't it be enough just to think about them?"

After my mother died, when I visited him once he started complaining that the worst thing were those letters and cards, he couldn't keep up any more. When my mother was alive she'd been the one to write; now it was down to him, because someone had to do it.

"She really knew how to write. Me, I can't manage it. When she wrote a letter it'd be three or four pages. I'd ask her, where do you get it all from, nothing happens around here for there to be anything to write about, even a card. There's not much space on one of those cards. But she'd always add things along the side or above the address. Me, I'd rather just say, nothing new here, what's going on with you. That'd do. It's a good thing these days you can buy cards with the greetings already in them, all you have to do is sign your name. Too bad there aren't letters like that, they'd make things a lot easier."

I couldn't understand it, then, when after his death I didn't find a single envelope in the house, no paper, nor any letters or cards to show that anyone ever wrote to him. Had he burned them all? It's possible. Because I also found no indication of him ever having written back to anyone. He didn't have anything to write on, or with. There was an inkpot, but there was no ink in it; I looked inside, it was all dried up. I even put my finger in; there was barely a trace of some dried-up remains on my fingertip, as if my mother had been the last person to dip her pen in it. There was no pen either, come to that, not so much as a pencil, or the fountain pen I'd once given him; there was no ball pen, nothing you'd need for writing. The woman I'd hired some time before to take care of him told me she would definitely have seen if he'd ever written anything, because she spent more time there than at her own house.

"One time I wanted to write a shopping list for the gentleman, and I had to bring my own pen. If he'd told me he wanted to write I'd have gotten him paper and envelopes, something to write with, stamps. For Christmas, Easter I'd have bought cards. And mailed them for him. I had to send my letters to my daughter abroad as it was. I used to go pay his bills for him at the post office, so I could've dropped off a letter or a card. He wasn't infirm. He looked after himself fine. Washed himself, shaved, changed his underwear. I never had to remind him. He remembered the day and the time of his doctor's appointments. When to take his pills. He filled the prescriptions at the pharmacy himself."

It was true. Whenever I came to visit, calling ahead of course – because while my mother had still been alive they'd gotten a phone – he was always ready for me, there was tea, he'd bought a cake, made dinner. When I talked to him I never felt there was anything wrong. He'd answer my questions straightforwardly.

"You have some nice flowers, I see. And the ferns have never looked so good."

"I water them, trim them, give them plant food."

"The snake plant's really grown."

"I repotted it."

"The araucaria was so small, now it's almost the size of a tree."

"Time goes by."

He no longer asked me so many questions, less with each visit, it seemed. I only realized after he was gone that he'd been moving more and more toward silence, further and further from words. His questions were never illogical though.

"So you're a professor already?"

"Almost."

"When will you be?"

"I don't know."

"Does it take such a long time from those Middle Ages of yours?"

"It takes a long time from anywhere."

"It wouldn't have taken so long if you'd been coming from the present day."

"All days are the present day."

"Maybe. I've not made the journey, I couldn't say. Was life possible in those Middle Ages?"

"At a pinch."

"Then it was like today. Like today."

"How's the yard doing?" I moved away from the subject of the Middle Ages because it would have taken too long to explain how people lived back then. How people live is the hardest thing to explain, not just today or then, but always and everywhere.

"The yard?" For a moment he seemed to be reflecting on the life we'd been talking about. "Go take a look. There are flower beds, paths, what's been sown and planted is growing. I have two apricot trees. Four black currant bushes."

"I thought you cut them down?"

"Well, but you remember the black currant jam your mother used to make? There isn't a single jar left, or you could've taken one. I went through the cellar, there's nothing. On the left-hand side the shelf was lined with jars of black currant jam. It's all gone. Underneath there were pickled cucumbers. And below that all sorts of things, I couldn't tell you what. Then on the other side there were plum spreads. We didn't have plums, but someone used to bring us them. Or maybe there were two trees, but they'd grown old and they had to be cut down. They're sweetest after the first frost. She'd make them without sugar. No one believed there was no sugar added. There's a few jars left, I'm saving them. Would you like one? It's delicious with farmer's cheese."

As I followed behind his coffin, a sort of film was playing in my mind with clips, fragments, snippets of memory summoned up by the imagination, which had formed them anew under the influence of his death. For who could remember how things really were, especially after so many years. The past is always subordinate to the moment presently being lived. And the present moment consisted of his funeral.

Out of all those clips and fragments and snippets I tried to piece together some picture that would encompass their life as it had been. Did my father trust my mother boundlessly, and it was only me who suspected she'd cheated on him? Did he never have any doubts? Or if he did, did he regard them as insignificant? Perhaps he was mindful of the weakness nature has endowed us humans with, and wisdom reminded him that what's most important is the capacity for forgiveness. They were so different in character from one another, not to say incompatible; it might seem surprising that they stayed together for life. But who knows, perhaps those differences gave them a sense of being complete. Though everyone believes – wrongly, in my view – that similarity between the personalities involved is what determines whether a marriage will last.

I even felt guilty that in my childhood I'd wanted their lives for myself. But what can you do, children want everything to be theirs.

They want to have their father and mother exclusively for their own, not only not to share them with anyone else, but also never to allow them a moment apart. Perhaps it's a token of the awareness – still unconscious at that age – that one day they'll leave us; from childhood we refuse to allow them to die. So the suspicions that arose in me back then might have merely been a manifestation of that desire for exclusivity.

When that man came and asked, Your husband isn't in?, it bothered me already. During his elaborate sales pitch to my mother I kept a firm eye on him. Then, when he opened his case full of all sorts of things, I felt as if with every little tin and sachet and vial and jar my mother was moving away from me. I didn't know what yohimbine was, I'd never heard the word, and perhaps I'd have forgiven her for asking what it was for. But he leaned in and whispered in her ear for a long time, and the whispering seemed fishy, as if the two of them were plotting against my father, and I'd lose my mother, and my father would lose his wife. Because the fact that my mother pushed him away with a laugh and said he was being dirty – that wasn't enough to stop me thinking he was showing her one thing, yet persuading her to do something else.

I felt a sense of pity for my childhood when I found out what yohimbine was. It happened when our blockhead, who Zbychu and I were coaching in return for sleeping three to a bed, was taking his exams. We were worried that if he passed we'd have to move out, and we had nowhere to go to. I'd put up notices at tram and bus stops as Zbychu had suggested, but at that point I hadn't had any takers. I'd already lost hope of any response, when one day the landlady knocked at our door and, poking her head in, said to us: "There's someone to see you."

A stranger came in. He looked to be about seventy, and was well turned out. He glanced around our tiny place and asked if he might sit down. He gazed first at Zbychu, then at me, then back to Zbychu; pointing at me, he said: "I'm guessing you're the gentleman who's looking for accommodation."

He explained he'd seen my notice at a bus stop, he even mentioned which street it had been on, and that was why he was here, though he wasn't interested in lessons.

"You'll forgive me," he said with a dismissive laugh. "Private lessons at my age? In what subject? Unless it was dying. But in that case I'd go to a priest, not to you. You're too young for those sorts of lesson. Plus, I'm in no hurry to die. In fact, I'm drawn more powerfully to life now than ever before." He sighed. "I could live and live. Back then, there was no time for it; other things were more important. But unfortunately life doesn't wait. I have three rooms with a kitchen, I could let you have one of them."

"The thing is, I don't have any money, that was why I said I could give lessons in return."

"I didn't say anything about money," he retorted. "Your youth is enough for me. Though don't read too much into it. You have no idea how hard solitude is. When you're young it's easier somehow. You know masses of people. Now only a handful are left. It isn't just that they've died; they've left, moved to a different city, gone abroad and stayed there. At a certain age, when you look around you it's hard to believe how many holes there are. I never married, I have no children, but I chose such a life. At least no one sniffed my shirt for perfume, looked for traces of lipstick on my collar, asked where I'd been, tried to catch me out. I couldn't have stood that. My only obligations were toward myself. Alas, it turned out that wasn't freedom but loneliness. I'm sorry, I'm talking too much." He took out a business card and laid it on the table. "My phone number's on there, as well as the address. If you accept my offer, as I'm sure you will, let me know."

At that point Zbychu spoke up: "Perhaps there'd be room for me too, sir?"

"Unfortunately I only have one free bed."

"We could sleep two to a bed. Three of us slept on this one."

"Well I never!" he exclaimed indignantly, as if unable to imagine not so much sleeping three to a bed in general, as two to a bed in his own apartment. "Why should I take you? This gentleman's a student," with a nod toward me. "What about you?"

"You mentioned you'd like to live a little, sir. Well, I could find you some yohimbine at a good price. I know a guy that sells it on the cheap."

"The impudence!" He jumped to his feet. "How dare you!" From the doorway he asked if I had a lot of things, because he'd pay for a cab.

The room wasn't large, but it was arranged as if in the expectation of someone moving in. Or perhaps somebody had already been living there – I could see at once that the armchair, for instance, needed re-upholstering, it was so worn. Later I noticed that the mattress on the bed had been turned. When I lifted it up to look underneath, I guessed that the bottom had once been the top, because what else could have made the depressions that looked like they were from sleeping bodies. A number of small details caught my eye. I'd learned my inquisitiveness from my mother, who often repeated: "You'll never feel at home the way you do here with your father and mother. You'll never sleep, or eat, like you do here, and even the walls won't be as friendly."

Yet none of this was of any significance in the face of the bed. I'd never seen a bed like it. The fattest married couple would have had room to spare. If it had been the three of us like in the previous place, Zbychu wouldn't have had to sleep the other way around, and we wouldn't have constantly been sliding towards each other, so squashed together it made our bodies ache. There was a tall headboard that had a dark inlay pattern in the center in the form of a star, and was crowned with an openwork arch, on the top of which were the carved figures of a man and a woman in an embrace. The bed was finished with a reddish-gold cherry veneer.

Whenever I was getting ready for the night, I'd start thinking about that bed. Where had he gotten it from? He couldn't have bought it in a store. It must have been made to order. You'd have to look far and wide for a cabinet maker capable of such a commission. Besides, cabinet makers had almost completely vanished with the appearance of industrially produced furniture. Had he inherited it, or what? It was precisely the "what" that most troubled me as I lay there, unable to stop wondering whose bed I was sleeping in. And whose mattress? The mattress was used, as I'd already realized, but the bed looked as if it had been made relatively recently. There was no sign of the veneer bulging or flaking, as happens with old furniture. Three people could have slept in it comfortably. That thought, with its faint hint of nostalgia, alarmed me at the same time. What if Zbychu suddenly appeared?

It turns out thoughts can bring bad luck too, for one day he showed up. The elderly gentleman had gone away; he hadn't told me where, only that he was leaving me on my own till the following day, and that I shouldn't let anyone in. I came back from the university. I'd barely closed the door behind me when someone knocked on the window of my room, which was on the first floor. I looked outside: it was Zbychu. He was signaling to me. He was so tall he didn't even need to stand on tiptoe: his head came up to the window. He was tapping on the pane and calling: "Open up!"

I opened the window. "What do you want?"

"Let me in."

"No, Zbychu. The woman next door will see and I'll get into trouble."

"I'll come in here, through the window. I'll get some shut-eye then I'll leave. I haven't slept in two nights. That guy of yours isn't there, he's away, I know."

How did he have my address? I'd taken the business card from the table right away, so he couldn't have seen it then. He must have tracked me down at the university and followed me. But I'd taken the bus, and I hadn't noticed him. True, it had been an unholy squeeze, but how could he have hidden even in such a crowd, a tall guy like him? I'd obviously underestimated him, despite the fact that we'd shared a bed. He'd surprised me with that yohimbine too. He clambered up and hauled himself in.

"Damn, you're in clover here." He looked around the room. On one wall there was a copy of a Modigliani nude in a wide gilt frame. "And I see you've got a naked chick. That's what I call living." He stared at her.

"Wonder how much you'd get for that frame? We could split it fifty-fifty. All you'd need to do would be to leave the window open at night. You wouldn't even need to wake up. I'm like a butterfly. I'd take my shoes off before climbing in. When the nights are hot people leave the window open. I sometimes sleep on a bench in the park, or when it's colder I go to the allotment gardens. There's always some empty shed there, half the time they aren't even locked. Once in a while there's food inside."

"So you didn't go back inside?"

"I changed my mind. OK, I'll just get some sleep. You can keep working. Wow, the bed's top quality too. Mattress, quilt. Don't try to tell me all this is for free. You're not coaching him, you must be giving him something else."

He stretched out, pulled the blanket up, and a moment later he was snoring. I felt helpless. The fact that we'd slept three to a bed somehow bound us; I couldn't just tell him to get lost. He woke up after a few hours, as the light was fading. He stretched so hard his joints cracked.

"Is it morning yet?"

"No, it's just getting dark."

"You see what it is to sleep on a bed like this. I wasn't out long, but it felt like a whole night." He got up. "I'll swing by again some time. If I brought you some sleeping pills you could slip one in his tea in the evening. Then I could crash again. I'd knock on the window like today, you'd open it for me, after the pill he wouldn't even hear. And think about that picture frame. See you."

He never did reappear; I didn't hear from him again. To this day I don't know what became of him. I once visited the landlady from the previous place to ask if he maybe came by there sometimes. He didn't. Her younger son, the one who sold everything his mother was given by the people she cleaned for, told me he'd seen Zbychu once on the street, but he got on a bus before the son could catch up with him, because Zbychu still owed him money from the horse with the wings.

In my room there was a desk with a lamp you could bend one way or the other, further away or closer, depending on whether you needed the light close to your eyes or overhead. At the desk there was an upholstered chair with a high back where you could rest your head, close your eyes and stop thinking for a moment, even doze off. There was also a two-door wardrobe that looked to have been made by the same craftsman as the bed: it had the same red-gold cherry veneer, with the same kind of openwork decoration at the top in the shape of a semicircle flattened into an arc. Inside, on one side there was room to hang a suit, on the other side shelves. My clothes didn't exactly fill the thing. A jacket, a sweater, a couple of shirts and undershirts, underwear, socks, and the trench coat I'd gotten from my mother's vacation lodgers when they sent the coffee and the ingredients she needed for her topielec. (At the previous place we'd kept our things in the landlady's wardrobe.) There was a separate entrance directly off the hallway to each room, to the kitchen, the bathroom, and the toilet.

But the bed was the most important piece of furniture. It healed me from the aches and pains of sharing with two bedmates. At first I was afraid to lie on one side or the other. I had the feeling that the moment I touched the mattress my whole body would begin to hurt. So I slept only on my back or on my stomach, and when I turned over

I lifted myself up on my hands, so I woke up at every change of position. It was torture, not sleep. The discomfort diminished night by night till eventually it was gone. But I never forgot sleeping three to a bed.

On the day I moved in and made myself at home, that same evening the landlord knocked on my door.

"If you should need anything, don't hesitate to ask. We have to learn to live alongside one another. I invite you to join me for supper in ten minutes. It'll be in the biggest room, across the hall."

During the meal, which was quite a spread – there was ham, butter, vegetable salad, bread rolls, tea in cups, for dessert donuts with rose filling – he let me know that we'd be preparing our own suppers and breakfasts together. In the morning he usually had a soft-boiled egg, farmer's cheese, and fruit spread; or would I perhaps prefer scrambled eggs? I said soft-boiled was fine, though in truth I would have preferred scrambled. He bought his bread, farmer's cheese, eggs, butter, and other things at a little private shop he knew. He'd already changed his order to two bottles of milk from the milkman. We just had to put out two empty bottles at night so he wouldn't need to wake us in the morning. As for dinner, it'd be brought as usual by a lady from one entrance down in the same building. The meals she cooked were tasty and healthy. You never had bloating after her meals, or diarrhea or constipation. He wasn't a vegetarian, but he didn't particularly like meat. He loved pierogis stuffed with cheese, or with strawberries or blueberries, when they're in season of course, because there's always cheese; he liked buckwheat with fried eggs and soured milk. His favorite soups were tomato soup, cucumber soup, and *krupnik* – barley and vegetable soup. "What do you like best?"

"The same – tomato soup, cucumber soup, krupnik." Though in fact I couldn't stand krupnik.

"I can see that as far as food is concerned we're going to get along. You shouldn't eat your dinners at the university canteen. There'll always be a dinner for you here. Whatever time you come back from classes. You can warm it over in the kitchen if it's cold."

One day after dinner, as I was just sitting down to study, he knocked on my door.

"May I? I'm not disturbing you? It's only for a moment. I wanted to see how you're settling in. And to say that once a week, on Fridays, there's a cleaner who comes. While she's doing your room you can move into the drawing room. That's the biggest room, we call it the drawing room. It's silly, but what can you do, it's a habit from my youth. Oh yes" – on the point of leaving my room he seemed to remember why he'd come there in the first place – "I forgot to tell you that this evening some friends are coming over for bridge. Do you play? Would you like to learn? That's too bad. It's a smart, enthralling game. I understand, you have an exam. Studying is serious business. In that case, I apologize in advance in case it gets a bit loud."

The part about being "a bit loud" worried me. If I'd had cotton wool I could have stuck some in my ears, I thought. That was what my room-mates at the dorm used to do; there were ten or twelve people to a room, and no one was considerate of the others. I didn't have any cotton wool, however. "A bit loud" sounded like you didn't know what "loud" means. Before they'd even picked their first cards up, it seemed, they started talking as if they were addressing one another from a great distance, not sitting around a table together. In any case, I heard almost every word they uttered despite the door being closed. I gritted my teeth and put up with it. But the voices rose with every hand. Then at some point in the game there were mutual protestations, though they sounded more like reproaches. As time passed and things became more and more heated, there were expressions of outrage, along with shouted accusations: someone hadn't followed the rules, hadn't discarded a card, hadn't bid that suit, and in fact they should have passed instead of upping the bidding. The voices rose from the depths of their throats, or even their innards; they were raucous, agitated, enraged. The shouts burst out one after another, like exploding shells. At a certain moment one of them appeared to throw his cards on the table, yelling: "I'm not playing with that moron!"

They must have managed to calm him down, because the game continued. It seemed to be getting quieter, but that didn't last long. After the next deal the temperature began to rise again and veer toward the same quarrelsome grievances, fierce disputes – who knows, brawls even. I waited for the rapidly approaching moment when somebody would be socked in the face. One of them in particular, with a high-pitched, wheezing voice, was abusing all the others. Maybe he was the best bridge player in the group. He insulted his fellow players every which way, cursing left and right. Or perhaps it was his way of trying to impart some authority to his asthmatic voice.

During the game I was unable to read anything at all. It wasn't only the sentences that escaped me; the very letters swirled like ants in a disturbed anthill. I read one page, then another; not only did I retain nothing, I couldn't even have said what I was reading about. I started over from the beginning, with the same result. Before my eyes I had only that anthill of letters. All at once there was a clink of glasses carried on a tray, and I felt hope. Someone was apparently concluding the first part of the evening: "That's enough bridge for today."

Another one of them greeted the glasses: "Hurrah!"

Drinks were poured, they drank the health of their host, and probably a couple of other toasts too. Then something worse than bridge began. The bridge game had at least occupied their attention and prevented them from talking too much, aside from the breaks between hands. Now, freed from the cards, they suddenly felt at ease, and one after another they began to open up their memories. Each of them was filled to the brim with such memories. I guessed they must all be about the same age, because each of them had a different set of memories. At first their recollections seemed to cover the same times, before the war, during the war, after it. But it soon transpired that when one of them abruptly hammered on the table with his fist, demanding confirmation of his own memory, they clashed, as if each of them had lived at a different time. They started accusing each other of falsehoods, lies, at best forgetfulness. It felt as if the various times themselves were in conflict with one another, challenged one another, while the central figures of the evening were merely spectators. With a little effort you could have heard the clatter of weapons, though it was only the glasses clinking together as the drinkers despaired that history was now taking place without them, unjust as always, in addition to excluding them because they'd grown old.

They didn't realize that it was only now, in their old age, in a small circle of friends – for what dangers can there be in old age other than sickness – that they were free to disagree among themselves, and even set their times against one another, though in fact those times had been shared. In their prime, perhaps occupying some important post, they had had to be in accord. It was only on their bridge night that they could permit themselves a difference of views. Even if the positions they'd held were relatively lowly – perhaps they'd been accountants, or planners, or benefits officers, and not in any enterprise of strategic significance but, let's say, in a cheese-making facility – still, consensus was the order of the day down to the lowest rung.

Yet I couldn't be sure of all that from their argument alone; I'd have needed to see them, observe their gestures and their expressions, their foam-flecked mouths, their eyes casting daggers. Words sometimes need support when they're constrained by gestures, expressions, mouths, eyes. These people, though, were seething, yelling over one another, interrupting, leaving things unfinished or unstarted. Elisions, syllables – a "fuck it" or a "Jesus Christ" – served as whole sentences. It was hard to figure out who was on top and who was underneath. In my mind I appointed the one with the high-pitched, wheezing voice as the manager, but I could be wrong. He may have been subordinate to someone who had held no position but was allied with someone else currently absent. In any case it's quite possible that in this ruckus they were trying to break free from a former hierarchy. Except that such a thing isn't so easy. Blood infected by a hierarchy like that circulates in you for the rest of your life.

They didn't go home till dawn. They banged around as they left, rattling door handles as if they couldn't find the exit. In fact one of them said furiously as he opened a third door, for there were three slamming sounds: "Is there no way out of this place of yours?"

Someone else opened my door and, seeing me sitting over my book by the lamp, grunted: "Sorry."

But instead of closing the door behind him, he opened it wider as if incapable of removing his body. He repeated: "That's to say... sorry."

After which, he gripped the door frame firmly with his other hand, pushed himself away, and shut the door with a crash as if this time his body had propelled him backward of its own accord.

I was preparing for an exam. I only had one to go, and the thought of leaving afterwards to spend the summer vacation at my parents' cheered me up. It seemed my landlord understood; he knew about the exam and so for a long time he hadn't had any guests over. He would meet his friends in a cafe or a restaurant, telling me he was going out and didn't know when he'd be back, because it was a bigger group, so I'd have to make my own supper, there was bread and cheese and butter, and so on.

One day, though, over dinner, toward the end of the meal, as if remembering something, he said: "Ah yes." He finished his mouthful and swallowed. "I wanted to let you know that tomorrow there'll be a slightly larger gathering here. It might be a little louder than usual, because there'll be ladies present. All the same, we'll try to keep it down, and you should be able to study. Or perhaps you'd like to join us, in which case we'll be glad to see you. Studying is one thing, but it's good to take a break every now and then. It won't harm your work. You'd be very welcome. Young people are always welcome. There'll be champagne, caviar, those are rarities these days. Have you ever had champagne? Exactly. I bet you've never tasted caviar either."

I admit I'd have gladly tried champagne, which my mother used to talk about from before the war, and also caviar – I'd heard once that it was the most expensive delicacy in the world. I tried to recall who had told me that and when. I was also curious who the ladies might be. Zbychu used to caution me that women were divided into mothers, widows, wives, fiancées, girls, and whores. Whores were a separate sex. They have the same bodies, but they're often infected. And I imagined to myself that those would be the sort here. But champagne and caviar for whores? I'd often seen them on the street, standing in the gateways of apartment buildings. Especially on my way home in the late evening, when they'd step forward and accost passers-by. Old or young, it made no difference. But it was enough for the police to put in an appearance; somehow or other word would get around, and then there'd be hide nor hair of any of them. Where had they vanished to? That I couldn't say. Sometimes there were roundups, but that didn't change anything. Two or three nights later they'd be back in every gateway. Plus, the roundups were never large scale. They'd pull in two or three girls at most, always those who were just starting and hadn't yet learned that you needed to get along with the police, sometimes share your earnings, and sometimes get in the police van without being arrested – they apparently always had a mattress back there.

The landlady's younger son, who usually came home late in the evening or in the middle of the night, knew in advance when the police were coming. He also knew all the girls from the gateways up and down the street. Laura, Señorita, Buns, the Flute Lady, the Duchess, Goosey, Softly – I don't remember all the names. He could have served as a guide: who stood in which entranceway, how much they charged, who you could haggle with and who stuck to their price. Who liked to take their time, who was in a hurry to get it over with. Who had the most business, who was barely scraping by.

"If one of you wanted, I could set it up at half price. And not with the worst one."

We suspected him of being a pimp, or at least in cahoots with the pimps and with the police. One time, when he was boasting about his connections in the gateways – and he liked to boast – Zbychu said to him: "Maybe I could join the firm?"

"There is no firm. You just need to know who, what, when, who with, where. And I've got a nose for it." He tapped his nose. "It's not in the head, it's in the nose."

"I've got a nose as well, but it doesn't do me any good."

"You probably blow it too much. You have to look after your nose."

It sometimes happened that, on my way back home at night from studying at a friend's place, someone would appear from one of the gateways and take me by the arm: "Hey, kid. Don't run away. You, I'll go with you for half the price. I want to enjoy it myself from time to time. And it looks like I would with you, though I can't really tell in the dark. It's just over there."

I pulled my arm free and quickened my pace. I heard her call after me angrily: "Hell with you! Young guy like you and you can't get it up."

I wondered if it hadn't been my former landlady's son who'd suggested which girls to invite from which gateways this evening. Maybe he'd actually brought them over himself.

People started to gather. At the beginning the men's voices were distinct from the women's. I listened intently, but I couldn't tell if the women were young or not, especially because their voices were drowned out by the men's guffaws. Even when I heard laughter that clearly came from women, I still wasn't sure whether they were young or old. One time it seemed one way, the next moment the other. Amidst the laughing and shrieking there was something like a drunken alto, but one of them might just have had a sore throat.

After a while the landlord knocked on my door. Barely poking his head in, he said: "We're about to open the champagne. Can I tempt you?"

"No thank you. I need to study."

"I understand." And he disappeared.

"Make it pop! Make it pop!" cried a man's voice.

The bottle opened with a bang as if a shell had gone off nearby. There was a general roar of approval. A moment later the host knocked on my door again, bringing a glass of frothing champagne.

"This is from the ladies. With wishes for a productive evening's studying." He put the glass down on my desk. "I won't insist, but if you'd care to join us we'd be delighted. The ladies would like to meet you."

Right, I thought; it must be the ones from the gateways. All at once a deep male voice began singing a song, and everyone joined in:

Then let's drink wine, my lighthorsemen
In broken glasses forgetting our lot

No one will know once we are gone
If we were happy or if we were not

And again from the beginning: "Then let's drink wine. . ." Then once more: "Let's drink wine. . ."

I thought the song would never end. I put my hands over my ears, elbows propped on the desk, thinking that maybe in such a way I could make it through – though I liked that song, my father would sometimes sing it when my mother made a fancy dinner for his nameday or her own, and she'd ask him to sing the song, especially if some of their friends had been invited. She liked to show off my father's voice, which was in fact pretty good. After all, he'd sung and played the guitar before they were married, when he and three others traveled around and earned their living that way. It was because of his singing and playing that she'd fallen in love with him.

There was a crash, probably from a glass being thrown to the ground, and a woman's voice rang out almost hysterically: "I'm taking my clothes off! I'm taking my clothes off!"

"It's too soon, we've only just had the champagne," a man's voice objected, and, no doubt turning to the host: "Come on, go fetch what we all brought. The champagne was the end of the introductions."

"What are you talking about, introductions?" came an indignant female voice. "You know me perfectly well! I'll introduce myself to you once I've undressed, you nitwit."

"What are you getting all bent out of shape about? That's what people say at the beginning. I mean, there has to be an official part and an artistic part. Did you never go on a works vacation? Everyone knows everyone else, but they still called it the introductions."

The glasses on the tray rang much louder this time; there must have been many more people present than during the bridge game. The same voice greeted the host as he brought in the drinks: "Finally!"

Things got merrier and merrier, louder and louder. People were constantly going into the kitchen or to the lavatory, leaving the door of the main room open. I stuck my nose in my book, trying to read aloud to myself. But I was unable to concentrate. Even though the words were anchored in print like a ship attached to the ocean bed, still they swung and danced as if they were being rocked by a storm and might come unmoored at any moment.

I couldn't study, and I couldn't go to bed – I wouldn't have gotten a wink with all the racket. Should I leave? Except I didn't have anywhere to go. To the station? Not there. As for going to someone else's place, they were probably all asleep by now. It was late, nighttime in fact. In my helplessness I imagined going from gateway to gateway and inquiring if one of the ladies there had an apartment. I'd ask her to let me stay there. I'd pay for the whole night. I didn't want anything in return, just to get some sleep. With one of them I'm negotiating the price, when my landlord wanders into my room without knocking, opening the door wide. He's swaying, his gaze is cloudy. He leans his hands on my desk. He's in his dressing gown; the gray hairs on his chest poke out when he bends forward. I might not have looked at his feet, but he staggered and I pulled a chair up for him. He was in stockinged feet, his socks held up with suspenders fastened under the knee. My father used to wear his socks with suspenders like that before the war. He refused to buy elastic socks when they came in.

"You get lost if you change everything," he'd always say.

"But you'll be more comfortable," my mother would try to persuade him.

"I'll be more comfortable later on."

True, socks were made of pure cotton and they were of such poor quality that they'd fall down the moment you took a couple of steps. Some people dealt with it by rolling their socks down over their ankles, which also looked awful.

My landlord didn't sit down. He lurched back and forth over the desk and said, slurring his words: "I'm terribly sorry, but the ladies are asking if you might join us. We're going to be dancing, and we're a man short for a pair. A friend was supposed to come – he's an excellent dancer – but he's sick. There's a phonograph, you can play your choice of records. Anything you like. You don't like dancing? That can't be. We love to dance. One of our friends here lost a leg in the war. With the right partner, he'll even dance the – what's that one that's all the rage these days? Whatever it is, he puts his crutch aside and goes out on one leg. Come on, say yes. Oh, that's too bad. Everyone'll be disappointed."

With bated breath, head bowed over my book, I listened for the music and the dancing to start. I'd stopped trying to read, I was simply waiting. And no doubt from the wait, a kind of creeping fear took root in me, all the more because out there things had mysteriously gone quiet, as if they'd given up on dancing for lack of one male partner. That didn't reassure me. Quite the opposite. The quiet seemed ominous, auguring something that was in fact hard to foresee. And I began to want whatever it was to finally happen. When you expect the arrival of some misfortune that is delayed, it's often the case that you long for it to finally come. It turned out I was right to feel that way.

The landlord came to my room again. One of his hands was stretched out in front of him as if holding onto the air; in the other he bore a glass of vodka. A good third of the liquid had spilled on the way, for the glass was oscillating in his hand as if it were dancing: "We're just drinking your health. Do please join us in the toast."

At that moment, through the open door I heard a man shout: "Long live youth!" Then everyone chorused: "Long live youth!" I believe they even said it twice: "Long live youth! Long live youth!"

"Can you hear how they're all missing you?" There was nothing I could do. I downed the vodka. "Shall I bring you another?"

"No thank you."

"Just for a moment," he said with a hiccup, almost begging. "The ladies refuse to believe I have a young person living here. At our age we're nostalgic for youth. You will be too one day. Youth is like a sun that's come out from behind the clouds and in a moment will hide itself once again. 'O moment, stay,' as the poet said. Life begrudged us that moment. We were young, but we had to be old at once. The war took our youth away. We didn't even know what it meant to be young. Then immediately after the war, life didn't go our way either. You'd understand if you'd been with us... What can I do to persuade you? You could have something to eat, taste some caviar. We still have another bottle of champagne. We put it aside specially – "

He was interrupted by the voice of a woman who sounded like she'd had too much to drink and too many cigarettes: "Tell him I'll come see him! I don't mind paying! He can have half my pension!"

"Ha ha ha!" There was general loud laughter. People applauded.

"I'm sorry," he said as if embarrassed. He left my room virtually on tiptoe, closing the door softly behind him, though he must have leaned heavily on it, for it creaked. "I'm sorry. I'll oil the hinge tomorrow."

I thought I recognized the voice that had smoked and drunk too much, and had offered me half her pension. One of the women waiting in the gateways had called out to me in just such a voice as I was walking home one evening close to midnight: "Hey kid! Wait up! You won't regret it!"

I wondered if it was the same person. But could she be retired already? It hadn't been long since that evening. Could time really be that relative? Or was everything simply getting muddled up in my head? Do you get a pension from waiting in gateways? As if to complicate my thoughts further, a girlish, larklike woman's voice sounded: "We should sing! We should sing!"

There followed a song that I knew well, and was my favorite among the songs my father sang:

Life goes by so quickly
Time flows swiftly past
A year, a day, a second
We'll all be gone so fast
Our youthful years will vanish
If not today, tomorrow
And then our hearts will carry
Mere ruefulness and sorrow

I'd been a child back then, but the image of my father singing the song had made such a deep impression on me that I began unconsciously humming along with them. I hadn't inherited my father's voice and I didn't like to sing, because whenever I did my mother would say, you're off key. On account of my father I was angry at them for singing so chaotically, as though each person were singing separately, and so there wasn't room for all of them in the same words, not to mention that the melody suffered too, as if the notes were bumping into one another. Some of them were singing out of tune. Of course, it could have been me who was out of tune, because you never hear your own voice as being off key. I stopped thinking about my father when they sang the song once more. They reached the end and began again. More and more hoarsely, but once again. Some had quieted down to a whisper, but then they started up again. Some voices finally fell silent; only three or four were left, and you'd have thought that in a moment the singing would fade and die, but someone with a deep voice struck up another song that began: "Hey! Hey!" It had the rhythm of a march and it livened everyone up. It burst out in defiance of the other, dying song, you might have thought, as if tearing itself from its embrace at the very last minute.

The walls shook from the "Hey! Hey!" The panes rattled in the windows, the lamp on my desk rocked. You'd think a column of soldiers in hobnailed boots were tramping along the pavement past the window to the beat of "Hey! Hey!" Why soldiers? Well, who else could be singing "Hey! Hey!" other than soldiers on their way to death? Someone started banging on the ceiling, so rapidly it was like shrapnel exploding on a tin roof.

I couldn't feel my own heart beating, I couldn't feel my breathing. The front doorbell rang, once, twice, three times, longer and longer. Then what sounded like several fists began hammering on the door. But "Hey! Hey!" was not to be overcome. Out in the hallway it was no longer just the jangling of the doorbell. The door itself began to groan under the pressure of bodies. It sounded like the handle was about to be pulled off; people were shouting, cursing, kicking at the door, which itself had done them no harm. Yet the song went on.

My numbness suddenly turned into rage. I ran out of my room and into the heart of the song, which broke off in an instant. I found myself in darkness: the lights were out. Someone closed the door behind me, yanking the handle from my hand, and the darkness intensified.

"Oooh!" came from every throat, though I couldn't have said whether it was an exclamation or a sigh. I started shouting in a breathless voice, as if I'd run to them from far away to let them know that someone was banging on the ceiling and hammering at the door. Then all at once I stopped being certain that someone really was knocking on the ceiling, ringing the doorbell and thumping on the door; perhaps I'd just imagined it, because it all seemed like a dream. The darkness, and them, and the song. Could I have fallen asleep over my book amid the hubbub? How was that possible? Sleep needs quiet, otherwise you can't cut yourself off from the waking world. Yet uncle used to say that he slept best when the enemy artillery was pounding the trenches, because then they knew they wouldn't be sent on a bayonet attack. Were they not falling asleep in preparation for death, though? Thinking that if they were going to die, let it at least be while they slept?

The larklike voice I'd heard from my desk exclaimed: "Let's put him inside the circle!"

To which another voice, also a woman's, which I'd not heard before, said: "Inside the circle! Yes!"

"Maybe champagne first?" I recognized the landlord's voice.

"No! No! Into the circle!" came all the other voices.

And the circle began to turn around me. A wave of sweaty heat blew over me, stifling me; I could feel that I too was perspiring. Sweat dripped from my forehead and nose, trickled down my chest and back. My shirt stuck to my body, my head was reeling and I couldn't tell any longer if the circle was moving around me or if I was rotating on my own axis. Even the thud from the legless man's crutch had stopped; the shuffling of feet grew louder and louder as the heat intensified.

"Old mister bear," one of the women chanted. The others took it up: "Old mister bear is sound asleep! Don't go near him, since we fear him." And once more, from the start, all over again: "Old mister bear...! Old mister bear...!"

It felt as if a centrifugal force was spinning me ever faster, that any moment now it would lift me up off the floor and I'd fly into oblivion. Then the woman's voice rang out again: "Turn the light on! Turn it on!"

The crutch thumped and there was a sudden blinding brightness in which for a moment I was unable to see anything at all. Gradually the glare thinned like rising mist. From it there emerged old naked bodies, drooping bellies, sparse gray pubic hair, sagging breasts, wrinkled thighs, swollen ankles, crooked feet. Perhaps as a consequence of the light, which was still dazzling me, I found it hard to tell the men from the women, as if old age had only one gender, neither the one nor the other. No one would have believed that those bodies had once conceived and given birth, and burned with passion. What was left for them? Champagne and caviar? What kind of shield is champagne and caviar in the face of death?

"That's not worth half a month's pension," came the same voice, but sneering now.

"Never mind your pension." The one-legged man came to my defense, anchoring his crutch to the floor. He turned to another woman. "Don't forget you used to be the best dancer at the plant. Dance with him."

A pair of hot, damp arms enfolded me.

"It's me," came an almost silky whisper.

"What record shall I put on?"

"Nothing. For us it's enough to hold each other."

She wrapped her body around me like an octopus. She was so hot she started to burn me, and my breathing faltered, becoming ever shorter and shallower. Where did such lust come from in old age? Evidently everything I'd known till then about the old was a drop in the ocean.

"I'll lead if you don't know how to dance. But don't be afraid of me. Imagine that I'm young. Is that so hard? Youth never goes away. It's our bodies that go away."

I could feel that old naked body fusing with me. And all at once a thought came to me: I'd never be old, I wouldn't let it happen. I'd kill my old age. And I started to turn faster and ever faster, till at one point she cried out in consternation: "What are you doing? This is madness, not dancing!" She tried to hold me back. But her arms weren't strong enough for the centrifugal force building in me, which tore me from her and threw me against the opposite wall. I struck my head against it and passed out.

Chapter 8

§

I found accommodations by chance.

I'd gone to the university clinic to make an appointment, for I'd been troubled for some time by a cough. As she wrote my name down in the book, the nurse – a young, decent looking girl – asked: "I don't suppose you know anyone who's looking for a room? The Housing Authority put people into more than half the rooms in our home, and we're afraid they'll send us even more."

"They don't assign accommodations like that anymore," I said.

"I know. But can you trust them? Today they've stopped, tomorrow they might start again. We have one room with a private entrance. We wouldn't even charge rent, maybe just for electricity, if we can only find an honest person. They'd need to take the train into town, but it's a good connection. I come in myself every day and I don't complain. Besides, lots of people take the train."

Despite her assurances, there were things to complain about. The railroad hadn't yet been electrified and there was only a single set of tracks, so the trains often ran an hour or more late, especially in winter.

Or when they pulled in they were so full – especially when an earlier one had been canceled – that it was hard to squeeze in, most of all in the morning when people were on their way to work, and in the late afternoon when they were going home. It was just as crowded in the last train of the day, in the evening. The railway workers were reluctant to update you, or they pretended not to know. They mostly just brushed people off, telling them a locomotive had broken down and was blocking the track till they could uncouple it and hitch up a new one. A train running late like that would get more and more delayed, since it had to wait at each station and let through the other trains so they could keep to their timetables.

Going to the theater or a concert, then, always brought with it the risk of missing the last train, which left ten or fifteen minutes after the show. Plus, you had to take a tram or bus to the station, and they didn't always run on time either. If I wanted to be sure, I'd have to leave the theater or the concert hall early, so I'd be checking my watch impatiently to see if I shouldn't be heading out already, or if I could watch or listen for a few minutes longer.

One time I didn't make it. I don't remember if it was a concert or a play that had me so engrossed. When I arrived at the station the last train had left. There was a freight train on one of the farther platforms. A railway worker was tapping the wheels, which meant it was about to set off. I asked him and he confirmed it was leaving, but it was a military transport.

I walked along the cars. All of them were sealed shut; there were no steps, ledges, or handrails. It wouldn't even have been possible to ride on the buffers, for there wasn't anything to hold onto. You'd have ended up under the car if the train stopped abruptly or took a curve too sharply. It occurred to me to ask if I could ride in the locomotive. The fireman was stoking the engine, while the engineer stood leaning out and talking to someone on the platform. I asked the fireman; he cussed and said: "Want a shovel over the head?"

So I went down to the back of the train. In the second to last car was the guard's cabin. A soldier was inside. The door was open and he was smoking. I didn't want to ask him for permission, because I already knew he'd refuse. The train set off, the soldier closed the door, and I grabbed the handrail and hopped onto the lowest step. The soldier opened the door and tried to push me off, jabbing at me with the barrel of his rifle.

"What're you doing? This is a military transport!"

I held on with both hands and wouldn't let myself be dislodged. As the train gathered speed, he gave up and drew back his gun, though he kept the barrel pointing at me.

"By regulation I could shoot you. But be my guest. Thing is, pal, how are you gonna get off? We're not stopping anywhere."

"I'll jump."

"Do you know how to do it properly? Jump in the same direction as the train, so you don't get dragged under the wheels. Where are you going?"

I named the station.

"I'd look at the map, but it's dark. How far is it?"

"Eighteen miles or so."

"That won't take long. But don't jump onto the platform. Wait till after the station, when there'll be an embankment. Turn around for now or you might get a spark in your eye. I'll tell you when you have to jump, you can face forward again then. I got a spark like that once, nearly lost my eye. Actually I sometimes regret it. I'd have been sent home. Now! Jump!"

"Long live our country, soldier!" I shouted in farewell, and I rolled down the embankment.

Years later – I'll already be walking with a cane, going down the steps one by one toward the old wild green valley that no longer exists – as I gaze at myself through my former youthful eyes, I'll doubt whether I have the right to say that it was me who jumped from a speeding train and didn't break a leg or an arm. I only lost two buttons off my jacket, and of course got wet from the fog-dampened earth.

The room was in a villa that stood at the edge of a wood. It was more of a summer home, with thin wooden walls; there was formwork on the outside, it's true, but the plaster was crumbling here and there. The place looked pretty old; at one time it must have been an impressive building, but now it was rundown, begging to be restored to its former splendor. On the south side the windows were large and sunny. On the second floor on that side there was a large balcony with a view, though I'd have been scared to go out onto it for it was coming loose. I never saw it being used by the tenants who lived in the two rooms up there. Just as well, because it could have collapsed under someone's weight. The former state of the balcony could be seen from the cast-iron balustrade richly decorated with stars and winding flowers.

I don't know what the upstairs rooms looked like. They were more of an attic, since there was no loft above them. The roof was steep and there were only small compartments adjoining the living quarters and serving as storage space. The tenants seemed decent, quiet people. A husband and wife with two small girls who were polite and well-behaved; in fact they were always being told by their mother not to make noise, not to clatter up and down the stairs.

The husband looked to be about ten years older than his wife. He left for work at dawn, or when it was still dark in fall and winter. He carried a well-worn briefcase which couldn't have contained more than a few papers; he came back in the late afternoon, which in fall and winter was almost nighttime, his briefcase always full of shopping. Sometimes the wife would take the girls down to the station to meet him, and then she would carry the briefcase home. Aside from his comings and goings to work I never saw him go anywhere, even on a Sunday. In the evening you could hear him strumming away at his mandolin and singing snatches of songs, sometimes together with his wife. I don't know who he was or where he worked. I didn't spend all my time at the villa either – I would leave like him in the morning and often come back late – so I didn't see everything.

The room I occupied could be entered from the outside, on the side of the villa, via a large walled veranda that was cluttered with junk: packages tied with string, broken chairs, baskets, and various unidentifiable objects. The top half of the veranda walls consisted of small square glass panes of various colors – yellow, red, green, blue – some of which were smashed. When the sun shone on the veranda, it was like a stained-glass window in a church. When it rained, though, or snowed in winter, everything on the veranda became damp.

My room too was cluttered. Almost half the area was taken up by a grand piano, which I was told used to be in the room next door that was now occupied by a couple with a baby not quite one year old who'd been born there; for them it would have been useful to have my room too, especially since the two rooms shared a connecting door. That door was blocked by a large wardrobe, which didn't entirely prevent sound from passing through. Behind the piano, against the wall there was a cabinet with glass doors that was filled with books. They were mostly romance novels, though there was also a handful of works by famous writers, including some of the greats, as well as a few books of philosophy: Plato, Aristotle, Spinoza, Hume, Kant, Nietzsche; and two volumes on occultism that I'd never heard of. From the contents of the cabinet alone I wouldn't have been able to say who the owners of the villa were.

There were three of them: a grandmother, her daughter and grand-daughter. The grandmother – Babcia – spent most of her time in bed. Her daughter was about fifty and still uncommonly good-looking. The granddaughter was the nurse. The three of them lived together in the biggest room, from which a large double French window led out into the garden. The kitchen, also large, was theirs too. The kitchen could be accessed from the yard through a small porch. My room was linked to theirs by another door. The door didn't close properly, so I heard many of their conversations, squabbles, sometimes full-blown arguments.

The space in my room was further encumbered by a huge armchair

that had seen better days. Above all it blocked the way from the veranda to the narrow bed where I slept. There was no way to either skirt
around it or move it aside; it was jammed between the piano and the
wardrobe blocking the door to the room occupied by the family with
the baby. The landlady, which is to say the nurse's mother, explained
to me that they'd had to move the furniture from the other room into
mine; previously both the piano and the armchair had been in there.
She told me I could access my room through their kitchen and their
room, since my bed was by the connecting door. But I'd have been
embarrassed to do so.

One time I did in fact go through the kitchen. The landlady was
washing her hair in a basin, naked to the waist. "Excuse me," I said.
I wanted to back out.

From under her soapy hair she said: "Could you pour some hot
water over my hair from that big pot on the stove?"

There was a bathroom, of course, but it only had cold water. If you
wanted hot water, you had to heat several pots of it in the kitchen,
carry it through to the bathroom, and pour it into the tub. It seems
they used to have a maid and then there was no problem, she heated
the water, carried it through and filled the bathtub. As for me, it made
no difference to me whether the water was cold or hot, so I washed in
the bathroom and sometimes took a bath there too.

After that incident, I preferred to clamber past the armchair to get
to my bed. The armchair was too heavy to lift out of the way. I came
up with another method. When my shoes were dry I'd hop over it by
placing a foot on the seat. If my shoes were wet or muddy I'd sit on one

side, twist my body and legs upwards, swing them across and land on the floor. Such was the journey to my bed. But I was young, my body was supple, and it was even fun to do.

The bed was the most dilapidated piece of furniture in the room. Truth be told, it wasn't adequate for sleeping on. Some of the springs were broken, and in the middle there was a dip; it was hard even to get settled, let alone actually sleep, in a hollow like that. I often woke up stiff as a board. What was worse, when I moved, under the weight of my body the springs poked through the mattress and jabbed me, often painfully. For the first few nights I got little sleep, remembering almost with nostalgia the time during my studies when I'd slept three to a bed. I determined to do something about it. I bought a bunch of newspapers, scrunched them up and filled the hollow with them. Then I got a few cardboard boxes from the grocery store and laid them over the newspaper. The first night after putting down the newspaper and the cardboard, I slept so soundly I didn't wake till around midday.

Aside from Babcia, the landlady, and her daughter, there was also a dog: a fine German shepherd called Mieszko, after the first king of Poland. He became my first friend at the villa. When I spent the day at home he'd sometimes come see me. He'd open the connecting door himself with a paw – it didn't close properly, so all he needed to do was push on it – then hop onto the armchair and sit there till Babcia called him. It might have been on account of him that I came to like Babcia. It's odd, because I couldn't stand old people. But Babcia took a shine to me too, and she'd often send the dog to bring me to her. Confined to bed like that, and in bad health, it was hard to guess how old she might be. Despite her age and her infirmity, though, you could see she'd once been beautiful. There were no wrinkles around her mouth, her eyes were still big and hadn't faded or shrunk into her skull; her features remained regular, with a slim nose. It must have been from her that the daughter had inherited her good looks, though they didn't look particularly alike in my view. I found the granddaughter nurse the least attractive. She was striking, but there was something unpleasant about her. Especially her eyes – they were handsome, yet seemed to look upon the world with disdain. She was often malicious, and clearly relished it. Her mother would sometimes bring flowers home that someone at work had given her, and she'd say: "Look what lovely flowers I got today."

The granddaughter would shrug indifferently, dampening her mother's joy: "What's lovely about them? They're just ordinary roses, ordinary gerberas, some other ordinary thing. He only bought you five? Cheapskate."

I sometimes tried to picture Babcia at her granddaughter's age. But my imagination wasn't up to the task. It shouldn't have been such a difficult task, but this particular old age simply rejected this particular youth, protected itself against it, as if the granddaughter's youth rendered Babcia's former youth invalid.

I didn't go to the university every day. Actually, I think I stayed home more often than not as I worked on my dissertation. When the daughter and granddaughter weren't there, Babcia would call to me from her room: "Come through, young man." Her voice was still clear, though she was a little hard of hearing.

"You need something, ma'am?"

"Bring a chair and sit down. Let me take a look at you. Give me your hand, young man." She took my hand in hers. "You have youthful hands. Smooth. Mine are dry and rustly." She would stare into my face, sometimes asking me to move closer. Then, when her gaze grew tired, she'd say in a weary voice: "Go now. I need to rest." And she'd turn her face to the wall.

One time she called me to her like that, then when I sat down beside her she looked at me with tears in her eyes.

"Why are you crying, ma'am?"

"What's left for me? No one even listens to me properly." Eyes averted, she stared ahead and sighed as if she had a lump in her throat. "Oh, how I loved, once. It's only now that I feel it. At the time I wasn't sure. And in love you pay for such uncertainty with your whole life. Only now, when it's too late."

"Who did you love like that?"

She looked at me with a gaze that was strangely penetrating for her old eyes.

"Maybe you."

I laughed. "Not me, ma'am. That isn't possible."

"You," she insisted. From the effort it took to utter that one single word, beads of perspiration appeared on her forehead. She virtually drove me away: "Go now. Leave me."

Afterwards I regretted not having accepted that I'd been the one she'd once loved. If I'd listened patiently to her confidences, perhaps I would have learned something about her life. Other people's lives can be useful to us. Who knows, maybe more than our own. Our own lives don't hold together when we try to gather them up, unless we find some fixed point from which we can watch them turning around us as if around an axis – see them flowing, getting ahead of us, retreating from us, leading us astray, speeding up or slowing down along with the planet.

I didn't think Babcia would call me in any more. But one day I heard her again: "Come through! Do you hear?"

Alas, when I moved the chair up to her bed the silence was suddenly broken by the sound of an accordion; after a few bars a hoarse sort of singing began. It was the man who lived with his wife and newborn child behind the door that was blocked on my side by the wardrobe. He was beginning a new accordion lesson. The thin walls of the villa, and the door that wouldn't close between my room and the room where Babcia was, let noise through like a sieve. Whenever somebody dropped something on the floor or a radio was turned up, not to mention arguments – it could all be heard throughout the house. When the accordion and the singing started up, even Babcia heard it.

"There he goes again," she said indignantly. "Why did God punish us with a tenant like that. I wanted to say something I forgot earlier on. Perhaps another time. Just remind me that I was going to tell you."

The accordion player's wife, quiet as a church mouse and always timid, would excuse her husband, explaining that he was learning to play so he could work at parties and weddings. The singing would come in useful too. They'd promised he could join the band, because they needed an accordion – he just needed to sharpen his skills a bit. He could earn a few zlotys, because the welfare office wouldn't give him any more. They said there was plenty of work, he should find a job. He'd always loved music, he sang in the children's choir when he was an altar boy. She sang too, that was how they'd met. She was a cleaner; she'd stopped work while the baby was breastfeeding, then afterwards she'd put it in daycare.

Even though the Housing Authority had imposed the tenants on them, from time to time the landlady would take them something to eat. She'd buy bread for them, or margarine, make extra soup and bring it over. The woman from upstairs, in turn, passed on diapers, onesies and other baby clothing left over from her daughters; she gave them a baby carriage, toys, and from time to time something to eat also. The husband had been a policeman; it seems he'd lost his job because of his drinking, though the wife denied it: she said a moonshiner had denounced him, claiming the husband had accepted a bribe. What was the bribe? The accordion. The moonshiner's son used to play it, but he died of consumption, so it was lying idle.

That may or may not have been true, but there was no denying the fact that he sometimes came home drunk, and then he'd make a scene, calling his poor shrinking wife every name under the sun, claiming she'd ruined his life, because some wealthy young lady had been in love with him, he would have been in clover, while now he had to slave away. Or he would have gone to music school, or hired a teacher. But he'd married a penniless wife with a single ragged dress to her name, and he'd had to join the police and go chasing criminals. He should have been in tails and top hat and patent leather shoes, and here he had to put on a uniform.

In fact, you couldn't tell exactly what went on; not everything could be heard through the walls and the door. I never heard her crying or calling for help. Nor did I ever see bruising on her face. She never complained about him, and always took his side even after the biggest row, saying that somebody had made him mad and he'd come home upset.

One day, he started in like that and all at once she rushed out of the house and set off running. He staggered drunkenly after her.

"I'll shoot you down! I'll shoot you down! Let this end once and for all!" He made a gun with his fingers and pretended to fire: "Bang! Bang! Bang! Fall down when you're shot, I tell you!" They ran around the yard, her trying to get away, him in pursuit. "Bang! Bang! Bang!" In the end he tripped over a tree root – there were several pines growing around the villa – and crashed to the ground.

She kneeled over him and begged: "Get up. Come on, get up. Stop embarrassing me. Let's get you into bed."

He had no intention of going to bed, though. He lay there without moving. She stroked his face and ruffled his hair tenderly, but it did no good. I had come out of the house, alarmed by the shouting and the shots. When I saw them chasing around like that, though, I decided not to intervene, because you never know: if I'd stopped him, she might just have told me to let him go, while if I'd protected her he would have lain on the ground anyway. She tried to lift him up but it was beyond her. He wasn't big, he seemed a weakling next to his tall and full-bodied wife. But an inert body, especially if it's lying down, is a lot heavier than you'd think. I lifted Babcia's body when she died, to move her to another bed – in other words, from the height of her bed, not from the ground – and I needed all my strength, planting my feet on the floor so she didn't get the better of me. Though perhaps it's even harder with the dead.

"Hey there, come help me!" she called. "He's small but he's heavy!"

I picked him up by the torso, passing my hands under his arms; she took his legs; and we carried his limp body into the house and put him on the bed. She was about to cover him with a blanket when he opened his eyes and sat up. He looked at her, looked at me, and said: "I'm heavy, aren't I?"

After that incident he seemed to change. He became quiet and submissive, stopped talking so much, stopped playing and singing; whenever he ran into me he'd thank me for helping his wife, shake my hand and salute me. He was no longer in the police but he wore a police cap with no markings or band, and he'd salute people when he said hello, even the little girls who lived upstairs. The most noticeable difference, though, was the fact that he started taking the baby on walks in the carriage. He became affectionate with his child, whereas previously he'd often shouted at it, saying he'd tear it apart if it didn't quit crying. It was as if he'd only now understood what it was to be a father. He stopped every passer-by whether he knew them or not – though as a police officer he knew everyone – and told them to look in the carriage and see what a lovely baby he had. He pulled the little blanket up when the weather turned cold, turned it back when the sun came out, leaned over the carriage and whispered blissfully to the child. He usually took a long time on those walks, to the point that his wife would go looking for him anxiously, asking people if they hadn't seen him, because he'd go wandering around the woods and the fields, losing track of time. He had no watch: he'd supposedly sold it to buy vodka.

Then one day he rebelled against himself. It started with the world being a piece of crap. I was home at the time. The fact that the world was like that was her fault. Then he began railing at his superior officers in the police, naming each one: "Lieutenant this! Captain that! He was no captain, he was a son of a bitch! And you danced with him on New Year's, you whore! I bet you screwed him! Kneel down here! Swear it!"

She knelt and swore as if she were the vessel of all the sins of this world. She never denied anything; it wouldn't have done any good, it would only have made him even madder. His rage always rose in an ascending line, then it fell off, often ending in tears. But God forbid she should try to comfort him at that moment, for he'd explode once again, more fiercely still. So she'd take the accordion, place it against his chest and slip his arms through the straps.

"Play a little, play, my darling."

One time he refused to let himself be subdued in this way. He'd already begun to play, but he suddenly roared: "I'm going to sell it! Sell it! The hell with music!" And he dashed outside with the accordion. She ran out after him, leaving the child wailing to high heaven, but she saved the accordion. The next day he was playing and singing again, which was a lot easier to bear than those scenes. From the things she said that I overheard from time to time, you could guess that his playing and singing gave her strength to live.

"When you're calm you play better and better. Couldn't we just live like that? It warms my heart to hear you play and sing. We'll be fine, don't worry. After I've weaned the little one and we can use the daycare, I'll go back to cleaning."

I felt sorry for them, and I hated them at the same time. But when he played and sang, my writing went well. Maybe I'd grown accustomed to it. I'd bought a molding board – the kind you knead bread on – and I'd sit on the bed, rest the molding board on my lap and write.

I left the villa before I finished my dissertation. And it may seem strange, but I missed the playing and singing. The part of the dissertation written elsewhere seemed less profound. My advisor confirmed it when I brought him the typed-up manuscript.

"The second part needs more work. It feels like it was written by someone else. The first part is richer, more probing, you draw bold conclusions. The second half is superficial, there's nothing revelatory in it. It's as if you were in a hurry to finish."

Could that inept playing and singing have forced me to greater intellectual effort? Could it be that, experiencing the difficult, tangled, often tragic daily reality of the residents of the villa, I'd had a deeper feeling for the harshness of life in a period as distant as those Middle Ages of mine? I had absurd ideas about hiring an accordionist to come play and sing for me. There were musicians on the street. Perhaps it wasn't just the playing and singing, though. Every day I imbibed those incidents, often seemingly insignificant ones, that memory ought not to have retained, that the organism almost automatically rejected, and that shouldn't have had any effect on what I was writing. Yet we soak everything up like a sponge, independently of our will or our preference. How could I have been influenced, for instance, by the husband's habit of wearing a police cap and saluting everyone? And yet I didn't find it at all funny, I even felt sorry for him when they wrote to say he had to return the cap. He stopped wanting to play and sing, he made another scene with his wife. He only calmed down when she went to the police station and asked them to let him keep it. They agreed on condition that he remove the peak.

Several years after I lived there, one day I ran into the granddaughter who was a nurse; we got to talking, and she told me that the accordion player had left home a few months before and never come back. They'd looked for him everywhere, but all they found was the peakless police cap. Now the wife played the accordion; she'd learned quickly, and actually played better than the husband had. Sometimes she'd sing too. She had a lovely voice, and her songs were beautiful. She wrote the music and words herself. Can you imagine?

I would have gone on living there, but they ended the arrangement. I offered to pay rent, but they said no. The mother might have agreed, she said she'd think about it, but her daughter, the nurse, told me firmly to look for other accommodation. For some time, in fact, she'd been behaving rudely toward me, which should have made me think, because before that she often invited me out for a walk in the evening, down lanes and wooded paths where there were no more houses. She took my arm, opened up to me, complained about her mother and her grandmother. She said her mother had a lover, while her grandmother had dementia. Plus, whoever heard of anyone living that long? When she'd taken to her bed the other two women had thought she'd soon be gone; a doctor they knew had promised them as much when they had him visit and take a look at Babcia. A month, two at most. Old people are sometimes healthy enough to go on living and living. So she'd have gladly left that house; it wasn't a place for normal people, a place that felt like home. Even sleeping with three people in one room was a strain. If it wasn't for the pills, she wouldn't have gotten a single night's sleep. Her only hope was that she'd marry and be taken away from there. But somehow she couldn't find the right candidate. She had someone, she liked him, but he was married and he wasn't prepared to leave his wife.

"How do you put up with it all?" she would ask me. "He must be wearing you out with that playing and singing. It wouldn't be so bad if he actually succeeded once in a while. He never will, because he's useless. What band would want him? There's no band. They're all just drinking buddies, they get drunk and talk about forming a band. Plus, on top of everything else there's the brat. How do you do it?"

Was she maybe hoping something would come from those walks of ours? And I disappointed her? I didn't see that to begin with. We hadn't been on a walk for a long time, then one evening I took the initiative and asked her if she'd like to go for a stroll. She said no, she didn't have the time. A few days later she refused again. I thought something had upset her, maybe she'd had a setback at work. She was unpredictable like that. Sometimes she'd be in a good mood, laughing and joking, the whole world could have cozied up to her, then all at once she'd become enraged if her mother asked her to brush her grandmother's hair: "Why can't you do it? She's your mother, not mine!" And there'd be an argument that was supposedly about her grandmother, but really was about everything, about life you might say, as is usually the case in such family disputes.

I learned a thing or two from those rows. For instance who the landlady's husband – the nurse's father – had been. He'd died at a young age of TB. His doctor had sent him to the mountains for treatment. The husband had wanted his wife to go with him, but she wouldn't, saying their daughter wasn't old enough for the journey. So he went alone, but someone told him his wife was living with a lover, and had left the baby in the care of the grandmother. He broke off his treatment and refused to resume it. He was a highly regarded architect with a successful career. He'd been the one who designed the summer villa where we were living.

Another time, they were just going to bed when they started quarreling. I didn't hear what had triggered it. The exchange grew fiercer with every word uttered on one side or the other; they cut each other with their words, injured one another, till in the end the mother slammed the door and ran outside. The daughter, her fury unabated, pushed open the door to my room without knocking.

"Go see where that crazy woman's gone."

It was pitch black outside; there was no moon, the stars were hidden by clouds. I went back into the house for a candle, lit it, and wandered among the pine trees. Step by step I circled the whole yard. All at once I tripped on a root; the candle fell from my hand and went out. I squatted down, felt on the ground and found it, but so what, since I had no matches with me. Besides, I couldn't see much more with the candle than without it – it shone in my eyes more than lighting the darkness. I went back into the house.

"Can you go out one more time?" the daughter said, all the time in a rage. "The last time she was on the ground on the other side of the fence."

And indeed she was lying just beyond the gate, by a lilac bush that had just bloomed, so its scent was overpowering. She was naked; she must have run out of the house before putting her nightgown on. Her daughter's words had clearly wounded her deeply; if she'd been standing on a riverbank or a cliff, she'd have jumped. Whereas at home, as she'd been getting ready for bed, she'd merely dropped her nightgown. I carried her unclothed and almost lifeless body into the house and laid her on the bed. The nightgown was right there on the floor. She didn't open her eyes. She was trembling all over.

"She's crazy, right?" The daughter was still beside herself. "You can't say the least thing to her. She gets all bent out of shape then she rushes off. How am I supposed to live here?"

The next day she got up and went off to work as if nothing had happened. I didn't know how to behave; I was embarrassed at having seen the mother naked. For a few days I headed out earlier than them, went to the university, and came back late. After that I'd wait till they left in the morning before I went to wash. If I came back earlier and they were already home, I didn't even go and make myself tea. Nakedness requires the understanding of someone's eyes. I had actually carried her naked in my arms, and that must have distressed her, since it was too much even for me to deal with; how could I look her in the eyes. Because carrying nakedness in your arms isn't the same as seeing it. You can virtually feel the blood flowing from one body into the other.

One day I came home late. They were already asleep, or at least the windows were dark. I decided to work a little to take advantage of the quiet. I sat on the bed, laid the molding board on my lap, then there was a soft knock at my door. I said: "Come in."

She was in her nightgown. She was carrying a glass of tea on a saucer.

"I saw through the crack in the door that you were still up, so I brought you some hot tea."

I sometimes made tea for myself when I worked later than usual at night. I'd tiptoe through their darkened room in my stockinged feet, certain that they were all asleep. And it sometimes happened that on the way to the kitchen I'd be stopped by a whisper from her: "I'll make you some tea."

She'd bring the tea through; she always had only her nightgown on. I found it natural: she wasn't going to get dressed in the night just to make tea. Her goodwill, for which I was grateful, took my mind off the fact that her nakedness showed through the nightgown. I was surprised how often she showed me such kindness. Perhaps she'd wanted a son and I was a sort of embodiment of him, since she lived in constant conflict with her daughter?

In the winter, even when it was bitterly cold I didn't light the masonry stove. I never felt the cold. I didn't wear gloves or earmuffs. Taking the streetcar from the station to the university, I'd perch on the steps with the other passengers, holding on to the handrail, because there wasn't room inside, yet neither my hands nor my ears would get cold. I slept under a thick puffy comforter that my mother had sent me; I'd pull it over my head, leaving only a little gap to breathe through.

She didn't just bring me tea. She offered a hot water bottle to keep my feet warm. One time I came home in the evening and it was like a sauna in my room; the stove was so hot you couldn't touch it. I went to thank her, and she said she couldn't bear to think of my coming in from the frost to such a cold room.

"I'll bring you some hot tea as well."

The problem was that the heat sapped my strength. I put the molding board on my lap, but I couldn't get down to work. I don't know whether I dozed off, or whether it was in a waking dream that I saw Babcia climbing the steps from the old wild green valley.

"It's just as well you're here," she said, "because otherwise I wouldn't make it to the top. There are too many steps for me. But wait a little, maybe I'll make it if I go slowly." It was as if the steps wouldn't move by beneath her feet. She put a hand on her chest. "See, I'm short of breath, my heart's pounding. Perhaps it's not the same heart that once loved you. Luckily it's still beating a little. It's still coming to you. Wait, so I won't have climbed up here in vain. Climbing up for nothing? A whole life, and for nothing?"

She was climbing and climbing, she still couldn't reach me. How many steps are there, I wondered. I'd never counted them. A pity. They seemed longer. Could it be that a new step was added with each passing year? Do steps grow like trees?

"Are you finding it hard to climb up too?" she asked, pausing on another step.

"For me steps like this are nothing, Babcia. I take them two and three at a time."

All at once she seemed to grow dizzy. She managed to take hold of the handrail.

"Two and three at a time, you say. Two and three at a time. When was that? I doubt you remember that we were the same age. You might have been a year older than me."

She didn't have many steps to go to reach me, but whenever she lifted her foot it wouldn't reach the next step. It was as if the step was retreating upwards away from her. She tried with her left foot and then the right, the same thing happened.

"I don't think I'll make it," she said. "I regret not having taking the way through town. I was even going to buy myself some press studs for my blouse. I remember I had a blouse with a wildflower pattern. I don't know if you'd like it if you saw it on me. People should remember blouses, not just wars; it would make life easier to live."

When she finally clambered up onto the next step, she said joyfully: "I managed. One step closer. Except I don't know if it's toward you. I need to get there so I can check whether it wasn't you who died back then."

She needed to find a little more strength within.

"I don't think I can go any further, though. I need to sit for a moment." She sat down, very close to me now. "I didn't think they went up so far. You've evidently lived too long."

"It's too bad you didn't come when we were young, Babcia. I waited here for you. Many times."

At that she jumped up almost jauntily from the step, and for a split second I saw her when she was young, in the blouse with the wildflower pattern.

"Stretch out your hand, I'll catch you."

I reached out, but my hand hung in the void.

How I ended up in her life I've no idea. It's been years since she died and I still don't understand. The villa's no longer there; they built a three-story apartment building on the site. The daughter and the mother died too, in that order in fact, yet I feel I'm living there still, on that sagging bed lined with newspaper and cardboard, and from behind the door hidden by the wardrobe I hear quarreling, or the sounds of the accordion and a song being sung in a hoarse voice. Every now and then, from the next room, through the adjoining door that doesn't close properly Babcia calls to me: "Come through."

I didn't live there long – less than three years. I might have stayed on, but one day after Babcia died they had another argument. At a certain point the daughter burst out: "Tell him he has to go. I'm going to move into that room, I'll lock the door and I won't have anything to do with you!"

"Tell him yourself."

From that moment, almost every day I was expecting to hear it from one of them. Yet the days went by; the mother brought me tea from time to time, the daughter asked how my dissertation was going and when I'd be done. Maybe they couldn't summon up the courage, or they were reluctant to part from me since I'd be taking away a small part of each of their lives. At times they were unpleasant and ill-humored, yet the state of suspension continued.

Out of the blue, Mieszko entered the picture. When I stayed home and they went to work, it was my responsibility to feed him and let him out to do his business. He'd come back of his own accord, I didn't need to go fetch him. He'd scratch on the French door that opened onto the yard; sometimes he'd whine if he thought I was taking too long to let him in, because it took a moment to lift the molding board with my dissertation from my lap and get up from the bed. Sometimes he'd come straight into my room, hop onto the armchair, curl up and watch as I put the molding board back in my lap and resumed my work. I couldn't help feeling that he'd have liked to ask me: "How far is it to those Middle Ages?"

But when he heard playing and singing from behind the wardrobe, he'd jump out of the armchair, pull the door open with his paw, go into Babcia's room and lie down by her bed, as if waiting for her to call me in: "Come through."

We don't know what dogs know about people. We impose our worlds on them, but they surely live in their own worlds, which are inaccessible to us. Dogs are joyful in different ways than us, they suffer differently; what do we know about their suffering and their joy? Though I sometimes had the impression that Mieszko lived in two worlds, his doggy world and our human world. For why was he so fond of hearing Babcia tell stories? It was as if he'd been at her side throughout her whole life. When he heard about somebody doing wrong to her, he'd bare his teeth, jump up and bark. Babcia would have to hush him.

"Stop it, Mieszko. There's no point getting mad when he's no longer alive. It was his family that wouldn't have me. They were rich people. They had land farther than the eye could see. If you'd been able to look from the sky, you'd have seen there was even more. While me, what was I? My father was a small-town doctor. Most of the people there were poor Jews; often he wouldn't take money from them because they could barely make ends meet as it was. And here God sends me this rich guy. I found myself pregnant with him, but I got rid of it, Lord forgive me. I never told the priest in confession. He wouldn't have understood. But you, you're a dog, you'll understand."

Mieszko may have understood, yet it made him even more restless.

"Settle down now. You've got a royal name but you're behaving like a common dog. And stop barking: he carried out his own sentence. I used to visit his grave till the war broke out."

When the mother and daughter were at work I'd always crack open the door from my room in case Babcia needed anything. In that way, the confidences she shared with the dog made their way into my writing. At times I was angry, because I was trying to concentrate on my work, and simultaneously I was eavesdropping. But when she called me through, I'd put my work aside with relief, go in and listen to her. I didn't believe her stories – I thought they were nonsense – but do you really not believe a word of it when someone confesses they used to love you? You deny it, but don't you believe it too? She's old, you're young, your ages have passed one another by; yet wouldn't you like to have lived in her life if such a thing had been possible? So when she died, the quiet she left behind wasn't the quiet that might be expected after someone's death. Her stories went on. Is that actually so strange? The dead tell their stories long after they've died, because no one can manage to tell everything while they're still alive. You'd have to live forever. A story doesn't know any such thing as an end, unless perhaps it's the end of the world. So millions of people keep on telling their stories, in the hope that they'll be heard. Besides, who knows if those stories don't actually delay the end of the world, which would already have come about long ago if there'd been someone to tell the story of that end, and someone to listen to it. So many wars, so much suffering and torment and despair: it all seemed to be inciting the world to end. So much hatred – for love too is often infected with hatred – yet the world continues to exist, seemingly despite itself. Is that not strange? So perhaps every event needs to see itself in a story if it wants to happen? And every person, if they want to exist? Even God – if He weren't told in a story, would He exist?

After Babcia died Mieszko continued to lie by her bed, though now the bed was covered with a red throw that had a green pattern, I think, or the other way around. I couldn't figure out what drew him like that. If a dog's imagination is like a human's, he must have been able to imagine that Babcia was still alive, lying on the bed instead of the throw. I'm justified in thinking so, because he'd often come in to me like he used to before when Babcia sent him to fetch me, if the accordionist was playing too loud for me to hear her when she called.

"Leave me alone. You can see I'm writing, and Babcia's dead."

He wouldn't listen. My unwillingness made him angry. He'd tug at the leg of my pants and growl; his eyes showed a single-mindedness that could have exploded in fury at any moment.

It was promising to be a hot, sunny day. The mother and daughter had words before they left for work. The mother asked the daughter if her chiffon blouse was all right for the heat that was forecast.

The daughter snapped back: "You can't get thinner than that. If you want to dress like a young thing then take off your shirt and bra and let people see your titties dangling."

An exchange of caustic remarks followed; it would have turned into a full-blown fight, but the train wouldn't wait. They didn't leave together as they usually did. The daughter went first, slamming the door behind her; the mother caught the next train. Before she left she came by my room to remind me to let the dog out, feed him, and give him a bowl of water since it was going to be hot.

"All right, out with you." I opened the door to the yard, and he looked at me in a disgruntled way, as if I were throwing him out. He seemed to want to lie down on the doorstep, so I pushed him out and closed the door. He stood there for a while. Perhaps it was the effect of the pane in the door, because glass can distort an image, but I thought I saw tears in his doggy eyes.

"What are you crying about? Dogs don't cry. You should be embarrassed. Off you go." I shooed him away. "You can come back in soon. What's wrong with you?" I walked away. His strange behavior troubled me, though. So ten or fifteen minutes later I went back to see if he'd gone. He was still standing there, his nose against the glass. "Scoot." And I walked away again. This time I waited longer. When I went back, he'd gone.

The next day I was meeting with my supervisor. I needed his help resolving some of the questions about my dissertation, so I had no time to think about why the dog hadn't wanted to move away from the door. In the end he'd gone, so everything was fine. No doubt he'd be back soon and would let me know by scratching at the door. I immersed myself completely in the Middle Ages; it was all the easier because of the quiet. There were no noises coming from behind the wardrobe, not even the crying of the baby. But the silence soon turned out to have another aspect, like a feeling of happiness whose other side is anxiety. I began to worry that Mieszko was taking a long time to return. The armchair was empty, yet he ought to have been lying there, watching me write. Once and again I poked my head out of my Middle Ages and listened to check he wasn't pawing at the door. In the end I set aside the molding board, got up and walked over to the French window. He wasn't there. At that moment I wouldn't have minded hearing the sounds of the accordion from behind the wardrobe, and the familiar raspy voice. Let it even be "The Blue Danube," a piece I hated, and with which the accordionist usually commenced his practice. I began unthinkingly humming the waltz. I believe I actually spun around a few times. In fact, I might even have lost myself in the dance, but it occurred to me that I ought to go out and look for Mieszko, for that was all I could do. I hoped to find him close by, right away. And as frequently happens, hope was accompanied by imagination. I guessed Mieszko must have met a she-dog, and that they were gamboling together. So it wasn't odd that his routine had been disturbed and he'd forgotten his usual habits. They could have ended up a long way from the house chasing each other.

I went to the next-door neighbor. The jasmine happened to be in bloom, and jasmine in bloom can stir sentimental feelings in anyone – so why not in a dog? Once when the jasmine was flowering, the accordionist stood breathing in its scent. He wasn't drunk at the time.

"Imagine playing a smell like that," he sighed.

I looked under the jasmine bushes to see if Mieszko might be lying there. The neighbor came out.

"You're welcome to some jasmine if you like. I'll cut you a few sprigs."

"No thank you. I'm looking for our dog."

"In the jasmine? You should look for him wherever he went missing. And if you do want the jasmine you should take it now or tomorrow, because it's already past its prime."

I went from neighbor to neighbor on both sides of the road, but no one had seen Mieszko. The hope that I'd find him quickly was beginning to fade. At one moment I was startled by the thought that he might have gone onto the railroad tracks to kill himself. And that he was lying dead between the rails, run over by a train. I don't know if dogs commit suicide, but my helpless imagination made such a thing possible. I followed the path alongside the railroad embankment, first in one direction then the other, almost to the next station each way. One time a local came past, then a freight train, but I didn't find Mieszko's body anywhere.

I went back to the house. I couldn't get past the idea that Mieszko had killed himself, if not on the tracks, then somewhere else. Perhaps he'd wriggled into some hiding place in the woods and decided to starve himself to death. But how would a dog know that something like suicide is possible? On the other hand, he'd heard so many stories about different deaths, including suicides, if only from Babcia. Too bad I hadn't counted all those deaths that Babcia had had to experience during her lifetime. And in general, how many deaths fall to one person throughout their life, before they too are greeted by death? I don't mean only those closest to me, but all those, however distant, whom I didn't know personally, yet whose death moved me. I couldn't remain indifferent even to the people from Babcia's stories, though in many cases I wasn't yet alive when they passed. They all only truly died in Babcia's stories: yesterday, the day before yesterday, tomorrow, the day after tomorrow, long ago, recently, and also after Babcia's death, when my memory summoned them back. No death occurs only once.

"Come through. Sit yourself down. Do you remember how we met?"

"If you want, I can remember, Babcia."

"Lean in closer, I don't hear well."

"I can lean closer."

"In the first war. I was a nurse, you were a soldier. "

"I've never been in the army, Babcia."

"You were then. Everyone was. There weren't any non-soldiers. That swine had jilted me, so what was I supposed to do, I volunteered as a nurse. Where do nurses come from in wartime? From despair after failed love affairs. One of them I remember, she'd caught her husband-to-be in bed with her maid of honor on her wedding day. They were getting married in the afternoon. In the morning she put on her gown and veil and wreath, and went to show him. She couldn't believe her eyes: in the very bed that had been made up for their wedding night, there he was with the maid of honor. She grabbed hold of a candle and set fire to herself. Luckily she'd forgotten to pin the rose to her dress. Her mother had taken the rose and run after her. She tore off the bride's gown and veil. 'What are you doing, daughter!' She was young and foolish, of course. She shouldn't have let him see her in her gown and her veil. Her whole body was covered in burns. How she would have lived with that, God knows. But the war broke out, and she enlisted as a nurse. After that man of mine, I signed up too. They assigned me to a field hospital. It was a sort of big tent. Whenever they brought in the wounded, the place shook with people groaning and shouting and begging. They'd lost arms, legs, their eyes were burned, their bellies ripped open. Some had lost their private parts. I thought to myself, there is no love in the world, there are only the wounded. One calls to me: 'Scratch my foot for me, nurse, it's itching like anything,' but he had no leg. Another one says: 'Nurse, lie down by me, I'm dying.' A third grabs me by the hand and won't let go, he tells me to repeat his name so I'd remember it. How could I remember, when every name in the calendar is in there. Another one wanted me to say the rosary for him because his hands were all bandaged up. There were some nuns with us, they lent me some beads. I knelt by his bed. I mixed up the beads; he corrected me but he got annoyed. Then the doctor comes up and snatches the rosary from my hand, saying there's no time for acts of compassion. War is work, not compassion. The doctor hadn't slept in three nights; he'd been amputating, cutting, sewing up the whole time. He told me to get back to work. One day, when I fainted for the umpteenth time, one of the older nurses told me I should pick one of the wounded and fall in love with him.

"'Love gives you strength. Fall in love with a wounded man and he'll be faithful to you all his life. Maybe that guy over there. His wounds aren't so serious. He'll live.' She pointed at you. 'He doesn't groan or shout, he doesn't beg.'

"You were asleep. It was such a homely kind of sleep, there was something inhuman about it. I thought to myself, no, he's not for me. I picked someone else. He wasn't severely injured either. But when he recovered he went back to the front and he died there. The older nurse, a widow, had killed her husband with a meat cleaver. She shared a prison cell with other women like her, who'd killed their husbands. But there was an ever-greater need for nurses, because the war was spreading, so they started taking them from the prisons too. They offered to commute the rest of their sentence if they volunteered. Soon even that wasn't enough, there was more and more killing. Between their trenches and ours there was a growing mountain of corpses, to the point that you couldn't see the other trenches. But they kept shooting at each other. One day, when they brought in another wounded man I fainted again. The widow says to me: 'You're too delicate. Life is going to be hard for you. You haven't seen the worst of it yet. Everyone needs tough experiences. I killed my husband; now that's behind me. If we survive all this we should meet up. You'll let me know how you're doing.'

"But she didn't survive. An artillery shell hit the tent. It spared me. Where was it that we met after the war? Oh, I know. You were in uniform. Your arm was still in a sling. At the next table a lady said, 'look at that handsome lieutenant, what a pity his arm's in a sling.' The uniform lay on you like on a shop dummy. Your collar was fastened up to the neck, as if it was cutting your head from your body. Once when they were bringing back the dead bodies, one of them was headless like that. Some high-ranking officer with cords, medals, tall boots, and spurs. You were in the cavalry too, I believe. Your spurs rang when you clicked your heels. How had you known I'd be there? It couldn't have been by chance. Where was it? Lord, where could it have been? I can hear music, they're playing the Blue Danube waltz. I see you looking from table to table. I try to draw your gaze. It passes over me. Some ladies jump up and hurry over to you. One of them kisses your arm in the sling. You try to pull it away from her lips, but it's immobilized. You kiss the lady on the forehead. I so longed for you to kiss me like that. I felt like I was once again a nurse in a bloodstained apron, in my cap with the red cross, amid the groans and shouts and pleas, the wounded and dying all around me. In fact I was wearing a fine cashmere dress. It had cost a lot. I had on a little hat. At the time small hats like helmets were all the rage. I was in high-heel shoes, and I had a string of pearls. A diamond ring on my finger. Before, I'd been to the beautician's, the manicurist's, the hairdresser's. They'd taken some of the war off me. Maybe that was why you didn't recognize me. I suddenly wanted to turn back time, so it would be wartime again and you'd see that it was me. My hands began to tremble. I took my cigarettes and lighter out of my handbag and tried to light up, but the flame missed the end of the cigarette. A man jumped up from the next table, took the lighter from my hand and lit my cigarette for me. He asked if he could join me. I said no, because he wasn't in uniform. I was waiting for you to come up and ask if you could sit at my table. I'd even forgotten that inhuman sleep of yours. I thought to myself that I'd been foolish to fall in love with someone else back then. The widow had advised me well. Now it might be too late. You were on morphine, that was why you were sleeping like that. Do you think that in war you don't have a desire for someone to come and hold you? I'd be exhausted after more than one sleepless night, my head would be spinning, yet my whole body – my whole exhausted, sleep-deprived, worn-out body – would long for someone to lie down by me and hold me. Sleep would be weighing on my eyes, but I'd resist, thinking I might feel someone's warmth in my body. Someone who hasn't lived through war knows nothing about themselves. The widow was right: love is the only way to prevent you from losing your humanness in that sea of tears and blood and dying. And perhaps the most permanent, for it bears the stamp of death. When it was over, though, I didn't feel relief. I wanted to live differently, yet I kept dreaming about the war. I lived a double life like that. Someone suggested I sign up for dance classes. Dance heals, give it a try. And my body, which seemed to have frozen in the war, loosened up. There was a dancer I partnered with in the lessons. I found him good-looking. I asked him if he'd been in the war. He told me his uncle was a general and he'd been able to avoid the draft. I thought, maybe someone like that will help me get over the war. So I married him. Where do you think my daughter and granddaughter came from? But one night I dreamed that we were making love back then, when my exhausted, sleepless, worn-out body finally got to sleep. And from that moment my heart beat only for you. Lord in heaven, could you not have appeared at that moment in your uniform, all glittering and bright? Instead of now, when it's time to die?"

Babcia died while the landlady was away on vacation. Before she left she'd had the doctor come and examine her mother.

"You're fine to go away," he pronounced. "Nothing bad is likely to happen in the next two weeks. Old people have a greater will to live than young folks. I'm here just in case. Your daughter can call me. Have this prescription filled; she should take it three times a day."

She asked the lady from upstairs to check in on Babcia too. The wife of the accordionist also volunteered to do so, for it was nothing just to pop across the hall. The granddaughter was going to take medical leave for the two weeks her mother would be away. So it can't be said that the landlady wasn't looking after her mother, or that she hadn't taken precautions so as not to have a bad conscience.

The granddaughter was patently bored during her mother's absence. Sometimes she'd take the dog out for a walk or to get the shopping; she'd cook once every two days, mostly soups. Whenever I stayed home, she'd come visit me. But she was usually on edge, irritable, as though something were nagging at her, and she never stayed for long. Often she'd jump up after she'd only been there a moment and virtually run out of the room as if something was about to boil over or burn in the kitchen.

For her part, Babcia didn't once call me through, or send Mieszko to fetch me, even when her granddaughter had to go out for a few hours, to extend her medical leave, she said. Was she afraid of her granddaughter? Or was she, as I suspect, already negotiating with her own death? How can a person negotiate with death, you might wonder. Well, at the very least by asking it to grant us the briefest of moments so we ourselves will know that we're dead. Why should other people have to learn for us that we've died? No one lived for us, they lived for themselves; it's our life, so it should be our death too. Why shouldn't we at a minimum have time to sigh: "It's good that I lived."

What a praise of life that would be. How people's lives would be enriched by it.

The mother was due back soon when her daughter, still bored, told me: "Tomorrow I'm having a little party for my birthday. There'll be a few people. Join us if you like."

I was so surprised I didn't so much as wish her many happy returns. Besides, she hadn't even come into my room, she'd just cracked open the door. All the time I'd lived there I didn't remember her ever saying anything about her birthday. Besides, both she and her mother avoided having visitors. The one room they had left, which was also their bedroom, where Babcia lay ill, was unsuitable for parties. Sometimes a girlfriend of hers would come by and they'd have tea together; that was it. I said I couldn't make it, that I had classes all that day at the university. I didn't, but I thought I'd go see a movie or even two, and I'd make it through the evening somehow or other. I'd come back on the last train, which arrived an hour before midnight. The birthday party should be over by then, since it was supposed to be just a small affair. The only thing that worried me was how Babcia would put up with the party. And what about Mieszko? There was no telling what he was capable of.

Alas: the villa was ringing with toasts, shouts, explosions of laughter. On top of everything else a phonograph was playing loud music. As usual, I entered my room via the veranda. I took my shoes off so they wouldn't hear me. I left the light off, went straight to bed in my clothes, and pulled the quilt over my head. I wondered: how can Babcia stand it all? Even if she were to call out and ask them – beg them – to quieten down, her voice was so weak no one would have heard her in all that racket. The quilt wasn't enough even for my ears. I started paying attention to the voices, trying to work out how many people were there. The more I listened, the more voices there seemed to be. I counted over twenty, though there wasn't room for so many people. A table, three beds, chairs, the dresser, the cabinet; there were only narrow passages to the beds, the kitchen, and to my room. The numbers I was counting had evidently gotten separated from the voices, yet I couldn't stop, I was caught up in the counting. It was only when Mieszko barked that I snapped out of it. I rose gingerly from the couch so the springs wouldn't creak and give me away. I decided to go out and walk around till the party finished.

There was a full moon and the sky was filled with stars; the air caressed my face. A night like that draws you into itself; you feel like melting away in it. So I walked and walked till I couldn't hear the villa any longer. I was surrounded by silence. At a certain point I stopped and began to listen intently to see if the quiet was real or just an illusion. I was startled by the crowing of a rooster. Then an express train thundered by, cutting through the night with its snaking lights. After that, pale signs of the coming dawn appeared on the horizon.

It's time to go back, I thought to myself. What will be will be; maybe it's over by now. Unfortunately it wasn't. The villa grew louder as I approached. No longer taking the same precautions as before, I went into my room. In fact, I slammed the veranda door so loudly its panes rattled. Dawn entered the room along with the hubbub.

I was just opening a window to air the place out a little when everything suddenly became quiet, as though they'd all turned to stone. Then came the alarmed voice of the birthday girl: "Go take a look. You're a doctor. Am I imagining it?"

There was a tense silence, as if before an explosion. Then a man's voice: "I'm afraid not."

The uproar returned with redoubled strength, but this time it was filled with consternation.

"We need to go! Now!" a woman screamed hysterically. "Death is in here!"

"Just a moment!" a hoarse bass voice slurred. "Let's have one for the road!"

They hurried out, to judge by the clatter of feet and the banging of doors. The granddaughter tried to stop them.

"Help me clean up, someone! You were all too happy boozing and stuffing yourselves with food, and now you're leaving me alone?" In the end, helpless and furious, she shouted: "Then I'm damn well going too!"

I thought about going through and at least kissing Babcia's hand to say goodbye to her. All at once the door opened. I broke out in a cold sweat. It was only Mieszko. He'd pushed the door open as usual with his paw. But he didn't come into the room. He stood on the threshold looking at me expectantly, as if Babcia had sent him to fetch me.

"No, Mieszko, I'm not coming. Babcia might not have wanted it. You're a dog, you don't need to understand."

I thought he was going to leap at me, for anger flashed in his eyes. But he merely shook himself and went away.

It was the day after Babcia's funeral that he didn't come home after I let him out. When the mother and daughter returned from work in the late afternoon their first question was: "Where's Mieszko?"

"He hasn't come back."

"What do you mean? When did you let him out?"

"Early in the morning."

"And he still isn't back? That can't be. We have to find him."

"I've been looking." I explained that I'd only just gotten home because I'd been out searching for him the whole time, but he'd vanished without a trace.

"God in heaven!" The mother actually put her hands to her face in alarm. "He's been with us since he was a puppy. He was still blind. I fed him from a bottle. Maybe he'll come back in the night. If not, we should go tell the priest tomorrow so he can make an announcement in church. Perhaps someone has him but they don't know whose dog he is."

"How's a priest going to help you?" The daughter seemed irritated by the priest. "Priests only worry about little human souls."

"How do you know Mieszko doesn't have a soul? We can give money for a Mass, let him announce it."

"Are you nuts? Something must be up between you and that boyfriend of yours."

They started going at it. They argued till it got dark. They were so intent on their fight they didn't notice me leave the room – for sooner or later I'd have been dragged into it. Listening to them through the door was bad enough, and I waited apprehensively for one of them to blame me for the disappearance of Mieszko. In the end the mother burst into tears and the daughter turned the radio on.

That evening, when the quarrel had passed, the daughter was the first to speak: "Come on, let's go for a walk. It's quiet now, maybe he'll scent us and come running. And as for the guy through there, tell him he finally needs to move out, it's his fault."

I didn't get a wink of sleep all night. In the morning I went to the university and applied for a dorm room, which I soon got with my advisor's help. Since the start of the academic year was still a long way off, I decided to visit my parents.

In the early morning, when I told them I was going on vacation the daughter asked: "So when will you move out?"

"When I come back."

I didn't have many things, but there was no way I could transport them all at once. First I took my winter coat, my overcoat, jacket, sweater, shoes, scarf, and cap. The next time, my books, notes, my unfinished dissertation, my underwear and various small things. Then finally the comforter that had helped me through the harshest cold. I was grateful to my mother for having mailed it to me. I hadn't wanted to take it. But she couldn't imagine me being able to sleep under anything other than a down comforter. I packed it up in the same Russia leather sack that she'd sent it to me in. The sack bore a huge stamp depicting a black eagle whose talons gripped a globe with a swastika.

"I tried to wash it out," she wrote. "I gave it a couple of goes, with lye even. It wouldn't come off. Stubborn thing."

She'd wrapped it in a thick layer of paper and tied it with string. I turned it inside out, but the stamp showed through on the other side. I went into town especially to look for some large sheets of packing paper. I had to hunt around, because no one had any. I saw a guy putting up posters for a production of Mickiewicz's *Forefathers' Eve*. I persuaded him to sell me a poster. I thought to myself, no one's going to give me grief over Mickiewicz. So I glued it over the eagle. I entered the train compartment, put the sack with the comforter by my feet, because it was too big for the luggage rack, and right away someone said to me: "Eve isn't one of our forefathers. You're saying bad things about our nation, buddy."

I left the molding board that I'd used to write on. I said goodbye to the mother and the daughter. I told them I hoped Mieszko would turn up. Maybe I imagined it, but I had the impression the mother's eyes were damp with regret; I was sure that at the last moment she had to hold back from giving me a hug. As for the daughter, all she did was make a face and say: "Bye."

The road to the station passed by the cemetery. I didn't have much time before my train, but I decided to go say farewell to Babcia. Her grave was by one of the side paths. As I approached, I noticed a woman dressed in black, leaning down and pulling weeds from the mound on one of the graves; near her, right by Babcia's grave a dog was lying. When the dog heard my footsteps on the gravel of the path it jumped up and started to move away.

"Mieszko, don't go! It's me!" I called. I dropped the sack with the comforter, thinking he might not have recognized me with the package, but he'd already vanished among the gravestones.

The woman straightened up and looked at me. She too seemed a little alarmed.

"What's wrong?" she asked.

"Nothing. It's the dog."

"What dog?"

"You know, the dog. He was here a moment ago, but he ran away."

"I've been weeding my husband's grave here, but I haven't seen any dog. You must have imagined it."

"I didn't imagine it. If he hadn't been here, he wouldn't have run away."

Chapter 9

§

Who could be calling at such a late hour? Phone calls would usually stop in the early evening. I was already in my pajamas and was just putting something to read on my nightstand – I always read for an hour or so in bed before going to sleep. I picked up the receiver. A man's voice asked if he had the pleasure of speaking with Professor Such-and-Such, and when I said yes, he apologized for calling so late, but he'd tried before at various times of day and there'd been no answer.

"I'm a busy man, sir. I must have been out of town. What's this about?"

He introduced himself. His name meant nothing to me. He mentioned the town he was calling from. That rang a bell. For a moment he paused, as if expecting me to give a joyful exclamation. Since I didn't respond, he added a few details that were clearly intended to entice me: he said the town had changed since my childhood, which surprised me, for what could he possibly know about my childhood. There were new apartment buildings and avenues, a park, a multiscreen movie theater, an arts center, several hotels; whereas the steel mill, which I must remember, had closed many years ago. He might have said even more on the subject of the town, but he seemed to sense my impatience, so he finally explained that they had a modest history club, with a dozen or so members, mostly retirees, for who else these days has time for outside interests, surely I understood. I didn't say yes, yet all the same, sounding more confident now, in the name of the club – he had been its president since his own retirement – he invited me to visit. He said they'd been thinking about it for a long time, but hadn't dared ask. They'd wondered if it wouldn't be better to write a letter, but they'd voted on it and decided to call.

I'd been determined to turn him down, but the story about the vote disarmed me. He wasn't sure of my reaction, so he continued his blandishments:

"When your book about the individual in history came out, we organized a discussion at our club. It was then that the idea of inviting you first came up. But we hesitated, because we thought you must be booked up for years in advance. Besides, what did our town have to offer that might convince you to come. Yet something happened out of the blue that I don't want to talk about now. I'll say only that we came across a trace of you in the town. In connection with which, we're planning a surprise which will surely please you, and might make the rather troublesome journey worthwhile. All the more because unfortunately we can't provide an appropriate honorarium. None of us has a car to fetch you here and take you back home. There is a direct bus, though, so we could agree on the time of your arrival, then we'd meet you off the bus and take a taxi to the hotel. As for that, we guarantee the best hotel in town, with four stars; the owner majored in history, and he's agreed to put you up for free during your visit. He asks only for a favorable word in the hotel guest book and an autograph on a special board he has in the lobby. Last of all, professor, could you let us know the title of your talk? We want to make a poster. Not this minute, but do think about it please. I'll call again, say in a week or two. It'll be a great day for us. We might even manage to invite the local media. We'd like to get word of your visit out to as many people as possible. Please say yes."

My mind was spinning so much from the call that I was incapable of either agreeing or refusing, especially because I don't like long phone conversations. I said simply: "Call back in a month. Not at night, though – I was getting ready for bed."

How could they have found a trace of me in their town? It worried me. Maybe I should have asked what trace it was, and made my decision based on that. A glass of brandy failed to calm me down. I switched on the TV but I didn't hear what was being said, I didn't see what I was watching, so I turned it off again. I tried the radio. There was some music on. But the thought of that trace got in the way. I went to bed in hopes that perhaps a dream would help me find the trace. Dreams know much more about us than we know about ourselves. For what do we know? And when we do know something, are we not merely stumbling about after ourselves?

For a long time I couldn't get to sleep. I tossed and turned, and didn't drop off till well after midnight. I woke at the crack of dawn, more tired than when I'd gone to bed. I was exhausted, not by having slept so little, but by the dream I'd had. I was standing at Needle's Eye without any hope that she'd come, when all at once she appeared and said: "I didn't think you'd still be waiting for me. Today I have the whole day for you. What shall we do?"

"I don't know. If I'd thought you were coming. . ."

"I wasn't supposed to. But I had a feeling it might be you waiting for me, not the old man. We have to move away from here; otherwise he could turn up at any moment and then I'll have to go with him, because he's been waiting longer. I know – let's go down by the river."

We'd been walking for some time along the levee when a man and a woman appeared, walking in our direction. The woman was barefoot. She was holding the man's arm, leaning in to him; he was explaining something to her and pointing. I had the impression it was me he was pointing at. They were old and wrinkled. The woman's hair was gray; the man was wearing a threadbare hat, perhaps he'd gone bald. But I recognized them as the vacationers my mother had let the room to years ago, then later they sent an overcoat for me and raisins, almonds, oranges, lemons, and chocolates for my mother.

I said: "Let's go down to the bushes, I'd rather not meet them."

The levee was steep and grassy; we almost fell as we walked down. We pushed our way through the dense willow brake, right to the edge of the river. A little sunny stretch of sand was waiting for us. We sat down, gazing in silence at the flowing water. We took off our shoes and socks and dipped our feet in. At that point several dead, seemingly poisoned fish started to rise to the surface and swirl around our feet in the water. I jumped up.

"Let's go somewhere else."

"It'll be the same everywhere," she said. "There's evidently no place for us."

She got up and began pulling small branches off the willows. She gathered a whole armful and stood with her face in the sun.

"Come here," she said. "Stand next to me. We'll take a picture. Smile. It'll be our wedding photograph. Move closer, don't be afraid. You see what a lovely photo it will be. Years from now we'll find it moving. We'll have left something moving behind, at least."

She laid the branches on a fold of sand untouched by any footprint.

"I'm sure you know that after a wedding comes the wedding night. Think about how we'll spend it. I want it to be on embroidered silk sheets, in a bedroom filled with flowers."

I looked away, because her body suddenly seemed to be emerging from darkness.

"Don't be embarrassed," she said. "I don't mind when you look at me. I belong to you now." She lay down, her head on the willow branches. "I want to feel you sate yourself on me. I need to tell you, though, that I'm not a virgin. As a child, in the camp I was raped. And don't be afraid if I get pregnant. I'll die before I give birth." She rose abruptly onto her elbows. "Why aren't you getting undressed?"

"I'm old, forgive me."

"That's not true, you're young. Look at the photo. You can't fool the camera."

"I walk with a cane now."

"There's no cane in the picture."

"But so much has happened since then. You can't remember it all. Time is moving in opposite directions for us. I had a wife, a son."

"I'm sorry for you, but we have to believe in life, however it was or is or shall be."

Believing in life – that's a hard, hard thing if you think about it. Perhaps that's why on the surface it seems simple, ordinary, banal. Yet it's the toughest of faiths. All the more so because there are only two perspectives in life: youth and old age. When someone's young they don't believe they'll be old, and when they're old they don't believe they were once young.

I kept thinking about the phone call, sometimes hoping he wouldn't call again, after I was so cool with him the first time. As I went back and forth about going or not going, my memory started bursting open, as it were, and out of it emerged an apartment in a two-story stone building, then a white house containing four apartments, a water tower along the way, and yet another apartment at the very end of a balcony that ran along the whole floor, past several other apartments. And out of the blue the same fear came back to me that I'd fled from by hiding my head under the blankets whenever they poured off the white-hot slag after a smelting at the steelworks, and a great flash appeared in the sky like an exploding star. My heart would beat so hard I could feel the blankets moving, even though at the time I was shaving and almost my whole life had passed since then. It did no good when my parents explained it was just the slag being poured off after the steel had been smelted, and since it was already night there was a big glow over the town as though the whole world were on fire. But it wasn't the whole world. If it had been, there'd have been fire sirens yet there weren't; church bells would be ringing but they weren't. The trembling I experienced went on for a long time, after the sky was dark again, and often it was midnight before I could get to sleep. Maybe that was why I'd come to dislike my childhood. And when memory sometimes took me back to it, I was never sure if it was my own memory. Especially because, as we know, every memory is composed of the memories of others and it's not possible to distinguish what's ours from what's borrowed or inherited. I have doubts, then, whether memory can be a guarantor of our identity.

A month went by and he didn't call, then a few more days passed. I was sure he wouldn't ring now, when suddenly, at the same time of night as before, the phone rang.

"I'm terribly sorry, professor. I was in the hospital, I only came home today."

He probably would have said more, but I interrupted him and surprised myself by saying: "I'll come."

He offered a date and a time and I agreed without even wondering whether I already had plans on that day. He suggested what he thought was the most convenient bus, though was the time not too early for me. That way, I could have an unhurried lunch in the hotel, then rest for an hour or two before the talk. Would I prefer a later arrival?

"No, I'll come on the earlier bus."

When I got out at the bus station I gazed around, but nothing looked familiar. A group of people came up to me right away. They introduced themselves as the entire board of the history club: the president, vice president, secretary, and treasurer: three men and a good-looking young woman. They handed me a bouquet of flowers.

"Welcome professor, welcome. And thank you for accepting our invitation. The journey wasn't too tiring? This way to the taxi. We'll take you straight to your hotel. Lunch is waiting. Excuse us for not keeping you company during your meal, but we've all already eaten."

The president and the young woman, who was the club secretary, got into the cab with me. It turned out she'd just graduated in archeology and was working on a dig nearby.

"The Royal." He tapped the driver on the back. "Take Dolna St. We'll show you something on the way, professor."

"We'll need to go the long way around – there's a detour."

"Then do that."

I was weary after the journey and didn't feel like visiting anything, especially since I had the talk that evening. I was still hesitating as to my topic.

"Could you stop for a moment by that derelict building?" the president said to the driver. We were on a narrow street where all the houses were single story, many of them crooked with age. The street was paved with cobblestones.

"It's no parking here," the driver replied.

"Just for a moment."

"I'll need to turn on the emergency lights and open the hood, pretend something's wrong with the engine."

Fortunately we didn't have to get out. The president pointed at the building and said: "In that ruin – well, it wasn't in ruins at the time, it looked nice – there was a photography studio, one of two in town. This one was more popular. Actually, the other one burned down during the war. When the owner of this place died, the municipality took charge of the estate. They gathered the photographs and negatives, even the ones on glass from long ago. They developed them, made new prints, and created an archive. He'd photographed all the official events and church celebrations in the town, the various dignitaries and the priests, but also ordinary people on the streets, taking a walk, in the parks, on benches, by the lake – we'll go there tomorrow perhaps. You can't come here and not visit the lake, where the whole town spends all its free time from spring to fall."

I cringed to think what they were planning to do with me. From what the president was saying, they seemed to have a timetable for my whole visit. When he called me, I should have warned him I'd be leaving the day after the talk. Now it was too late. Though perhaps I could try and tell him after all. It's just that they were bound to be disappointed, I might even appear ungrateful after they'd put so much effort and hard work into hosting me properly.

Meanwhile, the president went on: "A few years ago there was an exhibition based on the archive. Crowds came. In the photographs people recognized their great-grandparents, grandparents, parents, friends and neighbors. They saw their weddings, christenings, first communions. True, there weren't many whose memory reached back that far. The town has changed. Some folks left, others moved here and settled. In my view, though, something different has happened: memory is in retreat, so to speak. Let me give you an example. After the exhibition, our club organized a discussion on the subject of memory, during which one young person said that a condition of freedom is ridding yourself of memory. And that the young want to be free, as guaranteed for them by human rights. Can you imagine? Memory restricts their freedom. Incomprehensible. To go back to the exhibition, especially striking were the photographs of people about whom no one knew anything. So many individuals, faces, smiles, expressions of surprise or sorrow: yet who were they? Children, little girls and boys, young men and women, bald or gray-haired stooping men, decrepit old women – yet who were they? Jews from before the war, in front of their stores, some in yarmulkes and gowns and sidelocks – who were they? For they'd definitely existed. They can't be wiped from memory. They mustn't be. Memory at least has to preserve them. He even took pictures of the beggars outside the church. Let me tell you, when I saw that nameless mass of people, in the first moment I thought to myself: could the world have died?"

I didn't want to interrupt him, and the cab driver wasn't calling us back; he was still poking around under the hood. It was good after all that I'd come, I thought, if only for the president: such people still exist, and that means the world isn't dead. I didn't think twice about it when he said there'd been particular interest in a series of photographs of the ironworks: specifically, the pouring out of the slag after the smelting.

"How beautiful it was," the young club secretary said enthusiastically. "The glow, the fires. From the past, only beauty counts. That's the only thing that lasts. Beauty makes living worthwhile."

"If time allows we'll visit the steelworks too," the president said, interrupting the secretary's rhapsody. "It closed long ago, but it's still in excellent shape. They could start smelting steel tomorrow if they wanted. I worked there for many years as head of accounting, till my asthma forced me to retire." It was only now that I heard the wheezing of his lungs; previously I'd thought the hoarseness of his voice was caused by the torrent of words pouring from him ever since we got into the cab. "Actually there's something else I wanted to mention to you in connection with the photo studio. I should save it for later, though. You must be tired after your journey, professor." Yet he couldn't wait, and before we reached the hotel, which was situated at the edge of town, in the woods on the other side, at a certain moment he said: "We found a picture of you in the archive."

I started. "That's not possible." I felt a twinge of anxiety. "What picture?"

"From first grade. You went to the private school, right? Jan Kochanowski Elementary. It was located near the water tower, which is still standing. It's a historical site now. We don't have many of those here."

"If that's so, I was a child then. Over the years people change completely."

"But not enough that they can't be recognized, oh no. In any face, however old it is, if you look closely you can see the child in it. We took your face from a photo of the whole class, and when we enlarged it to portrait size, we had no doubt."

I felt powerless. I was well aware that objections would serve no purpose here. Should I just give in meekly? Sometimes that's the only way, for pointless resistance only makes our helplessness deeper and more painful.

"You're standing in the front row, which means you must have been one of the best students. They always put the best ones in front. We'll show you. You'll recognize yourself at once. You're wearing a white shirt with a ribbon tied in a bow under your collar – it must have been a national holiday – you're in short gray pants, white knee socks, and sandals. Your hair is short, with bangs. We framed it and added a caption saying, The Professor in Childhood. Unfortunately the school isn't there anymore. But there are plenty of other places connected with you."

When we finally reached the hotel I was so exhausted that right after lunch I took a nap. I asked the receptionist to give me a wake-up call an hour before the talk. They took me in another cab to the arts center where the history club had its office. It was a small room with a desk, a phone and a few chairs. The talk was being held not here but in a lecture hall intended for bigger events, conferences, ceremonies. When I entered the building they took pictures of me; in the lobby the local radio station asked me how it felt to be back in town after so many years. I answered that I didn't yet feel I was back. It was worse with the town newspaper. Their question presupposed its own answer, like leading a suspect to confess his guilt: what did I remember from my childhood in the town? I answered with a hint of annoyance that I hoped they would be the ones to remind me.

"What do you mean?" The man was actually offended.

"I'm sorry, but I don't have time now for reminiscences." I glanced at my watch. "Excuse me."

Something strange was beginning to happen around me. The photograph the club president had told me about in the taxi should already have given me pause. Were they not mistaking me for someone else? After all, what link could there be between childhood and old age.

You'd need a whole inquiry to prove that the first grader and the man giving the talk were the same person.

Quite a few people were there – the room was about half full. I was welcomed with a standing ovation. They sat me down at a table with a bottle of juice, a bottle of water, and a glass. Next to me sat the club president, who first invited one of the local bigwigs to speak – I didn't catch the man's name or position, I was so distracted by the idea that they may have invited the wrong person. In addition, the lecture I was about to give, and which I thought I'd prepared thoroughly, was falling apart in my head. I had a few humorous anecdotes in reserve, in case the audience seemed bored, but I started to doubt if anyone would find them funny. Even the title I'd settled on sounded uninteresting: "Is History Necessary?" I began desperately searching for an alternative.

To make matters worse, the official welcome on behalf of the town authorities, which I'd counted on lasting no more than a couple of minutes, went on forever. The last straw was when I heard at some point that tomorrow and the next day they'd be taking me to all the places I'd lived as a child. The speaker mentioned several streets, along with the numbers of houses and apartments, stating that this or that building was no longer there, and a new building stood in its place. "But we have photographs, so at least in that way we can satisfy the professor's memory. We have a photograph of the school where you completed first grade, a year before the war broke out. We have other pictures too. But first we'll visit the places that have survived. For instance the Rialto Cinema. Admittedly the cinema itself no longer exists. Or the water tower, you must have walked past it on your way to and from school, since you lived nearby at the time. We'll also go down to the lake; you must have spent time there with your parents, on Sundays if nothing else, everyone would go there on a Sunday. You may even have learned to swim in the lake, because all of us who were born here in this town learned there. Unfortunately the water that might have remembered you wasn't standing water but was flowing through the lake." He laughed at his own joke, and the audience laughed with him. "Or the town square: I'm sure you and your mom went there many a time, on market days at least, for eggs, butter, cheese, fruit, produce. So you must have heard about the incident that shook the town when one day, a market day precisely, the partisans shot to death the commander of the local Gestapo, a notorious swine, though they were all swine. The leader of the attack also died at that time – a lieutenant whose resistance name was Toni because of his Italian ancestry. His great-grandfather had died in the January Uprising. Time permitting, we'll also visit the former steelworks, one of the most important historical sites in the town. In the meantime we welcome you, professor, and thank you for agreeing to come.

"Ah" – he remembered something at the last minute – "we printed a detailed program of your visit. If you have any suggestions regarding the sequence, of course we can move things around. Everything's there: time, place, morning and afternoon, with breaks for a rest, for lunch and for coffee, point by point." He placed the program on the table in front of me. "Look it over when you have a moment. You can keep your copy as a souvenir."

I thanked him. Dismayed by what I'd heard, I began my lecture. It didn't go well. At times I didn't recognize my own voice; it quavered and broke. I kept coughing and clearing my throat, though I wasn't sick – I was just trying to give myself a moment to think about what to say next. My voice has always been clear and distinct, dignified even, I've often been told. I was never awed by a big audience, even an international one, for instance at conferences attended by world-famous names. While here there were just a few dozen people curious to see someone who'd spent their childhood in the town decades ago, as announced on the posters, on the radio and in the papers, rather than out of any interest in history.

Most of the audience looked a little bored; this was confirmed when I finished and there was only tepid applause. Some people didn't even clap. The club president, seeking to encourage a more enthusiastic response, rose to his feet and, opening his arms wide like wings, clapped his hands together with all his might above my head. Following the lead of the president, the local dignitary also stood up and applauded loudly. Yet this failed to liven up the audience, A few people close to the door got up and left without even waiting for the applause to come to an end.

"Does anyone have any comments?" I asked. "Or questions?"

"Exactly," the president chimed in. "There's plenty to talk about. Your talk was extremely thought-provoking." He praised different aspects of my lecture, saying that, wrapped up in our daily lives, we didn't realize these things until the professor pointed them out to us. So many questions sprang to mind. "Anyone? The lady over there at the end of the row – I thought I saw you raise your hand."

"Not at all," came the voice of a woman hidden behind other people. "I was just straightening my hairpin."

A few people laughed at the hairpin. The president didn't give up. He remained on his feet, looking around, his gaze seeking somebody who might have something to say.

In the end a hand went up.

"I see we have our first contribution. It's always hardest to get started. After that things go more easily."

A man stood up. He looked to be in his twenties, no older.

"I'd like to ask why we need to know about everything that happened in the past. It won't make it easier for me to find work. I've been unemployed for two years."

When I went back to the hotel I was dejected. I hardly ate anything for dinner; I just had some tea with lemon, and a glass of brandy. I didn't want any company, though the club president, and the young secretary, and the dignitary, and other people clearly wished to eat with me, all the more so because a meal had been prepared for a large group. I excused myself, saying I had a headache, that I'd had a hard day, and tomorrow would be demanding too. Of course, of course, they nodded, pretending to understand. We said goodbye, and the bigwig drove me back to the hotel.

For a long time I couldn't get to sleep. I didn't have a headache, true; but my thoughts were beating about my skull as if they suddenly felt imprisoned in there. How could I calm myself? I hadn't brought a book with me. In such situations a book would always come to my rescue. Nothing academic, but a love story say or a crime novel, or a biography. I turned the light on and looked in the nightstand drawer, but all I found was a color brochure advertising the hotel in several languages. There were photos of the place outside and in, of the restaurant, the bar, the kitchens, the conference room. A list of phone extensions and the rules and regulations for guests.

I began to look through it since it was all I had, and I might even have gotten to sleep, but I remembered the program the bigwig had handed me at the end of his introduction. I got out of bed, took it from my jacket pocket and set about studying it point by point, hour by hour. I only dozed off toward morning. I was woken by a call from reception to ask if I was coming down for breakfast. When I appeared, the restaurant staff were expecting me. The club president and the young secretary were waiting in the lobby.

It turned out the authorities had given us the use of an eight-person passenger van in which aside from the driver there were two other people, a man and a woman. We said hello and the president introduced them: Miss Klara and Mr. Kazimierz.

"Miss Klara helped us track down a friend of yours from long ago. She still lives where you and your parents used to reside. She's expecting us."

"And me? What about me?" said Mr. Kazimierz.

"It's true, Mr. Kazimierz played an important part too. He went through all the town rolls from those years. We identified several persons. Most of them are no longer alive or we were unable to locate them. All sorts of things can happen to people. But at least we managed to find a few addresses. Others live there now. One family – a young couple with a child – agreed for us to visit. They asked if they should give you flowers. We said we'd bring the flowers. Others refused, though; their places were a mess, so they said. But first we'll go down to the lake, after that to the town square; then on one of the streets leading off the square, in the fourth building along I believe, there's that friend of yours from childhood who's expecting us. She certainly remembers you, oh yes," the president rattled on. "She was touched. 'He's a professor now? I'd never have believed it. He used to go about all snotty-nosed, and now he's a professor. How about that. Wipe your nose, it's dangling there, I'd tell him. And now he's a professor.' It brought tears to her eyes. What can I say: childhood is always moving, the more so the further you are from it. Apparently, during the war the two of you used to sneak off and watch German movies on the sly. 'No one but Gestapo officers, prostitutes, and us two,' she said. 'They'd let us in without a ticket because the theater was more than half empty. Those times, my Lord. And now he's a professor. How about that.'"

I was about to object that I'd never gone to the movies with any friend, my mother wouldn't have allowed it, though sometimes she'd sigh and say she'd have liked to go see a film. After the war she made up for lost time. When they put on a movie at the plant where my father worked, she'd sometimes go to all three screenings: they'd always show it three times on a given day, so workers from all three shifts could see it. One time she told me in a letter that they'd shown *The Teutonic Knights*. There'd been crowds; the rec room wasn't big enough, and people had been sitting on each other's laps or on the floor, or they'd stood against the walls – they even opened the windows and people watched from outside. When the film ended everyone stayed put and shouted for it to be screened again. My mother was so taken with the film that she was still thinking about it. 'See what smart kings we had once. It'd be good to have someone like that now, because otherwise nothing will change. Burn this letter as soon as you've read it. When are you coming to visit?'"

There was no point in protesting. I couldn't prevent the visit to the former friend. I just said: "All kinds of things can happen."

Miss Klara unexpectedly took my side: "You're right. We're all adults here, so I can say this. In a marriage sometimes the husband has the pleasure, sometimes the wife. It's rare for it to be both of them together."

The driver laughed so hard he accidentally jerked the wheel. The young club secretary went bright red; the president peered off to one side as if we were driving past a road accident, while Mr. Kazimierz expressed his admiration: "As always, Miss Klara's painfully frank."

"What's the point in hiding it?" Miss Klara went on, clearly pleased with her own plain-spokenness. "Am I wrong? Then everyone's surprised when people get divorced."

We drove down to the lake and the president said: "We'll get out here."

"We can see the lake just fine from inside the van," I suggested timidly.

"Oh no, from the van you might not remember the lake. Ask people if they see anything through the windows when they're driving in a car. Or even if they do, do they remember it? The world goes by in a flash. Their life passes in the same way."

We stood on the shore of the lake, on a narrow strip of sand along the water's edge. Gentle waves, ripples really, washed against our feet. Miss Klara slipped off her shoes and stood there barefoot. At a certain moment she moved away from us and entered the water up to her ankles. She bent down and, taking the water in her hands as if she wished to rock it in her arms, she said: "Water's nicer to the touch than a man's body."

I didn't know if anyone aside from me had caught what she said. I was the closest to her, and she'd spoken in the direction of the lake, so her words were lost to the water. In any case no one let on that they'd heard.

"If someone wanted to drown themselves," she said, straightening up, "they'd need to swim all the way out into the middle." She pointed. "If you want to go in up to your neck, you have to go a long way from the shore. Beyond that you need a kayak."

"This year they found two empty kayaks," the young secretary said. "Last year I think there were three of them."

"Four," the driver corrected her. He'd just joined us after waiting behind for a while.

"An empty kayak is no proof of anything," the president said.

I don't know why, but hearing his words I imagined the whole lake covered in empty kayaks, one next to another. I heard them knocking against each other as the waves grew higher; they were creaking, rocking sideways and shipping water. This despite the fact that the day was warm, sunny, and windless, and the lake seemed to be drying up in the heat.

"A few years ago they found a letter in one of the kayaks," the driver said. "It was my neighbor's son. He was only twenty. No one knows what he wrote, because the letter had gotten wet. It was written in pencil and the words were blurred. The father tried and tried to find someone who could decipher it for him. Maybe you could have helped, professor? You said yesterday at the lecture that you deal with chronicles and letters and seals, in foreign languages too. His letter was just in Polish."

I started. What could I say?

"I feel for the father," I replied. "But you know, it's easier to deal with history than with someone's ordinary life. I have no gift for life."

"People mostly come to this point to bathe," said the president, as if trying to spare me from further explanations. "As you can see, everywhere else the shore's overgrown with sweet flag and bulrushes. You must have been here too. Did you know how to swim back then?"

"I don't remember. I've swum in so many lakes and rivers, in the sea. It's all mixed up in my recollection."

"Oh well. It's like our local VIP said yesterday, water has no memory. Too bad, because the lake would be able to tell all kinds of stories. Let's go to the town square now."

"The square?" Miss Klara said. "What's to see there? There's only the plaque marking where 'Toni' died. We're geniuses at dying, halfwits at living."

"Well, maybe tomorrow," the president said, glancing at his watch. "We're already late, and your friend is expecting us."

We pulled up in front of a two-story apartment building that from the outside looked recently renovated. It stood in a row of similar buildings. On the first floor there were storefronts with lavish, stylish displays. I imagined the building was the same inside. Yet when we passed through the entranceway into a small courtyard, I couldn't believe my eyes. Cobblestones with gaps, plaster crumbling on the walls, a heap of plastic trash bags in the corner, piles of empty cardboard boxes, a bin overflowing with garbage; plus, the place was littered with news-papers, empty bottles, potato peelings and other refuse, as if it hadn't been swept for who knew how long. Amid all the rubbish there was a latrine. It's hard to call it anything else. Two stalls, though stall isn't the right word either. On one of them the door had come off and was propped against the outside; the other door was hanging off its hinges. I can't say what the inside was like, but it wasn't hard to imagine. Oh, and on one of the stalls a board was missing from a side wall.

"The thing is, they ran out of funds," the president said in expla-nation. "Last year it was the anniversary of the town, and the money was spent on more urgent projects."

Along the upper floor ran a long wooden balcony; that too looked rickety. Luckily it had a roof. The doors of the different apartments opened onto it. An older woman was leaning against the balustrade, in an unfashionable hat with artificial flowers and a brightly colored floral dress. She looked down at us with a smile. From below she appeared to be missing some of her teeth.

"Watch your step!" she called as we started to climb the stairs. "Some of the boards are rotten. They were supposed to fix them, the bastards. One of these days they'll break and someone'll end up dead."

The stairs did in fact creak so much you were scared to put your foot down anywhere. We went up one by one, keeping several steps apart. The president led, trying one step at a time, then me, then after me Mr. Kazimierz. Miss Klara decided to stay downstairs.

"She must be from the authorities if she's afraid," the woman on the balcony snickered.

"I'm not from the authorities!" Miss Klara retorted. "I'm in heels. Oh, whatever." And she virtually ran up the stairs.

"She's thin," the older woman declared. "They'll hold up under her. On your way down, don't tread on the fourth step from the top or the fifth one from the bottom."

"This is the professor," the president said, indicating me.

"There's no need for introductions. We've known each other since we were children." She tugged her hand away when I tried to kiss it. "You needn't kiss this old hand. You should have done it back then. Back then I wouldn't have objected. I'd have married you even, if you'd have liked. But all you wanted was a peek." She screeched with laughter, revealing the loss of most of her teeth, as I'd noticed from below. "Remember: behind the outhouse you pulled up my dress, then I took my panties off myself."

Everyone looked away; only Miss Klara chimed in: "Unfortunately, that sort of showing comes to an end eventually."

"Like everything else, missy, like everything else. Sooner or later."

"Miss Klara, really – " Mr. Kazimierz tried to put in, but the president interrupted.

"You ladies are joking around, yet there's a young person present." He nodded toward the club secretary. From her face it wasn't clear whether she was embarrassed, scandalized, or indifferent. She seemed absent. "And young people need guidance."

"You have to guide yourself first," the old lady retorted. "But we didn't know how, so now it's the young people that are showing us how to behave." She turned to me and looked me up and down. "Well, you've really put on the years, but I know you. Do you recognize me?"

Unfortunately not, I was about to say, but to my own surprise, and in an over-enthusiastic voice, I asked: "Miss Irenka, isn't it?"

"No, it's Józka. But I'm still a miss."

"I'm sorry. Terribly sorry."

"No need to be sorry. People's names aren't written on their forehead. But I remember yours. I wouldn't dare use it though, now that you're a professor. They told me about that. I remember any name you care to ask me about. Including people that are dead. Go ahead, ask me. He's gotten shy. He wasn't shy back then." She gave her toothless screech once again. "I remember everyone who's lived here. I can name them all, apartment by apartment. Do you want me to?"

"There's no need," the president broke in. "That's not why we're here. Tell us where the professor used to live back then."

"Down there, at the end. They moved in when the Jews were taken away. There were a few Jewish families living here. In that apartment there, and that one. But come inside, we'll have tea. I baked a cake."

On a table with a white cloth a pot of tea was waiting. There were cups and saucers, a sugar bowl, spoons, neatly sliced cake. She poured the tea and served us each a piece of the cake.

"Help yourselves. I think the cake came out well. It's called a topielec. I don't bake it often, I don't have anyone to make it for. It's with raisins and orange peel."

At the word "topielec" my heart pounded. I lifted my teacup, but I could barely bring it to my lips.

"Try the cake."

"I wish I could, but I'm not allowed sweet things. I've developed diabetes."

"That's too bad. I made it specially for you. Your mama gave me the recipe when you lived here. I keep it in the book you lent me. Do you remember?"

"Of course," I said readily, though I didn't recall anything of the kind.

"Do the rest of you like it?"

"It's delicious," Miss Klara said.

"Do you think the people in the apartment would let the professor in to see where he used to live?" The president was remembering his role. "We could finish the tea afterwards."

"I already went and asked. 'He's not a Jew is he? Supposedly come to visit, then he'll make us give the apartment back.' 'A Jew? Lord no! I've known him since he was a child. I knew his mama and his papa.' They're all muddled up, those people, they're afraid of everything. Though there are worse folks. One low-life turned my father in. My father was the super here. We lived on the first floor. There's a toy store there now. They were taking away the Jews, and daddy hid one family in the cellar. We had a big cellar, with brooms, shovels, tools, cleaning equipment. It had a separate entrance down some steps by the entranceway, next to our front door. It had one small grated window that gave a little light. This one Gestapo officer that was responsible for the building would sometimes come see daddy. He'd want to know what was going on, who'd been doing what with who, ask if daddy hadn't seen or heard anything. And daddy would tell him, but not what he'd actually seen and heard, so as not to harm anyone. In the apartment behind you, to the left, there was a guy who'd been a policeman before the war. You must remember him, you used to stick your tongue out at him when he went to work. They had the nicest apartment. Now someone from the town authorities lives there, though I think he lost his job, because he hardly ever goes out. She works at the library and brings him books. I asked her one time, you're always carrying all those books, couldn't your husband help out? Actually they're for him, she says, he loves to read. At least he does now; I never saw her bringing books home before. If he doesn't have anything to do he should start a business, or drive a cab. If life hasn't made him smart, books won't. Cab drivers just drive around all day, and they're really smart people. They know everything about health, and about the next life. What it's like on the moon and beyond. And no one knows more than they do about politics, not even the politicians. Cab drivers know what people need, and what they deserve for the life they've led. Things'd be better if cab drivers were the government. When you don't have anyone else, you can open up to a cab driver. If I had three times my pension, I'd become a cab driver. You lent me a book once, remember?" She'd shifted topic back to me, and again my heart pounded. To shield myself from further questions – did I remember this or that – I lifted my teacup and emptied it.

"More?" she asked.

"Gladly." I thought in this way I'd distract her and she'd maybe go back to the cab drivers.

"I don't think I gave it back to you. Your family left before I was done reading it. There were two little kids that got lost in the woods, I remember. But I don't know what happened to them. I didn't feel like finishing it once you were gone. It was because of the policeman's wife that you had to move. I'd have given her what-for. One time she says to your mama, the only thing those Jews left behind at your place are bedbugs. And your mama ups and starts yelling at her: when you're gone you won't even leave the bedbugs behind, you witch. She was a heck of a woman, your mama. But after that she was afraid. She was always looking to see if they weren't coming for her. She'd ask me, Józka, she'd say, keep an eye out, let us know if need be. Not long after that you all left. You could have stayed, because that husband of hers, the cop, he was afraid himself. In those two apartments there was a pair of she-devils. Good-looking women, all very friendly. They took me in afterwards when I ended up on my own. All sorts of men visited them. Old men, young. One time there was a fellow had lost a leg, on crutches. He had trouble getting up the stairs. One of them went out and helped him up. She felt sorry for him. 'How're you gonna do the dirty when you can't even make it up the stairs?' That made me laugh. I often had a good laugh there. That Gestapo officer, they said he was a wet rag too. He was so fat they couldn't get him going. How did a fat guy like that end up in the Gestapo? You saw all kinds of men in the Gestapo, but most of them were slim. Plus, those black uniforms of theirs. Oh, I loved those uniforms. If our guys had had uniforms like that they might not have lost in the blink of an eye. They were the ones that took daddy and mama later on. Daddy liked the fat one and he liked daddy. He'd been a super before the war also, though in a bigger apartment building, he said. Sometimes he brought daddy cigarettes, and daddy made him tea. And he always asked him, will you be visiting the ladies upstairs? They're expecting you. And he'd go. He'd just tell daddy: mum's the word, or it's a bullet in the head. Daddy never told a soul. Though everyone here knew who did what. Somebody said something at one end of the building, at the other end everyone heard it. Sound travels through doors and walls here. People are always knocking on each other's door, telling them to keep it down. Nobody could sneak past without being noticed. The stairs creaked just as badly back then. The balcony creaked, all the doors. You heard every movement. Worst of all was in the night. All of a sudden someone's yelling at the top of their voice: 'Can't you walk quieter? Take your shoes off! You've gone and woken my kid!' People were on edge. But there were good times too. Life wasn't bad. You learned all kinds of things from shouting matches like that, stuff you'd never find in books. One time the policeman's wife says to your mama, 'You think we don't know who visits those two? I said to my husband, do something, it's a scandal. But he says, shut up and keep quiet. I'm telling you, I'm gonna move out and leave him if it keeps up like this. It's like Sodom and Gomorrah.' What had happened, the policeman had had to squeeze past this one woodsman when the woodsman was on his way to them. It's really narrow here – when you open a door there's barely room to push by, because the doors open outwards."

She got up and opened the door to show us. It was true: when the door was fully open it reached almost to the balustrade.

"Try it, one of you," she urged us.

Miss Klara volunteered; she got up and went out.

"Who wants to try and squeeze past? Maybe you, Mr. Kazimierz? You're the thinnest man here."

"Gladly, though I'd rather have been the woodsman than the policeman. Especially if you were inside."

"At that moment, the woodsman's coat opened and underneath it you could see a revolver. The policeman turned white. 'Excuse me, I didn't see a thing.' 'No sweat,' the other man says. 'Nil-nil.' At the time I didn't know what nil-nil meant. I asked my daddy. 'When they play soccer, nil-nil is when there's no winner or loser.' But daddy was afraid too. Everyone was afraid of everyone else here, though we got by somehow. There are as many things to be afraid of as there are people in the world, and everyone's afraid in a different way. The man that turned daddy in must have had his own fears. Maybe he didn't sleep at night, but just lay there listening. Maybe he had to get up and pee all the time because of his nerves, and the crapper's down there in the yard. I wasn't there when they came for daddy and mama and the Jews. I don't remember where I was at the time. I might have been at the movies. We used to go in the morning, remember? I often ask myself where I was then. How did I know he was the one who ratted on them? Because he looked after me afterwards. He lived right down there, third apartment from the end. God alone knows what I went through with him. He'd lock me in whenever he went somewhere. If it hadn't been for that I'd have gone to the Gestapo and asked them to take me too. One day he left and didn't come back. The two women took me in.

Then one time I overheard them saying they needed to do something about the guy's apartment while it was still vacant. They could give it to Andżelika and Dolores, who worked the street. You didn't do that well on the street; if they came here they'd be in business. Her, she's still a kid. Maybe something'll come of her. One day the fat Gestapo officer came to say goodbye, because they were sending him to the front. He complained that if daddy had told him, he'd have shot those Jews. Daddy would still be alive, and he wouldn't be going to the front. In those days you grew up three years for every year of life. So after the war, when they were looking for a super I applied. They thought I was too young, just a kid, but I told them I could handle it. I'd learned a lot from my daddy, they didn't need to train me. I knew the ropes. After that, I worked here my whole life. Though they didn't give me the old apartment, because they put a store in there. They moved me up here. Then I retired. I could still be working, I'm fit enough. Have another piece of cake each. Shall I make more tea?"

"Thank you, but we've taken up enough of your time as it is." The president glanced at his watch. "Is it really that late ?"

"You didn't take up any time at all. I could go on and on. You can't tell a whole life in a few moments. Even after you're dead you want to keep telling it."

"The thing is, they're already expecting us for dinner."

"Well, if you must, you must."

We got up, and she seized my hand.

"Do you remember my daddy?" Her pale, tired-looking eyes glistened with tears.

"Of course," I said. "One time he gave me a broom — no, I think it was a shovel — it was wintertime and he said, 'Finish clearing the snow, kid. I need a break.'"

I couldn't have told her I didn't remember, it would have been cruel. All the more because as I listened to her life, without meaning to I attached myself to her memory. I let myself be dragged into it, so to speak. It's always like that: when you hear someone else's life, you can't find a way out of it afterwards. You live in it like it was your own.

We were already on our way down the creaking stairs when she came out after us and called down: "Hang on a moment! You can each take a piece of cake. I made it for you! Why don't you want it?" And she burst into tears.

I felt drained when I returned to the hotel after dinner. In fact, I'd been unable to finish the dinner either. Every bite seemed to grow in my mouth. Eating like that is exhausting. You chew and chew and you can't swallow. So I made my excuses and said I'd go take a nap. I lay down hoping I'd doze off and start to feel better. Instead of sleeping, though, I began to reread the itinerary for my visit, item by item, hour by hour, and I had a strong feeling of dissatisfaction that something was missing in the program despite the overabundance of activities. What could have sparked my disappointment to the point that it felt bitter? I sensed it, but I couldn't put my finger on it. How would I last another two days, I wondered with trepidation. There were three items on the itinerary for the next day, one for the following morning, then a formal goodbye in the afternoon. I had to disappear somehow, it was the only way. But how? I'm not a magician, I couldn't make myself miraculously vanish, so I didn't exist and never had, and they'd only imagined me, like in a dream.

Maybe I'll go for a walk, I thought, when it gets dark and the lights go off in the hotel, and I won't come back again. But what about my suitcase? Should I leave it? I didn't have anything particularly valuable with me. Two changes of shirt, a spare pair of pajamas, two neckties, two pairs of socks, handkerchiefs. But what about the clothes I'd already worn? What about my toiletry bag, my shaving things, toothbrush, toothpaste, soap? (I always travel with my own soap.) If I leave them, then when I don't come back from my walk they'll think I've gotten lost. And they'll start searching the woods around the hotel. If I pack it all up and take it with me so not even the smallest object remains, how can I carry the case through the lobby? There's someone on duty all night at the reception desk. Even if they're dozing, those people keep their eyes and ears open. They'd see me with the suitcase and at once they'd make the necessary calls, and cause a hue and cry throughout the hotel. Especially since I hadn't signed the hotel guest book. Also, in front of the hotel I'd seen there was a uniformed guard keeping watch.

I turned off the light, opened the window and looked out. The room was on the second floor. It wasn't that high. I could drop the suitcase down, then go around the building on my walk and retrieve it. But what if it opened when it fell, how could I gather everything up in the dark? The night was warm and starry, the moon was full; some people might be sleeping with the window open. What if one of them noticed? It was so quiet you could have heard a pin drop – a suitcase would have sounded like an explosion. It wouldn't work. What could

I do? I turned the light back on and cast my eyes around the room for ideas. I went into the bathroom; my gaze fell on the cord of the hairdryer. Exactly: if I could find something like that that was long enough, I could lower the suitcase to the ground. I went back into the room, switched on all the lights, and started hunting around again inch by inch. I spotted an extension cord for the TV that ran along the baseboard from the power outlet behind the bed all the way to the opposite wall. But was it long enough? Well, just in case, I'd add my belt and one of my neckties, maybe both.

I packed my suitcase, knotted one end of the extension cord around the handle, tied the other end to my belt, fixed the necktie to that. I flipped off the lights, opened the window, and carefully lowered the suitcase. It reached the ground almost soundlessly, touching down no louder than if it had been an empty beer can. I closed the window, drew the shades, put on my jacket, and went into the bathroom. There was a small lamp right over the mirror. I checked my appearance, to make sure my face wasn't giving me away, because like they say, a guilty conscience needs no accuser. I imagined them combing the woods for me. Someone calls out: "He isn't anywhere! Maybe he hanged himself!"

Their flashlights shine on the trees.

"Look for oaks!" someone else shouts. "Oaks have low branches!"

The receptionist was surprised to see me. "You're still up, professor?"

"I'm having trouble getting to sleep. I'm going to stretch my legs, get some fresh air."

He unlocked the door for me.

"Don't wander too far away, though," he said solicitously.

The security guard repeated the warning: "It's a lovely night – very pleasant for a stroll. But please don't go too far."

I circled the hotel once or twice so no one would have any doubts they'd seen me. My suitcase was lying right by the wall. But I didn't take it for the moment. It was only on my third or fourth time around that I picked it up and headed into the woods. I was lucky in that the fencing was still unfinished, as I'd noticed the previous evening – the hotel had only recently been built – so I was able to leave the grounds without having to look for a way out. I stayed in the woods, walking parallel to the road at a close enough distance that I could see it. I joined the road itself only when I reached the end of the woods. I kept to the shoulder, remembering that if I simply walked straight ahead I'd end up near the bus station. Once I was close I just needed to turn left, carry on for a bit, take a right turn and I'd be there. Cars passed quite frequently, but no one stopped to offer me a ride; I didn't want to flag anyone down just in case the driver happened to have attended the talk the previous day and recognized me. I was a little dazzled by the headlights of the oncoming cars, but I stuck to the dip that ran alongside the road.

It was quite a ways to the bus station. I walked for over an hour, even though I was moving at a fair clip – for in my naïveté I was hoping to catch a late bus, or perhaps a nighttime line. Nothing doing: when I lit a match and held it up to the timetable, I saw that the next one wasn't till early in the morning. But I couldn't wait till morning, when someone might show up here at any moment, not having found me in the woods. Oh well: I'd rest for a minute then continue. Maybe I'd get lucky and find a ride along the way. It was a highway; perhaps someone would be going in my direction. For now I'd sit a while in the waiting room. The waiting room was locked though. I spotted a bench nearby. I sat down, resolving to press on soon. Yet the night was so agreeable I virtually sank into its embrace. I felt such a sense of relief that I would never have wanted to swap the night for daytime. I even thought to myself I'd have had nothing against dying on that bench, in the quiet deserted night. Though I was quite a few years short of fulfilling the Gypsy woman's prophecy. How many exactly? I'd have had to count up. It's too bad I didn't ask her back then what my death would be like. Because who knows, maybe she was a messenger of fate. Fate has all kinds of messengers. Sometimes it's a dream, sometimes chance. But at the time it would never have occurred to me to ask such a thing.

The moon was closer and closer, as if floating toward me. For a second I had the impression someone was moving on it. Could people be living there already? It hadn't been all that long since the first human stepped out onto it. Is Earth too small for people already? Or do they no longer know how to live here? Perhaps they're trying to reach God, to see whether He exists? I couldn't blame Earth though. Completely immersed in that night, for a moment I felt I'd ended up amid the stars, and the moon was to my right.

The sensation only lasted a moment, and was interrupted by what sounded like two people running toward me out of the darkness. I was alarmed, thinking they must be coming for me. Yet they came to a stop nearby. Right away I heard them.

"What's the big hurry?" It was a woman's scolding voice. "I'm not gonna do it standing up. I've changed, don't you know. I like comfort these days."

"All right, there's a bench over there."

"Someone's already on it."

"I'll tell the prick to get lost."

A big guy appeared in front of me.

"Piss off out of here."

I hunched over, trying to think of a way out of the situation, but I couldn't come up with anything.

"What are you waiting for, pal?"

I had a stroke of inspiration, the way you sometimes do when you're helpless: "For the police. They'll be here any minute."

He stepped back. I heard them hurrying away. Things didn't quieten down though. Less than fifteen minutes later, I heard somebody approaching the bench as if they too wanted to sit and rest. Unlike the previous couple, this person had a slow, heavy tread; each step was accompanied not so much by a tapping sound as a poking of the gravel in front. And in fact, when the walker was two or three yards from me I saw a white cane, and a dog by his side who was leading him. With his cane he tapped the bench, then my suitcase, which I'd placed by my feet, and he said: "I see you have a little suitcase."

The word "see" surprised me, since the cane, the dog, and the tapping all showed he was blind. I couldn't see his eyes as he was wearing dark glasses. His voice was hoarse and indistinct. He sat himself down comfortably on the bench beside me, sighed and said, more as a statement than a question: "If you have a suitcase it must mean you're traveling."

"Maybe," I said, so as not to have to continue the conversation. I don't like talking to strangers, especially at night. In addition, I couldn't be sure he wasn't just pretending to be blind – the white cane and the dog and dark glasses could be a front, and any second now he'd whip out a knife, press it to my throat and say:

"Give me your wallet. Your watch. What you got in that suitcase? Hand it all over or I'll stick you. Jacket, pants, shoes. It's a warm night, you won't freeze."

I mean, you hear about guys that'll strip you naked, kill you even, for a handful of zlotys. These days the world's filled with criminals of every stripe. As I waited anxiously for him to pull a knife, I resolved to grab my suitcase and shield myself with it.

"Just like me, just like me," he wheezed. "I can see we're kindred spirits. Sometimes you meet up like that." He pulled the dog closer. "Warm." The dog lay down on his feet. "Nice dog, warm dog." He leaned over and petted the animal. "My feet have been cold ever since." Maybe he was counting on my asking him, since when. Something in me warned me not to trust him, however, and I didn't respond, though it ought to have made me curious, because it was high summer and warm, yet here his feet were freezing. "Would you mind buying me a ticket?"

"A ticket?" I said. I was playing for time to get over my surprise. "Where are you going?"

"Same place as you are." I was even more taken aback. "Same place as you."

"I don't know yet where I'm going."

That didn't put him off.

"Like me. Just like me. I go wherever someone buys me a ticket for. And it'd be nicer to travel together. Whether you go one place or another, when there are two of you it's always nicer."

"Just like that, with no goal?"

"What goal could I have. I just want to reach the end."

I had no idea how to respond, so I said something that was probably foolish: "I'm thinking I might go on foot. I don't feel like waiting for the first bus. It doesn't leave till after five. What time is it now?" I glanced at my watch, which had luminous hands. "Just past one."

"Then I'll walk with you."

"Can you manage on foot?"

"Why shouldn't I. I'll always end up somewhere. Even that would be good. I don't have long left."

"Are you ill? What are you sick with?"

"The same as everyone."

"Meaning?"

"Life. Are you young or old?"

"What do you think?"

"At times you sound young, and others less so."

"Then maybe that's how it is."

He took off his glasses and rubbed his eyes with the back of his hand, blew his nose onto the ground, then stroked the dog again.

"What's his name?"

"Waluś. Same as me. Though there's no one left to call me that."

"It's a fine name."

"Now for instance, I'd say you're much younger. Before, when you said you didn't know where you were going, I thought you must be as old as me even."

"How old are you?"

"Why count? You can't make the years go backwards, or hurry them up. By night our age can't be seen."

"But you said before that you see I have a suitcase."

"Habit of speech. You get accustomed to saying, I see this, I see that, so you keep saying it. A word isn't like a hair – you can't grab it and yank it out. Once my eyesight was like a hawk's. It's hard to get used to not seeing any more."

"What happened?"

"Landmine. You know that song, 'Red Poppies on Monte Cassino'? It was there. I was a sapper. I knelt down. 'I'll disarm you in no time, you little beast.' The explosion was so bad I lost both my eyes, it took off these two fingers, and cut up my feet. Ever since then they're always cold. But I can sometimes hold things in my remaining fingers."

All at once a police siren tore through the night. A flashing light appeared in the distance and drew closer.

"Police," I said, my throat suddenly tight from fear. "Probably for me."

"Did you run away from somewhere? You don't look like you were in prison. I know people. Plus, the dog would have smelled it. But that's not a police siren. It's an ambulance. Someone's having a heart attack."

Chapter 10

"There seem to be fewer and fewer birds," he said, looking at the sky. "Yet there's no reason why that should be. Unless they're sensing something. Birds are always the first to know when something's about to happen."

"What's going to happen?" I asked.

"That I couldn't say. But I have some advice for you. There's a priest I know at the cathedral here, a classmate from high school. Go see him, mention my name. He might be able to tell you what's going on. Are you a believer? Though that doesn't make any difference in fact." He was about to carry on up the steps, but he glanced at me and said: "You know, yesterday – no, the day before – for a long time I had trouble falling sleep. And in that half sleeping, half waking state I saw you. You were sitting on a bench in the park. A moment later a Gypsy woman appeared on the path with a baby at her breast. The breast was enormous, perhaps at the cost of the other, whose outline was barely visible beneath her blouse. She went up to you, sat down, and tried to persuade you to have your fortune read. You didn't have the willpower to refuse. I was actually angry at you. Though I understand: people need a big effort of will to resist fortune telling. And who has such a strong will? That's why the world is awash in forecasts about the future. She took your hand and laid it in her lap, but it wasn't comfortable. So she moved the infant to the other breast, and then that one became enormous, while the first could barely be seen under her blouse. She passed her index finger over your palm. The finger was much longer than the others of her hand. But she spoke so quietly I couldn't hear anything. I guessed, though, that the number of years you have ahead of you depended on her words. Suddenly you jumped up and set off running. You wouldn't listen when I called out: 'Stop! Stop! Tell me how many!' Can you tell me how many now? Don't be afraid, I don't believe in fate. We walk up and down the steps, but can that be called fate? Yet do people actually know what they believe in? I doubt it. In the best case, it just seems to them that they know. Everything only seems to them. Plus, they only seem to themselves. Otherwise they wouldn't have come up with the word 'seem.'"

At some point I remembered about the priest he'd advised me to go see. I went by the cathedral a couple of times, but I missed him. Then one day I went again. The sun was burning, as if the door of a stove had been left open. The hot muggy air – a storm was clearly brewing – virtually forced me down onto a bench under a broad chestnut tree. I stretched out, linked my hands under my head and, thinking I'd lie there for a bit till I cooled down, fell asleep. In my defense I should say that for a month or more I hadn't gotten much sleep; it was strawberry season, and they kept transferring me from the drying plant, since there wasn't much drying going on, while there were so many strawberries being delivered that I'd sometimes work a shift and a half in one day. Consequently I was half asleep all the time. It wasn't anyone's fault – there was no pressure, I volunteered because I wanted the money. One day I almost lost my hands in the drying plant when I was cleaning out the pomace from the riddles and the overseer set the machine in motion. I jumped back at the last moment. On top of that I had to study, since I was applying to university. So I was always short on time. And where do you take time from when it's in short supply? Only from sleep.

I don't know how long I was asleep. I might well have slept on if I hadn't been woken by a stentorian voice: "Take your feet off the bench."

I opened my eyes, only half awake, and saw the priest. I sat up abruptly.

"Forgive me for waking you. At your age people still sleep like that. Not at mine. I'll join you, may I? Goodness, how hot it is." He took a large white handkerchief from the pocket of his cassock and mopped his forehead. "What was it you wanted?"

"Nothing."

"Nothing, yet you came to me? People don't come for nothing. Maybe you'd like to at least make confession? I won't drag you into the confessional. I don't like taking confession in there. Here, under the chestnut. In the sunshine, the open air, God will hear us better too. When I take confession through a grate I feel like a clerk, not a priest. We ought to be able to see one another's faces. Faces say more than words. In a face you can see words, not just hear them. God spoke in words that could be seen. When I take someone's confession, I confess to them at the same time. We're of the same earth, the same world, the same sins. I always carry my stole with me. See?" From another pocket in his cassock he took out a rolled-up stole. "Just in case someone stops me on the street and says they want to come to me to make confession. 'There's no need to come especially. We can go sit on the bench on that little square.' They accuse me of taking God out onto the street. But everything begins on the street. God began on the street just the same. Anyway, come see me sometime when you have a reason to. I have to be off now. Just don't leave it till it's too late."

Years later, long after I'd graduated from the university, I came home one time and decided that while I was here I'd go by the cathedral in hopes of finding that priest. I didn't really want anything from him. I had no intention of making confession. To me God was still a question, not an answer. It was scorching and humid, like back then; the sun was so hot you could feel it even under the chestnut tree. I sat down on the same bench as before and I began to feel drowsy like then, though I wasn't tired. Now I was older it wouldn't have been right to lie on the bench. Though at any age it's pleasant to stretch out. Our desires from long ago remain with us into old age, as if they were kept in a chest. And from time to time they make themselves known. Sometimes you feel you could run, though your legs aren't what they were once, or your heart. For instance when you need to cross the road and the light is red, but the cars on either side are far away. I tried once. The green light for pedestrians changed to red when I was still in the middle. The oncoming cars braked with a squeal; the drivers honked, opened their windows, leaned out and yelled, calling me every name under the sun.

Something tempted me onto the bench though, and I lay down and stretched out my legs. At some point I must have fallen asleep, because I heard his loud voice above me: "Take your feet off the bench. Honestly, at your age you ought to be embarrassed. So you came after all? Your conscience must be bothering you. No doubt it has its reasons. Though do you even know what conscience is? Have you ever thought about that?"

All at once someone started to shake me. "Hey mister, you've been asleep for ages. I already passed by twice. Wake up, it's getting dark."

I opened my eyes. A stranger was standing over me. At first glance he looked like a beggar. He was carrying a bunch of keys.

"If you wanted to visit the cathedral you should have done it before. I have to lock up now."

I rose to my feet and brushed off my crumpled jacket and pants.

"I'm the sacristan," he said. As if to prove his point, he brandished the keys. "Come by tomorrow, but earlier. It'll be open."

We went up to the doors of the cathedral. He selected a large key from the bunch, which rattled so loudly with every step it made your ears ring. He slotted the key into an equally imposing keyhole in the door and turned it once and twice, maybe even three times; the lock squealed at each turn.

"It needs oiling," I said.

"What for? It'll frighten thieves away sooner if it squeaks."

"For thieves an alarm would be better," I said.

"There was one. But it kept ringing for no reason. I'd have to get up three times in the night. Though whenever I get up I make the rounds anyway. Not always at the same time, because they could be watching. These days thieves are different than they used to be. They have their ways, and not an ounce of conscience. They'll steal the holiest things. One time this little brat hid in the pulpit. Goodness knows how he got in. He had bread and sausage with him, because he left crumbs and sausage skin there. They don't give sermons from the pulpit any more, so people don't often go up there. I arrived an hour or so before the first Mass, I opened everything up and aired it out. From time to time I genuflected in front of St. Vincent, because my name's Wincenty. I get up, go toward the main altar, and in the left-hand nave this pisswad is kneeling in front of Our Lady. His hands are together, I can see from his eyes he's been crying, he's mumbling a prayer. What happened to bring you here so early, I ask. 'Daddy died yesterday.' Poor child. Pray all you like. Then later it turned out the collection boxes had been emptied. The tops were pried open. An adult hand would have been too big, but a child's fingers took every last penny. You look like you're not from around here. I know everyone here."

"I used to be from here."

"You don't look familiar."

"It was a long time ago. You might not have been sacristan back then."

"That's possible. Before me it was my father. And before him, my grandfather. It's a good job. The salary isn't much, but it's a position for life. Free accommodation, and God is right there. I live across the way."

"That's really close."

"You know, I thought my son would take over from me. But he's a good-time boy. He came to visit one time, I ask him: 'So what work are you doing right now?' 'This and that,' he says. 'Only a fool sticks with one job.' 'What the hell,' I say. I was furious, mister, and I never get mad. 'I'm a fool? Me? You think your own father's a fool? Get out of my house! And don't come back till you've found yourself a job.'"

"Excuse me," I interrupted, suspecting this might go on for a while, now he'd opened up to me with his fatherly troubles. "Did you know this priest who used to be here. . ."

"I've known all the priests,"

"This one used to take confession on the bench under the chestnut tree. He didn't like to use the confessional."

"Ah, Father Jan. He passed away. I was already married with children when they sent him to some parish somewhere. Certain people reckoned he wasn't quite right in the head. When the weather was fine he'd bring folk outside and confess them on the bench, like you said. He did the same with me. One time I came to make confession with him, and he says, 'Let's go outside, the weather's nice and sunny, and it's dark in the church.' He wasn't a priest for today's times."

We passed through the railings, but when he tried to lock the gate he couldn't get the key in the hole. Every time he tried, the weight of the other keys pulled it downwards. As if the bunch was closer to his thoughts than to his hands. Or was the dusk veiling his eyes already?

"Here, let me try." I locked the gate and gave him back the bunch of keys. It really was heavy; no wonder he found it difficult.

"If I knew where he was buried I'd visit his grave. 'What sins do you have,' he said to me once. 'Come see me when you've collected a few more. I don't even know if I should make you do penance.' He wasn't for today's times. Where are you staying?"

"At the hotel by Needle's Eye."

"I'll walk you back."

I thought he'd be talking to me all the way. But strangely enough he didn't utter another word. It was only outside the hotel, as we were saying our goodbyes, that he stated: "You're the only one who's not forgotten that priest. No one else remembers him anymore."

The hotel had only recently been built. It was right at the edge of where the Jewish ghetto had been. On the other side of the street, on a kind of cut-off corner of a two-story apartment building, there used to be a workshop where they made jewelry out of banded flint. As far as I know, this is the only place on earth banded flint is found, in balls of limestone shaped like bread rolls. Its beauty comes from the fact that the patterns never repeat from one ball to the next. Each one is unique. It was mined as long ago as the Neolithic in the belief that it had magic powers.

I was always fascinated to listen to Mr. Cezary, the owner of the workshop, who introduced me to the mysteries of those often enchanting patterns, wavy lines and stripes in every shade of gray that only nature can create, and with which art cannot compete. The curving shapes seem to speak of the fate of the Earth, and at the same time of our human fates.

One time I commissioned a pendant and bracelet from Mr. Cezary, still hopeful that I'd give them to her when she came back from the sanatorium. When I picked up the order, I couldn't help but be enthralled. He'd designed and made the pieces himself, and had set the stone in the highest quality silver. Gold would have clashed with the flint, he told me; it would have ended up like fairground kitsch. My admiration pleased him – you could see it in his eyes and hear it in his words.

"Perhaps I should have asked who it's for. That helps the imagination. But flint has taught me to read people's thoughts. So I made it as if I'd placed the commission myself. We have to not know something about ourselves if we're to know something more."

Long before the hotel or Mr. Cezary's workshop, banded flint, along with the limestone from the cliffs where it was formed, was crushed for road surfacing. It was Mr. Cezary, though, who discovered its potential as jewelry.

"Let's take a stroll," he said when I walked up to him. He was standing in the place where in the future they would build the hotel, and which in the past had been the edge of the ghetto. When we found ourselves in front of the synagogue he stopped me. "Do you remember this synagogue?"

"Of course I do," I snorted. "I was in lodgings at the end of the street."

"Oh, right. You could say it's a monument to conscience. The only one in this town."

"Conscience?" I said in surprise.

"Do you not think conscience deserves a monument? Then you're still too young. The past continues to happen within us, making claims on our memory. It's quite possible, though, that at some point memory will come to an end, and people won't say 'where the ghetto used to be' but 'where the hotel is,' or 'where the flint jewelry workshop is.' Then only this monument will be left to trouble their conscience."

I felt sorry for him. I suspected he was playing some game against himself, in which I was only somebody he could visit his past with, who he needed so someone else would hear about what once happened here. I was relieved when we went our separate ways.

One day, years later, I would stay in that hotel when I came for the four hundredth anniversary of our high school, one of the oldest in the country; after years of renovations, it had finally been restored to its former glory. The celebration was to begin the following morning, so I had plenty of free time. I could rest up and go for a walk. Since I'd arrived at midday, I started with lunch.

The young waiter in the hotel restaurant brought me the menu and, as he stood over me, urged me to try the orange duck, a house specialty. He guaranteed it would be tender, without the tiniest bone. As for the soup, I don't recall what he recommended. I told him I don't eat soup; he tried to convince me to take at least a bowl of broth with a hard-boiled egg. When I said no to that too, he suggested a salad, or perhaps dessert; he listed all the desserts that were on the menu. They were all entirely fresh, and made from natural ingredients.

"I can see I'm not going to earn much from you," he said with a hint of disappointment. He revealed that along with their salary, which was low as everywhere, the servers received a percentage of each customer's order, thanks to which he was able to help out his parents. His father was retired; his mother had been a preschool teacher, but she'd lost her job when the preschool closed. It was inevitable: there were fewer and fewer children. Young people were leaving; there was no future for them, no work except in the glass mill, and even there the workforce had been cut by half. At one time, a few miles away there'd also been a sulfur mine after they discovered large deposits, but that too was on its last legs.

"Then you can put two entrees on my check, three even, three soups, three salads, three desserts. What do you have in the way of wines?"

"Everything, even the most expensive."

"Then I'd like the most expensive kind. Bring me a glass of it, then you can include the whole bottle on the check."

"I can't do that. It'd be dishonest."

"What's dishonest about it? I can order three meals and a bottle of wine for my friends, I'm expecting them right now. The fact that they won't show up is my problem. But you will put the order in, right?"

"Forgive me, sir, but I can't. If your friends come, I'll take their order. After all, they might choose something different."

"Extraordinary. I never met a server like you. I've been around a long while, and I've lost count of the number of meals I've eaten in restaurants, in this country and abroad."

"Perhaps you're testing me? Though I'm the one who needs to test myself. There's something unusual about you, sir. Don't take it the wrong way, but I'd almost say it's cruel!"

"No doubt you let a customer know whenever something isn't fresh?"

"Naturally."

"That it's a day old, or two?"

"Of course. Though in this restaurant, everything is fresh. Before, I used to work in a cafe where they had various ways of freshening up the dishes. Even the salads, which were sometimes two or three days old. That was why I left. Here, anything that wasn't eaten the previous day is given to the homeless shelter."

"What's your education?"

"I graduated from university."

"In what?"

"Philosophy."

"Philosophy? I didn't know they trained waiters in the philosophy department."

"Pardon me, I shouldn't spend so much time talking to one customer." He went away. A moment later he came back with a bottle of wine. He opened it at the table, poured me a glass, and left the bottle. He busied himself with the other diners. He was energetic, virtually sailing from table to table. He took orders, made recommendations, bowed, smiled, and brought the dishes promptly.

The restaurant manager came to my table. "How do you find the duck, sir?"

"It's excellent," I replied.

"I'm glad to hear it."

"That waiter — where did you find him?"

"We get a lot of applicants. We can pick and choose."

"I understand."

A moment later the waiter brought me a warm apple charlotte with chocolate and whipped cream.

"This is from the manager, on the house," he said. He was about to go away again, but I detained him.

"You say you majored in philosophy?"

"After than I completed a program for restaurant work. With a philosophy degree I wouldn't have had much of a future."

"Then why choose philosophy of all subjects?"

"For myself."

"And what did it give you?"

"Maybe it helped me become an honest waiter?"

"Interesting. Though I'm not sure I understand." I looked at my watch. "What time do you get off work?"

"Soon. I started early today. My co-worker should be here before long for the second shift." He glanced across the restaurant. Someone had just appeared in the kitchen passageway. "There he is now."

"Do you feel like going for a walk?"

There was something intriguing about him. It was so long since I'd been young that I'd actually forgotten what it was like. Perhaps over the course of the years even our earliest youth yields to old age, for that becomes the present, and nothing can protect the present from it. Or maybe our greed is stronger than time; or else time smooths out all the years that have passed since then and obliges us to live them again. So it may also be the revenge of the past?

"We could talk in a relaxed way. Not like this, between orders and tables. You're dashing about, bringing things, taking them away, writing up checks. Plus, your boss might get annoyed that I'm preventing you from working. That philosophy of yours has me curious. What do Plato or Aristotle have to do with serving tables?"

As he cleared my table, he glanced at me guardedly.

"I'll bring your check right away."

After a longish while – in fact, it seemed too long for such a small order – he came back. He placed the check on the table and was about to leave.

"Wait a moment," I said. "I'll settle up right away." I counted out the amount, along with a large tip, and went on: "Perhaps you'll come to understand me too."

"You'll have to excuse me, but I can't. I'm meeting a girl and I'm running late as it is. Luckily it's right by here, at Needle's Eye. She may be waiting already."

"Ah, right. Then you should run along, she may not be waiting anymore."

As I rounded the synagogue I noticed, on the side that faced the old wild green valley, a spray-painted sentence that I hadn't seen when I passed before: "We are small and vile, and yet beautiful, for we have our own faces." I wondered about the meaning of this line, and decided to copy it down. I reached into my wallet for a slip of paper, but couldn't find one. Oh well, I'll write it on the back of one of my business cards – I just need to make sure I don't give it to someone afterwards. But it turned out I didn't have anything to write with either.

I looked around: maybe somebody would come along and I could ask them for a pen or pencil. An elderly woman was walking by, laden with bags of shopping to the point that she was rocking from side to side. When I asked her if she had anything to write with, she retorted: "Why would I? What's in my head is enough for me." As she walked away she continued muttering to herself. "Wise guy, wants to write things down. Old man like him, and still dumb. People write all sorts of things down, then there they are pushing up the daisies."

With each step her speech became less distinct; she mumbled on, but I couldn't make it out any more. She quickened her pace.

Later on it turned out I'd left my pen in the hotel restaurant, on my table, though I didn't recall having noted anything down then. The desk clerk returned it to me when I went back to the hotel. I wondered what it could have meant that I'd left it there. For it must have meant something: there are no mistakes without a cause.

I wanted to fix the line from the synagogue in my memory. I began to say it in my head, hoping that at the same time its meaning would be revealed to me. I repeated it word by word, first only with my lips, as it were, then in a low whisper. By the time I reached the end of the street I was speaking it out loud to check if I had it. Luckily there was no one around, or they might have thought I was talking to myself. That was how I learned poems by heart in school: first in my mind, then with my lips, then in a whisper, and finally out loud.

Unfortunately there were always problems with learning things by heart, and especially with repeating them aloud. Six of us lived together in student lodgings, in a small room. Just how small it was, is best conveyed by the fact that we slept on iron bunk beds with rusty springs that creaked mercilessly whenever you made the slightest movement. The beds were supposedly left over from the ghetto, and only the mattresses changed, though the landlady denied it. She'd moved in here after the war; before then, after the ghetto was liquidated other people had occupied the place. Sometimes, when I couldn't get to sleep, and the bunks were creaking from bodies turning over, I'd have the impression that the beds were sighing, moaning and groaning, in the voices of those who'd died on them in former years. Sometimes, in the night I'd wake up drenched in sweat, terrified that I too was dying. As if the person who'd died on my bed had left death behind for me, since he didn't have anything else. Awake now, I'd try and imagine who he had been, what he felt, what he'd thought as he was dying. Perhaps he was whispering some poem, and he died with that poem? So it's good to learn poems, even if you have trouble retaining them.

The other boys who lived there weren't bothered by the fact that people could once have died on their beds. They slept soundly. The kid who slept on the top bunk of my bed would start snoring the moment his head hit the pillow – he was often so loud and raucous that the whole frame shook, and me along with it. Even if he fell asleep quietly, in the middle of the night he'd explode as though someone were choking him with a rope, and he was trying to loosen the rope with his breath. At those times I'd kick the springs of his bed above me, to which he'd respond, at most turning on his side: "Get lost. Go back to sleep."

A moment later he'd be snoring again, sometimes even louder. It made no difference whether he slept on one side or the other, on his back or on his stomach; all that did was change the tone of the snoring. His repertoire of sounds was exceptionally rich. I didn't know what to do about it. I asked him one day: "Do you know that someone died in your bed?"

"So what? Does that mean I'm not supposed to sleep?"

My other roommates also rasped and talked in their sleep. It could get louder than during the day in there. The oddest thing was that they never felt they'd had enough sleep. They'd drag themselves out of bed in the morning complaining, swearing, cursing the fact that they had to go to school. The landlady would hammer on the door and yell in her shrill voice: "Stop that swearing! High school boys, goddammit! You'll all end up hoodlums!"

Despite her predictions, everyone passed their exams and went on to university. I was the only one who didn't get in at the first attempt. Though after a year I stopped rooming with them and moved into the dorm.

The school anniversary reunited me with two of them for the first time since graduation all those years before. One turned out to be an artist, the other had risen to become a general, then when he retired he'd taken up beekeeping. He had an apiary with several dozen hives; he'd even written a book. He brought a few copies with him and gave one to each of us, with an inscription commemorating the times we lodged together. The book was titled: *Bees and Humans: A Comparison of Societies.* I haven't read it yet, though I keep promising myself I will. It's actually on my night stand, by the lamp, right next to me, nagging at me. We really should visit him some time, he said. He gave us his business card and wrote on it: "Come see me." Naturally he promised us a couple of jars of honey if we came. And he gave us a lecture about different kinds of honey. According to him, the most beneficial and most expensive is heather honey. I forget what it's good for, but it helps with quite a wide range of complaints. Next in the hierarchy is honeydew honey, then after that buckwheat honey. Though if you take as your criterion the ailments that humankind suffers from, the order might be different. He mentioned any number of different honeys – I don't remember them all.

Of the six of us who shared a room for a year back then, three had passed away. One, a mountain climber, had perished at a young age, during the descent from some peak in the Karakoram Mountains. In other words, he'd at least died after achieving success. The second had gone in a rather banal way: an auto accident. The third had been a doctor. He'd been working for a charity in Africa when, during a revolt against the ruling president, he was shot by one of his own patients, whom he'd saved from a deadly disease.

We didn't recognize each other at first. How could we. Our features had changed, our eyes; we'd forgotten one another's voices, our hair was sparse and gray. The general-beekeeper was completely bald – even his eyebrows had thinned out. The artist used to have a thick mop of hair that fell down over his eyes; now, it reached his shoulders to be sure, but it only grew on the back of his head. At times something familiar sounded in one or the other voice, but not in everything they said. In fact, at the beginning we didn't speak much, only mumbling something from time to time. And besides, everyone knows that a memory tired out by many years is not good at recalling the voices of youth, even if youthful tones resonate in one word or another.

As the oldest ones present, they gave us our own table. It was the table that loosened our tongues. At an event like that you can't sit long together without words, even if only mumbled ones. They seem to insist on emerging. So it gradually came out that we'd all lived together in the same lodgings. It's also the case that a celebration like that doesn't just force you to reminisce: reminiscences give it meaning, they justify the very fact that it's taking place.

True, we didn't remember first or last names or what we'd called one another – and it certainly wasn't by first or last name. For instance, there was a student in the year above us who was known as Titch, because he was the tallest kid in school and was an excellent basketball player. Anyway, we agreed to drink *bruderszaft* and switch to first-name terms, since we'd been familiar once before. After so many years of not knowing one another and, what was worse, of forgetting, it was hard to make the change without alcohol, and as everyone knows, drinking bruderszaft gives you courage, even if you sometimes slip up after you've drunk it. To avoid such mistakes we toasted two, three times; after the fourth we exchanged kisses on the cheek, shook one another's hand and clapped each other on the back. The general-beekeeper's eyes glazed over. The painter took out his handkerchief and wiped his glasses. I also felt the tears rising, especially when the painter – or maybe it was the general-beekeeper – as if trying to hide his emotion, said: "Of course I remember, how could I not. You were the one that used to memorize poems in the john."

It was hardly surprising. Each of us had been around a long while, and here all at once one life was meeting another, each perhaps filled with wounds. It wasn't easy to move abruptly to intimate terms with someone else's unknown life. So bruderszaft was necessary. With it, each of us cracked open the door to his life. I admit that things got lively, as if we were back in the lodgings and in our youth.

Yet when we began to recall that youth of ours, it turned out we didn't have enough memories in common to make it through the whole evening. Also, few of our memories agreed with one another. Each of us seemed to remember things differently. Either one person recalled something the other two didn't, or two of us remembered and the third didn't, or none of us remembered, even though all three of us should have. And so we began to argue, louder and louder, to the point that we started getting disapproving looks from the neighboring tables. At one moment someone called over: "Could you be a little quieter at the seniors table?"

The speaker's tablemate said: "Just ignore them, they're hard of hearing." Their whole group burst out laughing.

But there was also a pleasant moment when one of the youngest attendees, who must have graduated only recently, stood up, raised a full glass and, with an emphatic gesture in our direction, exclaimed: "Long live life!" He drained his glass; his tablemates greeted the toast with loud applause, after which they all rose and followed suit. We stood too, raised our glasses in acknowledgment, and drank in turn.

My head began to spin. The general-beekeeper turned his glass upside down as a sign he wouldn't drink any more. The painter, who turned out to have the strongest head of us all, poured himself another drink and downed it, saying: "Here's to you both."

We quieted down, but the disagreements continued. This time it was about who'd had which bunk. The painter claimed he'd been on the bottom bunk and that his bed had been against the wall with the only window, while I had slept above him, and he'd been the one who used to kick me, because he couldn't stand my snoring. He refused to accept that he wasn't the one I used to kick, because he slept on a different bunk, by the door. The general-beekeeper, in an effort to smooth things over, concluded in his version that all three of us had slept on the bottom bunks, while the top bunks were occupied by the ones who'd died. And that there was no point taking them to task for snoring or talking in their sleep. Now they were at rest. And since he wasn't going to drink any more, we should at least drink to them. He poured himself half a measure, and filled our glasses.

Those disputes of ours, though, had a deeper meaning that we were unaware of at the time. We'd exchanged first and last names, yet still an uncertainty remained that troubled each of us: how could we connect the names with our aged faces, which were so different from those of our youth? Was each of us actually the same person they'd been, though we were using the same name as back then? We could have taken the name of the one who slept on top, after all, because in our reminiscences we couldn't even agree on who had slept on which bunk. At a certain age first names, last names begin to separate from you, and when you're old you can only presume that that first and last name is you. In our quarrels, then, we were searching for confirmation that it was us who were meeting at the anniversary, not those who were no longer alive.

So we argued on. And not just about who'd been on which bunk. The other two even denied they used to drag themselves out of bed each morning complaining and cursing to high heaven, to the point that the landlady would hammer on the door. That absolutely wasn't true. Maybe I was mixing them up with the other boys, the ones who were dead. Or I'd been the one cursing and now I was trying to pin it on them. They didn't like school, on that much they were in agreement. The only people who like school are brown-nosers, and everyone knows what they turn into. You can see them plain as day, climbing higher and higher. But they never minded getting up. Remember: they used to jump out of bed to be the first at the washbasin. Each person got five minutes. The general-beekeeper was first up, he could already feel that military discipline. He got into it with the painter, who claimed he was up before anyone else. After him it was the general-beekeeper, then all the others. They put me at the end. I couldn't be bothered to object.

There was one washbasin for the six of us. If you didn't finish in five minutes, the next person would tip out your water, even if you were in the middle of washing. Then it was their turn. I don't remember: did anyone ever tip my water out because I went over my five minutes? Or if there wasn't enough water in the bucket because someone had forgotten to fetch it the previous day: what then? Exactly, what then? I don't recall. Oh yes: we'd go to the landlady and ask her for at least half a mug per person so we could brush our teeth and wash our face.

"I got up first because there might still be some water in the pail. Then I'd wake him." The general-beekeeper nodded toward the painter, who agreed and didn't agree, still unsure if maybe he'd been the one who woke the general-beekeeper. He gave up, though, and suggested another drink. We said no, so he poured one for himself and knocked it back with a jerk of the head.

"Now I'm certain you were the one that used to memorize poems in the can," he said, looking at me a little hazily.

"You'd send me outside when I practiced them out loud."

"Me? No way. I've always loved poetry. They call me the poet of the paintbrush."

"As for me, let me tell you a secret: I actually write poetry. I have almost a whole book already. And I've got a title: *The Bees.* Bees are the most poetical creatures of all, not excluding humans. If I believed in God, I'd say that God was the most poetical. But what can you do, in the army you weren't allowed to believe if you wanted promotion. It'll be dedicated to my late wife. She died a few years ago. We met when I was a noncom. I was a member of a reciting club. We gave a performance. She was sitting in the front row; when I looked at her I got stuck, and she prompted me. If it wasn't for poems I might not have become a general. Because it turned out she was a general's daughter. And the general, who soon became my father-in-law, liked poetry. He said that in peacetime, when he was bored, they would read poems. On his staff everyone read."

"Me, they call me the poet of the paintbrush," the artist put in.

"You already said."

"When?"

"A moment ago."

"What I didn't say is that every painting of mine is a poem. Houses, clouds, mountains, part of a street: it's all poetry. You should come to one of my openings: poetry. If I wanted to paint one of you, in your sagging faces I'd have to look for your youth, because it was my youth too. And that isn't so easy when you've both been marked by kitsch.

Because wherever you look, it's kitsch. We're all infected with it. We can't even imagine God except as kitsch. Is kitsch something you can believe in? These days, genius only exists in the blind."

He was talking nonsense and probably had no idea himself where it was leading. At some point the general-beekeeper broke in: "Enough now. Back to me. My wife, God rest her soul – "

"Which one?" asked the artist, hiccupping.

"I only had one."

"You can tell that by looking at you. I barely recognized you. Me, I have a rule: if you're getting old, find a new wife and it'll take years off you. That way you can go on and on."

"Not beyond death," the general-beekeeper retorted.

"How do you know? Eh? How do you know?" the painter replied, his hackles rising. "The doctors wrote me off. When they lifted me out of the car I was barely alive. I was hit by a semi. They had to cut me free. And I'm still here. With my old wife I wouldn't have had the will to live. You've a heck of a constitution, the doctor said. The body of a man ten years younger. And then I was already on my third. Wait, maybe my fourth. Whatever, one of them."

"I had one and as you can see, I'm still here too," said the general-beekeeper, refusing to yield.

That irked the painter. He poured himself a shot and drank it. He slammed his glass down on the table so hard the other glasses rang, and he muttered: "Thanks to my wives I'll outlive you both."

"Be my guest, if you want to live so much."

They would have continued sparring, and they might have made a scene because things were getting tense, but they were drowned out by the music which suddenly struck up. It was evidently intended for the youngest attendees. It was harsh and shrill. The whole room shook, and a moment later there was also the noise of dancing couples – chatter, squeals, giggling – so the two of them couldn't hear each other even if they'd started shouting. They let it drop.

I wondered what could have happened between them when they were young, because they hadn't seen each other since then. Whatever it was, it had lasted all these years till now. Something must have taken place, of that I was certain, the more so because they'd sort of pushed me aside. The trouble had flared up just between the two of them, to the point that they were snapping at one another like attack dogs. It must have been something painful: you don't hold on to ordinary grievances for so many years, especially into old age. Old age cancels out our youth, often turning grievances into longings.

If I'd lived longer with them in the lodgings I might have had a better idea of what had set them so much at odds.

I left the lodgings after one year, because of the food. On my own I certainly wouldn't have made the move. But my mother came to visit one day, and it was lunchtime. She saw what we were eating and she was appalled. A watery barley soup, then for the main course potatoes with hard-boiled eggs in a vinegary sauce. She made a scene with the landlady about what she was feeding us. It was no surprise I was so skinny that my jaw stuck out and my shoulder blades were poking through my skin! Plus, I was stooping because there was nothing to hold me up, my spine was so weak. Skin and bone.

"See: here, here, everywhere." She prodded at my body to show the landlady, who was just as furious as she was, and gave as good as she got.

"For the amount they pay they eat like kings. It's Friday today. What was I supposed to give them? Don't you want them to go without meat? Are you forgetting the Lord Jesus died on a Friday? You want him to be brought up godless? What kind of mother are you? As for him being skinny, the other boys eat the same food and they're strapping lads. Show us, boys!" she said, though it wasn't clear who to, because the moment the confrontation had begun the other lodgers had made themselves scarce. "Maybe he's got a tapeworm? If he has, he could eat cutlets all week long and he'd still be skinny."

"Do me a favor! Tapeworm, she says. The crook! A dog wouldn't want your food, lady! It'd get TB. Dear God!" she shook with worry. Then to me: "You're going to get X-rayed on Monday."

I went; the X-ray didn't show anything. In the meantime the dorm had some vacancies after the seniors graduated. I filled in an application and my mother delivered it herself, adding a note to say she urged them to consider me and hoped I'd be accepted, since at the lodgings where I'd lived in my first year I'd lost seven pounds and she was beside herself. I hadn't weighed myself, but that was what she wrote. She signed herself: His mother.

They didn't remember the confrontation. Though in fact how could they have, since they'd snuck away. But they spoke up in defense of the cooking, saying that at other lodgings it was often even worse, according to their friends. Neither of them could have moved into the dorm. The painter was from the country and his father had too much land, so he was classified as a kulak. The general-beekeeper had lost his father, but his mother sold alcohol illegally and had been given a year's suspended sentence. He might not have gotten a place at the university, but he volunteered for the army. They started him in the disciplinary brigade; he performed his duties so well they let his mother off. Anyway, both of them had to eat what the landlady gave them. But they each supplemented their diet. They bought bread, meat spread, black pudding, sausage, and often offcuts, meaning scraps of lunch meat that in private butcher's shops they would sell for pennies just before closing time. In those days there were still private pork butchers; they sold ham, baleron, sausages, whatever you liked. It was only some years later that everything was nationalized and at most you could find horsemeat sausage privately.

After their quarrel, conversation faltered between the two of them. It was another matter that we were in our cups, as the saying goes, and we'd grown drowsy. What can I say: at our age, after the umpteenth drink you don't feel energized but dispirited. True, the painter had done most of the drinking, while I'd drunk the least. But he too seemed oppressed by the loud music. In the end the band, tired and drenched in sweat, took a break and went off to eat. Soon afterward we were brought chicken drumsticks, fried potatoes and a salad, along with a glass of wine each. The painter had a shoulder bag with him; he took out a bottle of vodka.

"They served the vodka first, now they're trying to poison us with wine," he said. Pouring a half glass for the general-beekeeper, since that was all he wanted – I put my hand over my glass – he filled his own glass and emptied it in one, then poured another and hesitated whether to drink or not, ultimately holding back, it seemed, with a question directed at me: "What about you? You're not saying anything. How many wives have you had? One, two, how many? I remember you used to go with a good-looking Jewish girl."

"She wasn't Jewish," I said.

"Whatever. What happened to her?"

"Everyone called her the Jewish girl," the general-beekeeper said testily. "She must have been Jewish."

We were all in different classes – A, B, C, and D – so they might not have known it was because of her homework essay she was called that. Though word went around the whole school about it. The only boy in the same class as me was the one who became a doctor and died in Africa, shot by his own patient.

"Couldn't you have found a Polish girl?" The general-beekeeper emptied his half-glass. "Some of them were good-looking too. Remember, there was that, what was her name. She's a professor of medicine now."

"Dziutka," the painter supplied. "Your memory's failing, I see. You had a thing for her. You've forgotten her name because she wouldn't have anything to do with you."

"What's Dziutka short for anyway?" The general-beekeeper was embarrassed and was trying to cover it up.

"What difference does it make," the painter snapped. "My first wife's name was Justyna, but I called her Ustka, Usteńka." Out of the blue he started a sort of justification of those three or four wives of his.

"Don't think that I simply got bored and found a new wife. Art demanded it of me. If you're disloyal to art you're headed for defeat. Art needs youth. Youth is the lifeblood of art. How long can a wife retain her youth so you can be inspired? It can't be expressed in years, because for one it's longer, for another shorter. You can only tell when the work doesn't go well. Then it's essential to change. Otherwise you'll end up knocking on doors offering to paint wedding portraits, or doing pictures at church fairs. With a new wife, right away you feel a rush of inspiration within you, as if you were painting not just with brushes and paints but with your soul, your heart. Somebody once said to me that art above all requires solitude. That's not true. If the world didn't need art, God wouldn't have created women. Those bees of yours aren't the most poetical beings in the world: women are. If you ask me, God ought to be a woman. Because who gives birth to the world? Who suffers for the world? Women. They're our fate. Us men, all we're good for is warfare, revolution, turmoil of every kind. Our strength is only an illusion. God poured all his power into women."

"So you're a believer?" the general-beekeeper interrupted. "At school you didn't attend religious education, I seem to recall."

"Art is my faith. And everything is art, including God. Except that nothing in this world is worthy of Him. To put God on canvas – there's the thing. People try and try, but nothing comes of it. God refuses to even visit our imagination. And for that reason, in his place He gave us woman. He himself preferred to remain a mystery. If you don't take advantage of it, He'll take her away from you. My first wife – "

At that moment a tango started playing.

"Ah, a tango," he said.

"Not much of one," the general-beekeeper retorted. "The most beautiful tango is 'Jalousie.'" He started humming it, though the band drowned him out.

"You're off key," the painter said. "I met my first wife during a tango. And that was the most beautiful tango of all. It was love at first sight, as they say. She wasn't good-looking in the usual sense of the term, but she had magnificent breasts. These days breasts like that are usually fake. The whole world's become fake. Her, though, she'd been gifted by nature. She didn't dye her hair, didn't put on false eyelashes, didn't make her lips bigger. Everything was natural. If you could have seen those breasts. They weren't too high or too low, they didn't spread to each side, didn't sag, and between them it was like Queen Jadwiga's Valley. You remember Queen Jadwiga's Valley? If you stuck around for a couple of days we could go out there together. I'd have you over for lunch afterwards. I met her in a restaurant. She was sitting at the next table with three big guys. They started playing 'La Cumparsita,' which is the most beautiful tango of all. Not that 'Jalousie' of yours. I'm no weakling, I used to practice judo. I thought to myself, if it comes to it, I'll take the one on the left first. And I asked her to dance. She taught me the tango, because I didn't know how to dance it. Boy could she dance. A butterfly."

"And you divorced her?" the general-beekeeper said in surprise.

"She died. Three years into the marriage."

"I'm sorry."

"Don't be. I don't like feeling sorry. Her death taught me that art isn't immortal. I burned every one of my canvases. And I stopped painting. Because whenever I began work on some picture, I'd stand there paralyzed in front of the blank canvas, as if afraid of the first brushstroke. Yet the first brushstroke is like the first word that created the world. The first brushstroke is the germ of form. I don't know if you follow me."

"It's like with bees," the general-beekeeper said to show he understood.

"What do bees have to do with form?" the painter snorted.

"Oh, they do, they do. They have to do with everything."

They probably would have gotten into a discussion – an argument even – but at that moment someone went up to the band, waited for them to finish what they were playing, then took out his wallet and spoke for a moment to the saxophonist, who was the leader. He gave him a banknote and the saxophonist said into the microphone: "For Mrs Mariola from Mr Zygfryd, the 'Jalousie' tango."

Not everyone got up; most remained seated, as if the tango meant nothing to them. Because what kind of dance was the tango. It wasn't their past, wasn't their memory, wasn't their longing. Whereas to my surprise, our friend the general-beekeeper rose to his feet. We were sure it was because of the tango and that a moment later we'd see him gliding among the other dancers with a lady he'd perhaps singled out earlier just in case they played his beloved 'Jalousie.'

"You're going to dance?" the painter asked.

"No, I'm going to the bathroom," he replied. "It's the one pleasure left to me."

"Why's he in such a huff?" the painter said once he'd left. After a moment he added: "That's how it is when you've only had one wife." He suddenly perked up. "You know, I often stood for an hour, two hours, brush in hand in front of a fresh canvas, and all I did was drink straight from the bottle. Then I cut up the bare canvas with a knife. So I know what it is to lose a wife and not marry again. I often drank till I passed out. I stopped seeing anyone. People knocked and rang, I didn't open the door. I rarely got out of bed. At most to buy something to eat, and get more liquor. I stopped shaving. One day I looked in the mirror and I couldn't believe it was me. I pinched my cheeks, tore at my beard. I couldn't credit it. But it was all the same to me. Let my beard keep growing. And I went back to bed. The beard could cover me all over, they'd wonder who was inside the cocoon. Let me stink so much they'll back away from the door. It would have been worse for me than it was for him, though at the time I was still young. Then one day, I drained the last drops from a bottle and I couldn't be bothered to go out and buy another. Actually, I usually bought more than one. In any case, I thought to myself, maybe I have some meths somewhere. I didn't. Maybe I have some cologne. But how could I have had cologne when I wasn't washing or shaving. Even if there'd been any, it would have dried up."

"How could it have dried up?"

"How could it have dried up? You got me there. Whatever. Anyway, I realized I needed to save myself. But how? The only possibility was to find a wife. Hang on, was that the second, the third, the fourth maybe? Goddammit, I've had too much to drink. It's another matter that not each of them hurts the same way, and pain changes the order too. Let me tell you, I could make an exhibition out of my wives alone. But to find a wife, first I needed to wash, shave, tidy the place. I put out an ad for a cleaner. This poor little thing appeared. Her breasts were so small, if you hadn't guessed they were there you'd never have noticed them. A long nose, sunken eyes. In general she had too much bone and not enough flesh. But one time I see her when she's got her skirt hiked up almost to her underwear and she's kneeling on the floor, mopping up dirty water with a rag and wringing it out in a basin. As she's doing it her whole body is twisting and turning. Her broad bare feet had bunions. Her hair, though, was thick, long, and dark. She kept tossing it out of the way when it fell across her face. Then one time she flicks it back like that and I see beads of sweat like pearls on her forehead. Instinctively, almost in a reflex action I put up the easel, stood a fresh canvas on it and started to paint her. She must have sensed something, though she couldn't see what I was painting, her eyes were fixed on the floor. She raised her head abruptly from the basin; there was consternation in her eyes.

"'You mustn't. I'm not worth it. You can hire some other woman, sir. You took me on to clean.'

"'Go on with your work,' I said.

"She dropped the rag in the basin, jumped to her feet, lowered her skirt and burst into tears.

"'Why are you crying?'

"'I'm not going to clean for you, sir.'

"'I'll pay extra.'

"'I don't want your money.'

"'Then at least finish the floor.'

"'I will, but I'm not coming again.'

"'Does it hurt you that I'm painting you?'

"'No.'

"'Then what's wrong?'

"'What do you know about hurt.'

"I'm telling you: as I watched her hunched over on her knees, mopping the dirty water up with a rag and scrubbing the floor with a brush – because the floor was filthy – and not just with both hands but with her back, with her knees, with her feet, her neck, her head, maybe even with her thoughts, my image of her changed. There was something so intense about her it almost made me sentimental. Here's a droplet of the world, I thought, and she's washing my floor. I tried to give her twice as much for her work. She wouldn't take it.

"'The amount we agreed on, minus what I'm not going to do. It's just for the floor.'

"I took a wad of banknotes from my wallet and tried to stick them in her top. She slapped my wrist.

"'Take your hand away.'

"I was convinced she wouldn't come back, as she'd said. But I didn't look for another cleaning woman. The floor became coated in filth again – it stuck to your shoes. You wouldn't believe the mess. I kept losing things, then when I looked for them I'd make an even bigger shambles because I couldn't find them. But I started to wash and shave, and I painted from morning till night. I'd only go out briefly to buy food or eat a hot meal in the cafeteria next door. I painted over a dozen pictures, an entire cycle; I called it 'The Cleaning Woman.' I exhibited the work. Just imagine, I only managed to save that first painting, which had been so painful for her, from being sold. The rest went for prices that would make your head spin. Whereas before, I'd rarely been able to sell anything, and only for a pittance. Plus, the reviews – I'm telling you, my friend. Too bad I didn't bring them to show you. If I'd only known we would meet. There was just one blockhead who wrote that the title was bad. What kind of a title is 'The Cleaning Woman'? He didn't see any cleaning woman in the pictures, only form. But I saw her, you moron. She was cleaning at my place. I'd have punched that guy for saying the title was for cheap effect. To him it could have been a princess, it made no difference. The subject was only a pretext. Unless it was a joke. But on who? I don't paint as a joke. I put my heart and soul into it. I'd have to have been making fun of myself, calling myself names. Then, can you imagine, one day there's a ring at the door. I open it, and it's her.

"'I wanted to see what your place looks like now that it's cleaned, sir.' She came in, looked around, and she was horror-struck: 'Dear Lord, it's filthy! This is how she cleans for you? Where did you find her? And the floor – dear Lord.' She bent down and passed her hand across the surface. 'Even a scrubbing brush won't get that out. You've splashed paint on it. You need to buy solvent, four bottles at least. 'You've been living like this? You didn't hire a new cleaner, sir?'

"'Sir was waiting for you,' I said.

"She didn't respond. She was still glancing this way and that, as if afraid to look me in the eye.

"'Will you start work here, miss?'

"She didn't answer.

"'Would you like to sit down?'

"'I didn't come here to sit down,' she muttered.

"'Shall I make tea?'

"'I had some earlier.'

"She looked over the paintings – the ones hanging on the walls, those leaning against the chest of drawers, the chairs, anywhere they could be propped up.

"'Where's that one?' she suddenly asked. I was taken aback. She noticed my surprise and added: 'You know, the one that I wouldn't clean for you anymore because of it.'

"My first thought was to say I'd sold it.

"'You didn't sell it, I know.'

"I pulled it out from a stack of canvases and put it on an easel. She stood in front of it.

"'I wouldn't have come if you'd sold it.'

"She stood for a long time in front of the painting. She was wearing a nice dark blue skirt, a flowery blouse, beads around her neck, clip-on earrings; she had on red lipstick, red nail polish, and shoes with high heels. I'm telling you, I wondered whether she was the same woman. How could she be planning to clean, all dressed and made up like that, since she was sending me out for solvent? I didn't see that she'd brought a bulging plastic bag. I hadn't noticed it because when she came in she left it by the door, and I'd been staring at her and her alone since she arrived.

"'Then I'll go get changed,' she said. Taking the plastic bag, she went into the bathroom. As she walked away from me she added: "And you'll go buy solvent, sir. I'm not going to scrape the floor clean with my fingernails. Also, bring me some nail polish remover. I'll subtract the price.'

"There was something imperious in her voice. When she cleaned for me before, she'd sounded submissive, embarrassed. Perhaps her life had changed for the better, I speculated. Though I knew nothing about her life. Whether she was single, married, divorced, widowed. How old she was, where she lived, if she had any family. Whether she was from the country or the town. Who her father and mother were, whether they were still alive. Whether she'd had an education. Nothing. She was the cleaning woman, that was all. She came and cleaned, I paid. I'd never asked her any questions.

"When I came back from the store she was already kneeling like before over the basin, skirt hiked up, feet bare, repeatedly tossing her hair back, beads of sweat on her forehead.

"'First of all the worst dirt needs to be cleaned off,' she greeted me, without so much as a glance in my direction. 'Only after that the solvent. Put it over there. Did you buy nail polish remover?'

"'Yes.'

"'How much do I owe you for it?'

"'Nothing.'

"'What do you mean, nothing?'

"'It's a gift.'

"'I don't want any gifts from you, sir.' She'd already finished a good half or more of the floor and, as she wrung the cloth out into the basin she said: 'Over there it's already washed, you can stand and paint. We won't get in each other's way.'

"Let me tell you, I was gobstruck. I put up my easel meekly, placed a canvas on it and entirely automatically I began to paint those hands of hers with the red nails as they wrung out the rag with the dirty water over the bowl. I still have that painting. She can barely be seen; you wouldn't guess it's a human figure kneeling there, with what look like angels flying down from heaven above her. I may actually rework it because it might be better if, as she's wringing out the rag with her red nails over the basin, she were rising up to heaven.

"'I'm done,' she said. 'Now it needs to dry.'

"'Take a seat, miss,' I said. 'You can sit here. Is it miss or ma'am?'

"'Why do you need to know that, sir?'

"'You needn't say if you don't wish to.'

"'Why not. I had a husband, but he drank himself to death.'

"'Do you have any children?'

"'Children with a drunk? They'd only have been unhappy later. You read, sir, you know what kind of children come from drunks.'

"'Would you like to be my wife?'

"'Why not, I could be.'"

He didn't manage to tell me what happened next, because right at that moment the general-beekeeper came back from the restroom, announcing triumphantly: "I'm back," as if he was saying: "Veni, vidi, vici."

The painter replied: "You must have lost track of time in the dancing. That 'Jalousie' of yours ended ages ago."

"There was a line."

"You can meet someone in line just as well," the painter snickered.

"The ladies' and gents' are separate."

"You should have stood in the ladies' line."

The general-beekeeper snapped back: "What kind of painter are you anyway? I've never read anything about you."

The other man got mad.

"Well, what do you read! All you read about is your bees, and you think you know everything. You don't know shit. You're not a general, you're a prick. Come visit me and you'll see! Though actually no, I take back the invitation. I'd chase you away like a dog if you did come." He jumped to his feet, swayed and nearly fell. He walked unsteadily up to a table at the back of the room and asked a middle-aged woman to dance, though they weren't playing a tango but some frenetic number.

"So what happened to her?" the general-beekeeper asked.

"Who?"

"You know, the Jewish girl."

I didn't correct him. I wondered what to tell him. I was saved from answering by the middle-aged lady, who brought back the painter. She held him by the arm, as he could barely stand upright. As she put him in his chair – I doubt he'd have managed it on his own – she made no effort to conceal her indignation: "Suggesting I pose nude for him – me, a grandmother. The nerve!"

If it hadn't been for that incident, I probably wouldn't have replied to his question about what had happened to her. I'd often asked myself the same thing; it only brought me distress. I imagined all sorts of things: her dead body hanging from the fence around the ghetto after she'd almost made it over. Or that she was in a cattle truck, watching through a window barred with barb wire as the world slipped away from her. She presses her face close up to the opening, as if trying to fix that world in her gaze, till her blood runs from the barbs and drips onto the floor of the car.

Often, under the influence of those visions I'd get in my car, or later on catch a bus or a train, and go visit the old wild green valley in the vain hope that I'd meet her; at least it calmed my imaginings about what could have happened to her. Though it was also a reminder of how many years of life remained to me, according to the Gypsy woman's prophesy.

I returned to the hotel along a street that had crossed the former ghetto, and where for a year we'd shared lodgings in a tumbledown building that had survived the war, as we'd been recalling to the point of tedium during the gala that evening. I felt full of those memories and was wondering how much truth there was in them. Where the lodgings had been, now there was a small single-story building with an imposing sign over the door that said: "Photography Studio." I'd initially intended to go back via the town square, but lost in my thoughts – instinctively you might say – I'd turned into this street. I was a little tipsy, although I'd really only been sipping at my drink. Besides, on the square I might run into someone who'd offer unwanted help when they saw my cane and my unsteady steps. The square was lit up, and in bright light like that I'd probably have walked even more shakily. Here on the other hand, the few feeble streetlamps gave off no more than a faint glimmer, leaving the space between them scarcely lit. And here, at this hour I could expect not to meet another living soul. There was such an acute silence that I'd have sworn you could hear the houses standing there – for houses don't stand noiselessly. At a certain moment I took fright and looked around once and twice to check I wasn't being followed. All I heard was the sound of my feet. It was the first time I had the experience of being afraid of my own footsteps.

My thoughts returned once again to the evening I'd just spent. I was overcome by doubt as to whether they really were the same people I'd lodged with all those years before. Can a person ever retain a unity with their own self all the way to old age? Memories in old age seem untrustworthy, especially those from childhood and youth, though I myself am not free of such memories, which for some reason unknown to myself, I believe in. What lies behind the fact that we're so firmly attached to something that may or may not have existed, or which life begrudged us, and yet out of which nevertheless we've created a link to our longing? In that case, what is it that we feel nostalgia for? The entire evening with them at the gala, along with the music and dancing, and the joy emanating from people's faces whatever their age – effervescing, indeed, as the room warmed up – I found it all inexpressibly sad.

It may have been under the influence of these recollections, which the two of them in particular had shared so liberally, that I starting having doubts as to whether I really had once invited her to the circus. When I got my modest monthly pocket money from my parents, I'd ask her out to the movies or to a show. Various singing groups or theater companies came through town and performed. The circus was always a big event. To impress her, I spent everything I had on loge tickets. We were sitting right by the ring. The ringmaster, clad in a dark tailcoat, was slim and tall, with an aquiline nose and raven-black hair slicked down with brilliantine. In between acts he entertained the audience with card tricks. He offered us the pack and told us to choose a card. She picked out the king of spades. He took the card from her hand and walked around the ring, showing it so no one would doubt it was the king of spades. Then he replaced it in the pack, shuffled the cards and passed them to her, telling her to throw the whole pack at him. She did. As the cards flew at him like a scattering of stars, he snatched one of them out of the air.

"The king of spades, ladies and gentlemen!" he announced triumphantly to the audience, who were as amazed as we were. He was rewarded with enthusiastic applause.

"It was these lovely hands that picked it out," he said, coming up and kissing her hand, for which he was clapped again. "Take the card as a souvenir. Is this young man your king of spades?" That earned him yet another round of applause.

When the clown followed him in the ring I stepped outside, hoping the ringmaster would come out too. I walked around the tent but didn't see him. I was about to go back inside when I caught sight of a glowing cigarette tip nearby in the darkness. He was smoking and gazing at the starry sky. I went up to him. He drew on the cigarette again and again; each time, it lit up his face.

"Excuse me sir, can I ask you something?"

"Fire away."

"How do you do that? Catch the one chosen card from the whole pack?"

"Well, it's different spheres of reality. Most people live in the lowest sphere, the trivial one. I'd need to know which one you inhabit." He took out his cigarette pack and lit another. "I'm sorry, I didn't offer you one. Would you like to smoke?"

"No thank you."

"You have a very pretty girl. But you're not the king of spades."

When I asked them if they remembered the circus that came through, they contested it. Circus? What circus? They'd been to circuses, but only later, when they were away at university.

"It was a circus."

"Were there horses? Lions? A bear at least? Then you've never seen a real circus."

I regretted having gone to the gala. On the invitations it had said, gala evening, such and such a band would be playing, saxophone, bass guitar, acoustic guitar, clarinet, drums. It would have been enough to go to the formal part of the celebration, which had taken place in the morning, though even for that part I'd left before the end. It had been boring, not to say unbearably so. It consisted of welcomes and speeches from various high-ups, and the reading of telegrams from even loftier powers. Then after that, messages from alumni who were unable to attend, but were there in heart and mind. The school even got a medal for its four hundredth anniversary. I wondered: if a person happened to live four hundred years, could they put up with their life for that long? I doubt it. Though perhaps at that price they'd come to know the world better? I doubt that even more.

At some point they announced a coffee break; after the break there were going to be performances. The school choir would sing songs from the four hundred years that had passed since the founding of the school.

After which the school chamber orchestra would play excerpts from four works, one from each century. Oh yes, and the morning was to be rounded off by something they'd had to move to the end since the most important dignitary was running late, and he was the one who would hand out national medals to outstanding alumni. It seemed I was one of them, but I decided not to wait and, taking advantage of the coffee break, I left. I resolved, though, to attend the evening gala. I may have had a remote hope of which I myself was unaware.

As I walked back to the hotel I was tired, aching almost, from all the shouting and shrieking and the buzz of conversation, the ear-splitting music, and just as much from my two former roommates, who'd besieged me all evening with their recollections. In the program the lottery to pick the king and queen of the gala was still to come; I'd wanted to leave, but they stopped me.

With such a large number of people from so many graduating classes over several decades, it would have been hard to organize a vote. It had been decided, then, to hold a lottery. Two pretty girls from among the newest graduates went around the room with trays of wrapped candies. One gave them out to the women, the other to the men. Whichever woman found a blue bead in her candy would be the queen of the gala, while the man who found a red bead would be the king. The room filled with the rustle of candies being unwrapped and the accompanying excitement. I opened mine and my heart stopped. There was a little red bead along with the candy. Luckily I'd been discreet and the other two hadn't seen, as they were anxiously opening their own candies. The painter was annoyed: "I didn't get it."

The general-beekeeper said indifferently: "Neither did I. How about you? Show us."

I held up the empty wrapper. I'd managed to slip the candy and the bead into my mouth before they'd unwrapped theirs. Fortunately the candy wasn't hard; I crushed it with my tongue and swallowed it along with the bead. They were actually pleased that I hadn't won either.

"The bead evidently wasn't daft enough to pick one of us," the general-beekeeper said.

"The bead?" replied the painter in a huff. "You think the draw was fair? The bead went to whoever they decided on beforehand."

The queen was a good-looking young woman. She jumped up happily from her table. There was a round of applause. She looked around the room and called out: "Where's the king? Where's my king? Show yourself, king!"

There was a stir; people began to get up from the other tables, some were already moving about the room.

"We're looking for the king! The king has disappeared! Hey there, king, where are you? Everyone check their own table! King! The queen is waiting for you!"

"Let's have a drink," the painter said. "They must have picked some halfwit. He probably ate the candy and didn't notice the bead."

"Some people have a thing for candy," the general-beekeeper said.

I wasn't far from the hotel. All at once, in the gloom of the street I saw something like the end of a column of people being driven along with whips. They were moving away from me amid a hubbub of footsteps and curses. At the end, a dozen or so yards behind, she was running, trying in vain to catch up with the column. She was stumbling over the uneven pavement, tugging along a little girl much younger than herself. I quickened my pace as much as I could, but before I reached the hotel they'd disappeared in the darkness.